WAR OF THE SHADOWS

BLOOD & SHADOWS BOOK 7

BOOKS BY ALIANNE DONNELLY

BLOOD AND SHADOWS
Blood Moons
Blood Trails
Blood Debts
Blood Hunt
Shadow Hawk
Shadow Hound
War of the Shadows

THE REBEL COURT
Catch Me
Dearest Love
Sweetest Kiss

DAWN OF RAGNAROK
The Royal Wizard
Dragonblood
Prince of Deceit

THE BEAST
Bastien
The Beast

OTHER TITLES
Wolfen
Virtual
Function: L1VE

ALIANNE DONNELLY

WAR OF THE SHADOWS

BLOOD & SHADOWS BOOK 7

For the ones who were broken.

"Make it your business to understand who and what you're dealing with. In love as much as war, a spear will fell a wolf. But it won't do jack shit against a wildfire."

- Excerpt from the Evolutionary Gospel of Michael

HISTORY

2881-2895 — *War of the Stars*

Regional conflicts in the galaxy escalate into the largest, most destructive war in human history. The battle claims billions of lives, destroying entire worlds in the process. Fallout from untested weapons causes a severe and deadly breakdown in DNA integrity, which results in mutations, disease, and low birth rates. Unable to maintain a steady population growth, humanity faces extinction.

2899 — *Birth of the Interplanetary Council of Governance*

In response to the existential crisis, the sectors come together and form a new government with the express purpose of stopping and reversing humanity's decline. The Interplanetary Council of Governance (ICG) allocates all available resources toward medical research into the effects of the fallout, as well as potential treatments and cures.

2921 — *The Chem-Treatment*

After two decades of research and study, scientists have perfected the most viable solution to restoring population growth. When administered directly after birth, the "chem-treatment" stabilizes a child's DNA for the duration of their lifetime. However, while up to 90% effective, the genetic correction is not inheritable.

Chem-treatments become mandatory for every child born.

Genetic research continues. Over time, prison worlds are restructured into sophisticated laboratories where inmates are secretly used as involuntary test subjects in unethical studies designed to push the human body to its limits and beyond.

3000 — The Rise of Chem-Resistance

Eighty years of data indicate a declining trend in the effectiveness of chem-treatments across the population. This growing "chem-resistance" presents in different ways. In the worst cases, it causes genetic defects and lifelong diseases that do not respond to common cures. However, in other cases, it enhances physical or mental abilities.

While population growth remains constant, chem-resistance is considered a rare outlier condition. Treatments address the symptoms, but not the underlying cause.

3005 — Canaries in the Coal Mine

Two members of the ICG observe an increase in societal unrest, particularly in urban centers with high population densities.

With a gift for predicting the future, up-and-coming Senator Matthew Griffith blames the unrest on the growing number of chem-resistants in the population. He concludes that those with unique mental abilities (mind reading) will eventually unite and render existing laws unenforceable. He recommends that the ICG take action against them.

Secretly a mind reader himself, Special Liaison John MacMurphy recognizes the stigma against chem-resistants as the greater threat to society as a whole. He advocates for integration and social reform to address the current lack of resources for an increasingly diverse population.

The ICG takes their feedback under advisement and does nothing. All issues pertaining to chem-resistance and its impact on individuals and society as a whole are swept under the rug.

3006 – *The Shadows Are Born*

Senator Griffith begins building the brutal Shadow army in secret to further his political agenda. His troops are slotted into one of two ranks: Hounds or Hawks. The majority are Hounds, brute force foot soldiers with the sole purpose of wreaking as much death and destruction as possible. The much smaller percentage of Hawks are further honed into subversive infiltration operatives who undermine or eliminate target spaces from within, leaving no trace of their presence once the mission is complete.

To maintain absolute control, all Shadow soldiers undergo repeated treatments of electromagnetic-chemical mind control (EMC), which involves disrupting target neural pathways in the brain with electromagnetic shocks and a chemical injection that prevents them from reforming. This leads to memory loss and an unquestioning obedience to the Shadow directive. However, repeated treatments cause brain damage that can render soldiers obsolete, necessitating ongoing aggressive recruitment, often by force.

3007 – *The Special Unit*

Witnessing the rise of the Shadows under Senator Griffith's command, John MacMurphy realizes that genocide against chem-resistants is inevitable. Driven to take action and protect others like himself, he resigns from the ICG and begins to form the Special Unit (SU). The communal organization provides both protection and resources for telepaths, allowing them to integrate undetected within the general population. However, his obsessive focus on mind readers excludes all other forms of chem-resistance, leaving the majority of affected individuals to fend for themselves.

Outside of the SU's limited reach, chem-resistant individuals driven to insanity by the late onset of unique mental abilities begin to disappear from urban centers. Their absence goes largely unnoticed and unreported.

3018 — Green 24

Shadow outpost Green 24 is wiped out overnight. The lack of discernible exterior damage suggests the outpost was attacked from within. Of the six hundred soldiers on base, five hundred eighty-seven are found dead. The remaining survivors are psychologically compromised beyond any hope of rehabilitation. Those who don't suffer fear-induced heart attacks are eventually euthanized.

The incident is recorded as a telepathic attack and used as a case study in the ongoing radicalization of Shadow soldiers everywhere.

3028 [Blood Moons] — A Public Scandal

As more cases of chem-resistance arise, people begin to question the effectiveness of chem-treatments. Parents refuse them for their newborns. Protesters gather around clinics. The growing unrest leads to ostracism for chem-resistants whose differences are noticeable, good or bad.

Librarian and mind reader Dara Frost is arrested for reporting a crime she didn't commit. On the prison world of New Alaska, she is assigned to Dr. Amelia Chase, whose DNA studies revolve around shape-shifting. Dr. Chase's first and only partial success is Dara's cellmate, Tristan Hunt. Also a telepath, Tristan helps Dara hone her abilities and, in the process, reveals that he was the one responsible for the massacre at outpost Green 24.

When Tristan begins to transform and the murderer that Dara reported strikes again, proving her innocence, Dr. Chase and both of her patients transfer to a minimum-security prison for further processing.

Dara is exposed as a telepath and taken back to Earth to help John MacMurphy's SU find the real murderer. Tristan masters the painful process of shifting into a tiger and back, escapes, and follows Dara. He saves her life and kills the murderer, earning himself a special release.

Dr. Chase secretly leaks the experiments being performed in New Alaska to news outlets, sparking public outrage.

3032 [Blood Trails] — DNA Augmentation: The Chase Serums

Protests against the chem-treatment industry are turning into large "antichem" rallies on every major world. While a handful of communities embrace chem-resistants and make moves toward inclusion, most shame and shun them.

Without permission, Dr. Amelia Chase's sister, Hailey, changes the shape-shifting serum formula and uses it on herself. The new version takes effect immediately, but its most crucial part begins to degrade over time. On the run from the consequences of her actions, Hailey's body loses the ability to heal the damage of rearranging into a new shape. If left unaddressed, the transformations will eventually kill her.

Dr. Chase hires SU's Special Agent Jeremy Calen to find Hailey and bring her back for her own good. The sisters then work together to create a new serum that restores Hailey's healing abilities. Both serums only work on chem-resistant individuals.

3032 [Blood Debts] — The Chase Serums Perfected

Dr. Amelia Chase comes home after saving her sister's life to find a stranger with a gun in her apartment. Gabriel Connors is a gladiator in the brutal neomodern version of Rome. To get out, he needs Amelia to make him into a shape-shifter like she did with Tristan Hunt.

Amelia agrees under duress and proceeds to combine her research with Hailey's to restructure her original formula into two separate serums: one to enhance healing and one to produce shape-shifting abilities. Despite the Caesar's interference and the pair's abduction to Rome, both serums turn out to be a success. Gabriel and Amelia escape, and Rome falls.

3036 [Blood Hunt] — The Shadows Emerge into the Light

Antichem rallies have now evolved into full-scale riots in larger cities, prompting local law enforcement to take action to contain damage. It is clear that despite continued support from the ICG, the chem-treatment industry is finished as society teeters on the brink of full-scale conflict.

During an antichem riot, telepath and SU member Emma Calen gets trapped and abducted by the Shadows. She discovers that the army has developed technologies to protect itself against telepaths.

Shadow Hawk John Wayland is tasked with overseeing Emma's stay. But when she begins to break down, he defies all orders and escapes with her, taking refuge with the SU—the first instance of a Hawk defecting from the Shadow army.

With the whole galaxy on a tipping point, Tristan Hunt takes Dara and their children into hiding. Gabriel Connors and Dr. Amelia Chase quickly follow suit. Both couples disappear.

A faction of chem-resistants who were overlooked and rejected by John MacMurphy and his SU enters the spotlight, naming themselves the Evolutionaries. Guided by Michael, whose precognitive abilities border on prophetic, the chaos they create escalates antichem riots into a full-scale war with the Shadows.

Michael dies during an attack on the newly rebuilt outpost Green 24.

In a last-ditch effort to put a quick end to the conflict, John Mac-Murphy takes out his long-time rival, the Shadows' Commander in Chief, Senator Matthew Griffith.

It doesn't work.

John MacMurphy disappears.

In his absence, Emma Calen takes over as the Acting Director of the Special Unit.

3039 [Shadow Hawk] — Rebel Shadows

Three years into the war, humanity's worst traits shine once again. Infrastructure is in shambles. People suffer without access to basic resources. Having crippled society as a whole, the Shadows now focus their attacks only on the chem-resistants. Under the guise of reconstruction, the ICG turns a blind eye.

Deserted Shadow Hawk Finnegan Rowe returns to his hometown to find it in ruins. His old cohort, Latham Bigellow (also known as "Talon"), has assembled a radical and unhinged unit of rogue Shadows that terrorizes the region. Their primary target is Finn's childhood sweetheart, Laura McNally, and her small group of refugee survivors.

To get Laura and her people out, Finn summons the SU for help. They win the battle, but Talon escapes. The surviving Shadows opt to integrate into the SU. Finn deems Talon a persistent threat and assigns former Shadow Hound Vega Ortiz to hunt him down.

3039 [Shadow Hound] — The Catalyst

Quinn VanWarren was born with supernatural strength and a failing heart. After surviving Talon's reign of terror, he receives an artificial heart and a dose of Hailey Chase-Calen's regenerative serum. He then hires Vega Ortiz to help him uncover whether his ultra-rich family is secretly funding the Shadows. Having failed to locate Talon, Vega takes the job as her last hope of tracking him down.

However, during their investigation, Vega's target finds her instead. Talon launches an attack and is killed by a Shadow operative who has been posing as one of the VanWarrens for several years. Shadow Operative M (also known as Zach) then rescues Vega from near-death and abducts Quinn for the Shadows to reverse-engineer his unique mutation and the healing serum. The Shadow scientists are unsuccessful in replicating either.

With the help of her deserted Shadow friends, Vega stages a rescue and burns the outpost to the ground. Operative M is recovered and forced into an EMC treatment to erase his memories and reprogram his mind toward the Shadow directive. Upon waking up, he finds a recording of himself with instructions to run.

So he does…

January 2, 3040 - Chairo, Valhale 602

Four Earth-standard days without sleep.

Two without any sustenance.

A Shadow never stopped.

They'd never stop hunting.

There'd been at least twenty of them patrolling the Umbra Garde shuttleport, forcing Zach, formerly known as Operative M, into deep cover as soon as he landed on Valhale 602.

No communications, local or off-world. He didn't have anyone to call, anyway.

No database access. He'd memorized the city map. He could find his way to his final destination, no problem.

No transactions, though, was a problem that made him wish for the physical currency of ancient times.

No transactions meant no food or water. He'd been able to scavenge scraps from the food waste discarded by a restaurant the day before yesterday, but not water. Water was scarce in these parts. Rationed, and for hydration only. General hygiene was managed through different means.

The hunger Zach could ignore.

The thirst was driving him out of his mind. It would kill him in another day or so.

Which was unfortunate, because no transactions also meant no transportation or lodging. Valhale 602 was so paranoid that the only way for Zach to get a transport or catch some sleep was to break into something, which would instantly put his face on one of the thousands of security feeds around.

No, he had to keep moving.

Trouble was, he was starting to see and hear things that weren't there. Weakened almost to the breaking point, his body quivered with each dragging step. Paranoia had set in, and every time he looked up at the sky, the giant planet Vesta, anchoring Valhale 602 to its orbit, looked like it would smash the terraformed moon into dust at any second.

Worst of all, his disguise was starting to crumble. The clothes were filthy, reeking of dirt and sewage. Zach kept to the utility tunnels as much as he could, and only came out in side alleys with little to no foot traffic when the need for fresh air became too urgent. He'd circled and zigzagged long enough to be sure he'd disappeared. But there were no more utility tunnels, and he'd run out of time and options.

Around the next corner was one of the primary streets in Chairo. Pedestrian-only zone for three blocks in either direction. It had dozens of small shops and restaurants, as well as outdoor seating areas to encourage social interaction—something sorely lacking in cities of this size. And it was lunch time.

This was where everything had the potential to go to complete and utter shit.

Zach's face-changer had glitched out on him three hours ago. If the Shadows were still hanging around the city after four days, they'd get an alert the moment one of Chairo's security feeds captured Zach's face. He might have an hour, or he might have five minutes. His destination was so covert it hadn't raised a single flag with the Shadows so far, but it was still within the standard canvassing perimeter of his current location, and he didn't have a Plan B. Getting turned away from the door would mean game over.

No other choice. His body was out of time.

He had to risk it.

Zach rolled his head on his shoulders, then braced a hand on the wall to steady himself as the world continued to spin around him. It took a few seconds to get his knees to work correctly. Then he shoved his hands into his pockets, ducked his head, and strolled into the pedestrian zone.

Keep a safe distance from the genteel patrons. Maintain a slow pace to avoid suspicion. Don't scowl. Try not to pant.

With every second he dragged out to maintain a casual air, his sense of dread intensified. He was too dehydrated to sweat, but the feel of his filthy clothes sticking to his skin made his empty stomach clench.

A woman with bright red hair, feeding her child, gave him a look. Zach adjusted his path farther downwind.

He didn't dare look back, but he felt the mood shift behind him. She'd noticed he didn't belong. He needed to get the fuck out of there—fast.

Crossing to the other side of the open space, he pretended to window shop as he increased his pace the slightest bit. Enmity Row was the next street past the closest intersection—one more block.

It stretched out into eternity before him.

Zach kept his pace even, despite his knees wanting to buckle. He kept his breathing to a steady rhythm, forcing air through a throat that was so dry it hurt. He made himself turn away from tables where patrons had abandoned half-finished plates of food and glasses filled with melting ice.

As he turned his head toward a window display, the reflection showed him a familiar figure keeping pace behind him.

Zach stopped. Squeezed his eyes shut and opened them again.

The pissant Hound he vaguely recalled slicing up on Karem Shem now stood shoulder to shoulder with him. Several inches shorter, his eyes glowed a deep red. Hui smiled, and his mouth stretched too wide, tearing open across his cheeks where Zach had cut an eternal grin into his face as he died. Instant, bone-deep resentment made him want to smash Hui's pudgy, decomposing head like a pumpkin.

Zach ducked his head and kept going, straight through the hallucination.

The ghostly figure dispersed around him, only to appear at his side again, and this time Zach smelled the blood on him.

"How the mighty have fallen," Hui rasped, hacking a wet chuckle. "They'll catch you, you know."

Zach jogged across the intersection and kept jogging down the last block.

"They know where you are."

More and more people turned toward him as he passed. He didn't return their looks, but he felt them. Spotlights on his back, marking him as a target.

"*They're coming*," Hui said into his ear.

Zach broke into a desperate sprint.

He tripped over his own feet as he turned onto Enmity Row. The buildings evolved from quaint shops to street-level office spaces, their address numbers increasing along the way.

One-seven-nine-six.

One-eight-zero-zero.

He was a block away.

"Can't outrun the firing squad," Hui taunted and laughed, throwing back the upper half of his head to hinge his torn mouth wide open to the sky.

One-eight-four-four.

Almost there.

Zach's vision started to blur, going dark around the edges. He'd stopped breathing. His knees buckled, slamming him sideways into a load-bearing column. The resulting crack spiderwebbed upward as dust and rubble rained down on him. He shoved away, forcing more air into his lungs, pushing his legs back into motion.

It wasn't real. Just his exhausted, dehydrated mind playing tricks on him.

Hui had disappeared. His absence only made Zach more aware of how exposed he was.

Running out of time.

He stumbled along a sidewalk as it swayed beneath his feet, squinting at building numbers, but they'd stopped coalescing into coherent font.

One-eight-eight-six.

Zach read it four times to be sure before he reached for the door. He missed the handle by several inches and collapsed against the doorjamb as his legs gave out beneath him.

No, it couldn't end now. He was right there. *Right fucking there!*

Get up, soldier! Haul your sorry ass off the goddamn ground and act like the Hawk you are.

Were.

Zach braced a hand on the wall, but his muscles were done, and his fingers slid uselessly down the surface. Darkness closed in, and he didn't have anything left to fight it back.

So fucking close…

It was almost laughable.

He'd pulled off the greatest double-cross in all of human history only to die inches away from salvation.

Zach thumped his head back against the door, blinking up at the rosy planet looming across the sky.

Who are you?

"My name is…" One more breath dragged painfully down his throat. "Zachary VanWarren." He really did like that name.

Hui's corpsified face appeared before him, blocking out the sky. "You are no one."

"I am no one," Zach repeated. His face had gone numb. He couldn't feel his limbs anymore. A soft hum scrambled his thoughts, stealing the words from the tip of his tongue.

What do you do?

"How does it feel to have betrayed your brotherhood?" Hui demanded, his face screwing up with rage as one of his white eyes popped out of its socket.

"I did what needed to be done."

And no one would ever know.

Zach closed his eyes on a sigh that felt like it took his soul with it.

With a distant sense of separateness, he felt his body fall backward as the door opened.

January 3, 3040 – Imra Valley, Valhale 602

The call came in just after midnight. A familiar alert Raven Dello Russo hadn't heard in several months. She sat up and leaned to the side to reach for her com with a hand that wasn't there anymore. Muscle memory was a bitch.

She really ought to switch her nightstand to the other side of the bed. Not like Julian was coming back to use it…

"Yes?" No preamble. The people who called this particular com didn't bother wasting time on niceties.

"*Hope I'm not interrupting girls' night.*" Darrow Iridiae had as much personality in his voice as her bare walls. It was part of his charm, along with his genius-level intelligence and single-minded dedication to keeping their collective safe.

Nice of him to remember girls' night, but "That was on Friday." The one night every week when Raven was not allowed to think about anything other than the music pounding in her ears and the shimmery drink in her hand. Those were the rules, as set forth by Tessa Sinclair, best friend and the most ruthlessly upbeat dictator Raven had ever known.

"*Oh. Well, I hope I'm not interrupting anything…else.*"

"Well, I was just about to win the staring contest with my ceiling, so if you don't mind."

The short pause was laden with so much weight that Raven started to form an apology in her mind. Darrow might have stood witness at her wedding, but he was still technically her boss.

"*What's keeping you up?*"

Heart palpitations, hyperventilation, paralyzing night terrors, phantom pain that sent spasms through her entire body… "The usual," she said with a shrug.

He hummed in acknowledgment but didn't prod further. One of the many reasons she loved him like the brother she'd never wanted. *"We need you to come in. Got a new subject for you to analyze. He's…unique."*

"I'll be there in two hours."

"See you then."

One hour and fifty-nine minutes later, Raven walked through the front door at one-eight-eight-six Enmity Row, officially the Hilder & Pine Residence Complex. On paper, Hilder & Pine was an assistive medical care facility for long-term patients with chem-resistance complications. Established years before the war, it served a dual purpose of helping those in need while also providing a solid cover for the Special Unit's Valhale 602 home base. Darrow Iridiae wasn't just her boss. He was the boss of every telepath registered with the SU on the terraformed moon.

When the Big Boss called, you came running.

And when you found him waiting for you in the lobby, you braced yourself for a shit storm of epic proportions. "You've expanded since the last time I saw you," Raven said in greeting.

Darrow wasn't what one might expect a Big Boss to look like. Primarily, because he was seventeen years old.

No other organization in the galaxy would even consider appointing a minor to a position of such power, but that was why Raven loved the SU. They didn't discriminate. Three years ago, when the Shadows had fallen on their little moon, there'd been no time for elections. Most of them had been too busy saving their own asses to worry about order and organization. If it hadn't been for Darrow stepping up and taking charge, they all would have fallen apart.

He'd kept an eye on the sky while the adults had cleaned up the mess. He'd organized their forces to put the city back together while they'd mourned their dead and nursed their injuries. He'd set up new security protocols and given them some peace of mind in a galaxy mired in the chaos of war.

He'd earned his title many times over, and no one questioned his right to keep it.

Sometimes, Raven felt sorry for him. Wartime leadership was an unenviable position none of them had been trained for, and none of them wanted. Minor or not, Darrow was stuck with it now. And it took a visible toll.

In the six months since their last meeting face-to-face, he had stretched several inches in height and gained a new gravity in his pitch-black eyes. It didn't mesh with the awkward lankiness of his limbs. At least he'd let his hair grow out a little. Though the baby curls still clung tight to his scalp, making him look both younger and far older than he should.

"How have you been, Rae?" The solicitous concern was as stark as it was unexpected.

"Fine," she said, as she always did. It helped to be as clear as possible when communicating her lack of interest in discussing anything personal.

He nodded, then turned on his heels to lead the way to the elevator bank. "You need to be cautious with this subject." Another thing she loved about Darrow was that boundaries were sacred to him. He never pressed or crossed them.

She followed him into the elevator, shaking off the familiar buzzy sensation of a new, potentially dangerous assignment. "Tell me."

Darrow pressed a button, and a red light flashed across the panel, requesting an ID scan. Certain parts of the facility were only accessible to high-ranking SU personnel. It was as much for protection as it was for comfort. Sometimes, the people who got brought in had minds that could break an inexperienced telepath. It had happened before. But not here. Darrow never took chances with those in his care.

"He showed up on our doorstep around midday, filthy, dehydrated, and circling the drain. His ID chip has been cut out. We suspect he's a Shadow, but his mind is too, shall we say, disorganized, for a proper scan. We rehydrated him, and he's sedated, so the risk should be minimal. But if he is a Shadow, he could be a Trojan Horse."

"Understood."

Their war with the Shadows was about to complete its fourth year. While the grand violence of hovers exploding entire cities had stopped, the subtler assaults continued. They just didn't target anyone prominent or important, so no one reported them anymore.

Raven considered it a good thing. It meant they, too, got to play dirty. War was far more difficult to wage effectively while under the scrutiny of the public's eye.

The elevator came to a stop on Sublevel C, three floors underground. Darrow waved her out first. Raven stepped into the short hallway. There were only three chambers on this floor. One was a medical facility, fully equipped for any emergency treatment that might be needed during the study and interrogation process. The other two were holding cells with one-way observation glass, allowing outsiders to view the subject, who had no idea they were being studied.

They were not prison cells, in the strictest sense of the word, although the matter was often up for debate. To Raven's mind, the definition depended on the person occupying the chamber. More often than not, the holding cells housed unstable telepaths who were either overwhelmed by their abilities or had their self-control severely compromised. Sometimes, they walked in willingly. At other times, they were beyond rational thought and had to be confined *un*willingly. But their quarantine was always temporary, and for their own sanity.

Of course, exceptions happened. Sometimes, the subject was not a telepath, and their stay lasted as long as the SU deemed it necessary for the general public's safety.

Those were the cases for which Raven got called in. As the SU's interrogation specialist, her job was to scan, study, evaluate, and, when necessary, neutralize Factor 1 subjects. Those who presented too much of a threat for other telepaths to manage. It wasn't a pleasant task, but someone had to do it. And Raven would rather it be her than someone she cared about.

Darrow stopped in front of the second holding cell. Although he hadn't placed guards on the subject, he'd chosen the room farthest from the elevator.

Inside, the holding cell was furnished simply but comfortably. It had a bed, a small dining table with two chairs, and a separate bathroom with a sonic shower and a waterless toilet. No sophisticated entertainment consoles that could be hacked, but below the observation glass was a shelf filled with printed books and a few games. The automatic lights adjusted to simulate day and night, preserving healthy circadian rhythms, and the walls were decorated with fake windows framing tranquil nature scenes.

At present, the subject was lying on the bed. Adult male in his mid- to late thirties, with warm tan skin and black hair a shade longer than would be considered neat. As Darrow had said, he was unconscious, but he still exuded a sense of rigid order, essentially lying at attention. He had clearly been treated with care, no doubt washed, medicated, and nourished, but his body still showed signs of physical strain and stress. His lean muscles stood out stark against his too-tight skin. Lines creased his gaunt face, and dark shadows pooled under his eyes.

"Do we have a name?"

"That's one of the things I'm hoping you can find out. Facial recognition searches have yielded nothing. His face and biometrics don't exist in any official registry."

Definitely a Shadow, then. No one else went to such lengths to erase someone's identity.

"I performed the initial scan myself," Darrow continued, "but it was inconclusive."

Raven checked her glare. Scanning a Shadow whom Darrow suspected to be a plant posed an immense risk—one that the regional supervisor should not be taking. She said nothing because, despite his young age, Darrow hadn't gotten to his position by accident. Strong mental abilities ran in his family. His sister, Jessica, worked directly with the acting director of the entire SU collective as their chief of medicine, and, from what Raven understood, she was about Darrow's age, too.

But how curious that, even in an unconscious state, the subject had managed to hold on to something so fundamental and intrinsic. Names were usually the easiest things to glean. They were ingrained in a person's identity from birth and carved across every thought and memory.

Raven raised her hand and pressed it to the glass. It was more for balance than for amplification. Although she found it helped her navigate new minds when she had a physical direction to aim for.

Deep breath in, slow breath out.

She let the physical world fall away from her as her consciousness drifted toward their sleeping subject. Raven approached the boundary of his mind with caution on the off-chance he presented some form of violent resistance. If she did her job right, most people never noticed her invading their minds. The rare ones who did described the sensation as a gentle static and a sense of no longer being alone.

The Shadow's mind didn't have protective shields. Not uncommon among normies. But walking through his sleep was akin to passing through soft draperies. Not difficult, just disorienting.

They were all white.

Blank in a way she'd never encountered before, not even in other Shadows.

At times, she sensed ghosts around her. Never strong enough to manifest in a memory or dream, but enough to suggest the Shadow's mind wasn't completely blank.

Unfortunately, most of what she sensed didn't make sense. There were a lot of numbers and faint impressions of lingering pain. She smelled smoke at one point, and for a split second, the mindscape around her turned dark, with red lights flashing all around in an ominous pulse. Blood coated her hand in one instant, and in the next her chest felt light with what might have been wonder or joy as a long, sweet note of a song faded into silence.

She didn't pick up on any sense of a solid identity. Not even fragments of one.

Maybe she was too close.

Raven dispersed her mental presence from the tip of a spearhead into fine mist to blanket a broader expanse of the Shadow's mind.

Given a thousand guesses, she never would have expected to see what the bird's eye view showed her. It was like looking at a galaxy in its earliest stages of formation. Something she might find in the mind of a child still developing a sense of self. Except that a child's identity would form naturally as a result of their experience of the world. This, whatever it was, had a measure of intelligent design behind it.

Dust clouds of scattered experiences, thoughts, and ideas swirled in the void, slowly coalescing into what would eventually become solid convictions and beliefs. But it had an invisible hand guiding it all as if the Shadow was actively choosing the type of person he wanted to become.

A consciousness and a conscience creating itself.

From scraps of barely more than nothing.

In a fully mature individual.

Raven looked for the brightest lights, the strongest, most recent memories still lingering on the outer periphery of the swirling mass. She picked them out of the darkness and gently turned each fractal to examine its different facets.

Who are you?

The question wasn't hers, but something the Shadow had heard often as a challenge and a test. And the answer was at once a confident, "No one," and a more contemplative idea that sneaked tendrils of desire out into the vortex of his identity. A name that lingered like an exotic flavor on the back of her tongue.

Raven pulled back and extricated herself from the Shadow's mind, the memory she'd taken still firmly attached to her. A memory of what should have been the Shadow's last moments of life, when he'd declared his identity in direct defiance of everything he'd been groomed to be. A dying wish for something denied to him since birth.

"Well?" Darrow asked.

Raven took a moment to process what she'd sensed before she committed to its truth.

Whoever this man was, however he'd ended up across enemy lines, he was a world of trouble waiting to blow up in their faces.

"His name is Zachary VanWarren," she said, naming the lie he'd chosen as the foundation on which to build his truth. "And we're fucked."

January 3, 3040 - Chairo, Valhale 602

Darrow summoned his council to hear what Raven had to say and help him make a decision.

They hadn't had a council meeting in years. Not since the day half of its original members stood up and volunteered to sacrifice themselves for the good of the people.

Everything had changed that day. *Everything.*

The council meeting room encompassed half of the building's top floor, high above the main offices and dormitories. A convenient location for picking up the population's ambient thoughts to gauge the city's general atmosphere.

Not to mention, the glass walls offered spectacular views on all sides.

The city of Chairo nestled in a shallow desert basin, surrounded by coarse, light gray sand. The arid region made plants of any kind a luxury. Instead, residents infused bright colors into every wall and roof, turning the city into a jewel box. When the sun rose, as it did now, its light reflected off each building to form countless glittering rainbows.

The region experienced a short, three-month wet season from mid-December to late February, although 'wet' was a relative term. With temperatures dipping well below freezing at night and hovering just above freezing during the day, the precipitation was mostly snow and hail.

With peak storm season just around the corner, in a week or two, Chairo would transform into a living entity. All of the buildings were specially designed to absorb any excess moisture before it evaporated. When the clouds blew in after sunset, the city turned white with a layer of frost that disappeared as the sun rose in the morning. The daily "breath of water," as the locals called it, was a popular attraction for tourists.

"All council members present and accounted for," Darrow announced.

Raven turned away from the window and took her seat at the long table. As the reason for this get-together, her place was on Darrow's right.

"Let's come to order."

More than half of the current council members had never attended an official meeting. They were already in order, eager to be of use.

"The matter before us is called Zachary VanWarren," Darrow said.

"Of the Jericho VanWarrens?" The first to open their mouth was Ripley Parecourte, dressed today in all the imposing masculinity of a smart dark suit with a thick ring on each knuckle. They were a shameless flirt who made no secret of their love of bedhopping, but they didn't invite the intimacy of friendship even in its most casual forms.

Between Raven's lack of sexual interest and Ripley's emotional walls, they'd come to an unspoken agreement to keep their distance from one another.

Across from them, Xavier Higgins shifted in his seat, adjusting the sleeves of his caftan on top of the table. "Not exactly. There is a Zachary VanWarren tied to the family, but the identity appears to be a Shadow construct. It has no biometric data associated with it, and there's been no mention of it since the attack on Ela last year."

Granted, there were so many VanWarrens that knowing them all should have been impossible. However, the family was currently embroiled in a very public scandal that put everyone with their last name in the spotlight. Their subject must have used a different identity to get this far.

So why had he chosen to anchor his core sense of self in a fake name and an identity he couldn't even use in the first place?

"So we caught ourselves a Shadow?" Ima Ilani, their youngest council member after Darrow, must have been summoned straight out of bed. Her strawberry hair was still up in messy, haphazard buns, and her shirt was inside out.

Darrow shook his head. "He came to us."

Ripley straightened in their seat, as did several others. "Are we compromised?"

"We don't know," Darrow said. "Which brings us to the crux of this meeting: What do we do now? Raven, if you please."

Raven pretended not to see the quick, there-and-away glances pointed her way. Not her face, but the empty sleeve neatly pinned to her suit on the left side of her body.

To their credit, all the council members made an effort to conceal their pity. Raven was just too good at picking up on it.

Eager to get the whole thing over with, she focused her gaze inward, seeking the minds around the table. They were expecting her, but Raven preferred to stick to established protocols. She politely requested access before letting herself through the doors they'd left open for her. Once she was certain she had everyone's undivided attention—and that no one was attempting to take liberties with her thoughts and secrets—Raven pulled up the memory of everything she'd seen in the Shadow's mind and replayed it all for the council members.

She could have pushed the experience to them and let them sort it out, but the slow way was always best—fewer chances of something getting overlooked.

When she finished, Raven extricated herself back to the confines of her own mind.

Linking with other telepaths was easy. Detaching took effort.

Telepath minds were naturally inclined to connect and merge. The longer they remained connected, the more difficult it became to disconnect. While merging minds amplified telepathic abilities, it came at a high risk of losing one's sense of individual self.

Hive minds were dangerous, and telepaths spent their whole lives learning to safeguard against them.

No one wanted to lose themselves. But in extreme circumstances, sacrifices had to be made.

This war with the Shadows had created a lot of extreme circumstances over the years.

The council members remained silent for a while as they rebuilt their shields and reviewed what Raven had shared.

Then the debate began.

Darrow sat back and let them talk among themselves. He was only there to provide the swing vote, if one was needed. And since she wasn't on the council, Raven didn't get a vote. She'd done her duty by relaying what she knew. Technically, she could leave now. But she stayed put, letting the cacophony of voices wash over her to gauge how quickly she'd need to pack.

Xavier's agitation buzzed over the table. "This is a serious breach. He couldn't have found us on his own. Someone's betrayed us."

Jubal scoffed. "That is ridiculous. Who among us would be so stupid as to feed themselves to the wolves? And how could they have done it without *anyone* sensing a threat?"

"Subterfuge and sabotage are not the same thing," Orson offered. "If they thought they were acting for the good of the collective, no one would have noticed. We have poached Shadows from their ranks before. Perhaps someone simply got a little too ambitious."

After three years, the SU network boasted a good number of Shadows among its ranks—their acting director, Emma Wayland, was married to the first one ever to defect. They also kept tabs on several more who had decided to withdraw from the conflict altogether and go into hiding.

But never before had a Shadow without any prior contact or communication with the SU deliberately sought them out like this, let alone in a facility with no discernible ties to them.

"Are you willing to bet the lives of everyone at this facility on that assumption?" Xavier asked.

Ripley leaned forward, frowning in thought. "The motivation is irrelevant. Whoever revealed our location to him compromised all of our safety. We should notify the acting director immediately and begin moving the most vulnerable off-site."

Raven agreed.

Darrow and Orson did not. "Evacuation is confirmation," Orson said. "We need to find out whether we're a target before we make ourselves into one."

Ripley glared at him, but since Darrow didn't argue the point, neither did they. "Let's assume there's been no foul play," they said dryly. "His condition appears to be desperate. However he got here, he came for a reason. We need to find out what it is while we have him in custody."

Ima nodded in agreement. "Seconded. I also agree that the acting director needs to be notified immediately. We may not be the only ones who were compromised."

That was a sobering thought. Raven hadn't even considered that this might be part of an orchestrated attack. If so, they were even more fucked than she'd thought.

"Can we turn him?" Ima inquired, and Raven blinked to find them all looking at her for an answer.

She'd missed a critical conversational pivot point there. How had they gone from interrogating the Shadow to this?

"Into what?" she asked before she could think better of it.

Clearly, that had been the wrong thing to say. Xavier rolled his eyes with a frustrated huff, and at the far end, Jubal and Orson pushed away from the table altogether.

"I believe," Darrow supplied, "Ima is asking if it is possible to re-program Mr. VanWarren."

Right. That.

Reprogramming minds was part of Raven's job description. She hated it. Eradicating someone's past and giving them a chance to live a better life should have been a good thing. But every time she did it, Raven felt stained by the sins she erased.

"He was unconscious during our initial scans," she said. "I would need to do it again once he's awake to get a proper read on his mental state."

Darrow took a minute to think it over, his eyes darting left and right as if he was visualizing the complex decision tree before them. No one spoke a word, respecting his need for silence. When he finished his internal analysis, Darrow nodded to himself. "Thank you all for your time and input. I will notify the acting director of our situation, but unless other locations have reported a similar breach, I suspect she will leave this in our hands."

Reasonable. The SU had hundreds of locations on every inhabited world and then some. The acting director couldn't oversee them all. She would expect them to be able to handle one Shadow on their own.

"We will allow Mr. VanWarren to sleep off his ordeal. When he wakes up, Raven will take the lead on his case."

Raven nodded her grim acceptance. She pulled the assignments she did for a reason. No one else on this moon had the kind of telepathic framework she'd built up throughout her life. Most people trained for decades in just one telepathic discipline. Raven had mastered three. Something told her she'd need all of them to get through this.

"You will question him and see what you can find out about how he got to us, where he came from, and what he's after. If he can be swayed to our cause, we will use him. If it turns out his neural infrastructure is too damaged to accept a new directive, we will take the appropriate measures."

"Understood," Raven said. "The sooner we get to the bottom of this, the better."

"Take your time," Darrow countered. "If Mr. VanWarren is as dangerous as I suspect, I don't want you spending more than two hours with him on any given day. I'll pull a roster of names to test on him while you rest and regroup—which you will."

"It's too risky to involve others," she argued.

"They'll have armed guards and won't be allowed into his cell. He won't know they're there."

That was a lie. Or maybe just wishful thinking.

In any case, "I'm more concerned about them compromising"—tampering with—"the subject's memories."

"I'll keep the list short and vet every candidate with the council," Darrow said, meeting her pointed gaze head-on. "Will that satisfy you?"

No, it wouldn't. Someone had revealed their location to the Shadows. If it was someone at Hilder & Pine, giving anyone outside of this chamber access to the Shadow was irresponsible and potentially dangerous.

"The medical team treated him on arrival," Ripley pointed out. "Everyone already knows we have a new subject in custody. If we don't treat him the same as any other, people will talk. We don't want to cause a panic."

Training on subjects in quarantine, especially Shadows, was an

invaluable learning experience and standard procedure at Hilder &
Pine. Depending on the case, they might limit access on occasion,
but they'd never had a case that necessitated total isolation before.

Ripley was right. Damn it.

Raven inclined her head. "Your call, boss."

Darrow nodded to the council members, dismissing them with
whatever telepathic orders he didn't deign to have Raven hear.

They murmured their goodbyes and left without further argument.
None of them looked Raven's way again. As the last one out, Ima closed
the door behind her, leaving Raven alone with Darrow.

"Let me know what you need to work on the subject," Darrow said.
"I'll expect progress reports after every session."

"Two hours a day, starting at noon tomorrow. While I'm with him,
I want no one else on the floor."

"You'll need guards."

Raven smiled. "To protect me from the Shadow, or the Shadow
from me?"

Darrow glared.

"I'll also need his medical report."

"You'll have the file before you leave." Darrow shifted in his seat.
"Speaking of medical files, have any of the doctors updated you on…?"

"No."

He winced. "Me either. I keep pushing, but I guess my authority
only extends so far. Every time I call one of them, the condescending
pricks talk to me like I'm a child."

"I know you're doing everything you can. I appreciate that more
than you know."

She really did. Raven's missing arm was a constant reminder of the
worst day of her life and all the pain and suffering that had come after.
A replacement would go a long way to helping her forget and move on.

Maybe that was why she'd been less than proactive about it.

Part of her didn't want to forget.

Part of her didn't see the point.

"Well, if there's anything you need, you know how to reach me."

Raven accepted the dismissal and let herself out of the room.

By the time she climbed into her transport, the dash screen indicated a new file in her inbox and an upgrade to her security clearance for the next thirty-six days.

Raven sat back and let the autonav take over for the next hour and a half while she familiarized herself with Zachary VanWarren's medical file. She had the rest of the day to prep.

At noon tomorrow, she would be clocking in to the most intense assignment of her professional life.

4

January 4, 3040 - Persephone 5

There was no warning. The global defense alert system never activated. No one noticed that the communication relays had stopped working—because not all of their functions did. Only the ones that would make a difference. Even the weather satellites failed to detect the disturbance.

The news arrived from the night side minutes after the first attack, and seconds before the day side skies darkened with a massive fleet of rapidly descending shuttles. Flames and lightning coated their hulls, their orchestrated volley of plasma bombs blinding anyone foolish enough to look up.

Not that it mattered.

Two Earth-standard hours later, Old Port, Messina, Ursik, Station, Tehir, and seventy-eight other major metropolitan areas were reduced to ash and rubble. Plumes of toxic smoke rolled along with the air currents, raining corrosive acid on land and sea. Violent tornadoes ripped across coastal areas, wreaking untold destruction and claiming millions more lives.

Distress signals went out not from government agencies or even military complexes but from terrified citizens hoping to see the faces of their loved ones one last time. Their calls never connected.

A strategic strike on Mt. Vai activated the volcano that had been controlled through periodic lava drains for the last fifty years. Its eruption would have been felt three thousand miles away, had anyone there still been alive to notice.

Gerald Holdermann, a news reporter returning from vacation,

noticed the shuttle fleet emerging out of subspace moments before his cabin window shielded closed and his flight dropped out of the system.

By the time it emerged at its midpoint stop on Juneau, all of the news networks had already reported on the tragic, global-killer eruption of Mt. Vai and the quarantine declared on Persephone 5.

His report of inbound battle shuttles with weapons primed to engage got laughed out of every room.

No one believed him.

No one wanted to.

5

"It's noon," Raven said.

Ripley, too busy staring into the Shadow's cell, did not respond.

"I was clear in my instructions, was I not?"

"You were," Ripley replied, still staring.

"Then may I ask what you're doing here?"

Finally, Ripley blinked and turned their head toward Raven.

They were a uniquely beautiful individual with androgynous features that looked striking in both feminine and masculine makeup. With their deep love of transformation, Raven had seen them dominate a room full of criminals as a male, steal the power of higher thought function from gala attendees as a femme fatale, and command unwavering attention from everyone, at all degrees in between, simply by walking down a crowded street.

More than once, Raven had envied them the ability to step out of one persona and into another with such ease. Like shucking out of a skin that didn't quite fit the moment, or changing their colors the way some animals did to project something completely different, depending on their audience.

Unfortunately, despite their ever-changing outward appearance, underneath it, they were still a royal ass.

Today, they presented a stunning contrast to Raven's black suit uniform, wrapped in all white from head to toe, with their platinum hair slicked back.

It felt like a deliberate choice.

As was their current presence on Sublevel C.

"I am a member of the Chairo council," Ripley said. "If I feel it necessary to scope out a potential threat to our institution, I will do so. Also, I don't take orders from a contractor." For someone who'd been on the council less than a year, Ripley had quite the superiority complex.

"But you do take them from Darrow."

Ripley graced her with a smile that turned their kohled eyes into near-iridescent chips of aquamarine ice. "For now." Yet, instead of leaving, Ripley turned back to the cell. "Your subject is awake. He has an interesting mind."

Raven waited for them to elaborate. She could have looked for herself, but without knowing what Ripley was up to, the risk wasn't worth it.

"I wish you luck with him," they said as if their interest had just run out. "I'll be eager to read your report."

"I'll have it to *Darrow* before the close of day," Raven replied sweetly, then stepped aside to nod Ripley toward the elevator.

The council member swept past on a waft of their signature desert bloom perfume, a cloying scent that lingered in the air long after they left.

Twelve-oh-four.

Raven was late.

She hated being late.

As soon as Ripley had cleared the level, Raven shook herself off and approached the Shadow's holding cell.

He was, indeed, awake. He'd also decided to strip down to the thin, white shorts the medical team had put on him after his exam. Raven had already seen all of his physical scans; she knew what he looked like, from the shade of his skin and every mark on it, to the flowing lines of honed muscles. But there was a defiant vitality about him that no scan could capture.

Zachary VanWarren looked at ease, strolling back and forth within the confines of his cell, his expression nearly meditative. But Raven's skin prickled at the tension he exuded with each barefoot step.

Twelve-oh-six. Time to say hello.

She scanned her ID against the lock and stepped into the cell.

The Shadow stopped his circuit and faced her with a charming grin. It froze on his lips as soon as he saw her. "It's not you." He sounded more intrigued than disappointed.

The door closed and locked automatically. Raven pulled out a chair and made herself comfortable at the table. "My name is Raven Dello Russo. I am an interrogation specialist for this branch of the Special Unit."

He cocked his head, dropping a strand of black hair over his eyebrow as his dark brown gaze swept her from head to toe. It didn't linger. It also didn't miss anything. "Where's the other one?"

"Other one?"

"The one who's been prodding at my brainpan for the last hour. Clumsy. One might say, discourteous. Doesn't seem like your style, so why are you the one who walked through the door? And what happened to the other one?"

His summary fully encompassed the danger a Shadow presented. He'd not only clocked the telepathic intrusion into his mind, but also inferred from its style traits and characteristics of the intruder—and he wasn't far off the mark about Ripley. He'd even profiled Raven within seconds and correctly deduced from just her entrance that he was dealing with at least two separate individuals before she'd said a single word or gone anywhere near his mind.

He was observant, intelligent, and physically as flawless as a human being could get without losing their humanity. He had the build of a habitual swimmer, with powerful limbs and a broad chest. His facial features were even and striking. His coloring suggested origins in a region with abundant sunlight. He had a narrow nose and sharp M peaks to his upper lip. His initial exam hadn't revealed any evidence of surgical augmentation. He was simply a fluke of genetics, as all pretty people were.

Except, in his case, good looks were a weapon. And, if the crooked half-smile and wicked spark in his eyes were any indication, he knew it, and knew how to use it to his advantage.

"Would you care to take a seat?"

"I prefer to stand," he said, flexing his abs for show.

Raven ignored the posturing but made note of his body language.

He kept his distance, his hands clasped at his back. He didn't attempt to intimidate her, and made no threats, verbal or physical. From his unconcerned demeanor and his astute assessment, Raven concluded his rank among the Shadows to be Hawk.

Unlike the foot soldier Hounds, Hawks received additional training to turn them into infiltration specialists. They worked alone and, as such, were highly lethal weapons in and of themselves.

"Let's start with something simple. What is your name?"

He grinned at her. "Raven. Not a name you hear often outside of Earth these days. Who clipped your wing, Blackbird?"

"Do you expect me to be unsettled by the nickname?"

"Would Carrion work better?"

"I'd much rather know what to call you."

The Shadow leaned forward a little. "Guess."

It wasn't an invitation so much as a dare.

Raven decided to take it. Keeping an eye on him just in case, she split her focus to let herself into his mind.

Immediately, the goddamn Shadow dropped her into a lurid scene. Flashes of naked bodies writhing on a massive bed, white silk sheets crumpled and pushed aside. A passionate moan echoed in her ear, shuddering through her frame. A pale hand fisted into thick black hair; a muscled back flexed as lean hips curved in and up, a pair of long, pale legs locked around them.

If he'd had any telepathic abilities, Raven would have felt the slide of skin against skin and smelled the musk of sex permeating the air. As it was, the close-up of his mouth sucking at her nipple was enough to make her body react physically, her brain supplying what his had failed to provide.

Raven blinked herself back into the cell to find the Shadow's smile had turned contemplative. "Definitely wasn't you before."

"I'll take that as a compliment," she said.

"You should. So? See anything interesting in there?"

People who'd had dealings with telepaths in the past often looked for ways to keep their thoughts safe from unwelcome intrusion. The usual techniques involved concentrating on one specific item in their vicinity or repeating nonsensical rhymes. But here, again, the Shadow proved himself to be a step ahead and above with his mental deflection strategy.

It wouldn't work in the long run, but Raven didn't imagine he ever needed it to. He only needed to throw a telepath off their game long enough to make his move.

So why hadn't he?

"The name you chose is Zachary VanWarren."

Thankfully, she'd managed to get at least that much during her scan last night. Let him think she'd seen past his surface thoughts. It wouldn't do her any good to let on how well his counteroffensive had worked. She hadn't been prepared for it—this time. She wouldn't make that mistake ever again.

"But it's not the name you were assigned at birth. Care to explain?"

The Shadow didn't show any outward signs of surprise, but Raven could tell she'd caught him off guard. She endured another measuring once-over and noted his continued lack of interest in her handicap. Then the Shadow closed the distance between them and seated himself at the table with her. "Can you detect lies?"

"It's one of my specialties, yes." More of an offshoot of one. Raven had a rare ability to compel people to think and speak only the truth. She could detect its neural pathways and shut down any distractions to prevent someone from using them to disguise it.

"Good. Use it."

She gestured for him to proceed.

"The name I was assigned at birth is Operative M. I am the product of an unsanctioned breeding program on Prime Gama. I was adopted into the Shadows directly after my umbilical cord was severed, and served as a Hawk from age twelve. Two years ago, I discovered a security flaw in the Shadow operating systems, allowing me to access restricted accounts. I used this access to learn some things they don't want anyone to know. I also used it to transfer ownership of several primary bank accounts to separate entities under my control, then staged a double-cross to bring down a minor outpost and destroy a database of ongoing research into DNA grafting."

He didn't blink once.

"You…robbed the Shadows?"

"To be more precise, I financially crippled them."

"You understand they will dismantle you bone by bone."

He shrugged. "That's why I'm here. There's no safer place for me to take refuge than with the Shadows' greatest enemy. Tell me I'm lying."

He wasn't.

That was the scariest part.

This man had just given her everything to prove he was, if not with them, then at least against the Shadow.

Which wouldn't help them one single bit when the Shadows came to exact their revenge.

Dammit, they should have killed him while they'd had the chance.

Zach watched as the interrogation specialist they'd assigned to him did the math in her head. She was a fascinating specimen. Five and a half feet in flats, all buttoned up in a suit that might as well have been armor. Skin like the palest marble, and black hair cropped in a harsh straight line just above her shoulders. Her almond-shaped eyes, the color of golden honey, looked straight through him out of a doll-like face that was too sweet for the harsh, expressionless mask she put on for his benefit. She may have been named for a scavenger, but her personality was all predator. She didn't waste an ounce of energy, entirely focused on the hunt. Graceful, probably deadly.

In many ways, she reminded him of a Shadow Hawk. The same rigid neatness in look and dress, the same discipline and personal distance. Her mental touch had felt like a brush of down feathers across his entire being. No comparison to the bludgeon he'd felt before. Raven Dello Russo wasn't a professional in her field. She was an artist.

Zach didn't think she ran the facility, but he knew authority when he saw it. If he wanted to claim sanctuary with the Special Unit, he'd have to convince their interrogation specialist of his worth first.

Curious about her arm. She didn't appear to be self-conscious about it, but she didn't seem inclined to discuss it, either. Maybe that was his in. Since his more seductive strategy had failed to impress her, he needed to switch gears. If he could get her to open up to him about her past, he could build on her trust to smooth his way into the SU.

"Why did you come here?" she asked. "Why this branch?"

"I don't know."

"Lie," she declared. "Try again."

"Not a lie," he countered. "I probably had a good reason for it at some point. But after the outpost on Karem Shem went up in flames—with me still inside, by the way—my CO put me in the chair and wiped my memory. All I have is what I recorded for myself as a failsafe. I got a lot of account numbers, limited information on Shadow presence and recent movements, a new identity profile, and the address to your offices here in Chairo."

If they hadn't moved him. Zach had no idea how long he'd been under. He could be at the opposite end of the galaxy, for all he knew.

"Speaking of Shadow movements, there were an awful lot of them at the shuttleport when I landed. I am ninety-seven percent sure I lost them, but you might want to have your people put out an alert."

"Thank you for the warning. Where did you get our address?"

"I don't recall."

"Were you in contact with anyone from our organization at any point in the past?"

"I don't recall."

"Do the Shadow know we're here?"

He frowned. "The point was to get away from them. Why would I run to a location I knew to be compromised?"

Her mental touch swept across his mind, raising goose bumps down his back. It felt like a caress, and Zach had to steel his spine against melting.

Then it withdrew, and his interrogator abruptly changed the subject. "What happened on Karem Shem?"

Zach didn't figure telepaths for complete idiots, but it was possible they might have gotten a little overconfident from their past victories. Now that his life depended on them taking proper precautions, the way she'd dismissed his warning about Shadows in their city concerned him just a smidge.

Then again, maybe she didn't feel like discussing it with a prisoner, which was fair.

"My past self didn't deem those details to be necessary for me to remember. I know I had a prisoner there, and I know I was using their systems to avail myself of their funds." He grinned. "I remember I got stabbed."

"And that is a good thing?"

"The woman who did it came right up to me and shoved her knife in my gut." He couldn't keep his satisfaction out of his tone.

The interrogation specialist looked unimpressed.

Clearly, she didn't understand. "She looked me in the eye and twisted the knife," he explained. "In my *gut.* Among the Shadows, that's practically a love poem." Up close and personal. And the eye contact! Sublime. "I don't care what anyone says. She was into me."

The confounded woman twitched an eyebrow.

Zach sighed. "I guess you had to be there."

"What happened then?"

He shrugged. "The infiltration team shot the place to shit and made off with my prisoner. Reinforcements arrived shortly after, evacuated the survivors, patched me up, and then put me in the chair."

"Who was the prisoner?"

"Not included in my self-brief. Knowing myself fairly well, I assume it's because I'm not supposed to go near them anymore."

The interrogation specialist considered this for a moment, then changed the topic. "You chose a rather high-profile name for your secret identity."

Yeah, he'd figured that out about an hour after making his quick exit. The VanWarrens were all over the news. Overnight, a good number of VanWarren businesses had shut down or declared bankruptcy, and watching the family's public lives implode on screen had become the entire galaxy's favorite pastime. Debt collectors had primetime shows centered around them showing up at a VanWarren house to pick apart their valuables in payment. Half of them weren't there, so they got to break in and cash in on the added entertainment value of showing off how the ultrarich really lived.

Every other day, one of the patriarchs released a statement about how they'd been targeted for a systematic attack and were working with the authorities to locate the culprit and bring them to justice. Right after those recordings, a team of lawyers and police officers followed up to refute their claims and deny any malicious activity against the VanWarrens.

It was all very entertaining.

And it made Zach's life a living hell.

The mere mention of the name VanWarren put him in the spotlight and in the Shadows' crosshairs. He'd already burned multiple identities to get this far. At some point, he'd like to adopt the name permanently. Alas, as much as he liked it—and he really did—until the war came to its bitter end, advertising it was not the smartest idea.

"It would appear my past self miscalculated a bit on that score."

"What is your mission here in Chairo?"

"Do you always wear all black?"

"We're not talking about me."

"Well, Blackbird, I gave you everything you need for now. So if you want to keep chatting, you'll have to give me something in return."

She drummed her fingers on the table—once. "I prefer a standardized wardrobe. It makes my day-to-day life simpler."

"Because of your arm?"

"Because I consider fashion a waste of time."

Now who's lying?

"What is your mission here in Chairo?" she asked again.

"I want protection."

"Why did you betray the Shadows?"

"I literally just went over that. What happened to your arm?"

"You told me *what* you did. Not *why.*"

Zach grinned. Clever. "The answer will cost you, Blackbird."

She had a knack for keeping her inner thoughts to herself, but he still picked up on her rising frustration. Raven Dello Russo was accustomed to poking at others, but not having them poke back at her. "Three years ago, the Shadows took down the global nav network. An oncoming transport accelerated out of control and collided with mine. I got pinned, and my arm was crushed beyond salvaging."

"Were you knocked unconscious in the collision?"

"The answer will cost you, Shadow."

"I feel no allegiance to the Shadows. Not even the manufactured kind. Guess it doesn't work on me."

It was true, as far as Zach knew. The Shadows might have made him, but for whatever reason, they didn't own him the way they did so many others.

"No," she said. "I was not." It took him a second to realize she was answering his question.

"How long were you stuck there?" If the entire nav grid had collapsed, every vehicle on Valhale 602 would have either stalled or crashed. Civilians no longer had to complete training courses on operating vehicles. The vast majority of them wouldn't know how to handle one without automatic navigation.

That included first responders.

"What was your last assignment for the Shadows?" she shot back.

Zach decided to be generous. "Can't recall. I just know there was a sharp pivot that changed the mission objective to target acquisition and damage control."

"Three hours and forty-seven minutes," she said.

And it was a damn good thing Zach was sitting down to hear it.

Four hours, pinned inside a transport with her arm crushed beyond repair. Fully conscious.

"Were you alone?"

"Where did you escape from? Which outpost?"

"Were—you—alone?"

"Telepaths are never alone," she said. But her eyes darted downward for a blink.

Lie.

Zach flexed his fingers underneath the table.

Raven cocked her head. "I sense you've become agitated."

Agitated? Yeah, you could say so.

"The sooner you answer my questions, the sooner we can both go our separate ways."

Funny, how that didn't help the *agitation* at all. "Planet 7439 in the Halo system. It's terraformed, but not accessible to civilians. Only way in or out is with Shadow shuttles. I ditched the one I stole as soon as I touched down on Jericho, and stowed away on a mass transit shuttle to Mars 2, then to Earth, and then here."

Each of those planets had a strong Special Unit presence. He could have walked out of the shuttleport on any of them and made contact with the local cell within hours.

He'd come here for a reason. Even if he didn't remember what it was.

"Thank you for your cooperation," she said, and, despite calling him agitated, Zach sensed she was eager to get away from him, too. "Is there anything else I should know?"

He needed a hook. If he let Raven run away in her current state, she would never come back. And he needed her to come back. "Yes," he said, fixing a grin on his face, and giving his imagination free rein to set the scene. "Before you and I are through, you're going to beg me to fuck you."

He knew she wouldn't be able to resist looking, so he pictured himself throwing her on the too-soft cot they gave him. He imagined tearing her out of her black suit and pinning her good arm over her head while he fingered her pussy and tongued her nipples.

He could get her dripping wet for him, writhing and begging for him to let her come, cursing him for keeping her on the edge until her entire body shook for release. The quiet ones always turned unabashedly feral in bed. His cold and distant Blackbird would *burn*, he was sure of it. She would claw and bite him bloody and—

There she was. The brush of invisible down over his skin made him rock-hard as he imagined her coming on his hand, screaming in his ear, bucking them both up off the cot. So much passion, so tightly contained behind her professional mask of disinterest.

Oh, he'd very much enjoy breaking it down.

Bit. By. Bit.

The object of his sordid fantasies leaned forward, a sultry smile teasing at her lips. "Not unless you somehow get really good, really fast," she purred.

And his mind took a sharp turn south, with her thighs around his ears, and her delicate hand fisted in his hair, holding him in place as she rocked her pussy against his mouth. His body jerked in the hard chair as every single one of his senses engaged full force, from the feel of her skin against his face to the sound of her cries.

The air became too humid to breathe—he was more than happy to drown.

The lights flickered out—he didn't need to see anything but her.

He lost all sense of time and space, his head spinning and his body twitching with insatiable need. He wanted to bury his dick inside her. The silken sheets he thrust against were nowhere near enough to sate him—and *sweet heaven,* but she was just as demanding.

Zach groaned, palming himself under the table, aching as if *she'd* edged *him* for hours. Still fully immersed in the vision, salivating for a real taste of her, he blindly leaned in to meet her over the table, desperate to know if she was as delicious as he imagined—

The vision disappeared.

He blinked in the sudden brightness of his cell to find Raven standing from her seat, all business and no give. "Oops, would you look at that? We're out of time."

And she walked straight out the door without a backward glance.

7

Raven kept it together until the moment the door closed and locked behind her. She crossed the hallway and leaned against the opposite wall, her heart rate taking its sweet time to slow down. Her knees felt weak, and she sweated beneath her suit.

She hadn't even lasted the whole two hours in there.

Raven was a grown, mature woman, not some blushing virgin. The fantasies the Shadow had spun for himself didn't bother her. But the truth behind them had thrown her. Yes, he'd used them to shield his inner thoughts, but in doing so, he'd revealed something else.

It had been a long, long time since anyone had looked at Raven with that much lust.

Three years, to be exact.

She didn't like it.

She didn't, dammit!

One hour and twelve minutes left on the clock for today's session. Sublevel C was under constant surveillance. No doubt, Darrow would know she'd ended the session earlier than scheduled. He'd want to know why.

Well, boss, it appears I have somehow become the object of the prisoner's sexual fantasies, and I'm not sure how to handle it.

Playing into them had been a mistake. Raven had meant to distract him enough to get deeper into his thoughts, but in the seven seconds she'd managed to hold onto it, Raven had only caught a pretty melody she'd never heard before.

In retrospect, three years might have been too long to abstain from any form of physical intimacy. If the state of her body was anything to go by, crossing her legs tightly would set her off right now. And the fact that she'd been brought to this by a *Shadow* added a thrill to the shame and made her all kinds of conflicted about it.

But she could handle this.

She was a professional.

Raven pressed her forehead against the wall to better feel the texture. She took a deep breath of sterile air with a hint of disinfectant. The sound of her heartbeat thudded in her ears as she licked her tongue across the edge of her teeth. Physical sensations that were real. Not a fantasy. Not a telepathic red herring to lead her off the straight and narrow.

It took longer than she would have liked but after a few minutes, Raven's knees steadied and the butterflies in her abdomen settled. Because she was a goddamn professional, and she would not be thrown like this by anyone. Much less a Shadow.

He stood for everything she despised. He was the face of her pain and grief. All she had to do was remember.

The shock of a blaring alarm as her transport suddenly swerved out of control. The sharp explosion of metal crumpling like paper, and glass exploding at her face.

The last time she'd looked into Julian's eyes. The last kiss he'd pressed to her temple, whispering words of love before walking away from her for good.

The agony of rousing out of a chemical coma in a hospital bed, knowing that nothing would ever be the same again; that she'd lost more than she could ever rebuild.

There.

Her spine straightened. Raven rolled her shoulder and tipped her head back on a sigh.

There it was, the tragedy of her existence—it kept going.

The Shadow was nothing more than her latest assignment. He would be gone in a few weeks, one way or another, and then none of this would matter anymore. Her life would go back to its usual routine, and she would forget all of this.

She'd slipped. It happened to the best telepaths. Wouldn't happen again. She'd take a minute to compose herself, then go to a drop-in office upstairs to make her report. Then she'd have the rest of the day to get her head back in the game and come up with a strategy for her second session with the Shadow tomorrow.

Walk away. Take a breather. Regroup and come back.

Easy enough.

Against her better judgment, Raven turned to face the glass.

The Shadow had moved from the table to the cot. He'd shucked off his shorts and was now sprawled out across the mattress, head thrown back, eyes closed, muscles flexing as he stroked his hard cock.

And Raven froze, tracking the movement of his fist up to the swollen head, down, and down to the base. She was several feet away, on the other side of a glass wall, but she might as well have been in the room with him. Her rapt gaze missed nothing. She traced the veins as they bulged and disappeared beneath his grasp, and her breath caught to see a bead of precum collect at his tip. She watched him swirl his thumb through it, then twist his fist over the head before stroking back down the length.

This was wrong.

She shouldn't be watching this.

Then again, he'd started it with his lurid fantasies. It was practically an open invitation.

He cupped his sac and arched a little while his fist continued to pump up and down the length of his erection at an ever-increasing pace.

Raven's vision blurred as her consciousness split, floating straight into his mind without her say-so. She dropped into *her* version of the fantasy, but *his* point of view. Her thighs all but drowned out her breathy moans. She could almost feel her intimate flesh against his lips. The pleasure the Shadow derived from the act bordered on obsession. He was single-minded in his task and fervid about the looming result.

As he registered Raven's presence in his mind, his skin erupted in goose bumps. The fantasy vision of Raven screamed her climax, bucking against him, but he clutched her to his mouth to ride out the orgasm with her.

And then the imagined pleasure became real, chasing Raven back to herself in time to see him make himself come.

Raven stumbled away from the cell and made a dash for the elevator, her body riding the sharp edge of a climax she'd experienced in her mind but hadn't quite reached physically. The son of a bitch had felt her snooping. He'd been waiting for her to float right into his trap.

She fumbled with the ID scanner and jabbed at the floor button until the doors closed. Her face burned, and her hand shook.

Too soon, the elevator opened on Darrow with his arms crossed over his chest. "You're off the case."

"What?" Raven shook her head. "Why?"

"*Why?* Did you really ask me that?"

Get ahold of yourself. Raven pressed her lips together and sucked in a sharp breath through her nose to cool her insides. She was probably glowing red right now. Short of taking a long stroll through the industrial freezer in the kitchens, she couldn't do anything about it without drawing more attention to her obvious distress. "I can handle him."

"He is a Shadow with a dangerous attraction to you."

He didn't know the half of it. He'd only heard and seen the conversation she'd had with the Shadow in his cell. He wouldn't have been privy to anything happening inside the Shadow's mind because the lower floors had a Faraday layer between them, keeping telepath minds on their respective sides of it.

"I'm taking you off this case. End of discussion." Her seventeen-year-old boss turned on his heels to walk away.

It pissed her off. "If I can't get through to him, no one will," she snapped, following him to his office. She slammed the door behind her for good measure.

Darrow tended to overcompensate for his age by keeping his work environment and relationships as impersonal as possible. He hadn't changed a single thing in his office. The walls were still empty, painted in a flat beige tone. He hadn't moved his desk from its original position at a right angle to the door and the window, facing the far wall. He didn't have any books on the shelves, or knick-knacks on his desk. The trash bin by the window was always empty, and the name plate on his desk still showed his title as Jr. Liaison because he'd never gotten a new one made.

Darrow rounded the desk to snap open the window shades. "Your skills are not in question here."

"Then there is no discussion to be had. Every subject resists initial contact—you know that. This one just happens to be more perverse about it than most. He had no malicious intent. It was all a defense mechanism."

Nothing about his fantasies had indicated intent to harm. If anything, he seemed to get off on the idea of bringing her pleasure. Mind-boggling, out-of-the-world pleasure. As a Hawk, he would have been trained in the psychology of desire and how to use it against a mark. But what she'd seen in his mind hadn't felt like a cold manipulation. It had felt like something a person would scribble onto the pages of a secret diary. He'd meant for her to see the act. He hadn't intended for her to pick up on how much it appealed to *him*. And it had. Which meant she could use it against him.

"It's a hook I can use to build rapport. As long as he's receptive to me, I can work him. I've got this under control."

Darrow paused halfway into his seat to do a double-take at her. "Are you…*flattered* by his interest?"

Deep breath. "I'm going to give you a chance to rethink what you just said to me and correct course."

He flushed, looking away. "I didn't mean to imply you were compromised."

"No, just that I'm so desperate for attention I'd be willing to entertain it from a Shadow. We'll skip right over you speculating about my personal life and finding it lacking, shall we?" She wouldn't insult him by accusing him of crossing the line and peeking into her mind without her consent. Normally, she would have felt it if he had—except she wasn't at her best at the moment.

Darrow sat and steepled his fingers.

Raven didn't bother taking a chair. She didn't plan to be there any longer than necessary. "There is no one better to process the Shadow than me," she said. "Unless you want to try brute force and risk destroying the integrity of his memories in the process."

He took a couple of seconds to think about it, but in the end, said, "No. We need to learn what he knows."

"Then you'll need me to fill in the blanks, because what he remembers might not be enough on its own."

One of her three specialties was memory reconstruction. She could visualize fragments of remembrance like pieces of an elaborate puzzle and rearrange them into their correct place. Even if the picture missed entire chunks, this method of realignment gave the subject more clarity. It minimized the mind's tendency to exaggerate, omit, or fabricate to make the incomplete story make sense. It was tricky, intensive work, and one of the prevailing causes of burnout among telepaths.

Darrow glared at her for the reminder. He was cornered, and he knew it. "Regardless of what he does or doesn't know, your safety is my first priority."

Not a potential traitor in their midst, not the other Shadows lurking in their city.

Raven's safety—which wasn't compromised in the first place.

What was he thinking?

"I'm cutting your time slot to an hour a day. You'll attend *mandatory* meditations before and after your sessions with the Shadow, and I'll be monitoring the situation the entire time you're in there with him."

"I'm not a child."

"No, you're my employee. And I have just outlined what I expect from you for the duration of this assignment. You got a problem with that, tell me now."

The precautions were reasonable.

But they still rubbed Raven the wrong way.

Nevertheless, as long as Darrow was in charge, Raven had to follow his instructions to the letter. Telepaths were too dangerous to be allowed free rein. The rigid order the Special Unit had built up since its inception was in place to protect not just them, but society at large.

Raven nodded. "Understood."

"And I still want that first report by the end of the day."

"You heard the whole conversation. I didn't delve deep enough to gauge what he omitted, but everything he said out loud was pure truth. We should look into the Shadow presence in Chairo and route them off-world."

"I already have people on it."

"His memory is definitely impaired, and his sense of self is fragmented. He might not remember his SU contact, but if I can put enough pieces of him together, something might float to the surface." It was possible that the traitor's face or voice still lingered somewhere in his subconscious mind, and he'd lost the connection between that person and his current predicament. "I also caught a few leads from his personal life that I want to follow up on. But nothing solid yet."

"Impressive progress for the first session."

"As I said."

He shifted in discomfort. "Very good. If he truly deserted from the Shadows, and you can vouch for his intentions…?"

"Based on everything I've seen so far, Zachary VanWarren is absolutely a threat by virtue of the fact that he is here. But he has no active intentions to harm me or anyone at this facility. I'm more concerned about how he got here in the first place. What did the acting director say?"

"No other locations have been compromised. We're to handle this as we see fit."

That was a relief. "So what are your orders? Should we consider evacuating?"

He stared at his desk for a moment, then said, "No."

"Are you sure?" she pushed.

He gave her a quelling look. "Why don't you let me worry about security?"

Raven stifled a flinch. Darrow didn't like having his authority questioned. Although, to be fair, he never compromised when it came to matters of security. If he said he had it handled, he did.

"Focus on rebuilding VanWarren's memories and see what comes up. If anything does, I want to know immediately. And I mean it, Rae, your safety takes precedence over anything else. If he acts inappropriately toward you again, I will rectify the situation. Am I making myself clear?"

As a lance telepath, his method of rectifying involved scrambling someone's mind until it stopped sending signals to their body to live. It could be the cleanest form of execution or a prolonged torture, depending on the infraction. Another reason why the entire SU collective had been so accepting of him taking charge during the attack—regardless of his age, Darrow could hold his own.

"Crystal."

"Good. Now go home. Meditation tomorrow."

Raven headed straight for the elevator. She needed isolation to decompress and shake the Shadow out of her thoughts.

On the ground floor, Ripley leaned against the front desk counter, flirting with the receptionist. At Raven's approach, they broke off from the conversation to smirk at her. "How was it?" they teased.

"Darrow has my report. You can get it from him."

"I'm sure I will," Ripley said as Raven passed them. "Be sure to let me know if he turns out to be too much for you to handle. I'd be happy to step in for you."

Ass.

Raven wriggled her fingers in a wave, not bothering to look back. In her transport, with the council member safely closed away inside the building, Raven still felt their parting cackle claw at her spine.

8

The simulation window meant that Zach's holding cell was underground.

They'd given him fabricated wood furniture—breakable into pieces sharp enough to use as a weapon.

The dumbwaiter cubby, where his meals got delivered three times a day, was wide enough to squeeze through.

He couldn't find the surveillance equipment, but half of the doorside wall was definitely made of observation glass. It would be too thick to shatter by hand or any tool short of a percussion grenade, but it would put his every move on display to anyone outside of his cell. This presented an obvious liability.

Overall, not a bad setup for a sophisticated prison cell designed to make the prisoner feel at ease.

But they'd given him a rudimentary, fully charged digital tablet. Compared to the sophisticated devices on the market these days, the tablet was a fancy paperweight. It could play media and had a library of content to choose from. Unfortunately for the SU, just because its networking software had been disabled didn't mean it wasn't there.

If he wanted to, Zach could use it to hack into the building's security network in a matter of minutes, unlock the door, and walk out.

Of course, escaping a building full of mind readers wouldn't be a simple matter of hacking a few security protocols. Plus, having finally made it inside, Zach had no intention of leaving unless they forced him to.

He'd expected more telepaths to come by after the interrogation specialist left the day before, but he hadn't sensed anyone else rooting around in his brainpan until the lights had dimmed and he'd knocked out for the night.

He'd dreamed of her. A strange, whimsical vision of cold and collected Raven Dello Russo in a pink and white sun dress, swinging hard and fast on an old-fashioned wood-and-rope swing in a massive willow tree. She'd laughed, head thrown back, two good hands curled around the ropes. Whatever that meant.

What he wanted to know was whether she'd dreamed of him, too. And whether her dreams were anything like what she'd pushed at him yesterday. *Whew!* A vision like that made a guy wish he could read minds right back. He'd bet she'd thought of him at least once after she'd left.

Would she admit it if he asked?

Likely not.

Killjoy.

Having placed the digital tablet on the bookshelf and set it to display the current time, Zach watched the minutes tick by, waiting for her to return—because she *would*. He'd given her enough information to whet the SU's appetite. They would want more. The only question was how hard she'd have to fight them not to replace her for her own safety—because they'd try, and Zach had a feeling she wouldn't let them.

At noon on the dot, the cell door opened and the woman of mystery walked in, dressed in the same black-on-black suit she'd worn the day before. "Hello, Mr. VanWarren."

"Hello again, Blackbird. You're right on time." Zach motioned for her to sit at the table set for two. He'd saved the plate and utensils from breakfast and split his lunch portion into two. A dozen pages from one of the books made for a decent enough tablecloth, and he'd managed to detach the bathroom night light to fashion a lantern in place of candles.

"What's this?"

Zach shrugged humbly. "I like to treat my partners to a morning-after breakfast." Then he grinned. "Was it as good for you as it was for me?"

"No," she said.

Zach clutched at his chest. "Ouch."

Raven pulled a small device out of her pocket and placed it on the table. A timer. She set it for one hour and activated it. "Shall we sit?"

"Will our time together have restrictions now?"

She inclined her head at the timer. "One hour."

"Their idea, I assume."

She didn't bother responding.

Zach took his seat opposite her. "I know they're watching us, so this bit of intel is for them: If I wanted to hurt you, I wouldn't need an hour to do it."

"Noted."

"And this bit is for you: I don't want to hurt you."

"The record shall so reflect."

"For said record, do please verbalize that I am telling the truth. I know you're already in my head." He felt her there. It was subtler than yesterday, a warm not-aloneness rather than a physical sensation. But Zach instinctively knew it was her. He left himself as open as he could as a show of trust.

"You're telling the truth," she confirmed, displaying no reaction to it one way or another. He might as well have made a casual observation about the table between them.

"Then shall we eat?"

As with everything else about his imprisonment, the nourishment provided for him was wholesome in nutrition and generous in portion. He hadn't touched a morsel of anything yet. The meals they'd sent him yesterday had stayed in the dumbwaiter until the surveillance officer decided to send them back again. This morning, in anticipation of his guest, Zach had dumped out his breakfast into the dumbwaiter to free up the plate and utensils. That time, they'd gotten the message and sent it back right away.

He was starving.

But these people didn't trust him, so he couldn't trust them, either.

A suspicion Raven confirmed when she looked over the spread he'd put together for her and didn't pick up her fork. "I've been given detailed instructions on how your case is to be handled going forward," she said instead, and Zach detected a hint of resentment in her tone.

"Our sessions are to be timed. If my exit is delayed for any reason, security will seal this room and neutralize you."

Which would mean neutralizing her as well. It made sense if they considered him a big enough threat. The Shadows would do no less if their roles were reversed. So why did it bother him?

Because soldiers were expendable. Telepaths shouldn't have been. The Special Unit was supposed to be better than that. They were supposed to care about and *protect* their own.

"When I am not here, other telepaths will be given access to scan you from outside your room. You won't be allowed to see or hear them. But you'll likely feel them when they work on you. Only I will be allowed into your room. This is for your safety as well as theirs."

Right. Because he was a Shadow. And everyone who worked in this building had probably known someone who'd died a horrible death at the hands of a Shadow. Some, maybe even before the war had officially begun.

Zach harbored no illusions about making friends here. They hated him on principle—and they were entitled to their hatred. It was a miracle they hadn't killed him already. He should be grateful for that; maybe he should show some humility or remorse. But neither was his style, and he couldn't keep himself from poking back instead. "Getting territorial over me so soon, Blackbird? I'm flattered. Although I must say I'm starting to feel like a rat here. I don't mind being in your clutches, but I draw the line at performing tricks for an audience." His mind was not an open circus attraction.

"Rest assured, no one is here to be entertained."

"That's comforting."

How did she manage to stay so detached? What had her bosses said to her to put so much iron back into her spine? Granted, his focus had been somewhat compromised yesterday, but he could have sworn he'd seen her sashay out of the room after giving him the worst case of blue balls he'd ever felt after, what? Less than ten seconds?

Now she was all walled off again. Whatever progress he'd made with her was gone.

"You're not a refugee, Mr. VanWarren. You're a prisoner of war until we decide otherwise. Provocation of any kind will be considered an act of hostility against us."

"Does that go both ways, then? Should I consider the way you left me yesterday cruel and unusual punishment?"

She shrugged. "Play stupid games, win stupid prizes."

Zach's mouth twitched into a grin before he could stop it. There she was. Her bosses might have put a leash on her, but Raven Dello Russo was no one's pet. She would play by their rules only as far as she liked, and stars help anyone who pushed her too far.

He loved a woman who gave as good as she got.

His stomach growled.

Raven heard, and her gaze dropped to his midsection for a second before she twitched an eyebrow at him with an unspoken question: *Why aren't you eating?*

"I'm going to need you to take the first bite."

"I see."

It seemed to be a reasonable enough request because she finally picked up her fork and stabbed it through a piece of sauce-covered meat. She used it to scoop up some vegetable mash before bringing it to her mouth. Zach watched her lips close around the morsel so tightly the fork slid out clean of the tiniest speck.

Hunger suddenly became a secondary concern.

Her jaw worked to chew the bite. His gaze stuck on the column of her throat as she swallowed, then shot right back to her lips as her tongue peeked out for a quick swipe over them.

Yesterday, he'd imagined all kinds of naughty things as a way of insulating his mind from telepathic touch. Today, those thoughts came all on their own, and Zach forgot where he was as his imagination picked up where Raven had left off after their last session.

He imagined feasting on her pussy to slake his hunger, while her thighs muffled her sweet, sweet cries. He would make her quiver, and then pull her down on his lap, onto his cock to feel the clutch of her orgasm firsthand. He would chase down her tongue and suck it into his mouth while he drove himself into her as deep as she could take him and—

"…things I'd like to discuss today."

Zach blinked the daydream away. What had she said?

Fuck, he was hard as rock again, and this time, he had no one to blame but himself. He'd felt Raven's mental touch retreat the second she'd confirmed his honesty. This one was all on him.

He needed to get his head on straight.

Raven watched him as if waiting for him to respond. He had no fucking idea what she wanted from him.

Shifting around in his seat, he leaned forward and picked up his fork. Maybe he just needed to get some food in his belly. Raven showed no reaction to the bite she'd taken, so it should be safe. "What's that, Blackbird?" he asked, then stuffed a forkful of food into his mouth to stall.

Raven frowned a little. "Mr. VanWarren—"

"Call me Zach."

Invisible down feathers brushed across his forehead. He felt her sink into his mind and settle over the surface, watching and waiting. "Why?" she asked.

"I like it." He really did. "A nice, normal name." For a nice, normal guy. "Reminds me of…" Something he didn't remember. He didn't *want* to remember. The pain he felt in the void of the memory was enough to tell him some things were better left forgotten.

Tendrils of warmth sank into his head, and a random parade of people from his past scrolled across his mind's eye. Some of them, he almost remembered. Others were reduced to vague impressions.

Raven was fishing.

"The woman who stabbed you?" she guessed, but she sounded doubtful.

Zach burst out laughing. "If she heard you say that, she'd probably stab me again." All in good fun.

Raven cocked her head. "The woman from the song, then." Her mental fingers brushed up the back of his neck and along his scalp. They dragged up a bittersweet ache, the muted joy of a connection cut short before it fully formed. A deep sense of loss. "Tell me about her."

Zach felt a gentle tug, a subtle twist, but the sensation slipped through his thoughts with nothing solid to grasp onto. "There's nothing to tell," he said and took another big bite. It was true. Zach didn't remember who the woman was, what she looked like, or why pieces of her song kept playing through his mind day and night. He'd searched the archives already and hadn't found anything. All he had were small fragments. Not enough to identify the song or artist. Part of him liked that. If he couldn't find it, he could pretend it had always been his alone. A gift—the only one he'd ever received.

But another part of him raged against the universal void as an insult. Humanity *should* know her song. Every soul in the galaxy should hear those sweet melodies. They should be sung to lovers and children, in life's quiet moments when nothing mattered but the warmth of another person beside you.

"There must be something," Raven said with gentle insistence. "Your mind carries so few core memories, and you pick and choose them with intent."

As she spoke, the song fragments pieced together into half of a chorus that hummed through the humid night. He could almost smell the fragrant mix of tropical flowers and cooked meats. His vision darkened around the edges into shadows of swaying trees and starlight.

"You chose to hold on to the song for a reason. The person who played it for you must have been someone of significance in your life."

The muted hum of many voices floated across his mind, disrupting the song and pissing him off. He remembered total tunnel vision, but the target of his undivided attention remained a shapeless blur.

Maybe she had been important. Zach would never know.

Shadows didn't get to have people of significance. Only two possibilities existed for what might have happened to her. Either he'd removed himself from her life for her own safety, or the Shadows had removed her for their convenience. Neither was something Zach wanted to contemplate.

"She was different," Zach said. True again. For whatever reason, a fragment of her memory had stuck where so many others had faded away.

He finished his plate of food in silence.

Raven didn't press him any further. They'd reached the end of the road on the topic of the mysterious song woman.

When he pushed his plate away, Raven nudged hers toward him.

"You're not hungry?" he asked.

"Not as hungry as you."

Zach checked the timer. More than half of their time had elapsed. She would leave soon, and he hadn't gotten a single bit of personal information from her. "Have you ever had a lover feed you in bed?"

She sighed. "This again?"

Zach held up his hands. "I'm just looking for a little quid pro quo here. You poked at a subject I'm sensitive about. It's only fair that you share something equally intimate to restore the balance of our relationship."

"We don't have a relationship."

"*Yet.*"

She rolled her eyes at him.

Zach grinned. "Indulge me."

"No," she said. "I am neither a child nor debilitated. I am perfectly capable of feeding myself."

"You shouldn't be. Not if he did his job right. Or she," he amended.

Her soft presence retreated from his mind, leaving him oddly bereft. He hadn't expected her to fall for the same trick twice, but come on. Shutting him out completely was such an overreaction. He just wanted to make a point—that she hadn't been fucked the way she deserved.

He'd never said he'd to be the one to fix it.

That was a date four or five kind of topic.

Raven changed the subject. "I reviewed your medical scans and test results."

Naturally, they would have done a full work-up on him first thing to ensure he wasn't a biohazard. The Shadows did have protocols for such things. Infect an underperforming Hound with a virulent strain of a violent disease and send him to the enemy. Two days later, no more enemy.

"It would appear that you escaped from the Shadows shortly after an EMC treatment. Our medics found traces of those chemicals in your system."

"Makes sense."

"Do you feel any lingering side effects from them?"

"I wouldn't know." The Shadows didn't bother following up on EMC treatments. They didn't give a shit about side effects. And even if he'd had any, how would he know which part of the treatment was causing them? What was the difference between a migraine from getting your brain fried and one from a chemical cocktail being injected into it? Pain was pain. You pushed through and carried on with the mission.

"I would like to suggest a detox treatment to filter out the chemicals and give your brain time to heal. We would sedate you and submerge you in an oxygenated detox solution for a few days. The treatment is experimental but has been tested on patients with brain damage similar to yours. The results have been positive."

"I'll pass." The last thing he wanted was for more people to fuck around with his brain. Especially people whose definition of "positive results" would be loose when applied to a prisoner of war they wouldn't hesitate to neutralize, as Raven had called it.

"Perhaps you shouldn't think of it as a suggestion for *you*, but for my superiors."

In other words, the choice wouldn't be his.

A Shadow like him would have done the same to prisoners in his care many times in the past. But being on the other side of the equation now, he had a new understanding of and appreciation for how much it fucking sucked. "Have I not been cooperative enough?"

"I think you can answer your own question."

Zach pushed aside Raven's plate and leaned over his elbows on the table. "Then let's try round two. I promise to be a good boy." Now that he knew what she liked, he could make it so, so good for both of them.

The timer zeroed out and beeped an alarm. Dammit, did she have the thing sped up double-time? It felt like she'd just walked in here fifteen minutes ago.

Raven tucked it back into her pocket and stood from the table. "Good day, Mr. VanWarren."

She was out the door before he could correct her to call him Zach.

"You appear to have an issue with respecting my boundaries," Raven said to Ripley outside of the Shadow's cell.

The council member once again stood at the window, watching the prisoner despite Raven's instructions to keep the level clear while she worked with him. Today, they were wrapped in a tight, light blue dress with black pinstripes. The skirt's short hem ended a few inches above their knees with a split on one side halfway up to their hip. Their hair was arranged in delicately messy waves around a face painted with the softness of classical feminine beauty. It almost worked, too, except they couldn't quite disguise the apathy in their eyes.

Since no response seemed forthcoming, Raven pushed. "You already scoped out the subject once. What are you doing here again?"

"Checking on your progress." Ripley didn't look away from the prisoner as they spoke. "I read the report of your first session with the Shadow. It felt incomplete. You wouldn't be withholding vital information from us, would you, Raven?"

The only thing Raven had left out was the nature of the Shadow's mental shielding strategy. The SU would need to know he had an effective way to distract and deflect telepathic probes, but Raven didn't feel it necessary to spell out the details of Mr. VanWarren's sexual fantasies about her. A verbal confirmation of his interest in her was enough. The rest, Raven considered a personal matter and not up for public opinion.

"Why are you so interested in the subject?" she asked Ripley.

At last, the council member tore their gaze away from the observation glass to smirk at her, a thin wave of platinum hair casting shadows over their right eye. "Deflecting now? Careful. If I didn't know better,

I'd think you really have been compromised."

Yet they hadn't answered her, either.

"I wouldn't blame you, you know. As far as weapons are concerned, the Hawk is…effective. Almost as if he was molded specifically for us."

For us, for us echoed across the silence in Raven's mind, ringing with a disturbing flavor of truth. The pointed words felt like a hint toward something larger. But with lust dripping from Ripley's every word, their meaning went no deeper than the surface.

They were horny for the Shadow. End of story.

Raven almost rolled her eyes. "Your weakness for a chiseled physique will be your downfall one day."

Ripley chuckled. "I do enjoy your wit. But don't for one second pretend you're better than me. You lost that right years ago."

What?

"The rest of the council may have their heads up their asses with pity over you, but I know better. I *expected* better from you. And what a disappointment you turned out to be."

Truth. Deep, bitter, and laced with enough resentment to mentally set Raven back on her heels. Worse, they seemed to know that Raven had no idea what they were talking about. The naked challenge in their eyes dared her to try and find out.

If she did, they'd bring her up on charges, and Raven's career would be over.

Raven didn't have the time or the patience for this bullshit. If Ripley couldn't come out and have a direct conversation about whatever bothered them, they could keep chewing on it until they choked. "The feeling is mutual," she returned evenly. "The next time you interfere with my assignment, you and I will have a problem."

Ripley drew themself up and closed the two steps of distance between them. At several inches taller than Raven, with high heels adding a few more, they towered over her, the full force of their temper pressing on her as they glared down the length of their nose. "I'm curious what you think you can do against me. And how far you think you will get if you attempt it."

"Believe me when I say, you don't want to find out. Stay—away—from—my—subject." It was wrong, borderline illegal, but Raven couldn't stop the thin thread of compulsion from snaking out with the verbal command. A civilian might not have felt it, but it would have been enough to make them back off with an instinctual need to put some distance between them.

A telepath with considerable gifts of their own, Ripley blinked and backed up all of one step before the compulsion registered, and the wrath that took over their face made Raven brace for impact. "You *dare!*"

"Before you start climbing your high horse, I want you to remember one thing. My service record with the SU is spotless. I have interrogated eleven Shadows over the last three years, and not once have I behaved half as unprofessionally as you have in the last two days. If bring this up to Darrow, it won't be my head on the chopping block. Consider your next steps carefully. I wouldn't want you to trip and fall on that pretty face of yours."

Something sparked across their expression, there and gone in a blink. Surprise, and a hint of something else. Anticipation maybe? Admiration? Or victory? Couldn't have been relief—that would make no sense. Either way, it jarred her as much as their vitriol. Raven didn't appreciate mind games, especially ones that made her feel like a toy being played with.

Because it wouldn't do to let Ripley see how much the exchange had rattled her, Raven took her leave without a backward glance. If Darrow was still watching, he'd have caught every word of their conversation. She'd let him handle it.

And if he wasn't, Raven would have to have a word with the security team. They could disable the elevator for her and prevent anyone other than her from accessing or leaving the level for her designated one hour a day. It would put her at greater risk, but Raven wasn't worried. The Shadow had meant it when he'd said he didn't want to hurt her. Despite what Ripley thought, he posed no danger to Raven—on any level.

She was more concerned about Ripley's apparent obsession with her subject.

And their confounding animosity toward Raven.

Had the council member ever spoken to her that way in the past?

Raven couldn't recall. But it didn't bode well for their future working relationship.

Something to keep in mind.

As he had the day before, Darrow waited for her when she emerged from the elevator. He didn't look any happier than he had the first time. "So. Detox?"

Raven nodded. "As it is, the Shadow's mind is too fragmented to get a proper read on him. I tried to rebuild a memory that had a strong emotional anchor in his psyche today, and the pieces just slipped through my fingers. The chemicals in his system are interfering with his ability to coalesce. If we allow his brain to heal, his memories will be easier to access."

Not to mention, his mind would be much safer to study while he was unconscious for the procedure. No more deflection. Only dreams. Raven still wouldn't trust a junior telepath near him—stars only knew what kind of horrors a Shadow would dream about—but if properly supervised, apprentice telepaths could be given access to him. It was a good plan.

Darrow seemed to agree. "I think we can set that up. I'll need some time to confer with the medics and make sure we have everything we need. Give me a few days."

"No problem."

"About Ripley…"

Raven's irritation from earlier resurfaced full force. She hadn't planned to say anything, but since he'd brought it up, "Yes, let's discuss Ripley. Because if there is a mole here, based on their interest in the Shadow, I'd be inclined to suspect it's them."

Darrow shook his head. "The acting director herself recommended Ripley and endorsed them for the council seat. They're too smart and too connected for something like that. But I'll talk to them and get them off your back."

"Will they comply?" They hadn't before.

"If not, then you won't be the only one who has a problem with them. We've never had to do it before, but I'm not opposed to replacing council members if they refuse to follow the rules. No matter how powerful their friends are."

Good enough for Raven. "Thank you."

Darrow nodded. "Go. Meditation. It didn't sound like you made much progress with the Shadow today, but I'll still want your report after you're done."

"Yes, sir."

Given her current state of mind, a few mindful breathing exercises wouldn't be a bad thing.

It just pissed her off to no end that, between Ripley and the Shadow, it wasn't the Shadow compromising her mental and emotional balance. With a subject as dangerous as a Hawk, Ripley's interference put Raven's life and the lives of everyone in this facility at risk.

Darrow had better deal with them and fast, because if he left it up to Raven, Ripley would be getting carted out of the building with their mind in tattered pieces.

~

Raven had left her plate mostly untouched. But she had sucked that fork for one single bite. Zach picked it up and put it in his mouth, pretending he could taste her on the tines. He tongued the gaps between them until the metal warmed and his stomach reminded him that he'd only finished half of his meal.

He was about to dig into the second half when the cell door opened again, admitting an individual he hadn't seen before.

Stunning dress, pretty, feminine face, and a seductive smile, but eyes as cold as ice. Between one step and the next, their femme persona slipped for the briefest moment, revealing a hint of masculine strength. They made him think of a slick ambush predator poised to strike.

His hackles went up instantly, and he clutched the fork like a makeshift knife. "You're not supposed to be in here."

"Aren't I?"

The bludgeon. Zach could tell by the tone of their voice and the way they rudely seated themself without invitation that this was the person who'd let themself into his brain yesterday before Raven had arrived. "Are you the bad cop to Raven's good cop?"

"Who are you?"

The question snapped his spine straight. He didn't feel the telepath's mental touch, but the way they stared at him, the snake knew exactly what they were asking. And they expected a specific answer in response. "Like I told your colleague, my name is Zachary—"

"Who—are—you?"

Zach ground his molars to keep himself rooted in the chair. This person knew which buttons to push and showed no hesitation in doing so. Zach didn't need anything more to classify them as a threat. And he had to battle down a powerful urge to launch across the table and open their neck with the fork's dull handle.

They wanted to provoke him into a violent response.

It was working.

Zach palmed the fork's tines and thought of Raven's calm, unaffected face to steal a bit of her self-control for himself. "Whatever you're after, you're not getting from me. I'll only talk to Raven."

The telepath stared him down, and he felt the first stab of intrusive pain at the back of his head. "Who are you?"

Zach breathed through the sensation and imagined throwing the table across the room to get at them. He would grab them by the throat, yank them out of the chair, and pin them to the locked door. He imagined their face going red and their eyes bulging as he squeezed until he felt their pulse cut off. He pictured bruises blooming around his hand, and blood vessels bursting in their eyes as he strangled the life out of them. They would fight, of course. But what could a gangly civilian do against a Shadow?

Telepaths tended to lose control of their most effective weapon when their bodies had to fight to stay alive. This one wouldn't fare any better. Their body would betray them. Their mind would falter.

And he would enjoy every second of watching them writhe. He would savor their helpless terror as they pissed themself. He would watch the light fade from their eyes, and it would be the most satisfying thing he'd ever done in his life.

And then he would take his fork and use it to tear open the telepath's chest, rip out their heart and dump it down the toilet.

Zach could tell by the widening of their pupils that the telepath had seen his fantasies. Their breathing changed, and sweat sheened their skin.

He made sure to let every ounce of his satisfaction show in his thoughts and on his face.

"Who am I? Are you sure you want to know?"

The telepath shoved away from the table to put some space between them. They were unsteady, their artfully mussed hair now giving them the look of someone at the end of their rope, but they still managed to look down their nose at Zach. "Raven will remain your handler for as long as we decide to let her. I suggest you don't get too attached."

Zach tilted his head the way Raven had done earlier and imagined stringing the telepath's entrails across the observation window for a bit of decoration. "Is that a threat?"

"Yes," they hissed through clenched teeth.

Zach nodded. "I will remain in this cell for as long as Raven is my handler. The day another person walks through the door, I'll stop playing nice."

He pictured the telepath's hand and the ID chip embedded in it—the universal key to all locks in this facility. Should he feel like it, he could sever said hand and use it to let himself out of the cell in seconds. From there, he only had to locate the nearest utility panel, disable the building's security protocols, and initiate an emergency biohazard cleanse.

Two minutes, max. Unless they had guards stationed right outside his cell—doubtful—no telepath could take him down before he was done, and they wouldn't be able to undo the damage after. The building would lock down, and everyone not inside a utility panel—everyone other than him—would get vaporized.

And that was just one of many strategies he could employ to fuck with them.

"Don't come back here," he said. "You don't want me as an enemy."

The telepath, who hadn't bothered to introduce themself, ran a shaking hand through their hair, then swiveled around and marched out of the cell, taking their mental probe with them. Zach imagined they broke into a run as soon as the door locked between them.

Whatever meal they served him next would likely be drugged in retaliation.

Hell, if the bludgeon decided to tattle on him, he might end up dead before the day was through. But at least now they had an understanding between them. Zach had come to them willingly and, while he didn't expect them to treat him as an honored guest, he didn't intend to subject himself to cruelty.

He'd remain civil as long as they did.

And if they decided to suspend civilities between them, Zach would show them what a Shadow Hawk was truly capable of.

Not like he had anything to lose, anyway.

10

January 5, 3040 – Mars 2

The Historical Society of Technology and Advancement had to petition the local authorities every six months to keep a series of old communication relays from being destroyed at the farthest edge of the solar system. They were big and unsightly but ultimately harmless. And while they were still functional, the relays provided an excellent learning opportunity for tech students all around the moon.

The night of the attack, four of those seventeen relays picked up a disturbance significant enough that two hundred and eighteen amateur techies called in an alert.

The warning perhaps saved a half-billion lives.

It gave the authorities two and a half hours to sound the alarm and evacuate a good portion of their citizens to solar storm bunkers deep underground.

From there, they watched dozens of shuttles rain destruction on city centers, utility stations, and military bases. They listened as armed foot soldiers disembarked and swept outlying areas, gunning down hundreds of survivors without ever speaking a single word.

They didn't return fire.

To do so would have alerted the enemy that there was still someone left to fight back.

Someone with a small army of tech students terrified enough to hack the global com systems and send out a warning as far as their illegal, sub-frequency signal could reach.

11

As recently as a few years ago, meditation sessions for telepaths had been conducted in groups to foster cooperation and a sense of community. The idea was similar to some 20th-century religious practices, except that no one appealed to a higher power. Instead, the sharing of space during one's most vulnerable moments was thought to engender trust. You couldn't ask for help if you didn't trust the people around you.

Another thing the war had taken from them.

Seeing a group of telepaths willingly go too far into a merge, never to extricate from it again, had made the rest of them reluctant to risk it.

Now, SU telepaths meditated during scheduled sessions, but each in their own, shielded space for safety. Their sense of community stemmed from group activities such as games, lectures, dinner parties, and outings. They were voluntary, but each member of the SU, telepath or otherwise gifted, was strongly encouraged to select at least two per month for participation.

Raven hadn't attended one in years.

Meditation pods were on the level below the council chambers and on the rooftop above. When the weather permitted, the rooftop sprouted hexagonal Faraday glass cells. The glass allowed for an unobstructed view, but was charged with a Faraday field to block out telepathic frequencies.

Raven preferred the one with a view of the desert. The light gray dunes shifted formation every two weeks or so, depending on the winds. She found it calming to track their progress—eastward in the spring, and southward in the winter months.

This morning, each rooftop pod had been supplied with a thick, heated blanket. The sun was up, but partly obscured by the planet Vesta, and a layer of white frost covered the ground. Few people bothered to come outside during these times, which meant Raven had nearly the entire rooftop to herself.

She went through her mental exercises, then attempted to focus on her breathing, but her thoughts kept wandering down into the bowels of the facility and disrupting her patterns.

The Shadow's lack of a personal history troubled her. She'd never met anyone whose development had been so severely sidetracked. By all rights, it should have caused far more issues than he displayed, and Raven couldn't tell which part was the construct—the way he remembered his upbringing, or the seemingly functional and rational adult individual he was now. The two didn't fit together.

A delicate chime announced the end of the hour. Raven replaced the blanket for the next person and emerged from her pod. While the wind barriers kept the rooftop comfortable, the dry winter chill still prickled at her face and neck.

Across the sea of glass hexagons, she spotted a familiar face.

Uh-oh.

Tessa Sinclair crossed her arms, staring her down as she waited for Raven to drag her feet over. She had her signature, *I am the consequence of your actions* look on her face, which never boded well. They were supposed to have had their girls' night last night, but Raven had turned off her coms to focus on the Shadow case. She'd woken up this morning to seventeen messages from her best friend, ranging from concern to outright fury at being stood up.

In Raven's defense, she'd planned on calling Tessa back after her session today.

Apparently, Tessa hadn't felt like waiting.

"You couldn't be bothered to tell me you're on assignment?" she demanded. "I had to find out from Darrow?"

Raven flinched. "I got busy?"

"Too busy to send a message? Unacceptable." Oh, she was really mad.

Not that Raven blamed her, given their history. Tessa was the sweetest person in all the worlds, but she took no shit from Raven. That was why Raven loved her, and why she wouldn't have wanted anyone else standing beside her at her wedding. Tessa had dragged Raven out of bed, out of the house, and back into work after her accident. She'd come by three times a day to make sure Raven ate something and checked on her every hour, on the hour, every day for months, just in case Raven got any ideas about making a permanent exit. Girls' night had also been her idea, to force Raven out of isolation and back into the rhythm of living.

And, after putting in all that work, she tended to get snippy whenever Raven had anything in the slightest way resembling a relapse.

"I'm sorry?"

"And you're group-meditating now? What is going on!"

"That wasn't my idea. Darrow's forcing me."

Some of Tessa's anger dissipated. She finally unclenched to tuck a thick strand of rich, honey brown hair behind her ear. "He's forcing you? Why?"

"This particular assignment is…different."

It was also classified, and Tessa didn't have the security clearance. She was neither a telepath nor an SU employee. Darrow had to pull a lot of strings to get her admitted as a patient with one of the doctors who worked in the medical ward and he only allowed her to freely roam the rest of the facility because of Raven.

Tessa was the unfortunate type of chem-resistant. Looking at her, you'd never know there was anything wrong. She'd been blessed with a statuesque beauty reminiscent of Renaissance paintings. On the inside, however, Tessa was a mosaic of replacement body parts that kept failing. Every time she underwent a life-saving organ transplant, the medics corrected one issue, and her body decided to create three others. Last summer, they'd given her five more years to live, warning that she might not make it through another transplant operation.

She was thirty-two years old to Raven's thirty-five.

Girls' night wasn't just for Raven's benefit. No part of their friendship was, which made it that much shittier whenever Raven had to drop off the face of the moon because of work. She usually made more of an effort to give Tessa a heads-up. The Shadow had just gotten more into her head than she cared to admit, and it had simply slipped her mind this time. "I can't really talk about it."

"But you're okay," Tessa pushed.

Raven gave her a cheery thumb-up. "Never better." She nudged Tessa through the door to get them moving. As much as she loved her friend, she had an appointment to get to. "How are *you* doing?"

"As you'd expect. Heart's still ticking. Bloodwork is getting wonky. They're threatening me with a bone marrow transplant."

Raven's gut twisted. "How long?"

"I've been testing every day for two weeks—"

"You get on my ass about missing one girls' night, but don't think to mention *that* for two weeks?"

"If I talk about every little thing that goes wrong with my body, that's all we'll ever talk about. And no, thank you."

Dammit. She needed to pay more attention. Tessa deserved better from her.

"Docs say if the progression stays consistent, I have a few months."

"Fuck."

Tessa gasped, tugging her to a complete stop. "Raven Dello Russo! What have I told you about swearing?"

Raven rolled her eyes, dutifully quoting, "Keep it classy, or keep it to yourself."

"So?"

"Fucking assfuck motherfucker fuckity fucking fuck."

Tessa stared her down for a second, then nodded. "Better."

"Is there another treatment they could try? Pharmaceuticals? UV therapy? Magic spells?"

"If there were, you know they would have tried it already. There are just too many chem-resistance variants and not enough experts to study them."

Since chem-resistance wasn't a uniform disease, it didn't have a universal cure. It functioned more like genetic evolution in real time, Nature testing different mutations to see which ones worked best.

"They're doing the best they can." Tessa breathed in deep and exhaled on a sigh. She didn't seem outwardly bothered by the news. "It's alright, really."

"No, it isn't."

Tessa grinned. "I love the way you cling to denial. But, Raven, you'll have to let me go eventually. You know that, right?"

"Eventually could be three decades from now. You don't know."

Tessa grasped Raven's empty sleeve, pulling her to the side to let the next group of meditators pass them in the hallway. "It will be sooner rather than later," she said soberly. "And I need you to be okay with it."

Something was off. "What aren't you telling me? You're not thinking of doing something stupid, are you?"

Tessa bit at her lower lip. Where was her enthusiasm? The ever-cheerful outlook on life? Her usually bright gray eyes were so empty. Raven had never seen Tessa like that before. Not even after the attack. She'd been sad then but defiant, too, determined to fight—despite Raven, if necessary. Now, she looked like she had nothing left to fight with or for.

"Tessa. Come on."

"Do you know what makes a person?" she asked, resuming their walk to the elevators. "Do you know where our souls live? It can't be just in our heads. Otherwise, I wouldn't feel like pieces of me are going missing every time something gets replaced."

Organ transplants no longer required donors. New organs were grown using the patient's own DNA. It reduced delays and lowered the risk of rejection. For the most part.

"I'm a doll stuffed with things that shouldn't be there. I don't *feel* like myself anymore. Even when everything's going right, it still feels wrong."

They got in the elevator together, and Tessa pushed the button for her floor. She didn't speak again until the doors closed and they were alone. "I made the appointment."

"Tessa, no."

She shook her head. "It's not worth it. Life should be *lived*. Not endured. I don't want to keep enduring."

Raven had felt that way since their whole world had gone to hell. She'd had Tessa to hold her up. But she still wasn't sure it had been worth it. She couldn't be expected to return the favor now. How could Raven convince Tessa to keep living when she still had to keep convincing herself almost every other day.

"Let me talk to Darrow. He can make some calls. He has connections everywhere. There is no way someone isn't working on a solution somewhere in the galaxy."

The elevator stopped. Tessa stepped out and turned back to Raven, with sad eyes and a serene smile. "You'll be okay. You're so much stronger than I ever was. Just do me a favor?"

"Anything."

"Don't miss me too much."

The elevator door closed between them, leaving Raven shaken. It took her a full minute to scan her ID and proceed to Sublevel C. She barely noticed the security override she'd requested. Once she exited on Sublevel C, the elevator would remain there until she scanned her ID again to return to the upper levels.

It also now tracked traffic on and off the level and showed her a readout of today's activity. Three telepaths had gone down and come back up, the most recent one half an hour ago. The level should be clear for her.

Tessa's news had obliterated whatever good her meditation had done. Raven was in no shape to deal with the Shadow's mind games, but she couldn't skip a session, and she couldn't let him see a hint of vulnerability. He was too good at exploiting them.

She took a few seconds at his window to get her shit together.

The Shadow lounged on his cot, scribbling into a book. He didn't look happy about it. No doubt, he hadn't appreciated having so many other telepaths traipsing through his mind. Raven had recognized two of the three names on the list. As trainees, their mental touch likely wasn't subtle, but Darrow wouldn't have allowed them near a non-telepath subject unless he was sure they wouldn't cause pain or harm.

The third name, she'd never seen before, but that wasn't out of the ordinary. People filtered through the Chairo center on a regular basis. The SU didn't collect strays, and they didn't coddle anyone. They trained people to be self-sufficient, slotted them into employment opportunities, and sent them on their way.

"Are you coming in, or what?"

Raven startled. She hadn't gone anywhere near his mind, and he couldn't see her through the one-way observation glass. How did he know she was there?

She scanned her ID at his door and stepped inside. "Hello, Mr. VanWarren."

He'd set the table for two again, and hadn't eaten any of the food.

"One minute past noon," he said, not looking away from his book. "You're late. Something the matter?" All flirting appeared to have been suspended. His face was hard, and so was his voice. Something had angered him.

"Why would you assume something's the matter?"

"You're never late, unless something's wrong."

"You've met me a total of two times before today, and I've been late one of those. Today makes my rate of tardiness sixty-six percent."

The Shadow cast her a look that said she wasn't fooling anyone, then did a quick double-take. "What's wrong?"

Raven pulled out the timer and set it on the table, already counting down the hour.

"Ah, of course. We don't talk about you unless I earn it. Fine. Let's talk about me." He turned the book toward her. "Who's this?"

Raven gaped. Using only a pencil, he'd drawn a portrait of Ripley with the accuracy and detail of a black-and-white photograph, capturing their aloof arrogance down to their cold, pale stare. But something about the way he'd drawn their eyes and the tense set of their mouth gave the impression of masked fear.

Stall and deflect. "I didn't know you were such an accomplished artist. Is that a common skill among Shadows?"

"Nice try. Who is it?"

Raven shrugged, taking her usual seat at the table. "How would I know? It's your drawing. Maybe someone from your past?" She brushed the prompt across his memories.

His surface thoughts churned over Ripley's visit in his cell yesterday, while Raven had been discussing them with Darrow several floors above. Raven fought back her instant flare of unadulterated rage and pushed deeper, but her probe didn't stick to anything else. She sensed no discordance that would hint at memory tampering, either, aside from the same incoherence that affected his entire mind.

As far as the Shadow was aware, he'd met Ripley for the first time yesterday.

And their audacity pissed him off as much as it did Raven.

His jaw muscles twitched as he set down the book, but he remained on the cot, staring her down. "I want a name, Blackbird."

"And I want a bionic arm. It looks like we're both doomed to disappointment."

Shit. She shouldn't have said that.

The Shadow's expression blanked, as if she'd surprised him. "Why can't you have a bionic arm? It's a common enough procedure."

He wouldn't talk about anything else now, until she answered. Fantastic. "I'm on the waitlist."

Any other day, her lack of a functional left arm would have ranked on the same level as a change in the weather. She noticed, but didn't pay it any attention unless it struck her with sudden phantom pains. But after Tessa's announcement, her empty sleeve suddenly felt a lot emptier. The prospect of losing another piece of her life made Raven acutely aware of all the ones she'd lost already. She couldn't get Julian back, and she couldn't make Tessa stay. But a bionic arm should have been attainable and, all of a sudden, Raven didn't feel as complacent about it anymore.

The Shadow raised an eyebrow. "The waitlist? I thought you people were connected out the ass end of the galaxy. Are you telling me you can't find someone to do it? Or that you can't manipulate them into doing it sooner?"

Dammit, she shouldn't have said anything.

He stood off the cot to sit at the table with her. "I'm waiting."

So was Raven. And today it bothered her as it never had before.

But Darrow had already tried everything he could to get her care, and the specialists refused to give him the time of day, despite his position. "A lot of people lost lives and limbs during the war, Mr. VanWarren."

"Zach."

She ignored the correction. "A lot of highly connected and influential people. People whose health and comfort take precedence over mine. We don't manipulate others to make our own lives easier."

"Bullshit."

"I'm telling you the truth."

"Oh, I can tell *you* believe it. But it's still a lie." He leaned over the table and lowered his voice. "People prioritize those they fear, and control those they need."

"If I wanted to abuse my gift to jump the line, I could have. I chose not to."

"Naturally. Because that's what people do when they lose a part of themselves, right? Shrug it off and move on. And, let me guess, the people in your life didn't fight on your behalf, either, because their moral compass always points north, too." He scoffed, shaking his head. "Can't have people bending those pesky rules—that would be *wrong*."

"Yes," she replied. "It would be wrong. Power like ours comes with an unforgiving weight of responsibility. We have rules, and we enforce them for a reason. If we don't police our own, someone else will, and innocent people will suffer for it. I wouldn't expect someone like you to understand."

"Understand what? Rules? Consequences for breaking them?"

A flare of bitter darkness dimmed the room around them in her mind's eye. Raven hadn't touched his thoughts, but their conversation must have pulled up a lot of severe trauma for her to pick up on it without trying.

"Believe me, I understand. The difference is, I don't give a fuck."

"Of course not." Shadows didn't care about any rules other than their own. Their moral compass boiled down to one directive: complete the mission by any means necessary.

"Rules don't mean shit when it's someone you care about," he declared, every word ringing with so much conviction it rattled her. "You do whatever it fucking takes to make it right, no matter what it costs you. When it's someone you love, *no one* is innocent."

Raven stifled a flinch. He didn't blink, staring straight into her soul, and she felt unaccountably lacking beneath his scrutiny.

Reading her like a book, he smirked. "Or maybe that's just me."

Raven looked away first, knowing he'd consider it a victory. She needed a second to compose herself. Despite the darkness in him, or perhaps because of it, his fervor on the topic shone bright, spiking fear through her gut at the prospect of ever finding herself on the receiving end of his wrath.

But it came with a traitorous hint of wistful envy, too. How different her life might have been, had she had someone like him on her side.

And right on the heels of that thought came guilt. She'd had Julian. He'd given up his life to make her world safe again.

The Shadow sat back, the cloud of his memories receding. "You weren't waitlisted because others are more important," he said. "You were waitlisted because it benefits your people for you to believe you're less than. They know that if they give you back your wing, you'll fly away as fast as you can. And you're too powerful an asset for them to risk setting loose."

Now he'd gone too far. "Why would I fly anywhere? The SU has been good to me. I have a job that pays me well, a support system—"

"A gilded cage lined with down. Still a cage, Blackbird."

Divide and conquer. And they'd been getting along so well.

"I think you're drawing too many parallels between my experience and your own. They're not comparable."

"Aren't they? The longer I'm here, the more I'm coming to realize your people and mine are both exactly the same. Their methods might differ, but the end result doesn't. Your people just make it feel more palatable. One could argue the Shadows are superior to the SU in one aspect: at least they're honest."

"You're grasping."

"Ask your boss. Point blank. Ask him why you're still waiting for your arm. The war's been dwindling for a while now. All those important people should have been checked off the list ages ago. So why are you still missing a limb?"

There was the master manipulator Raven had been looking for. A Hawk on top of his game, seeking out vulnerabilities to exploit. Three sessions, three different strategies to get into her head. Raven found no fault in his approach. It was seamless, each strike an extension of the previous. When sexual desire had failed, he'd made himself into a diplomat to appeal to her emotional side. She'd shown her hand by revealing a crucial detail about herself, and now the Hawk would use it to turn her against her own people.

Masterful.

Because, as much as she hated to admit it, his question was valid. When the Shadows had come, they'd targeted society's most vulnerable parts: infrastructure, communications, food production, and medical centers.

It had only taken one coordinated attack to cause catastrophic damage— but it had informed the SU's defense strategy going forward. They hadn't lost another medical center or infrastructure hub since the beginning of the war. And, while the losses they'd suffered were all terrible, they hadn't been insurmountable.

Hospitals and medical centers continued to operate. Patients continued to receive treatment, and lives continued to be saved.

And the SU was, indeed, connected out the ass end of the galaxy. In fact, they had their own army of scientists and medical professionals—a number of them worked in this very building.

So why hadn't Darrow been able to pull the right strings to get Raven her bionic arm?

These kinds of thoughts would lead to trouble. She could not and would not let the Shadow get the upper hand. Rather than play into his game, Raven changed her own. "I've received approval for your detox treatment."

The Shadow studied her for a few seconds. "Congratulations. Explain to me how it's any different from EMC."

"EMC damages brain tissue and destroys neural pathways. The detox reverses some of this—inasmuch as it can."

He shook his head. "Not buying it."

"Not selling anything. However, I can see you're still resistant to the idea, so I brought you something as a show of good intentions."

The moment she reached into her pocket, Zach readied for an attack. Good intentions, his ass. These people didn't even value their own, much less him. He still couldn't wrap his mind around how calm and accepting Raven was about being denied a routine medical treatment.

Also, her blatant lie about not knowing the telepath who'd stopped by to fuck with him the day before. Raven wore her mask well, but he'd started picking up on her tells. An extra blink, a twitch of her fingers, the way she tilted her head at a slightly different angle, or the way she spoke a fraction of a beat faster or slower. They were all subtle, which only made the game of spotting them more enjoyable.

Like right now. She was aware of him watching her every move, so she moved slowly as she extracted a small crystal cube from her pocket and placed it on the table between them.

A data crystal? "What's this?"

He felt her gaze on him, but not her mental touch. She wasn't attempting to manipulate him, but she was curious about his reaction. He didn't have one to give. Whatever she'd discovered about his past wouldn't make the smallest difference to Zach. He wasn't the same person anymore. He *chose* who he wanted to be.

Raven retrieved his digital tablet from the bookshelf. She set it on the table to free her hand so she could tinker with its functions. Having cleared the clock, she navigated to an entertainment screen and picked up the crystal cube again.

"You are correct in one observation," she said, holding the cube a couple of inches above the tablet. "Our organization is well-connected. We have access to databases the general public doesn't even know exist. And you did choose a very prominent name for yourself, Mr. Van-

Warren." She said his name like a clue to what she was about to reveal.

After a dramatic pause for effect, Raven lowered the crystal cube onto the glowing square on the tablet.

The instant the first notes of a song filled the cell, Zach shoved away from the table so hard he toppled his chair.

It was his song—*her* song—played by a full orchestra. The acoustic resonance and soft background noise suggested it had been recorded during a live performance. No vocals, but the assortment of musical instruments rendered the melody at once grandiose and deeply personal. The song was sweet and romantic, with a hopeful lilt that went straight to his chest.

"Where did you get this?" The lyrics teased at his mind, but try as he might, he couldn't grasp on to anything more than a lingering hint of a vocal tone, and a sense of wonder and beauty.

"As I said, the SU has extensive resources."

Zach tore his gaze away from the little crystal to find her frowning at him, and he realized he'd backed himself against the far wall. His heart raced, and his face felt stiff. He couldn't have telegraphed a weakness better if he'd written it on the observation window in his own blood.

He wanted to smash the data cube into pieces. He wanted to play the song over and over for the rest of his life. And he still had no idea why.

"Please," Raven said softly. "Sit."

Zach's knees refused to bend. But he couldn't stand there all day. Staring at the crystal as if it would jump up and bite him, he righted his chair and lowered himself into it.

The crescendo built up to a dramatic burst of sound, and then it got quiet for a beat.

Two.

Three.

Zach held his breath, waiting.

A solo violin finished the last few bars in a slower tempo, dragging out the final note to tease at his heartstrings until it faded into silence.

Raven removed the cube from its placeholder to prevent it from looping back for another replay. He expected her to pocket it again, but instead, she placed it on the table and slid it toward him. "This is for you," she said. "One piece of your memory I can restore without any manipulation whatsoever. Now, I know you will try so, to spare you the frustration and"—she tilted her head to the left—"heartache, you should know the digital device we provided for you is restricted to a specific network loop. It can't access any open or private databases."

She'd dangled a carrot in front of his nose, then yanked it out of his reach.

"You know who she was," he guessed. *Was*, because, without any additional information, he already knew the song's composer was dead. Living artists didn't get orchestral renditions of their work. And the ones who went out of their way to commission one sure as shit didn't pay for it to sound so funereal.

"Yes," Raven confirmed. No attempt to correct his assumption. Which was a confirmation.

Fuck, it fucking hurt.

"If you cooperate with the detox treatment, when it's finished, I'll tell you her name."

Zach's "*Fuck*" came out on a disbelieving huff of breath. He let his head drop back on his shoulders and stared at the ceiling, counting his heartbeats by the sharp pangs radiating out through his chest.

He felt…guilty.

The composer was a stranger to him, nothing but an idea in the farthest recesses of his mind. And still, Zach somehow knew her death hadn't been gentle, or inevitable. And he'd somehow had a hand in it.

Whatever "healing" they thought the detox tank could perform on his brain, they couldn't guarantee that it would restore the memories he'd lost.

But there was a chance.

Raven expected him to jump at it, assuming he would want to remember the woman who'd affected him this way. It's what a normal person would want. People who lost loved ones grasped at straws to hang on to the smallest pieces of them.

Zach wasn't normal. And if a simple song could hurt this much, did he want to risk uncovering more?

"The treatment will take a few days to set up," Raven told him. "You have some time to think it over."

"And if I refuse?"

She shrugged. "You'll still end up in the tank. But you'll lose your chance to learn her name. You strike me as a man who knows how to weigh his options. What do you think your odds are of finding her on your own if you don't remember?"

Decent.

Assuming he ever walked out of here. With access to public databases, Zach could conduct his own research and find out whatever the hell he wanted to. With the data cube she'd so helpfully provided, he could isolate the source the same way she had.

But it wouldn't be without potential risks. With the Shadows still hunting him, any activity on the broader public networks could draw their attention.

Zach stared Raven down, looking for a weakness to exploit, and found none. She held all the cards, and she knew it. The solicitous concern in her eyes in no way counterbalanced the cruelty of her strategy. He wanted to hate her for it, but hell if it didn't turn him on a little.

They still had a good amount of time left for today's session.

Rather than answer her, Zach replaced the data cube onto the digital tablet and started the song over.

He played it three more times, and all the while, neither he nor Raven spoke a word. Zach cycled back and forth between searching his mind for another hint of the composer and watching Raven's reaction. She kept her mind to herself, using patience and silence to draw him into a confession.

At first, anyway. After a few minutes, her spine loosened the slightest bit, and the focus of her gaze shifted to a spot on the table. She lost herself in the melody, same as him, and it pleased him how much she enjoyed it.

Eventually, the timer ran down to zero again, but Raven stopped it a second before the alarm went off and disrupted the song. Without a word, she stood from the table, heading for the exit.

"Raven," he said, stopping her before her hand had come close enough to unlock the door.

Her entire being tensed. Good. She was paying attention.

"The person I drew is no friend of yours. Watch your back."

Raven didn't go back to the meditation pods. She headed straight out the door, avoiding eye contact with everyone she passed along the way. As soon as her transport peeled away from the curb, its com chimed with an incoming call that included a system override. It initiated without her command, Darrow's face filling the front windshield.

"Do we need to revisit taking you off the case?"

"You tell me," she returned, in no mood to be lectured.

A light scrape along her scalp signaled his attempt to read her from a distance. She forcefully shoved back. Being her boss didn't give him permission to take liberties with her thoughts. And Raven didn't feel particularly forgiving at the moment.

Whether it was her violent reaction that clued him in or the look on her face, whatever lecture Darrow had been about to deliver died on a sigh. "I assume you have some questions for me."

"Let's start with Ripley."

"They submitted to a scan after you left yesterday. I didn't see any red flags. As for their visit with the Shadow, technically, they are qualified to engage and cleared for full access. And you only requested that the floor be empty while you're working on him. They didn't break any rules, but they went to some lengths to bend them. I docked their pay and wrote them up for insubordination. One more infraction, and they're gone."

By the book. Darrow wasn't a fool. If he'd had proof that Ripley was in any way acting against them, they wouldn't have gotten off with a slap on the wrist.

She still didn't like it. "As the lead on his case, I should have been notified as soon as it happened."

"I noted the incident in his file."

Which Raven hadn't reviewed since finishing yesterday's report. Why would she? Interrogations weren't a group project. The Shadow's file was a record of her work for Darrow's review.

"And the rest of what the Shadow said?"

"You know I never held anything back from you, Rae. My resources have always been at your disposal."

She hated this.

Raven wasn't a trusting person to begin with, and, as much as she wished they hadn't, the Shadow's comments had gotten under her skin. But at the same time, she couldn't say that Darrow had skimped on her care or isolated her from the others in the Chairo unit. Raven had done that all by herself.

Maybe it had been a mistake. She'd willingly put herself out of sight and out of mind. She'd made herself easy to forget about until they needed her. Her grief had been too heavy for her to deal with anything else.

She could have pushed harder. But part of her hadn't wanted to get better.

Part of her hadn't wanted to wake up again at all.

"I need a couple of days' leave." Tessa's news had shaken her, and that could spell disaster around a subject as smart and unpredictable as the Shadow. She needed some time to process, maybe look into possible treatment options for her friend. It was a long shot, but she couldn't just sit there and wait for the clock to run out.

Darrow nodded. "Whatever you want. I'll have one of the other—"

"No!" Shit. Too loud. But too late to take it back. "No one else goes down there while I'm out."

She read Darrow's anger before he spoke a word. He measured his words and maintained an even tone, but his youthful temper was written all over his face. "We can't afford to lose momentum now."

"Why?"

"We never located the Shadows he warned us about. No one has seen, heard, or sensed them. But we know they haven't left. If I put out a moon-wide alert within our ranks, it'll cause a panic and tip our hand."

"So you're just going to let us all fend for ourselves?"

"Don't put words in my mouth, Raven. That's not what I said. We're already rehousing the most vulnerable residents off-site, and I have two teams of eight sweeping the city and the surrounding area. I also doubled our security at the center and stationed additional lances around the neighborhood just to be safe."

All lances shared the same gift as Darrow—the ability to make a mind stop giving the body instructions to live. Official cause of death: spontaneous cardiac arrest.

It was a job none of them had ever imagined they would need to create. And those who took it did so out of a sense of duty to protect those who couldn't defend themselves. But something about it had always stuck Raven as wrong.

"Two days," she told her boss. "The Shadow can cool his heels until the detox tank is set up. Then we'll put him in it, and I can resume my study. I'll make up for lost time while he's unconscious." And unable to distract her. "But I don't want anyone else tampering with him in the meantime."

Darrow narrowed his eyes at her. "Be careful that you don't trip yourself into a trap over the Shadow's pretty face."

"You seem to have a great many misgivings about my ability to handle this case, boss. Why is that? What aren't you telling me?"

The look he shuttered so quickly lent truth to the Shadow's accusations, tempting Raven to take a peek at his thoughts. She resisted by reminding herself of the consequences of such an attack on her supervisor. Getting fired would be the least of her concerns. To compromise a high-ranking officer like Darrow was tantamount to treason. She'd end up tried and put down on the spot.

"*Is* there something you aren't telling me?" she pressed instead.

"Take your two days. I'll let you know when the detox tank is ready. Ripley won't be authorized to see the prisoner while you're gone. But I'm not going to sequester him from the others. I have telepaths to teach."

Half-truth, and she didn't need to read him to hear it in his voice. He only insisted on the Shadow remaining accessible to spite Raven and put her in her place. To remind her that she answered to him, not the other way around.

Funny, how the structure of their work relationship didn't feel as comforting as it once used to.

She was still thinking about it when her transport stopped in her driveway.

Raven stepped out onto the winding path tiled with rocks and followed it through the sand garden to her front door. The house was too big for her. It had been built for a family, the first structure in a new neighborhood that never got completed. The friends who should have joined her and Julian in their little community had never made it past the planning stages. More than half had lost their lives in the war. The other half had chosen to relocate to safer worlds, underdeveloped communities that wouldn't attract Shadow attention. Now, Raven had twenty acres of desert all to herself and a cavernous house filled with regrets.

The open living space echoed with her every step. An artificial fireplace radiated light, but the heat came up from the floor. The south and west walls were floor-to-ceiling glass for as much natural sunlight as Vesta permitted. In the moon's current position around the planet's orbit, it wasn't a lot.

Raven slipped off her shoes and went downstairs. The master bedroom was at the far end of the hallway. The two additional rooms should have been guest rooms and, eventually, kids' rooms. Now, one of them served as her office, and the other remained closed at all times. It held all of Julian's things. Even after three years, she couldn't bring herself to get rid of them. This house had been his dream. It was still his home as much as it was hers.

"System initiate," she commanded as she stepped into her office. With most technologies in her life being voice-activated, she only had a desk to hold up an augmented keyboard for some occasional typing. "Open file 37724."

The screen wall displayed the file with separate entries for each of her session notes. A subfolder with the SU's seal contained all the information they'd gathered about the Shadow prior to Raven taking over his case. A second one with her initials served as a repository for her own research notes.

"New entry. Time stamp with current date."

A separate partition opened up with a blank section at the top and the date and time stamp she'd requested. The cursor blinked, ready for her dictation. The bottom section would display the waveform of her voice recording for redundancy and fact-checking purposes. The cadence of an investigator's voice provided crucial information about their state of mind—the subject's effect on it.

Raven thought about what to say and drew a blank. "Upon locating the musical fragment sourced from the subject's memories, I decided to use the information as leverage to gain his cooperation. The song appeared to have a profound effect on the subject. He had a powerful emotional reaction and developed an instant obsession with it. When presented with the opportunity to gain insight into the song's composer in exchange for his cooperation…"

The Shadow's furious, almost pained expression flashed through her mind. It made her feel like a criminal for using his obvious grief against him. She couldn't shake it.

His self-control was admirable. If someone had told Raven they had a recording of Julian's last words, but she'd have to do something loathsome to earn it, she probably would have torn them apart.

It was a dirty tactic unbecoming of the values the Special Unit stood for.

But this was war, and the time for holding on to their moral high ground had passed.

"The subject did not immediately reject the idea, which leads me to believe my strategy will eventually yield the desired results."

Once they put the Shadow into the detox tank, Raven would have unfettered access to his mind during its most vulnerable stages of subconscious healing. In theory, it would be a prime opportunity to reprogram his thoughts and desires to more closely align with the SU's directive.

However, that kind of tampering could also cause damage. Human minds didn't have a backup and restore option. Too much of one's personhood resided in inactive portions of the mind which couldn't be mapped, even by a master telepath. Accidentally disrupting a core aspect of the person's identity could cause a catastrophic domino effect and destroy the very information they wanted to extract.

"The subject has been given a recording of the song, and further sessions are on hold until the detox treatment is prepared. To maximize the effectiveness of subsequent sessions, they will be extended to three hours a day. To preserve the integrity of the subject's mind, it is my recommendation that no other telepaths be allowed to access the subject during the treatment except under controlled conditions and my supervision."

Then, because she was still irritated, she added, "Council member Ripley Parecourte's breach of established protocol has compromised the subject's emotional state and undermined my progress with him. I recommend suspending all further telepathic testing by third parties, except under my direct supervision."

Was that everything?

"Personal observation. While the subject is understandably guarded, he has not responded negatively to detention. His apparent comfort and sociability would suggest a subconscious desire for interpersonal connection. While I do not believe his, shall we say, *romantic* overtures to be genuine, I do believe his intentions toward the Special Unit to be neutral, if not completely positive. Further study is needed to confirm. Close entry. Save in file and send to Regional Supervisor Darrow Iridiae."

The screen displayed a confirmation message, then shut down automatically.

For the next two days, Raven threw herself into research mode.

First, she set the AI trawl to search all databases and public resources for alternative treatments for Tessa. It returned archaic torture methods like dialysis and bloodletting, and a slew of holistic remedies that had no supporting research. Tessa wouldn't get better by taking daily walks in the sun and drinking raspberry leaf tea.

It only took fifteen minutes for the system to inform her that in cases where a blood marrow transplant was deemed necessary, no alternative treatments existed. Unique genetic defects could only be corrected with unique therapies on the genetic level—in cases where it was impossible at all.

And yet, chem-treatments existed.

If 29th century scientists could have come up with those, then modern-day experts had to be capable of producing a cure for chem-resistance.

So far, the only thing they'd been able to confirm was that each variant was nuanced and specific to the individual and therefore required a custom cure. Only someone with massive clout and unlimited resources could afford that—assuming they lived long enough to reap the benefits. Everyone else was left to suffer and die.

Frustrated, she ordered a pack of raspberry leaf tea to be delivered to Tessa's place later today and switched gears to her subject research.

She read everything there was to learn about the VanWarrens, and the man who'd infiltrated their ranks so seamlessly they hadn't noticed.

Zachary VanWarren appeared to have had a stormy history with the family, including a business deal gone wrong, and what had been labeled as a terrorist attack on their residence on planet Ela.

Very little about the attack had been shared publicly. However, the VanWarrens blamed it for their subsequent financial ruin, so, naturally, that became the next trail of breadcrumbs Raven followed. She didn't believe in coincidences or miracles. The timing was suspicious enough in and of itself, but the strategy matched her subject's escape from the Shadows: a physical attack, coupled with a financial hit. Could he have had a hand in the Ela disaster?

When her eyes started to lose focus, Raven called it a day to get some sleep. But she went right back to her office the second she woke up the next morning. A deep dive into the Ela law enforcement databases led her to several legal and financial documents bearing their official seal. Raven ran them through her system to condense the hundreds of pages into summaries while she worked on tracing the origin of each one. All of them had a comprehensive record of every time a recipient accessed the documents and every time they sent them on to someone else.

And that trail led her to the recording, which linked them all to their sender.

The moment the woman's face appeared on her screen, Raven recognized her as a Shadow. Unlike her prisoner, she made no effort to conceal her predatory nature.

The digital signature identified her as Vega Ortiz VanWarren, and her cold little smile said she knew her direct stare would unsettle the viewer. She was counting on it.

"Play," Raven prompted.

"Greetings," Vega VanWarren said, her tone giving Raven instant, very unpleasant chills. *"I should probably say something like 'I hope this message finds you well,' but I think by now we can all agree to dispense with the bullshit..."*

Raven's jaw slackened by degrees as she listened to the woman rip the massive and highly popular clan of entertainers apart word by word. She'd left no loose ends. The attack had been quick, efficient, and merciless. Raven had no doubt they'd deserved it, but still...

She compiled everything into an envelope and added it to her file, marking it as URGENT AND SENSITIVE. Darrow would want to see this.

Vega VanWarren was ruthless and vicious, and might have more in common with Zach than just their shared surname. If she could single-handedly destroy an empire in revenge for disowning her husband, based on how the SU had treated their Shadow prisoner so far, what would he do to them, given half a chance?

January 8, 3040 – Breckenridge, Danai

The mirror wall captured images at a rate of one every five seconds. It even had a hologuide of the most ideal poses for Hansel to display his muscles. He'd tanned specially for this, and the gym full of other muscle-bound people mid-workout served as the ideal backdrop.

"Hey, check out Mighty Mouse over here." A big, meaty fist bumped him on the shoulder, then pushed to shift him out of alignment, ending the photoshoot.

Hansel rolled his eyes at Uriel and stepped aside to let him take a turn.

"Lookin' good, man," Uriel said, striking the first shoulder pose. The mirror's hologuide identified him by his features and switched profiles so the new photos would be saved to his account. "Finally hit up that aug clinic like I told you?"

"Some of us don't need medical assistance to get buff, El." And some didn't have the luxury of building muscles just for show. Some were living on a shoestring budget, taking care of three young girls, one of whom was paralyzed from the chest down.

Treatments were expensive. The equipment tended to break down after several months, necessitating costly replacements. Gemma's specialized levchair had stopped levitating six months ago. It was now a heavy eyesore in the corner of her room, because Hansel couldn't lift the damned thing to dispose of it.

Between college, work, and taking care of the girls, Hansel hadn't had time to figure out how to repair it. It was easier for the rest of them to carry Gemma from spot to spot instead. Not like she ever displayed any overwhelming desire to go outside anymore. And she kept getting lighter…

Uriel laughed. "Yeah, right. Cuz muscles like that grow on trees, eh?" He twisted to show off his back. "Come on, we're all friends here. No one's judging."

Hansel crossed his arms, flexing his pecs for good measure, doing his best not to laugh. "I'm serious. This is all hard work you're looking at. Fourteen straight weeks of hardcore bootcamp finally paying off."

Fourteen weeks of almost no sleep, while Issa and Ophie shouldered his responsibilities. They were just kids. At a fresh twenty-three, Hansel barely felt like an adult himself. But he was all they had. And he was determined to make a good life for his sisters. A damned good life. If that meant working a little harder, a little longer, then so be it.

With his new physique, he would have a lot more options available to him. Augmented fitness models were a dime a dozen, but feats of real physical strength could get you into contests that paid better than any job out there, just for participating. And between those, Hansel now had enough experience and knowledge to work as a personal trainer. Rich people paid through the nose to have pretty young things come to their houses and spot their squats. Sometimes they paid for more, too. Hansel felt sick to his stomach thinking about it, but if it helped make Gemma's life more bearable and freed Issa and Ophie to be kids again, Hansel would do it. He would do anything.

Anyway, it was all worth it to watch them giggle with glee when he flexed his biceps for them and let them all hang from his neck and shoulders as he spun them until they cried laughing.

"Yeah? Go and do a pull-up, then," Uriel taunted. "Bar's right there beside you." And leg pose.

"I mean, I don't wanna make you look bad," Hansel teased.

"Oh, I insist." Bicep pose.

Hansel shrugged. "Fine. Watch and weep, loser." He grabbed the bar by two fingers on one hand and sent Uriel a wink and a kiss as he pulled himself up. He made it to five before his hand started to cramp. Not a record, but enough to prove his point.

"Well, I'll be damned. Where did you say you went again?"

Grinning from ear to ear, Hansel opened his mouth to tell him when a dull *bang* went off behind them and the gym filled with thick, stinking fog. He gasped on instinct and instantly began to choke and gag.

Alarms went off everywhere, sirens drowning out the sound of people screaming around him. Uriel staggered and fell so hard he knocked over a leg press. Hansel's knees gave out, and he dropped to all fours to retch, his entire body shaking from the gas. He couldn't tell up from down, but he sure as hell noticed when Uriel got snatched backward from three feet away, disappearing into the fog.

Hansel panicked. He crawled sideways, looking for a safe corner. For all the work he'd put into making himself bigger, he now did his best to shrink as small as he could. Hands over his ears, he squeezed his eyes shut and wept.

Rough, hard fingers clamped around his arm. With a sharp yank, he went flying, slamming face-first onto the floor. A knee to his back immobilized him. A merciless hand in his hair jerked his head so far back he thought his neck would break. Through the thick fog and the tears streaming from his burning eyes, Hansel couldn't see much more than black silhouettes with little blinking blue lights.

The needle in his neck barely registered.

But the speed with which the darkness descended convinced him he was about to die.

15

For two days, Zach split his lunch into two portions to irritate his pretty, traumatized interrogation specialist. Only for her to not make an appearance. Just as well. His meals weren't worth sharing. Instead of real food, his jailers had served him nutritional bars and a cocktail that made his bowels run. All designed to keep him nourished while prepping his body for the detox tank.

When not visiting the toilet, Zach spent his time playing his new favorite song.

He ought to stop doing that. For one thing, they'd be watching his every move. Giving them insights into his weaknesses was a bad idea. Yes, he'd already memorized the song down to the last note, but he still didn't want to risk them taking the cube from him if they got testy.

It was a pathetic self-soothing technique, anyway.

But he couldn't make himself stop. Each time he played the song, it hurt a little less. He couldn't mourn someone he'd never met, but appreciating her work seemed like an appropriate way to pay his respects, circumstances being what they were.

That one memory gap bothered him the most. Not knowing who she'd been, and who she'd been to him.

Not his mother—too convenient.

A sibling, maybe? A cousin?

A lover?

The sense of loss had a particular flavor to it that he couldn't identify. His regret wasn't only tied to her death. There was more. Something he'd missed. Or possibly something he'd neglected.

Zach kept trying to figure it out through the melody of her song, but it was like banging on a vault door without knowing what it contained. It would be valuable, but perhaps not in the way he expected or wanted.

And where the fuck was Raven?

Her absence felt more sinister than just an attempt to make him sweat the detox tank. Had they taken her off his case? Had she taken herself off?

Had she finally realized her beloved Special Unit wasn't so special after all and left them?

That would suck.

They'd started becoming such good friends. She could have at least said goodbye. Maybe left a forwarding address.

A Shadow having friends. What a concept.

Several hours past noon, his cell door opened.

He shoved to his feet, ready for battle.

When Raven waltzed into his room as if nothing was wrong, his initial fight instinct melted into irritation. She wore the same hairstyle, the same black uniform, the same neutral expression on her face, and somehow, she still looked different. More purposeful.

"You're late again," he informed her. "Two days and three hours…" he trailed off.

Raven wasn't alone.

The door remained open after she passed through, admitting three big men in riot gear, pointing weapons at him.

And standing outside his cell was the bludgeon whose cold eyes Zach would pluck out of their skull at the earliest opportunity if they didn't stop staring daggers at the back of Raven's head.

Raven noticed the direction of his gaze, looked over her shoulder at the person, and silently made them move out of sight.

Not out of mind, though. Their intrusive mental fingers poked at his forehead in a steady rhythm, irritating the shit out of him.

"Good afternoon, Mr. VanWarren," Raven said, distracting him. "Have you had enough time to consider my offer?"

Her guards raised their weapons a few inches. They meant business. If he didn't give her the right answer, they'd knock his ass out to force his compliance.

"I have, and there's no need for all this. I'll submit to the procedure willingly."

They'd do it whether he consented or not, but at least if he was conscious while they moved him, he could get a better idea of the facility's layout and security.

"Excellent. Mr. Jawali, it looks like we won't be needing the gurney after all. Mr. Leethe, the handcuffs, if you please."

One of the grunts produced thick metal shackles out of his pretty belt purse. They weren't connected to each other or to anything else. Electromagnetic cuffs worked on motion detection. There would be a set perimeter in which Zach could move—presumably out of arm's reach of anyone else—as long as he moved slowly. If he crossed over the boundary, the cuffs would electrocute him. If he moved too quickly, say, to throw a punch or grab an uninvited individual by their scrawny neck, the cuffs would electrocute him before he made contact. Depending on how paranoid they felt, the shock could be mild enough to set him back on his heels or strong enough to stop his heart.

"A security precaution," Raven explained.

"A building full of people who can make my brain drip out of my nose needs me to be in cuffs to feel safe? I'm flattered, Blackbird." But he didn't like the idea of being bound in the presence of the bludgeon out in the hallway, whose name he still didn't know.

"You will also be blindfolded for the transfer."

Meaning, this part of the facility didn't have a proper medical station. Good to know.

Zach searched Raven's expression for a hint of what bothered her. Something did. He could see it in her rigid posture. She almost stood to attention. She'd never looked this uncomfortable around him before.

The guards were standard-issue security grunts whom Raven knew by name and while she'd spoken to them with authority, it had been tempered with the kindness of familiarity. They weren't strangers to her, and they were clearly dedicated to their duty to keep her safe. No reason for her to be uneasy around them.

Had to be the bludgeon, then. Raven must not have expected them to be here for this, and it was throwing her off.

Zach offered his wrists to Mr. Leethe. "Shall we, then?"

Leethe holstered his weapon and stepped forward, only close enough to snap the cuffs around Zach's wrists. The edge of each one flashed green, indicating they were active. Solid brand. Good make. A reliable model with a single key to unlock it, which could be anything from a fingerprint to a physical pin engraved with the release code. Short of finding that, Zach wouldn't be getting out of the cuffs on his own.

Mr. Jawali looked to Raven for further instructions.

She nodded to him, and he stepped out of the room momentarily to retrieve a blackout helmet. Like the cuffs, once the helmet was on his head, Zach wouldn't be able to remove it on his own. It would obscure his full field of vision and muffle sounds to keep him disoriented during transport. He'd have to count his steps and hope they didn't put him in an elevator or vehicle, or he'd have no way to track their speed to estimate travel distance.

Mr. Jawali checked with the other two guards before he stepped toward Zach.

The tapping at his head intensified.

The guard lifted the helmet.

Zach reared away.

Jawali jumped back, and the other two stepped forward, charging their weapons.

Zach ignored them, looking pointedly at Raven. "Remember what I told you." *Watch your back.* He didn't expect her to hear it; he couldn't feel the soft brush of her mental touch, only the bludgeon drumming on his head like it was their favorite pastime. It made his eye twitch. Not because he couldn't handle the annoyance, but because Raven appeared unaware of their interference. That was dangerous.

Raven tilted her head a couple of degrees, her eyes darting quickly to the side and back. Then her chin dipped to indicate she understood. "Mr. Jawali, if you please."

The guard approached again, slower this time, and lifted the helmet with shaking hands. Zach held Raven's gaze until the helmet lowered over his head and his world became darkness.

16

The Shadow's willing cooperation made the guards twitchy. Raven tried to keep them calm as much as she dared without dulling their instincts too much. They'd need to have their wits about them for the transfer.

Ripley didn't like or approve of her methods. Raven didn't care. They shouldn't even be there.

Unfortunately, for security reasons, Raven needed backup. Following established protocols, she'd put in a request with plenty of advance notice and got told that none of the other council members were available, and no one else had the necessary clearance.

Darrow couldn't risk exposing himself, and he wouldn't allow Raven to handle a Shadow prisoner transfer on her own, no matter how co-operative he pretended to be. Since Ripley had already compromised their identity, he'd had no other choice but to amend his restrictions on them. They still weren't allowed near the Shadow unsupervised, but until further notice, Ripley was officially the only one cleared to act as Raven's backup whenever necessary.

Far be it from Raven to question her superiors, but what the fuck?

Never would she have thought the day would come when she'd look at her own people as anything other than her allies.

Maybe it was a sign. It might be time to leave Chairo and move on somewhere else.

But she'd see this last assignment through to the end first.

With the Shadow prepped, Raven nodded to the guards. They moved single-file: Jawali at the front, followed by the Shadow, with Leethe between him and Raven. Ripley and Mr. Kangalai brought up the rear.

Ripley had agreed to this arrangement most readily, which made

Raven suspicious. She gave the signal to move out, and the guards maneuvered the prisoner into the hallway with as little contact as possible to steer him in the right direction. Following behind them, Raven decided to trust her gut.

The elevator opened.

Jawali tugged the Shadow inside, and Leethe followed.

With her foot on the threshold to prevent the door from closing, Raven turned her palm toward the Shadow and reached out to a specific part of his mind.

Her third specialty, and the rarest one of all: a natural gift for mental shields. Raven could get into a telepath's mind as easily as a civilian's, regardless of their protections. A crucial skill for someone in her profession. However, she could also create mental shields in others, which she usually did to protect compromised minds until they gained control over their abilities. Once the shield was in place, no one else could breach it without killing the person in the process.

It only took a second to get a solid anchor, as much of a pause as Raven could risk without tipping Ripley off. Once she was rooted, she stepped into the elevator. She began to weave her web, starting at the base of the Shadow's skull, where his instinctual, emotional animal brain resided—the easiest part of a person to read and manipulate.

It didn't take long to complete the weave. She was done by the time the elevator came to a stop. As the final step, before she followed Leethe out on the medical floor, Raven fashioned a lock with strains of his favorite song, and the name he himself didn't know yet.

No doubt, he'd felt her working on him, but he didn't falter a single step as the guards steered him through the open medical center toward the far back, where a detox tank had been placed in the quarantine room.

Similar to his cell, the room had been augmented to lock for additional safety, which it did as soon as they were all inside. Only then did Leethe remove the Shadow's helmet.

He squinted in the brightly illuminated room, turning a full circle to study his surroundings. There wasn't much to see. The walls were solid and bare. Only essential equipment had been brought in, so he had nothing to convert into a weapon, and security feed strips lined the upper edge of the walls to canvas the room from every angle.

Four more guards stood by in the corners, a safety precaution for the two medics who would be putting him into the waiting tank. It was upright—the only kind they'd been able to get on short notice—and made of thick glass. The clear fluid inside varied between the faintest shades pink and orange, depending on the angle of the lighting.

"Cozy," the Shadow observed.

"As I explained, you will be sedated for the duration of your detox," she said for everyone's benefit. "This is to minimize the stress of breathing the oxygenated detox solution. It will be enriched with all the nutrients your body needs to preserve your health."

"If you would, please remove your clothes," said Dr. Vernon. He'd been with the Chairo SU for fifteen years now. A solid man with zero pretensions. But he had never treated a Shadow, and addressing one made him visibly nervous.

Instead of answering the medic, Zach turned a questioning look at Raven. "Didn't get enough the first time?"

The other medic, a younger man named Immanuel Zyxon, stepped forward. "Foreign materials can contaminate the solution and cause pneumonia and other infections to take root. We will need you to remove everything, including the cuffs, and go through a sonic shower before you can enter the tank."

He grinned, still watching Raven. "Will you come scrub my back for me?"

"Well, you have been a good boy. So far."

He threw his head back and laughed, causing all the guards to jump, weapons ready to take him out.

"Only the patient is allowed through the shower," Dr. Vernon said, frowning. He tended to be somewhat literal.

"Mr. VanWarren," Raven prompted, indicating the shower stall at the end of a sterile tunnel leading to the tank.

"Call me Zach," he said. "Just once."

The way the collective emotional echo resonated throughout the room, he might as well have asked to do filthy things to everyone's grandmothers. The guards itched to shoot him. The medics wanted to get out of there, and Ripley's irritation prickled at Raven's spine, demanding her attention. Unless she missed her guess, Ripley had discovered Raven's shield around the Shadow's mind, and they weren't amused. The way the Shadow ignored their presence didn't seem to help, either.

She decided to play along with him. Holding his gaze, Raven said, "Undress for me, won't you…Zach?"

No one but her noticed his dark eyes soften over his wicked grin. They saw the way he flexed his impressive muscles as he pulled his shirt off over his head, but missed the way he let it drop slightly in front of him, as if offering it to her. They saw him stare at her unblinking while he toed off his shoes and pushed down his pants, unabashedly revealing an erection that pointed straight up. But they wouldn't know how hard he focused on every nuance of her reaction.

The mental shield she'd constructed for him wasn't connected to her, in the strictest sense, but it was still, in a small, abstract way, a part of her. In such proximity, it acted almost like a gauge of his mental activity. She couldn't tell what he was thinking, but she sensed how much and how hard he was thinking about it.

The moment he'd gotten his sight back, his mind had flared with a burst of activity she would have expected of someone performing a quick study of his new environment.

As he looked at her now, his thoughts were a low, intense hum. She had his full, undivided attention, something a man in his dangerous profession could rarely afford.

"Please step through into the shower, sir," Zyxon said. "If we can kindly get his cuffs removed?"

One of the guards stepped up to take hold of Zach's wrist and unlock the cuff.

He didn't react, allowing the man to do the same with the other one, never once breaking eye contact with her.

"Sir?" Zyxon prompted again, keeping a prudent distance.

Zach winked at her, breaking the spell. He passed through the shower and into the tunnel.

Vernon waited for him at the other end, the tranquilizer ready. "The sedative will have a fifteen-second delay. Once I inject you, please climb up the ladder and lower yourself into the tank. Do not jump.

Your weight will submerge you to the appropriate level. You will be sedated by the time you run out of breath."

Zach held still for the injection, then obediently climbed up the ladder and out of the tunnel. He sat on the ledge, swung his legs over, and found Raven again, at the back of a small army of guards who'd stepped up to shield her. "I'll be dreaming of you," he said, and carefully lowered himself into the tank.

His eyes closed as soon as the liquid swallowed the top of his head. Air bubbles escaped from his mouth and nose on a final exhale of air before his lungs expanded to take in the liquid solution. His vitals spiked as his body struggled to compensate for the solution's higher density, then settled into a steady, calm rhythm.

"Well done, everyone," Raven praised. "You may go back to your stations now. Drs. Zyxon and Vernon will monitor the patient for the duration of his treatment."

The guards murmured their goodbyes and left.

Ripley didn't.

Not that Raven had expected them to. "Something I can help you with?"

"Interesting strategy."

"I don't know what you mean."

"Of course you don't." Ripley sneered. Per Darrow's orders, Ripley was not supposed to interfere with Raven's subject in any way, except in the event of a catastrophic security breach. They couldn't say anything about the shield Raven had constructed for Zach without admitting they'd poked around where they shouldn't have. Darrow was a patient person, but he had his limits.

So did Raven. If the council member refused to play nice, Raven would play dirty. And she would make them regret the day they'd decided to poke their nose where it didn't belong.

Ripley stared her down a moment longer, then said, "Consider this a lesson. In complicated times, unpleasant consequences do not absolve us from making difficult decisions." Then they turned and strolled away, tossing back, "I look forward to reading your next report."

"Good day to you, Council Member Parecourte."

And good fucking riddance.

January 10, 3040 – Chairo, Valhale 602

SUBJECT:	Zachary VanWarren
	AKA Operative M (Shadow Hawk)
SEX:	Male
AGE:	38
STATUS:	Partial sedation with measurable brain activity, indicating REM sleep

SESSION 4

With the shield in place, Raven could no longer sink and absorb herself into Zach's mind. She had to open a door and walk through it.

She entered into the darkness of an echoing hallway. Her telepathic self didn't have a shape or form, but as she moved down the corridor, the sound of her footsteps echoed ahead of her.

Eventually, the darkness receded a little as dull red lights appeared overhead. The hallway, lined with doors, split into different corridors every once in a while. Raven marked her path at each intersection to make a mental map for herself.

This appeared to be a place from his past. One of the Shadows' outposts, maybe, but which one? The layout appeared to be bland and uniform. Exactly the way a sprawling military institution would want to keep things. Variety only bred discontent, after all.

Wandering around wouldn't get her anywhere. Instead, Raven chose a door and opened it, stepping through into a memory.

The disconcerting red of the hallway faded into drab gray. Gray walls, gray floor, gray ceiling. A gray desk in the middle, with a child dressed in a gray uniform sitting at it, swiping across a bright digital screen.

She heard heavy footsteps marching back and forth, but didn't see a person attached to them.

The boy was blank-faced, sitting almost completely still. Only his hands moved over the screen, and only enough to perform his assigned task.

The footsteps stopped. "Time," an older man said.

The boy straightened in his seat, putting his hands in his lap.

The screen slid across the desk, turning away from him. Then the boy's head snapped to the side, his hair flying out of its neat arrangement as the invisible man slapped him across the face. The screen then swiveled back toward the boy. "Again."

This was Zach. A memory from his childhood that seemed to hold some significance. But even as she watched the boy resume his work, shedding not a single tear as his cheek turned bright red, the ceiling began to disintegrate along its edges.

Raven sensed a presence beside her before Zach, as he was now, took shape, dressed in a plain white T-shirt and pressed, dark blue uniform slacks. Standing at ease, with his spine straight and his hands clasped behind his back, he watched his childhood self perform the task again, as ordered, while the ceiling disappeared and the walls began to melt down around them.

The invisible man checked his work, still finding it unsatisfactory. He slapped Zach once, then a second time across the other cheek, and repeated, "Again."

By now, the walls had disintegrated, leaving only the boy at his desk and the door at Raven's back floating through the darkness of a black void.

Adult-Zach blurred and streaked as he swiveled on his heels and walked away from the memory, fading through the door like a ghost.

"Wait!" Raven rushed out after him, sensing the memory collapse into nothing as she emerged back in the red hallway.

He'd destroyed it.

A core memory of his early development, and he'd chosen to rip it apart and scatter it.

His determined, long-legged stride forced her to run after him. She didn't have time to properly mark her path, throwing out haphazard flags every few steps as she struggled to keep up.

His shape wasn't solid, as if he couldn't decide whether he wanted to be there or not. He led her deeper into his mind, from one hallway to another, and then through a different door.

Raven caught it before it slammed shut and stepped through into bright sunlight.

She found herself alone in a field overgrown with tall grasses and flowers. As far as she could see, rolling hills spread out like bright green dunes, dotted with great big trees.

There was Zach again, a few years older, running through the grass, his cheeks red and his eyes bright with excitement. He ran up to a tree and climbed the gnarled knots of its trunk to the first branch, then caught the next one above it and pulled himself higher, and then higher into the crown, until he perched on a branch so thin it bent and groaned beneath his weight. He looked out across the landscape, an almost manic smile stretching across his face. When he whooped to the sky, Raven smiled.

"That's how it should have been," the adult version of Zach said, appearing next to her out of thin air. "That's what I want to remember."

"But it's not real," she said. As beautiful as the scene was, she felt the artificial construct of it. The scene wasn't anchored to anything. It had no roots in reality. The gossamer threads that had woven it into being were purely emotional. Threads of longing, sadness, and defiance.

"Reality is what we make of it," he replied, watching his imaginary childhood self hop and climb back down the tree. "We can choose how we see the world. We can decide how we see ourselves."

The child dropped to the ground and dug into the dirt between two thick roots.

In the distance, a scattering of houses sprouted across a hill and a dark red road snaked through the grasses to mark a well-traveled path. The scene became more complex as structures emerged from the landscape and people appeared like mirages, filling it with movement.

Each new detail solidified the construct a little more.

"We are who we are," Raven said.

"No," adult-Zach replied sharply, turning his head to look straight at her. "We choose. We decide. We build ourselves up from what we can accept and what we can't. The second you let someone else define your character, you lose it."

"Are you lucid right now?" He shouldn't be. His mind wasn't experiencing a regular dream. He'd been sedated into a mild chemical coma. All of this should have been random.

Come to think of it, Raven shouldn't be seeing or hearing this version of Zach at all. Had something gone wrong with the sedation?

Zach smiled at her. "Hello, Blackbird."

"How is this possible?"

He tapped his temple. "Guess EMC has more side effects than the Shadows ever bothered to study. Not that I'm complaining."

The child version of him shouted in triumph, having unearthed an ancient treasure chest. He used a large rock to break the rusted padlock and fumbled with the latch to open the top. Raven couldn't see what the chest contained, but child-Zach's excitement was contagious. She felt happy in this scene, for all that it was fake. It made her wish she could make it real for him.

Child-Zach extracted his treasure, hugging it to his chest as he came away from the tree, heading toward her and adult-Zach. Raven shifted aside, not wanting to stand in child-Zach's way, since he was effectively a ghost with no awareness of her.

But the boy altered his course to compensate, smiling right at her.

However Zach had constructed this scene, it was no longer just a dream. Raven had no idea how to classify it, or even how to understand what was happening. Sleeping minds shouldn't be lucid this way. Dreaming minds shouldn't be aware of telepathic intrusion.

Neither version of Zach should be interacting with her, but both were. Meaning, anything she said or did would become incorporated into Zach's memory. It felt dangerous to breathe the wrong way.

Child-Zach stopped a few feet in front of her and puffed out his chest as he offered her a little glowing ball.

She looked to adult-Zach for guidance and found him watching her with a hint of a smile of his own. So much for his help.

With no better alternative forthcoming, Raven accepted the gift from child-Zach. "Thank you." The ball of light settled in the center of her palm and melted into her skin. Its warmth raced up her arm and, as the light dissipated, something else took shape. A left arm and a left hand cradling her right. It started out transparent but solidified in moments until she could feel it as well as see it.

"I think child-me would have liked child-you," adult-Zach said.

Raven didn't know what to say to that.

Child-Zach grinned from ear to ear. "One day, I'm going to grow up and become a superhero!" he proclaimed. "I'm going to fight monsters and make people safe."

The scene froze, down to the last blade of grass. All of child-Zach's enthusiasm froze with it, leaving adult-Zach's wistfulness and a deep sense of loss.

He'd imagined himself into cognitive dissonance. The goodness he craved didn't match the darkness of his actual life. She sensed that he still wanted to hold on to this fictional version of a childhood well-lived, but his grasp on the fantasy was already slipping.

The skies turned dark, shrouded by heavy clouds. Thunder rolled in the distance—and so did the landscape, rumbling and breaking apart the same way the Shadow memory had.

"We should go," Zach said, turning his back on it all.

Raven followed him through the exit into the dark-red hallway. "We are who we are," she said, as gently as she could. "Fighting our own nature only leads to pain."

At the next corner, Zach stopped. "You did something to me. Back in the real world, before I went under. What did you do?"

Taken aback, Raven fumbled for words. "I… I just… I mean, Ripley was—"

"Ripley? Is that their name?"

Shit. Too late to take it back now. "Yes."

"I felt them poking at my brain, and then I felt…warmth. And it stopped." He turned to face her. "You did that."

"Yes."

"You trusted me over them."

That was going a bit far. "I trusted my instincts. Ripley has been interfering with my work since the day you were brought in. I don't know what their intentions are, but I don't like it."

"You protected me."

"I protected the integrity of my work with you."

He gave her a look. "You protected me," he insisted. "I won't forget it."

Raven nodded.

"How much time do we have?"

As if on cue, the breadcrumbs Raven had left for herself flashed a bright white. "Time moves differently in dreams. I've been here for hours." And she'd pay for it later.

"Does it hurt to walk through people's dreams?"

"Not exactly. It's more like an intense workout. I'll be drained and tired, but not in pain." Barring a dehydration headache and a stiff back.

"I'm glad," he said. "Means I get to see you again soon."

The breadcrumbs flared brighter, and the red lights momentarily turned into blood stains all over the walls. Raven gasped when a dead soldier appeared on the floor at her feet.

"Don't mind him," Zach said. "He can't hurt anyone anymore."

"Who was he?"

Zach cocked his head at the corpse, then nudged it over with his foot. The man's face was cut from ear to ear, his jaw hanging loose, exposing a swollen, purple tongue and the black hole at the back of his throat. "Someone who didn't deserve to breathe."

Raven blinked, and the body changed. Now, the face was whole, but his hair faded from brown to blond, and his neck opened up, pumping out fresh blood. His eyes snapped to Raven, and she jumped back.

Zach's booted foot came down on the man's head, crushing it to mulch. He stepped over the rest of him and took Raven's left hand to pull her away. "Let's get you out of here."

He followed her breadcrumbs all the way out to the solid wall of her shield. He wouldn't be able to see it, but he might sense its boundaries. The door appeared as a black liquid portal. All she had to do was step through it to get back to herself.

She turned to Zach to say goodbye.

He cupped her face with his free hand and pulled her up into a kiss. His mouth softened as it moved over hers, the harsh pressure of their collision easing into a teasing caress before he retreated completely.

Raven blinked, disoriented, at a loss for words.

Zach gave her a crooked grin. "I'll ask forgiveness some other time." Then he lightly chucked her under the chin to close her mouth and nudged her toward the portal. "See you soon, Blackbird."

Raven backed out of his hold and out of his mind to the sight of him walking away hand in hand with the ghostly copy of her he'd held onto.

Raven opened her eyes to Darrow glaring at her from a new chair set between her and the detox tank. "It's true, then. You really have lost your goddamn mind."

Her back was killing her, and her legs had gone numb sitting on the hard office chair the staff had brought in for her. With her mind still adjusting to being back in her physical body, Raven struggled to unstick her tongue from the roof of her mouth to speak.

Darrow wasn't in the mood to wait. "Fraternizing with a Shadow? Really? That's how low you—"

Her hand flew of its own accord, striking Darrow across the face. It was weak and caused her lower back to spasm, but she turned her wince into a snarl and held his gaze in open defiance.

His eyes went wide with shock.

"That is the last time you speak to me like that," she rasped. Also, the last time she'd allow him to blindside her and treat her with such complete disregard for her safety. Getting between her and a subject while she was working on him? Attacking her the second she came up for air? No. They had protocols in place to ease the transition back and forth whenever a telepath worked such intense assignments. They were required for a reason.

Raven had been sitting there, unmoving, for three and a half hours. She should have had a table set out for her with food and drink. She should have had a junior telepath in place to help her realign and get back into the movement of her body after such a long session. Not to mention, a trained medic on standby in case something went wrong. Dehydration, muscle cramps, and blood clots were just a few of the physical risks, not counting the mental risks she took to do this in the first place.

Raven only had Darrow with his pissy attitude and a sense of another presence outside the door. Likely Ripley, waiting to gloat over Raven's punishment.

Darrow wouldn't be there now unless they'd thrown her under the bus. And he wouldn't be this angry unless he'd confirmed the claims firsthand. Meaning, not only had he chosen to overlook Ripley's multiple breaches of protocol, he'd committed two of his own. First, by trying to insert himself into the Shadow's mind while she'd worked on him, and second, by withholding Raven's aftercare.

This from the man—the boy—who constantly attempted to reassure her that he was on her side, and that anything she needed, he would get for her if and when she asked.

Darrow stood up, the icon of offended authority, and drew back his thin shoulders. "Did you forget who pays your salary?"

"The Special Unit pays my salary," she retorted, shifting her torso from side to side to relieve some of the ache in her lower back. Her voice might be hoarse, but her brain was fully functional. "Just like they pay yours. Having a higher rank doesn't give you the right to insult me. Control your temper, or I'll do it for you."

"You have some nerve—"

"Strike two." Raven rolled her head on her shoulders, rubbing the back of her neck.

Darrow's face darkened, and his nostrils flared. A muscle twitched in his jaw as he clenched it hard against more insults. It took him far longer than it should have to get himself under control, which Raven attributed to the maelstrom of puberty hormones. It didn't excuse his behavior.

Having accepted his position as Regional Supervisor, he had assumed the responsibility to act accordingly.

Still glaring at her, he pointed a shaking finger at the detox tank and the Shadow floating inside of it. "Explain. And you better make it good, Raven, or I swear, I'll call up the council and bring charges against you before the day is out."

"You forced my hand. You asked me what I would need to work the Shadow, and then overruled me. You cut my time with him in half.

You restored Ripley's access despite them repeatedly disregarding my orders—and yours. The subject showed clear signs of distress at their presence, which led me to believe that Ripley was provoking him *while I was in the room!*"

Her shout echoed, setting Darrow back. It surprised even Raven. She'd just admonished her boss for losing his temper, and there she was, doing the same. She sucked in a deep breath through her nose and released it, bringing herself back under control. "At every turn, you question my integrity and ignore or countermand my very reasonable requests, but still expect me to do my job as if nothing's wrong, so I did what I had to do. I secured the subject against further tampering that might interfere with my work. I don't know what you and Ripley are up to, but it stops now. I won't have my safety compromised or my reputation shredded because you have some bug up your ass about me working with a flirty Shadow. You want to fire me? Fire me. You want to bring me up on charges? Do it. And you can kiss your chances of getting intel out of him goodbye. No one is getting through that shield but me."

The silence of his stare was oppressive. Darrow didn't like one word of what she'd just said, but, short of killing her, he couldn't do anything about it. "This isn't how we do things, Raven."

"I agree. So why don't you do your job and stop obstructing mine?"

His and Ripley's interference since the Shadow's imprisonment was no small matter. Raven could bring it up to their acting director and have her sort it out. She had a feeling Darrow would fight tooth and nail to keep that from happening. Emma was married to a former Shadow herself. She'd created the precedents and protocols for processing deserted Shadow soldiers with a fairness most telepaths had opposed in the beginning.

Predictably, Darrow turned the tables back on her. "Report."

She almost rolled her eyes. "The subject's dreamscape is as unpredictable as his waking mind. He is still in the process of pruning his identity. I experienced it firsthand today. He dismantled a formative memory from his childhood with the Shadows."

"So it's true, they really are breeding soldiers now."

Raven rolled her shoulder and pushed herself up to stand. Darrow didn't help. "As far as I can tell, they've been doing it for decades. The memory was…harrowing." She described the scene she'd witnessed and how Zach had disintegrated it into nothing, effectively purging it from his consciousness.

"Why would he do that?"

The better question was *how* had he done it? Trauma survivors commonly used memory repression as a coping technique, but that wasn't what Zach had done. He hadn't shoved the memory into a dark corner of his mind; he'd utterly destroyed it.

"I think he wants to be someone else. And I can't coalesce his memories while he's still deciding which ones he's willing to keep. Not without his cooperation." The fantasy of a happy childhood, dreams of becoming a superhero—a good person—had twisted Raven's heart. It felt too personal to share with Darrow.

"Anything on who sent him our way?"

"No. That chase might be a lost cause. I keep looking for hints, but he has no recollection of anyone tied to our address prior to his arrival. Depending on when the contact happened, the memory might not have had time to embed before the EMC treatment burned it out of his head." Either that, or he'd destroyed it himself to protect his source.

"So we're dead in the water."

"Not at all. He still has caches of information we can use. Not to mention all the money he stole from the Shadows. I could pull it out of him, but I wouldn't recommend it. Right now, he's cooperative and slowly building trust. If we break that, we risk losing everything."

"You think he can make himself forget the information before we access it?"

"Without a doubt." Which led her to the bigger issue. "Darrow, he's awake in there."

His head swung around to the tank. "He's sedated."

"He was lucid when I encountered him. He recognized me and interacted with me." She hesitated. "His file said his DNA is stable and locked. Is that true?"

Darrow swung back around to her. "Of course it is. What are you saying?"

"I don't know. But there's something different about the way his mind works. I have never seen anything like it. Anomalies this intense only happen in chem-resistants." Meaning, someone was lying.

And it wasn't Raven.

Darrow rubbed the bridge of his nose. "Ripley says one thing, you say another. Who am I supposed to trust?"

The hell kind of a stupid question was that? "Neither." Obviously. "You do your own thinking and decide for yourself." Darrow was usually so eloquent and confident that people found it easy to forget he was still a teenager. But at times like this, he really showed his age and lack of experience. "I think you should call the acting director."

"No," he snapped. "She has enough on her plate. We can handle this ourselves."

Raven watched him wage some sort of internal struggle for a moment. Her knees still felt too weak to walk away, and her senses were still a little frayed around the edges, but she recognized signs of a crisis in Darrow, and it didn't put her mind at ease. Given his volatile state, the wrong word could set him down a very dangerous path.

She chose her words with care. "You've led our community with utmost care and professionalism for the last three years. You've proven yourself more than capable. There are too many of us here to follow a leader we don't believe in. We believe in you, Darrow. There is nothing left to prove. Everyone makes mistakes. A good leader has to be able to admit them. It's the only way to fix them and move forward."

His gaze met hers again, filled with dark fire, and Raven knew she'd fucked up. "You think I made a mistake."

"I just—"

"What was my mistake, Raven? Checking up on you to make sure you were safe working on a Shadow, or assigning you to his case in the first place?"

Raven sighed, too tired to rehash the same argument a third time. If Darrow wanted to throw a temper tantrum, he could do it while she got herself something to drink, since he appeared disinclined to provide. With that less than comforting thought in mind, she turned for the door, mentally bracing for another confrontation with Ripley pacing out in the med center.

"You keep talking about your reputation, but it wasn't you who joined the merge. You weren't one of the five who brought down the Shadow fleet and restored order here."

Ice settled in her bones. She heard it creaking as she faced her boss again. "You're right," she said, her face numb, and her phantom limb screaming in agony. "It wasn't my sacrifice. If it had been, and it was Julian standing here instead of me, you never would have dared to say those words. You want to know what your mistake is, Darrow? You used to trust the people you chose to have around you—you chose them *because* you trusted them to know what they were doing. I used to be one of those people, remember? What's changed?"

"The Shadow is—"

"Just another subject for me to interrogate using whatever method I deem most effective."

"No, Rae. This one is different. You're different with him."

She frowned. "Are you jealous of him?"

"I'm just thinking about what Julian would say if he heard you ask the Shadow to strip down for you."

Raven recoiled as if he'd struck her. Pain bloomed in her chest, so intense she couldn't take a full breath. "Julian isn't here," she said, her voice quivering. "And I am done with this conversation."

She rushed out, ignoring whatever else he shouted after her, shoving past Ripley, and half-running for the elevator. She was hyperventilating by the time she emerged on her floor. Her feet dragged, tripping over themselves on the way to her temporary quarters. She barely made it inside before her knees gave out and her body collapsed into shuddering sobs.

There was one skill which every telepath always mastered: identifying the emotional weak spot that would bring their opponents to their knees.

19

January 12, 3040 – Chairo, Valhale 602

SESSION 5

The mindscape Raven entered was completely different from before. Instead of a dark hallway, she found herself in a bright, cheerful bedroom with an old-fashioned stuffed teddy bear on the fluffy bed, and a bay window framing a view of ocean waves crashing against dark gray cliffs.

The room exuded calm, comfort, and safety.

And Zach wasn't in it.

Raven was so thrown, she reached for the door handle with her left hand—only to find that she had one again. Fully formed and as much a part of her as a real one would have been.

Not her doing.

She stepped out into a massive Viking lodge where an enormous fireplace took up the middle of the room, and thick animal skins covered the floor. Giant windows looked out at a snow-capped mountain range in the distance. Wooden beams crisscrossed above her, making the ceiling feel impossibly high, and wrought iron sconces and chandeliers flickered with candlelight.

"All it needs is a giant Christmas tree," she said to herself, unsure what to make of this.

A moment later, an evergreen burst out of the floor by the windows and grew to nine feet in seconds, spreading thick branches that sprouted colorful ornaments and glittered with lights.

"Do you like it?" Zach asked, appearing out of nowhere beside her.

"What is all this?"

He shrugged. "I figured if you're going to be coming by more often, you should have a place of your own. Not like I don't have the space."

"I'm not here for me, you know."

He smiled at her. "I know. So what's on the agenda for today, Blackbird?"

Raven couldn't remember.

"Do you want to take a tour? Maybe have a snowball fight outside? If you don't like the view, I can change it." A tropical beach replaced the mountains.

Raven immediately recoiled.

Zach chuckled, and the mountains came back. He added a thick blanket of snow and big, fluffy snowflakes floating down from the sky for good measure.

The fireplace crackled, adding a warm scent of smoke to the cozy atmosphere, and two steaming mugs of spiced cider appeared in Zach's hands. He offered one to her.

This was why she was here.

Everything he did, the speed with which he changed the scenery, and the level of detail in all of it was so far out of normal that Raven didn't know what to make of it. She felt the textures, smelled the scents, and heard the ambient soundscape as if it were all real.

People didn't dream this way. They didn't imagine this way. A mental construct, by its nature, always had a level of ambiguity and vagueness. Its edges softened around the periphery of one's focus, where consciousness couldn't quite fill in the details anymore. That's how the mind recognized it as separate from reality.

It had to be another elaborate distraction. She needed to get back on track with her objective.

"The treatment is starting to work," she told him. "Your scans show the EMC chemicals have filtered out of your system almost completely, and your brain activity has stabilized a little. You're on track to fully detox in five more days."

"I can feel it. My mind is…sharper."

"I need to know more about the Shadows."

The mugs disappeared, and Zach offered her his arm. "Then let's take a walk."

Raven didn't take it.

He didn't seem to mind, keeping in step with her as a long hallway extended out from the living space, lined with ornate wooden doors, flickering torchlight, and rough, worn floors.

Raven approached the first door, carved with two trees twined together. When she reached for the handle, Zach caught her hand. "I don't think you're ready for that one yet."

"Why? What is it?"

"Let's go over there." Still holding her hand, he pulled her along the hallway, past several other doors, to one carved with the image of an ancient warrior wielding a battle ax. He opened it and stepped through into a memory.

Another bland, empty room, another nightmare from his formative years. This time, he was older. Maybe twelve or thirteen. His hands, wrapped in white tape, curled into fists as he squared off against a big man with obscured features.

Young Zach launched an attack, only to be struck down by his opponent. He hit the floor, his cheek reddening, but his eyes were determined as he pushed himself back up.

"Again," the man snapped.

Young Zach squared off again. He tried a different attack, kicking up at his opponent's side.

The man caught Zach's leg, then grabbed his belt in the other hand and threw him like a sack of potatoes. Zach landed on his back, breath knocked out of him, but the man kept coming, raising his booted foot and stomping it down on Zach's middle.

She heard something snap as adult-Zach flinched beside her. His face was set as he watched the scene, eyes hard, mouth no longer smiling. But he kept watching, with his shoulders squared and his hands behind his back as if he'd been ordered to.

"Again," the man barked, sounding more agitated.

Young Zach struggled to get back up. He favored his right side, holding his ribs. His face was flushed, and his eyes glittered with unshed tears, but he clenched his teeth and squared off a third time.

The man caught Zach's punch in his fist, twisted his arm until it cracked. Zach's white sleeve tented and bloomed red as his broken arm bone stabbed through. His sharp cry, so young, so full of pain, broke something inside Raven.

But the man just shoved Zach away and shouted, "Again!"

She couldn't watch this anymore. "Destroy it," she said, turning away. "Like you did the other one."

"No," adult-Zach replied. "This one has to stay."

Instead of crumbling, the memory took root, anchoring itself in place. She felt it solidify in his identity, a core piece of who he was and always would be.

"Why?"

"Because I'm going to need it for what's to come."

Behind her, young Zach whimpered softly, trying hard not to cry as the man kept barking, "Again! Again! *Again!*" faster and faster as the memory of the ruthless beating sped up until a soft thud silenced it.

Only then did adult-Zach turn away and open the door for her. "We can go now. He won't be getting up anymore."

Raven shivered when she emerged into the safety of the ancient hallway. "Who was that?"

"My CO."

"I want a name," she growled. "Show me his face." If the son of a bitch wasn't dead yet, she'd make him wish he was.

"His name is Rajeev Sandoval. Serial number 047432. Earth-based ID number 339-EICG-47086753-8751 Delta."

"Delta?"

"Government suffix. Makes all his personal information classified."

"Not for me."

Zach caught her arm, stopping in the darkness between two sconces, in front of a door carved with swirling knots and symbols. "Raven, no. Promise me you won't go after him."

Sandoval's disembodied voice echoed through the hallway, "Again…" His presence haunted Zach even when he wasn't consciously thinking of him. "Again… Again!"

Zach glared over his shoulder, stepping into Raven as if to shield her. The voice quieted.

"I'm not afraid of him," Raven declared.

He turned back to her, his dark eyes searching. "You should be. Sandoval's not like the other Shadows. He was the first Hawk they ever turned out. He's sharp, capable, and utterly ruthless."

"He's a bully."

"He's a monster," Zach corrected. "If he catches you sniffing anywhere near his profile, if he starts hunting you, he'll never stop. And Sandoval won't just kill you. He will *obliterate* you and everything you hold dear."

Raven tilted her head. "Are you worried about me, Zach?"

His shoulders relaxed and his eyes softened. "Of course not, Blackbird."

Lie.

She felt it shuddering through the walls around them, undermining the integrity of the entire construct. A wooden beam cracked above them and resolidified almost immediately.

"Let's move on," he said, ushering her through the door into another memory.

The first thing she saw was a beautiful naked woman sprawled across a couch, her long hair draped over the armrest, her leg stretched down so the tips of her toes touched the floor. She was generously curvy, the soft lighting burnishing her skin in shades of gold and copper.

And there was Zach, sitting at an easel, sketching her shape with a piece of charcoal. Raven estimated his age at sixteen or seventeen, old enough to get visibly aroused by the subject of his painting, yet his face remained expressionless.

After a moment of silence where the hiss of a brush over canvas provided the only sound, Raven started picking up on a soft thud of boots on carpet. The rhythm became louder, more insistent, until she recognized the CO's now familiar pace as his invisible presence marched left and right at young Zach's back. She felt him watching every move Zach made, every stroke he committed to the canvas, every flicker of his gaze over the woman's prone form.

"Art class," adult-Zach said.

"The Shadows trained you as an artist?"

His mouth twisted into a sardonic smirk. "You wouldn't believe how wet women get over artists. If you can make her feel beautiful, desirable—*desired*—you're that much closer to winning her trust. And a woman who trusts you will give you everything. She'll do all manner of sordid things for a picture and a smile."

Young Zach's painting had taken shape. He'd captured the woman's softness and sensuality, exaggerated the lighting to give it more drama and romance, and the woman couldn't stop staring at it. She'd come around to see it for herself, one hand on his shoulder, the other pressed over her chest. When Zach offered her the painting, the woman melted.

Straight onto his lap. Her naked limbs curved around him, and her hair draped all over him as she kissed him flush on the mouth.

With the CO still in the room, watching.

Only, he'd stopped pacing. His judgment thrummed across Raven's skin. His approval was at once sickening and a relief. Zach had done what had been asked of him. He'd completed the mission to the CO's satisfaction.

And this was part of it.

"She was my first," adult-Zach confessed.

Raven lowered her gaze, having no desire to watch Zach lose his virginity to a woman he'd manipulated on his CO's order.

As the combat training memory had done earlier, this one also took root and became part of his identity.

Raven didn't need to see it.

Leaving him to his work, and his younger version to his pleasure, such as it was, she stepped out of the memory back into the hallway.

Zach followed on her heels, closing the door behind him. He leaned against it, watching her. "Art is the one thing they taught me that doesn't have to be inherently evil."

Raven nodded. "I get that. My husband was—"

"You were married?"

Why the hell did she keep doing that? She *knew* all of this was a manipulation tactic. He'd deliberately chosen memories to rattle her emotional state, and still, Raven kept falling for it, revealing things she'd never intended to say.

"He died," she said. End of story.

Except, not for Zach. "Tell me about him."

The wall at her back shifted as a new door took shape. Not the same type of ornate wooden portal as the others. This one looked fresh, lighter in color, with a gleaming silver handle. An invitation.

Curiosity got the best of her. Raven put her hand on the handle and felt an immediate tug at her consciousness, enticing her to walk through. With Zach behind her, she entered a place of all white. A blank canvas for her to fill, isolated from the rest of his mind so it wouldn't interfere with his sense of self.

"Was he a telepath like you?" Zach asked.

"He was…gentler."

The white around them filled with soft blurs of colors and the distant hum of voices. Raven let the memory coalesce, pulling from herself to fill the void with people. A group of children chased a swarm of flying toys around the room. Their desks were all pushed out toward the walls, and half-finished arts and crafts projects lay scattered across the floor.

At the far end, sunlight speared through a soft cloud of chalk dust as the teacher cleared the board. His shoulders quaked with silent laughter while he pretended not to hear the kids go wild.

When he turned around, his familiar features struck her straight in the chest. Julian hadn't been as handsome as Zach. His face had been round, his nose a little too big, his body softer. But there'd been so much kindness and love in his eyes.

"He taught telepathic control through creative expression," she explained. "Psychic abilities can manifest at any time. It's a lot easier to teach a child self-control than it is to convince a fully-grown adult that they aren't crazy, but will be if they don't learn how to work with their gifts. Julian had a unique way of connecting with people. He could spend an hour with someone tearing out their own hair and leave them calm enough to fall asleep. I can't… It's impossible to explain to non-telepaths what a miracle that can be."

The memory wavered from one place to another. Now, they were outside in the square. The day she'd met Julian, standing in line at the most popular restaurant to pick up their lunches. He'd cracked some lame joke that shouldn't have made her laugh as much as it had.

Their first date, out in the desert, with nothing but a blanket and a set of ornate lanterns to set the mood. Julian had pointed to the sky and made up ridiculous names for the constellation he traced, talking about how he would travel the galaxy one day and see every single inhabited world.

Their wedding day. Walking out of the registrar's office hand in hand with their witnesses following behind. They shared a quick kiss and a quicker goodbye before they rushed back to their respective jobs.

"He was the head teacher in our school. But they always pulled him in for the most heartbreaking cases. People who'd turned to drugs to silence the voices. People who'd accidentally killed their loved ones during sleep. People who thought they were possessed and tried to kill themselves. Julian took the jagged pieces of them and put them back together into something beautiful. That *was* his art."

Another scene: Raven and Julian dancing among snow flurries on the night they went to see the plot of land they'd just bought. He'd called it a good omen, precipitation of any kind being so rare in these parts.

It faded away into the last day she'd seen him, half out of her mind from pre-surgery meds. His face was a blur as he leaned over to kiss her. He'd promised to make it all better. To make it safe again.

"I'm sorry we didn't have more time…"

He'd left before she went under. She hadn't understood until she'd woken up days later that his goodbye had been forever.

"Chairo was in chaos from the Shadow attack. Our entire infrastructure was down. Nothing worked. People were hurt, hungry, and terrified. Everyone was in too much shock to cope, let alone act."

Unintentionally, a new scene took shape, filled with dust and smoke. A city in ruin, its people wailing in the streets, flinching away from strangers, too scared to accept what little help was offered. They chose to suffer on their own, rather than trust each other.

"We needed a reset, or we were all going to die."

Five telepaths had stepped up to the task of taking down the Shadows. It should have ended there; they should have stopped after it was done. But there'd been panic left in the wake of the attack. Untreated, it would have left the moon in shambles for decades to come. Millions more would have died.

Instead of letting go, the five had chosen to hold together far longer than was safe, knowing it would be the last thing they'd ever do.

"I love you, Raven… I'm sorry…"

They appeared in a circle around Raven and Zach, each face haunted and streaked with tears, but set with a deadly resolve. Their joined hands clutched tighter as they closed their eyes and faded away into a vision of Chairo rising from its ashes, more colorful than ever before.

Wailing cries became joyous laughter. Crushed transports turned into monuments to honor their fallen. The skies cleared, the sidewalks rolled out clean, and the city resumed its normal rhythm of dance, having forgotten the tragedy that had almost brought it to ruin.

A waft of wind echoed with sighs, marking the silent death of five heroes who would never be acknowledged for their sacrifice.

No one could ever know. No one would ever trust people with that kind of power. Telepaths who fell into a merge ended their own lives as soon as it was safe to do so, leaving no trace of themselves. Leaving their loved ones without closure.

Maybe that was why Raven still had trouble coming to terms with Julian's absence three years later. She'd never seen him die. She'd never had anything to bury. Without physical confirmation of his demise, her heart and mind were in constant battle, the one struggling to move on while the other insisted he might still come back.

"He died to save the entire moon, and here I am, wishing he'd let it all go to hell instead."

Everything faded back to white, stranding Raven in the void, a stark black stain with her left sleeve pinned flat to her side and a hollow where her heart should have been.

"I need to stop it," she told Zach. "I need to know what you know, so I can help put an end to all of this." She needed to do *something* that mattered. To make up for the fact that it should have been her, not Julian, making the ultimate sacrifice. She'd always been the stronger telepath. It should have been her stepping up.

Phantom arms closed around her, a warm presence pressing into her as invisible lips touched her forehead. She told herself it was Julian's spirit coming back to absolve her of her guilt. But the ghost had a hardness to it, an edge of anger too far out of character for him.

Zach was watching. "We'll stop it," he said, and Raven suddenly felt too exposed beneath the intensity of his dark gaze.

She swept past him back into the hallway, her left arm filling the sleeve as soon as the door closed behind Zach.

The sconces flashed white, a warning that her time was up.

"I have to go," she said. But at least she had a lead to take back with her.

"One of these days, you'll have to stay long enough for me to show you something beautiful."

"Alas, you already gave me a primer for your seduction tactics. I'm afraid I won't be falling for your artful ways."

Zach grinned. "Good. At least now I'll know that when you do fall for me, I'll have earned it for real."

Raven rolled her eyes and headed back the way they'd come. She flushed past the art lesson door and turned away from the combat one. At the end of the hallway, they emerged into the living space. Night had fallen outside, turning the Christmas tree and fireplace into a fantasy backdrop. It beckoned with the promise of a cozy evening cuddling on the couch.

Nope! Wouldn't work on her.

She was a professional, and Zach had already shown her all his cards. She wouldn't let him manipulate her this time.

To make her point, Raven pretended to get lost and reached for the door he'd steered her away from earlier. With all the confidence she could muster, Raven walked through as if it were her door, her bedroom sanctuary, and her exit out of Zach's mind.

Instead, she stopped dead in the middle of a different bedroom.

This one was darker, with heavier furniture and a bed draped in crimson silks.

And on that bed, a made-up copy of Raven rolled her hips as she straddled a copy version of Zach and rode his cock with wild abandon, head thrown back, and passionate cries coming from her throat.

Copy-Zach watched her in that unblinking way of his, only this time, there was a feral hunger in his eyes and a sense of triumph in his smile as copy-Raven came on top of him.

He surged up to claim her mouth and, without missing a beat, flipped her onto her back, driving himself into her, smothering her scream as another orgasm overtook her.

And they were only getting started.

Raven stumbled backward out of the room and slammed the door shut.

"Told you, you weren't ready," Zach said.

Raven had to lean back against the opposite wall for balance. She fought her breath into a steady rhythm, refusing to look at Zach's smirking face. The bastard was completely unrepentant. He enjoyed her reaction, but made no move to capitalize on it.

Moans and groans floated through the closed door, and Raven had to swallow back an answering moan of her own. The energy in that room had been almost a physical sensation, and her mind reacted to it as if it had been her real self in there, fucking Zach as if there was no tomorrow. She teetered right on the edge of coming so hard her knees threatened to buckle.

Pointing a finger at the door, Raven opened her mouth, and a squeak came out. She cleared her throat and tried again. "That's a fantasy."

"Yes," Zach confirmed.

"But it's genuine," she said as the sounds behind the door ratcheted up to another crescendo.

He'd built that scene for his own pleasure and put it in a permanent place at the forefront of his mind. It wasn't like the constructs he'd used to distract her when they'd first met. As erotic as those scenes had been, they'd been disconnected from him in all but the most superficial ways.

The scene behind that wooden door was as solid and anchored as his memories. It wasn't real, but he'd made it as close to real as possible with the power of his desire.

He shrugged. "So?"

"*So?*"

"I'm not apologizing for it, if that's what you're waiting for. I warned you not to look. This one's on you, Blackbird."

Raven shut her mouth.

She stared at him, at a loss for words, and he held her gaze right back, while their fantasy doubles went at it, the sound of their coupling echoing through the hallway and living space, sometimes muted from behind the door, other times sharp and clear, as if they were right at her ear. And the whole time, Zach didn't say a word. Didn't move an inch from his irreverent lean against the wall, arms crossed over his chest. And he never looked away.

The world blurred around her, taking on a red hue. Raven slumped forward as her grip on her telepathic projection began to fray. She'd loitered too long.

Zach straightened out of his slouch. In the next instant, his hands pinned her shoulders against the wall, and he frowned. "You need to go," he said.

Raven nodded. Words floated away from her. She was starting to lose it.

Bracing her against his side, Zach walked Raven to her door, another fancy wooden portal, carved with an intricate image of a bird in flight. He ushered her through into the sanctuary of her empty bedroom. Beside the window, a floor-length mirror rippled, marking her exit.

"Get some rest, but don't leave me here alone too long," he said with a wink. "Who knows what manner of naughty things I might get up to while you're gone?"

Bright light shone into her eyes, and Raven flinched away so hard she nearly fell out of her chair. Luckily, Dr. Zyxon had excellent reflexes. He caught her by the shoulder and righted her. "There you are. I was starting to get worried."

Raven squinted at him through the blinding glare still floating around her vision. "Hey, Doc."

"How do you feel?"

"Hurt," she mumbled. Her head was splitting open, and her body felt like she'd been asleep for days. She couldn't feel her legs, and her lower back was one big knot of agony.

Dr. Zyxon produced two small blue patches and pressed one to each of her temples, massaging them to help the painkillers release faster.

Raven hummed her appreciation as her migraine began to ease. "Thank you."

"You're welcome. Let's get you up and walking, shall we?" He eased an arm around her and lifted her to her feet. He had to carry her for the first few steps until the numbness in her legs gave way to pins and needles. They walked a couple of circuits around the room while the doctor reported, "I came in to get new readings on our patient and noticed your timer had run through to red. You were almost an hour late coming out."

That explained the migraine.

"The patient seems to be doing well. No adverse reaction to the detox, his metabolism has stabilized, and his brain activity looks good. Are you okay to eat something?"

Raven nodded out of habit, but her stomach was still in knots. When Dr. Zyxon walked her over to the food table, she could only manage a few sips of lemon water and a couple of salty crackers. "Has Darrow been by?"

"Not today. But you do have a visitor waiting for you outside, whenever you're ready."

Raven groaned. "It's not Ripley, is it?"

Dr. Zyxon chuckled, handing her a small cup of hot, thin soup to sip on. "No. I think you'll like this one."

Raven choked down a few more bites of food and walked around the room a bit to get her joints working again while Dr. Zyxon checked the detox tank and Zach's vitals.

"You know," he said, "we register heightened brain activity whenever a telepath is inside the mind of a patient in the tank. Dr. Vernon says it's evidence that the telepath is hard at work, but I tend to disagree."

"Oh? Why is that?"

He cycled through various screens on his device. "I just think maybe people get lonely, all alone in their thoughts. When I look at those spikes, they look happy to me. Like someone is excited to have a visitor, you know?"

Raven smiled. "That's a nice way to look at it. But in this case, I'm afraid Dr. Vernon's assessment is more accurate. Your machines can't detect emotion. And our subjects aren't usually aware of our presence when unconscious. What you're seeing is largely just neurons being activated by the telepath to achieve the desired outcome."

"Maybe," Dr. Zyxon conceded. "But this one is different, isn't he?"

"Why do you say that?"

When she completed her circuit back to the tank, he tilted his digital device toward her. It displayed a 3D brain model and a surface waveform charting Zach's brain activity spikes in different regions. Dr. Zyxon swiped his finger across the screen, reversing the timeline several hours to before she'd begun today's session. "You see this? The low peaks and valleys indicate a resting state. Not quite sleep. Let's call it idle mode. Here is where you started your session." The churning waves spiked three times higher and lower in an erratic pattern for the hours she'd worked with him. "You can see where the peaks spike and cluster—that's where the most intense work took place. The smaller ripples afterward repeat the intense patterns. Almost like a review. I see it as you going over your work before moving on to the next task."

Raven nodded to validate his assumptions. She'd done none of the work this session. It had all been Zach.

"Now look here." He tapped out a few commands, then the screen split, showing a sped-up replay of her session at the top, and the active scan below it. "This is his brain right now. You see it?"

"What am I supposed to be seeing?"

He traced his finger in the air up and down like a conductor, then swiped again, expanding the session timeline to spotlight a specific segment. "The pattern is repeating, only slower."

"Meaning…?"

"Subconscious replay, maybe? The patient checking your work in his dream state?"

But was Zach dreaming? Was he even asleep right now? "Fascinating."

He grinned, proudly pulling back his shoulders. "I thought so too. I'm writing a dissertation on the subject of mapping telepathic activity. I think one day we will have the tools to identify where and how a mind has been altered. It would revolutionize therapy."

Only in the utopia of his dreams.

The real world didn't suffer telepaths. It didn't care how much good they could do. All it cared about was that telepaths had the means to control people without them knowing.

Raven wished she could say their fears were unfounded.

If Dr. Zyxon's vision were to come to fruition and science developed a way to detect telepathic interference, it would only stigmatize the very therapies he praised and ostracize anyone who sought them willingly to improve their lives.

"You should go. Your visitor is waiting for you."

"Thank you, Doctor."

He'd given her a lot to think about. Not just where their Shadow subject was concerned, but everything the Special Unit had done and was still doing. There would always be people who used their gifts to make their world a better place. But power was only ever as good as those who wielded it, and humanity had demonstrated over and over throughout history that the right gift in the wrong hands always wrought catastrophic destruction.

In the end, no matter how much they evolved, humans continued to prove themselves nothing more than vicious, selfish animals.

"You look like your dog just died."

Raven blinked at Tessa, waiting for her in the med center. She was pale, with dark shadows heavy under her eyes, and the aged pink sweater she wore didn't do her complexion any favors. "Hey, I didn't know you were coming in today."

Tessa shrugged. "Yeah, I was going to visit you out in the desert after my checkup, but they told me you were onsite now, so here I am! You wanna hang out? Get some dinner and have a sleepover or something?"

She was buoyed with excited energy, but her smile had a fragile edge to it.

"I could use a girls' night."

"Excellent!" Tessa put her arm around Raven's shoulders and swept her to the elevator. "Which floor?"

"They gave me one of the on-call suites up on hundred and eighteenth."

Tessa selected the floor. "What do you want to eat? My treat."

"My food is comped while I'm on assignment, so it's *my* treat. And you choose."

"I say we go nuts and have a little of everything. I haven't had pizza in years." Because her digestive tract couldn't handle wheat. "And I always wanted to try those creepy crustacean things from the Karos system. I heard there's a new place in town that imports them."

The elevator opened on Raven's floor.

"Chocolate cake for dessert?" she suggested as a test.

"Yes! With passionfruit jelly and fresh berries." None of which she could have.

Raven got a sick feeling in her stomach as she led the way to her suite.

She found Darrow waiting for her by her door. He started to say something, but Raven glared at him, shaking her head. Whatever he wanted, it could wait.

Thankfully, he got the message and pasted a smile on his face. "Hey you," he greeted Tessa with an affectionate hug. "Missed your face.

Did I hear something about chocolate cake?"

The two of them hadn't always been friends but they'd gotten a great deal closer after Raven and Julian's wedding. Standing witness at the ceremony had bonded all of them into a makeshift family, and Raven would never be able to express how grateful she was to have them both in her life. While Tessa and Darrow didn't hang out as much nowadays, Raven still felt deep affection between the two of them.

Tessa beamed. "We're having a girls' night in!"

"Does that mean I'm not invited?"

"Nope! No boys allowed."

"You break my heart."

Tessa rolled her eyes. "You'll live."

Darrow laughed. "Fine. We'll just have to do a family dinner some other time. Order whatever you want on the house. Raven, don't forget your meditation. I'll check in with you before your session tomorrow."

She nodded, fighting to ignore the grief in his smile as he walked away.

The on-call suites were comfortable, but generic, with practical furniture and no frills. The only personal touch Raven had brought with her for the duration of her stay was a framed photo of her and Julian at their wedding feast.

Tessa picked it up, some of her enthusiasm waning. "I always loved this photo. You look so happy. But then, Julian always had that effect on people."

"He really did," Raven agreed. "It was a good day."

Tessa chuckled. "Do you remember the caterers brought in double the order, for some reason?"

Yeah, that hadn't been by mistake. Raven and Julian had invited all of their colleagues from the SU to the feast. But the day before, they'd received word that three telepaths on three different worlds had disappeared without a trace overnight. With the entire organization in a panic over possible Shadow abductions, a level red alert had been issued, and most of their telepath friends hadn't been able to make it.

"I still say we should have had a food fight."

"Julian donated the untouched food to the boarding school. The kids had a party. He was their favorite teacher for the next year."

Tessa made a face. "Of course he did—which was the right thing to do. Ugh. Living with him must have been torture. He was always such a saint."

Raven laughed. "Julian was very far from a saint." Even though he'd died a martyr.

But that was enough reminiscing for one day.

"Go ahead and put in the food orders. I'm going to get cleaned up."

"And change into your comfy PJs!"

A full spread was laid out on the floor by the time Raven came out of the bathroom in the fluffy onesie she hadn't worn since her first girls' night with Tessa years ago.

Tessa raised one corner of a faux fur blanket Raven didn't recognize. "Darrow sent a care package. There are facial masks, chocolate-covered fruits, and champagne, too. I think he's trying to buy his way into our club."

Raven tucked herself in next to Tessa and accepted a glass of champagne. "I'm surprised he didn't send any Bliss."

Especially because, according to the update Darrow had shared while she'd been in the bathroom, this was going to be Tessa's last girls' night. Her end-of-life appointment was scheduled for tomorrow morning. Her medical team had doped her up enough to keep her energized and pain-free for her final farewell, and tomorrow, they would end her pain for good.

"I'm not allowed," Tessa grumbled. "Docs say recreational drugs and therapy drugs don't go together. But I won't stop you if you want to indulge. Go nuts. You only live once, right?"

Raven swallowed past the lump in her throat. "Right." She couldn't start crying now or she'd never stop. Tessa shouldn't have to console her. Girls' night was supposed to be a celebration of love, sisterhood, and all the good things.

She clinked her glass against Tessa's. "Cheers."

They drank and then dug into the mountain of food. "So… I got a peek at your subject when you came out earlier. Hot damn, girl."

Raven choked on a bite of cake.

"Please tell me his mind is as sexy as his bod. There's nothing worse than a pretty face over an empty head."

Unconscious or not, her subject was still a classified case. Raven wasn't allowed to talk about him with anyone outside of Darrow and the council. But what did it matter now?

Truth be told, she could use a second opinion to make sense of what the hell Zach was thinking.

"Ooooh, she blushes! Tell me everything. Everything you can," Tessa amended.

Her excitement was an artificial construct, a desperate attempt to make the most out of every moment.

It wasn't fair.

But it worked.

"He's so different than what I expected," Raven confessed.

Tessa refilled her champagne glass and scooted closer, her eyes bright and encouraging.

Raven managed a chuckle. "Keep in mind, this guy is a Shadow."

"Minor detail. Totally eclipsed by the *major* one between his legs. Please continue."

Raven told her about Zach's recent EMC treatment and what the detox tank was doing—all of which Tessa waved away as unimportant.

"So he's damaged. The best ones always are. Can you fix him?"

"That's the thing, Tess, he's fixing himself."

She explained the concept of memory reconstruction and how Zach was effectively doing Raven's job for her by pruning and solidifying his own character map.

"Wait," Tessa said. "He's sedated, but awake?"

"More or less. I can't tell how aware he is of the outside world, but inside his mind, he's fully conscious."

"And he's just letting you waltz through his thoughts willy-nilly?"

"He practically rolled out the red carpet." Worse, he'd carved out a place just for her, the way a person would empty a sock drawer or closet for their partner to store their belongings.

"Is that normal?"

Raven shook her head. "I don't understand him. It's like he *wants* me in his mind."

"What's to understand? Sounds like he likes you. People do that, you know."

"Not like this."

Sexual desire, Raven understood. It could be powerful and instantaneous, but it was superficial and often didn't last long term. Affection developed over time.

And neither should have been on the table for someone she was interrogating. Raven's job was to invade his memories, root out his secrets, and, if need be, rearrange his mind to suit their purposes. Nothing he'd done on his own so far posed a risk to the SU, so she hadn't interfered. But, sooner or later, they'd reach a crossroads that would force her hand. It would alter him on a fundamental level. Regardless of how small a change she wrought, as aware as Zach was, he would notice, and he might spend the rest of his life questioning his own reality.

And he knew all this. He knew Raven was the last person in the world he should trust with his most secret thoughts and memories.

But, for some reason that likely had a lot to do with his unconventional upbringing, the Shadow didn't appear to care. "It's like he met me and decided, 'Yep, this is my person.' It has to be fake."

"Does it, though? Just because you're emotionally closed off…"

Raven glared. "Peek into enough brains and you eventually start to see patterns. Is there an occasional outlier? Sure. But, for the most part, people follow a relationship-building roadmap that's almost programmed into our DNA. It can be expedited, but not skipped completely."

Tessa slowly set aside her champagne. "Who said anything about a relationship?"

"In a weird way, he did." She described how he'd rearranged his mind to make room for her, the details he'd augmented solely based on her reaction, and how he'd studied her the whole time as if he'd been the one interrogating her.

Tessa hung on her every word. When Raven got to the part about Zach's little fantasy, she squealed and threw her arms around Raven, wriggling them both back and forth and squeezing tight enough to hurt.

"What is wrong with you?" Raven choked out.

Tessa pulled away and shook her by the shoulders. "Holy shit, girl, do you even realize what you're saying?"

"Yeah, that the Shadow is a master manipulator."

Tessa scowled. "You're an idiot. I love you, but you are." She jumped off the couch and did a little dance, then dropped to the floor amid the food. She swept a bunch of cookies off a plate and piled the dish with slices of various cakes and pies. "This guy gave you an arm, Raven."

"So he considers me deficient without it." He wasn't the only one.

Tessa beaned her with a cupcake.

"Hey!"

"He gave you an arm because *you* feel deficient without it."

"I'm starting to regret this topic of conversation."

Tessa returned to the couch, raising an eyebrow at Raven.

Rolling her eyes, Raven pulled back the blanket so Tessa could get under it, then endured having a piece of chocolate caramel cake stuffed into her mouth.

"There," Tessa declared. "That'll shut you up for a minute. While you're chewing on it, I want you to chew on something else, too. What if—and stay with me on this one—what if, just this once, you decided not to finish someone's thought for them? Let's explore that crazy concept, shall we? Take everything you've seen inside this guy's mind as exactly what it seems. No more, no less." She ticked the items off on her fingers. "He not only let you into his thoughts but welcomed you there. He put your comfort over his own self-preservation. He showed you who he is, knowing it's not for the faint of heart. *And* he clearly communicated his interest in you. This guy is a freaking unicorn."

"He is a *Shadow*." More than that, he was her assignment. "Nothing he thinks or does can be taken as what it seems." His continued existence depended on the outcome of this interrogation. If Darrow decided he didn't like Zach, it wouldn't matter how cooperative he'd been. He wouldn't leave the building alive.

Of course he would do everything in his power to ensure the people interacting with him liked him. Of course he would attempt to seduce Raven to get her to side with him.

Of course it was all fake.

Tessa set the platter of cakes aside. "Raven, I'm going to be saying goodbye to this life tomorrow."

Raven's stomach knotted, the bite of cake turning it sour.

"I know you already know, and I appreciate you pretending you don't. It's okay. I know that no matter what happens, you'll be just fine. You are so, so good at taking care of yourself. But…" She sighed, hugging her knees to her chest. "I still worry about you."

"You just said—"

"You are so good at taking care of yourself, you forget that people aren't meant to be all by themselves."

"I let you take care of me."

"Because I made you. But that will end tomorrow. And, when it does, I'm afraid you'll go back to the hermit cave I dragged you out of. I don't want that for you. You need another person in your life."

"I had my person, Tessa, and he was taken from me." And tomorrow, she would lose her other one, too. Strangely, as much as it hurt to think about not being able to see or speak to Tessa again, there was a hollow kind of acceptance in it, too.

Maybe some people just weren't meant to have people in their lives.

Maybe Raven was one of them.

"No, sweetie. Julian wasn't taken. He chose to walk away. Noble as it was, *he* made the choice to leave you. He chose to save the world and left you to pick up the pieces alone. Hate me all you want for saying this, but I think you deserved better. You deserve someone who'd set the world on fire if it kept you warm. A saint like Julian would never do that. But a villain might."

21

January 13, 3040 – Chairo, Valhale 602

SESSION 6

Raven's seaside room had changed views to brown deer frolicking through a snowy clearing. The bed frame was now made of thick, natural wood instead of elegant white, and an evergreen wreath with four burning candles adorned the dresser. She barely noticed.

Emerging from the room, Raven made a beeline for the massive couch and sank onto it, hugging her knees to make herself as small as possible. She just needed a few minutes to herself.

The warmth from the fireplace battled with a nighttime snowstorm happening outside the windows, giving her chills and making her feel overheated in turn.

Zach appeared in a crouch on the floor in front of her. "What's wrong?"

"I laid my best friend to rest today," she said.

The dam broke. Raven couldn't keep her face from crumpling, so she hid it against her knees, sobbing her heart out.

Zach made a rumbling sound, and lightning cracked outside.

Next thing she knew, he was on the couch and she was in his lap, crying into his shirt.

He didn't ask any questions; he didn't say a single word. He just held her tight and let her grieve while the fire crackled and the storm raged, until her time ran out.

January 14, 3040 – Somewhere Else…

Hansel woke up to a loud mechanical roar of a landing shuttle. His eyes were swollen almost shut, and his mouth tasted of copper and bile. The cabin shuddered with a rough impact, jarring him almost out of his seat, but the restraints kept him in place.

Hansel pried open his sticky eyelids.

He was alive. His body felt like it had been pummeled all over after an eight-hour workout, but he was alive.

His relief quickly morphed into gut-twisting terror when his blurry vision cleared enough to make out his surroundings. The cavernous hull was filled with saddle-like standing seats. Hundreds of them. And each one had another terrified person strapped in so tight they couldn't move. Their feet were clamped to the floor. Their hands were cuffed in front of them. Band restraints strapped their torsos to the meager backrests at the waist and across the shoulders. Some had an extra strap around their heads and black tape over their mouths.

The engines shut down, along with the air filtration system, leaving the stench of fear and human waste to cloud around him.

"The fuck…" Hansel's mouth was too dry, his throat too raw to speak properly. But at least he wasn't whimpering like so many of the others. He strained against the bands around him, but even with all his new strength, he couldn't budge them a hair.

The lights came on, stabbing pain into his retinas.

Those who were still conscious screamed as the cabin doors opened wide on a trio of masked soldiers in dark blue uniforms, pointing weapons at them.

The first row of seats released, their occupants crumpling to the floor like old-age marionettes. More soldiers marched in to drag them out. Some by their arms, others by their hair, kicking and screaming.

When they were gone, the now-empty row of seats folded down, and the second one released.

Half of those people were awake enough and desperate enough to put up a fight. Three of them charged the soldiers guarding the door. They got gunned down instantly.

As soon as the smell of charred flesh hit the others, the cabin went deathly quiet.

No one else tried to escape after that.

Row by row they went, meek little lambs, trembling before the wolves.

Hansel had a good ten minutes to come to terms with his fate and breathe down the panic before his turn came. He was proud of himself for managing to stay upright when the seat released him. His knees were jelly, his insides were soup, and his heart hurt from beating too hard, but he only trembled the slightest bit as the soldiers marched him past the trio of shooters into a long hallway angled down.

They passed him from one team to another, shoving him roughly along the way to keep him moving. He didn't resist. There was no point. He didn't see any doors or windows along the way.

The corridor spat them out into an open space almost too big to comprehend. They could probably fit multiple shuttles in there if they tried. Instead, the floor was divided into partitions with a considerable amount of open space around each. No place to take cover. Too many armed soldiers kept watch over the procession.

It didn't stop a woman four places in front of him from trying to make a run for it. She shoved out of the line and stumble-sprinted off to who-knew-where. They let her get all the way behind one of the white tents that dotted the space, almost as if to make her think she was getting somewhere.

She tore down a cloth wall when they killed her. It draped over her body, mercifully hiding the hole charred clean through her chest.

The shooter dragged her by the ankle to a pile of debris not far away. He deferred to another one, hauling a body over his shoulder so he could dump his burden first.

Corpses. It was a pile of corpses, growing by the minute.

Hansel looked away.

Two men in white lab coats bottlenecked the prisoners. Each person got scanned and then directed to the next station.

It was much colder here than in the shuttle cabin. Still wearing his gym shorts and trainers, and nothing else, Hansel clenched his teeth to stop them from chattering.

The scanner's light passed over him from head to toe. The medic didn't even bother looking at him when he ordered, "Yellow Six."

Another soldier shoved Hansel to the left. "Follow the yellow line."

Six more were spaced out along that yellow line. All of them armed, their fingers on triggers.

Hansel obeyed when they told him to take off his shoes and shorts. He went through the sonic showers as ordered and put on the white hospital pants and shirt they gave him when he came out on the other side, absurdly grateful to be clean and covered.

His bare feet and calves cramped by the time he joined another line waiting to enter one of the white tents. He couldn't tell where it let out, but it sure wasn't the same way it let in. None of the people who stepped through the tent flap came out of it.

Then it was his turn.

A pair of soldiers dragged him to a chair and strapped him down tight before resuming their stations a few feet away.

The medic was a young woman who looked as scared as Hansel felt. She was ashen, her trembling hands cold as ice when she pushed his head toward the backrest and strapped it in.

"Please," Hansel begged through gritted teeth. "Please, don't do this. I have a family. I have three younger sisters waiting for me back home." They had to be scared to death, all alone in that shithole of an apartment. What would happen to them? Who would take care of them? Hansel was all the family they had left. "They need me. Please!"

The medic gulped. "I'm sorry," she whispered, forcing a mouthguard between his teeth. She wiped her nose on the back of her sleeve, then scanned him again.

Hansel couldn't turn his head to see the readouts, but out of the corner of his eye, he caught a flash of red.

"Heart rate elevated, blood pressure high." The medic's voice trembled, but she went through her little checklist, despite Hansel whimpering through the mouthguard. "Both within acceptable limits. No underlying issues. Physical condition optimal. Adrenalin and cortisol levels elevated, but within acceptable limits. Green light to proceed."

Hansel couldn't get enough air. He started thrashing around, fighting the restraints, fighting for just one full breath. It got him nowhere.

Sweat sheened the young medic's face as she came back and reached for something above him. He smelled her nervous sweat beneath the acrid scent of disinfectant that clung to her like perfume.

Look at me, he tried to say, but the mouthguard had suctioned onto his teeth, sealing his mouth shut. *Please, look at me—see me!*

As if she heard him, her pretty brown eyes met his, and she hesitated. *Please, don't do this...*

She blinked rapidly, licking her pale lips. "It'll only hurt for a minute," she said, settling a delicate white band over his forehead, aligning the rounded bumps at his temples. "Try to pass out. It's easier that way."

Hansel moaned, tears and snot running down his face. His body vibrated, muscles tensing and cramping, while a litany of prayers cycled through his mind.

He should have paid better attention in Religion class. He shouldn't have been so cavalier about higher powers. Maybe if he'd taken the time to get to know one, it might have been more inclined to help him now. Maybe—

White hot pain seared through his brain, burning away the end of his thought, and the beginning, and everything in between...

January 15, 3040 – Chairo, Valhale 602

A new document had been added to Zach's file. It had Darrow's ID attached to it. Had he learned something relevant about Zach's medical history? That had to be it. There was no way Zachary VanWarren wasn't chem-resistant in some way. She wouldn't be surprised if it turned out he really was some form of a telepath. Mental abilities could manifest at any time, most commonly around puberty, but who knew how a lifetime of repeated EMC treatments might have affected his mind's natural evolution?

Raven opened the document on the wall screen.

Wait…

She stared at the ICG database watermark across the front page. It took up a full quarter of the wall in front of her, glaring its accusation in the spread of wheat stalks and stars around the perimeter of a faded Earth and a bold CLASSIFIED & CONFIDENTIAL stamp across its face.

He wouldn't…

It wasn't even a document page; it was an image of one. The SU had limited access to governmental databases, both in scope and time. Only leadership and certain investigators had the required access clearance. Darrow had it, but his council did not. Due to the nature of her assignments, Raven also got temporary access while on an active Shadow case, but she'd never been dumb enough to use it.

Every time they did, their ICG liaison was notified, and they had to submit a report of what they pulled and why. It was for their own protection. Given the ICG's paranoia, no one wanted them to think the SU was overstepping their bounds. That would be a quick ticket to extermination.

Besides, it wasn't as if one could just log in and go exploring what the ICG's been up to. To obtain information, they needed to know where to look and what to look for, and they only had five minutes at a time to find it. It was good for confirming what you already knew, not so much for learning something you didn't.

Except, of course, when your position gave you direct access to members of the ICG who were familiar with the system, and you managed to learn the database infrastructure from their minds.

Raven swiped to the next page and stared at the name printed thick and bold across the top.

He'd done it. Darrow had accessed the ICG's confidential databases and pulled Rajeev Sandoval's file.

She frowned. *Files*. Multiple. The same face, but different names, titles, and biographies. Every preformatted page included standard information one would expect to find in a personnel dossier, except people usually only had one.

Raven scanned through the pages. The most distinctive thing about the profiles—aside from the fact that there were twelve of them—was a glaring lack of personal information. No next of kin, no listed associations, no history of medical procedures or treatments. On their own, the profiles documented the unremarkable lives of very private individuals who had somehow circumvented all biometric security screenings involved in the hiring of a government employee.

The bigger problem was that all of the profiles overlapped. Rajeev Sandoval had started his career as a high-ranking army officer—and simultaneously, a liaison to the Mars 2 ambassador on Jericho. At the end of his active army career, he'd taken up a new profession as a bodyguard to the late Governor Hirei on Persephone 5, where he'd also worked as a second assistant to another ambassador at the same time. When his term as liaison had expired, Sandoval had advanced to personal assistant to a junior senator in the ICG, while also serving as an advisor to—shock and awe—former Senator Matthew Griffith. The Shadows' creator and first Commander in Chief.

With so many characters so closely interwoven within the ICG network, it was a wonder no one had ever noticed the overlap. Then again, the ruling body currently consisted of nearly four hundred thousand core members alone. They didn't even know each other, and, for security reasons, they were never all on the same planet at the same time. It was entirely possible for someone with Sandoval's training to get around established security protocols and go unnoticed in roles that would have kept his face off-screen.

No one cared about the personal assistant fetching drinks and ordering transports.

This was what a true Hawk looked like: everyone and no one at the same time. A face you never remembered, even when you looked right at it. Someone nice enough, productive enough, obedient enough, and forgettable enough to blend in with the background.

And all the while, the spy carved himself a path toward his target. But who—or what—was it?

Being the first Hawk ever trained, according to Zach, made Sandoval the oldest one still living and active. Either he was that good, or he'd been trained for one specific mission. At sixty-eight years old, he'd survived forty-two of them in a career that usually resulted in death after ten to fifteen. And, on top of all his public roles, he'd apparently also had the time to serve as Zach's commanding officer.

Whatever his special mission, it would be one for the history books.

Darrow had taken a massive risk to retrieve this information.

It was vital information to have, but Raven couldn't shake Zach's warning from her mind. What if just having it was enough to put a target on all their backs?

Raven stretched up and out of her seat. It was well past her bedtime, but she couldn't sleep.

Someone had cleared away the leftover food from her girls' night with Tessa, and her suite had been cleaned spotless. But the blanket still covered the couch, and the movie they'd watched was still paused thirty minutes before the end.

The whole place felt like a tomb.

Unable to stand it any longer, she wrapped the blanket around herself and went up to the roof for some fresh air.

Chairo's night scene was famous far and wide. Tourists came from all over Valhale 602 and other worlds in the sector to experience the fervid celebration of life.

It hadn't always been like that. Before the war, Chairo's residents had mainly adhered to a daytime routine and retreated to their homes and beds at night. Ever since its rebirth, the residents appeared to have decided not to take a single moment for granted. Sleep was for the dead. The living had better things to do.

A big, fluffy snowflake landed on Raven's eyelash. She looked up at the sky and couldn't spot a single star. Powerful light beams swept across a thick cloud cover, reminding Raven of the winter in Zach's mindscape.

His attention to detail was so incredible, Raven wondered whether he'd constructed the scene based on a real location. Could such a beautiful place exist somewhere out there?

If it did, she wanted to see it one day.

It had a unique soundscape that made the whole world feel softer, tucked beneath thick covers. Childlike in its purity, but wild and unpredictable at the same time.

It felt safe.

A sanctuary for a mind that hadn't known much peace.

Raven could use some of that.

Turning away from the bright city lights, she looked out over the dunes endlessly rolling toward the dark horizon. A few miles away, the cloud cover broke, allowing a shaft of reflected light to spear down. The planet Vesta was in its most dramatic season, with massive storms churning over its surface, painting it in a rainbow of light pinks and deep, crimson reds.

She'd used to love those colors. Now they reminded her of years of bloodshed.

Stepping into one of the meditation pods, Raven activated its wind barrier and sat on the provided pillow. She'd already done her required meditations for the day, but her mind was still restless.

Raven closed her eyes and let her thoughts wander. She imagined herself soaring like a bird over the frozen dunes, swooping up toward the unreachable pink giant in the sky. Her shoulders relaxed and her spine curved, sinking her upper body into her hips. Raven felt her weight press into the pillow and breathed deeply, teetering on the boundary between consciousness and sleep.

Despite the wind barrier, the night's chill kissed her nose and cheeks like an old friend, and she sank deeper into her visualization, letting it carry her up and up toward the looming Vesta. The higher she climbed, the lighter she felt, until her grasp on the vision frayed.

At the upper limit of her ascent, when she could see red lightning flaring across Vesta's face, Raven let go, let the vision's current carry her away from her restless wakefulness as she dropped straight down. She felt the wind rushing past her, but not its wintry chill. The thrill of watching the ground get closer tickled her belly, threatening a hypnic jerk that never came. She never hit the ground. Instead, her arms extended at the last second, and she caught a breeze that swept her back toward the city, glowing bright and magical in its desert valley nest.

And then she blinked, and the world was gone.

Raven found herself at the periphery of a dark universe, watching a galaxy take shape before her. Only it wasn't dust and debris coalescing toward the center. It was a cloud of memories. Thoughts, ideas, and dreams. Echoing sighs, and bright, cheerful laughter, punctuated by the booming pressure of explosions and weapons fire. A triumphant whoop turned into a cry of agony. A tormented groan became one of pleasure.

No longer painful and slow, Zach's self-actualization had ramped up to lightning speed, recovering pieces of himself and cobbling them back into place without any interference from Raven.

"What do you think?" he asked, appearing beside her.

"How is this possible? How are you doing this?"

"Does it matter?"

It should. A mind shouldn't be able to consciously restructure itself this way, much less separate itself from the already impossible task to examine its progress from a distance. Zach shouldn't be there.

"If it makes you feel better, I don't think I could have done any of this without the detox." He grinned at her. "Feel free to say, 'I told you so.'" He winced and rolled his shoulder. "By the way, that twitching thing is annoying as hell."

"Part of the detox tank's design. It creates a low voltage charge to make your muscles contract so they don't atrophy while you're immobilized." Another thing he shouldn't be aware of.

And it still paled in comparison to what he was doing here and now. The center of the galaxy wasn't a shapeless blob of light anymore. It had started to take shape. Still too soon to make out what it would ultimately become, but the foundation was solid, and the building blocks were already falling into place.

Raven slowly shook her head in wonder. "People get to choose who they become." That's what he'd told her. "Who are you turning yourself into, Zach?"

A memory flew past them, brushing against Raven's ear with heart-wrenching sobs and the feel of a strong anchor wrapping around her. It streaked across the swirling mass, heading straight into its center with incredible speed. When it crashed into place, the impact rippled outward, altering the trajectory of an entire cloud of memory fragments, forcing dust and debris off their edges so they could fit together.

"Someone worthy," Zach said, and the soft strains of his song echoed around them. Not the orchestral melody she'd given him, but the hum of a sweet, feminine voice, sounding out the notes where he couldn't recall the words.

"Of her?" she asked.

Zach turned to her, his dark eyes reflecting the galaxy of lights straight into her soul. "No…"

~

Raven woke up with a start to find a stranger's face above her, his hand on her shoulder. "Ma'am? Are you okay? Do you need help?"

She was still on the snow-covered roof. Raven's wind barrier had kept her upper body dry, but she was soaked and freezing from the knees down, despite the gentle heat rising from beneath her pillow.

She groaned. "What time is it?"

"Eight in the morning, ma'am. Should I call for a medic?"

Now that her body had awakened, the cold had sunk its teeth deep into her bones. Raven nodded. She wouldn't make it off the roof on her own.

Within seconds, a crowd of people surrounded her and covered her in blankets. Someone took off her shoes to warm her feet. Someone else offered her a flask of steaming hot tea, but Raven's hand was too numb to take it.

Minutes later, she sweltered in a reheater suit in the med center, while Darrow paced back and forth, lecturing her on the idiocy of going outside at night in the middle of the coldest winter of the last ten years.

Raven tried to pay attention, but between the constricting heat sack and the sterile air, she was too uncomfortable to give him the responses he wanted.

Her mind didn't fully kick in until Dr. Vernon came by to check her over. "You were lucky," he said. "The wind barrier activated the meditation pod's heated base, and your weight on the sensors kept it active well past the one-hour timer."

If she hadn't used it, if she'd fallen asleep in a slightly different position, or rolled off the sensor, Raven might have frozen to death before the morning meditation session had gathered up on the roof.

There'd been a time, not too long ago, when she would have been disappointed to have woken up at all. She still didn't feel an overwhelming sense of joy to be alive. But at least she wasn't wishing not to be. Raven supposed that counted as progress. "Thanks, Doc."

"Hydrate and take it easy for a few hours. And next time you want to meditate at night, maybe do it indoors." He patted her foot before slipping out through the curtains, leaving her alone with Darrow.

Eventually, her young boss calmed enough to take a seat beside her bed. "Julian would have been heartbroken to see you this way."

"Stop."

He didn't. "I promised him I'd take care of you. I should have been there for you. I shouldn't have let you go into another session while you're grieving."

Strangely, it hadn't even occurred to Raven to skip her session with Zach. She'd wanted to do it. She'd been relieved to escape her mind for a few hours.

Darrow took her hand in both of his. "I wish you had come to me."

Raven wished she'd had the presence of mind to do so while Tessa had still been alive—when applying a bit of extra pressure might have done some good, opened some more doors.

But she'd been too distracted by her own misery to pay much attention to Tessa. Raven had failed her. And now it was too late to fix it. Regret, remorse, guilt—none of it changed a damned thing. Tessa was still dead. Thousands of other chem-resistants still suffered without adequate treatment. No one cared, unless the patient had the potential to contribute in some way—and even that was a questionable prerequisite.

Raven pulled her hand free and fumbled with the fastenings of her reheater suit. "Get me out of this thing."

Darrow sprang into action, undoing clasps and detaching tubes. He helped her sit up and pull her arm free of the vest, then had her lie back again so he could tug the medical garment off her lower half.

As soon as she was free of it, Raven breathed a sigh of relief. Her limbs felt like gelatin, and her spine wouldn't stay straight when she sat up, but at least she wasn't suffocating in the artificial heat anymore.

"Did you get my notes?" Darrow asked.

"I did."

"What do you make of it all?" He seemed eager for her response, humming with an almost childish need for approval. He'd done this for her, she realized. As if to make up for overstepping their mutual respect.

Raven didn't reply.

"I'm looking into the details some more," he continued. "But if this guy has ICG overrides that high, he has friends in places he shouldn't. This has to be handled carefully."

An epic understatement.

Having slept on it, in a manner of speaking, Raven now had enough mental distance to look at the situation with a clear head, and she didn't like what the clues seemed to spell out.

The Shadows' first Commander in Chief, Senator Matthew Griffith, had created the army in secret. When his Shadows had come into the light, the ICG had publicly shunned him and removed him from his senatorial post. All records of his army should have been archived from their servers as part of their official stance of dissent.

The fact that Sandoval's file still existed at all, much less with such a high classification, could only mean one of two things. Either Sandoval, the first Hawk, had infiltrated the highest levels of government without anyone noticing, or the ICG had reconsidered their dissent and chosen to side with the Shadows against telepaths and other chem-resistants.

Raven wanted it to be difficult to believe, but truth be told, it would be right in line with their policies since the last war.

The innovative chem-treatment of the late 29th century might have started as a way to heal the population, but sometime in the last few generations, it had turned into a vehicle of control.

And it had failed. The whole reason the Shadows had attacked in the first place had been to put down city-wide riots of billions of everyday citizens rising up against the chem-treatment industry and everything it stood for.

But if the ICG had thrown their support behind Sandoval, he wouldn't need multiple personnel files with governmental security overrides.

No, the far more likely explanation was that Rajeev Sandoval, the first and oldest Hawk, had secretly replaced Senator Griffith as the Shadows' new Commander in Chief.

Raven paused on that thought, a cold weight sinking into her gut.

The SU's campaign against the Shadows was only effective because the Shadow forces were fragmented and couldn't function without centralized leadership. If Sandoval had stepped up to fill that role, then the war they thought they were winning was about to get much, much worse.

And none of them were prepared.

24

Later that day – Chairo, Valhale 602

Darrow forced Raven to take the day to recuperate from her near-freezing before he allowed her into Zach's mind again. But his idea of recuperation was to make her sit through another council meeting so he could inform everyone about the Rajeev Sandoval situation.

Raven took careful note of each council member's reaction. Most of them were consistent with any sane person facing the prospect of the Shadows regrouping for a new round of organized tactical warfare. The council members hummed with a discordant clash of fear, anxiety, righteous anger, and grief.

All except one.

Ripley Parecourte appeared curiously composed as they absorbed the news. They didn't twitch an eyebrow as they watched Darrow with a diplomat's patience.

Raven tried to alert her boss to this, but her polite nudge got shut down hard. She clicked her teeth together until her jaw ached while the rest of the council debated how to proceed.

It took hours.

Ultimately, the council decided to inform their acting director immediately. With the majority carrying the vote, Darrow conceded, even though he didn't look happy about it.

Raven was relieved.

Ripley showed no reaction whatsoever, as if none of it bothered them. As if it were all a stage play they'd seen before.

Darrow made the call with all of them present. They all watched the welcoming smile on Emma Wayland's face fade as she listened to

Darrow explain the situation. They all saw her go so pale, her freckles stood out stark across her nose and cheeks.

"You did what?"

Visibly taken aback to be cut off mid-sentence, Darrow shifted in his seat. He cast Raven a glance in a knee-jerk cry for help.

What did he expect her to say?

Emma Wayland looked away from her recorder to motion to someone off-screen. Raven heard movement somewhere near her, then the unmistakable thump of boots on the floor and the rhythm of heavy footsteps rushing away.

"Director, it's clear we're in uncharted territory here," Darrow said, his youthful uncertainty clashing with the authority he tried to convey with his voice.

"You knocked at the kraken's shithouse," the redhead snapped. "And you want what from me now?" Her furious gaze turned to Raven. "Didn't the chameleon warn you not to change colors?"

Raven gulped. "He did," she answered, because the words might have been random, but the question was pretty direct. Zach had warned her not to go poking into Sandoval's files, and Raven had recorded and highlighted his warning in her notes.

Darrow had chosen not to listen. The way he hadn't listened to any of her recommendations since he'd assigned her to this case.

The acting director slapped both hands over her face and rubbed hard. She took a few deep breaths to get herself back under control, and then she faced them all again, her expression grave but resolved. "Charlie Foxtrot," she said.

Darrow's hands curled on the table. "We can't—"

"Start now. Move fast. Do not stop." She bit out the words one by one, using small ones to make herself understood.

"What's Charlie Foxtrot?" Ima asked, looking back and forth between their director and Darrow.

Emma Wayland only stared him down and nodded once. Then she whirled away a second before the connection shut down.

"What is Charlie Foxtrot?" Ima repeated, sharper this time.

Darrow's throat worked on a dry swallow. "Emergency evacuation protocol."

At the far end of the table, Xavier gasped.

"This is ridiculous!" Jubal barked, shoving out of his seat.

"Sit, my friend." Orson reached up a calming hand, but Jubal shook him off.

"It's paranoid and alarmist!" Jubal insisted. "She wants us to evacuate? Because of *one Shadow*? Does she even realize how many people we have here?"

Ima clasped her hands together, pressing them to her mouth.

Darrow allowed Jubal to rant without saying a word. Emma Wayland might sound loopy, but her mind was scalpel-sharp. She knew exactly how many people Darrow had here, and she knew what it would take to move them all. She wouldn't have ordered him to do it unless she had a good reason.

"How much time do we have?" Raven asked him softly.

Darrow shook his head.

Orson's voice now clashed with Jubal's and Xavier's, trying to reason out the situation and only managing to make it worse. When Ima joined the fray, Raven knew all order was lost.

Darrow tapped on his side of the table to activate his console and began typing in commands. Raven picked up on bits and pieces of thoughts as they slipped past his shields. Luckily, he'd already rehoused a good fifteen percent of their people off-site. That still left hundreds of staff members and medical residents, all of whom would need time to vacate the building.

The emergency protocols were designed to manage the evacuation gradually over several days, minimizing panic and potential casualties. Darrow overrode those commands and queried the AI to recalculate for the most expeditious solution while maintaining order.

For all they knew, the Shadows were poised to attack at any moment. The bunkers underground might hold out during a direct attack, but they weren't built to withstand a prolonged siege. The safest course of action was to leave Valhale 602 entirely. As Emma Wayland had instructed, everyone had to move fast. And they couldn't afford to stop.

The AI running the scenarios generated a new estimate of twenty-eight hours to vacate the building and three days to completely clear all registered SU residents from Valhale 602.

But it didn't account for the moon's civilian residents.

Raven's skin prickled with goose bumps, and she looked away from Darrow to find Ripley watching her. Still wholly unbothered, their serene mask still firmly in place.

The knock at her frontal lobe signaled their request for direct communication.

Against her better judgment, Raven met them halfway, making sure to keep all her private thoughts to herself.

—*Complicated times. Difficult decisions. How does it feel to have more sense than the person in charge of keeping us safe?*— Ripley asked. The question itself felt like a coded message with multiple meanings.

—*What are you talking about?*—

—*I'm simply pointing out that even you, a disabled and emotionally compromised contractor with no leadership experience, would have handled this mess better.*— Ripley's telepathic voice conveyed a careless shrug, but an echo of ghostly impressions flashed through Raven's mind at their words. She sensed that she could have prevented this from happening. Except it felt dated, as if Darrow's disastrous mistake had been years in the making. And Ripley placed the responsibility for it on her. —*After all, you did try, and your counsel was dismissed at every turn. If only you'd tried harder.*—

What a disappointment you turned out to be…

—*No one is infallible. Darrow has never let us down before,*— she reminded them, deeply disturbed by their insinuations. They bordered on mutiny.

—*Until now. Now, he has compromised the safety of everyone in this facility, possibly everyone in the city at large. Did you notice our acting director turned to you for an explanation? Wonder why that is. Maybe she knows things would have turned out differently if you were the one calling the shots. Maybe she's wondering why you aren't.*—

They nodded at Raven in respectful deference, as if they'd just delivered some profound compliment. Then their deep red lips twitched and, for the life of her, Raven couldn't tell if it was to smirk or scowl.

25

That evening – Chairo, Valhale 602

The evacuation orders went out immediately, starting with school groups and chronic patients. The med center hummed with tense activity as staff members went through their transfer procedures for each patient and checked them off the list.

Raven weaved between multitasking androids and harried nurses in stained scrubs. At the quarantine door, the scanlock denied her entry, flashing an angry red, ACCESS DENIED.

"Mr. Iridiae has revoked our special patient's visitor privileges," Dr. Vernon informed her, reading through a checklist on his device as he passed her by. "I'm sorry, Ms. Dello Russo, but I'm afraid no one is allowed in."

Raven gritted her teeth. —*Darrow…*—

—*You should be packing, Rae.*— His telepathic presence sounded frayed.

—*The Shadow is still my case.*— And she still had work to do.

—*Not anymore. We're shutting down his detox in ten hours and twenty-seven minutes. I'm having him transferred to the VSS.*—

The Vesta Space Station had once been the first port of call for Valhale 602's colonizers. Since its shutdown almost two centuries ago, it had been transformed into a monument to humanity's early spacefaring days. Fully automated, the VSS continued to orbit Vesta and became an annual tourist attraction whenever it crossed paths with the inhabited moon.

—*And then I'm going to blast his location all over the public channels so his Shadow buddies know exactly where to come pick him up.*—

Raven's stomach clenched in a cold fist. —*You're going to use him as a decoy.*—

—*I'm going to do whatever the hell I can to buy us more time.*—

—*What about the intel in his brain?*— If nothing else, he had access to all the accounts he'd stolen from the Shadows. He'd been truthful about that. Enough money to financially cripple the Shadows was enough to fund the SU's every last effort and put a quick end to the war once and for all. It was worth pursuing.

—*No longer relevant.*— Darrow replied.

Because they now had much bigger problems.

Darrow must have picked up on her frustration because suddenly her mind felt smothered in a mental hug. —*It wasn't your fault.*—

—*Excuse me?*— He was putting this on her?

—*The Shadow played you. It's what they do. He dangled Sandoval in front of you, knowing we wouldn't be able to resist.*—

Raven had resisted. She'd had no intention of poking her nose where it didn't belong without first establishing a safe base from which to do so. She'd planned to get more intel from Zach before she went anywhere near a database search.

—*No one blames you for this. We just don't have time to wallow,*— Darrow assured her. —*Go home and pack whatever you can't leave behind. I want you on the first shuttle out with the kids.*—

To hell with that! —*I'm not done here.*—

A Hawk was worth more than a momentary distraction. He'd done enough damage to the Shadows to make him an asset for the SU already. But if she could convince him to fight on their side, it could significantly improve their chances of survival.

And she wasn't just thinking of the telepaths. If Sandoval came after them, everyone on the moon would be in the line of fire. The SU owed the civilians as much protection as they did to their own. And it pissed her off that Darrow hadn't even considered the city of Chairo in his evacuation plan, let alone the rest of the moon.

There was no way Zach didn't know something useful about Sandoval. The man had as good as raised him. Somewhere in his memories, there had to be a way to stop the first Hawk before it was too late.

—*I said no, Raven. I locked that door for a reason.*—

—You realize I don't actually need to be in the room with him to get into his mind.— Although it would make the process easier, not to mention safer.

Something like a sigh shivered across their link. *—Let it go. It's done. He's not your problem anymore.—* He shut down their connection to make his word final.

Raven clenched her hand into an impotent fist. All around her, the med center slowly cleared out. Patients hugged their doctors in gratitude before they stepped into the elevator. Nurses hid their frustration behind professional smiles. Custodial bots swept away discarded materials, cheerfully apologizing every time someone ran into them.

She blinked away the stinging blur and worked out the tension in her jaw. This shouldn't be happening. None of it.

One of the security guards who'd escorted them up here was on watch by the elevators. Raven caught his eye and waved him over. Derek Kangalai was a sweet man with a husband and three kids to support. No telepathic abilities to speak of, but he was very quick on his feet and very, very good at his job.

Raven carefully set the mental groundwork for him as he made his way through the mayhem toward her. "I'm so glad you're here. I think I'm locked out."

Mr. Kangalai frowned. "Yes, Ma'am. We got orders to lock down quarantine."

"That's what I mean. I know his visitor privileges have been revoked and his treatment is suspended until we clear out, but he's still my subject. I need to get in there."

He scratched the back of his head, and Raven pulled back slightly on the compulsion. "We were told you would be taking medical leave for a few days."

Truth. And it pissed her the fuck off. "Do I look like I need medical leave?"

From the face he pulled, she definitely did. Raven raised an eyebrow in challenge and snaked doubt through his convictions. Just enough to remind him he still answered to her as the lead on the Shadow's case.

"Look, I could work from out here, but with everything going on, it'd be better for everyone if I weren't in the way. I just need an hour or so. Already cleared it with Darrow."

He huffed a breath, still hesitating.

"I'll get you a case of those fig cakes you like so much."

With a scowl, Mr. Kangalai put his hand to the scanloc. "Two."

"Done. Thank you!" She slipped into the quarantine chamber and sent the guard back to his station, taking away his memory of their short interaction. She'd still get him the fig cakes, but he didn't need to have her little rebellion on his conscience.

What mattered was that she was in. Raven smiled her defiance up at the security feeds. If Darrow was watching, he could get himself down there and drag her out by force.

Something told her he had other, more important things to keep him occupied at the moment. Probably shouldn't waste it. Raven sat on the floor facing the Shadow's detox tank and closed her eyes.

~

SESSION 7

If possible, the central nest of the Shadow's mind had become even cozier since her last visit. It pissed her off. She didn't have time for this manipulation bullshit anymore. It was time to do what she'd been hired to do. Whether he liked it or not.

"Where are you?" she called. Her voice came out muffled as if echoes didn't exist in this dreamlike reality.

A log split in the fireplace, casting up a shower of golden sparks that looped in intricate patterns in the air before fading out.

She stomped across the space to the massive glass doors and shoved them open. The scene disappeared into a black void that tugged her toward an infinite nothing. The oubliette of Zach's forgetting. The place where he sent unwanted memories to die.

Raven slammed the door shut and took off down the ornate hallway instead, grabbing each door handle as she passed. None of them budged, as if they'd grown roots into the frames.

"Van Warren!"

The hallway extended before her, a dozen new doors sprouting along its length, but the sconces became scarcer, creating an illusion of a path that faded into darkness.

She ran straight into it, shouting for him. "*Van Warren, where the hell are you!*" The shadows swallowed her voice as she passed door after door that refused to open. They were a series of cauterized wounds. The last remnants of memories he'd excised from his mind.

At last, a small light flared in the distance. Raven picked up her speed, racing for it as it grew and grew and—

—she emerged in front of the fireplace, the Christmas tree mocking her with a tinkling chorus of its many bells.

A sense of unease crept along her shoulders.

She whirled around the way she'd come, but a solid wall blocked her way. No one there.

Raven shook off the feeling and considered her options. There was only one door she hadn't tried. It would be just like him to hide in the one place she didn't want to be.

Raven scowled at the carving of entwined trees from across the chamber, and in the next blink found herself right in front of the entrance to his fantasy.

A soft thump against her spine gave her pause as she reached for the handle: her heart throbbing an extra beat in her chest.

The subtle nudge of fear made her recoil for all of five seconds. "Not falling for your tricks." It was *his* mind. *His* fear. A defense mechanism to make her think twice before going where he didn't want her. Did he really think it would work?

Darrow might be satisfied with running away, but Raven wasn't. Sandoval would catch up to them eventually, and Raven needed to be ready for him when he did. She needed what Zach knew—now. And if he refused to share, well, her talent for puzzling together pieces of memory worked just as well in the reverse. She could tear his newly constructed identity into shreds.

With her whole weight and no small amount of mental effort behind it, Raven inched the door open, fighting the groan of its suddenly ancient, rusted hinges.

She stepped across the threshold into a thick, heavy darkness that echoed with the sound of deep, measured breaths.

There was that sense of unease again, more intense this time, like a hand closing around the back of her neck. Her scalp prickled with static.

She shook her head and pushed the feeling aside.

How long had she already been there? How many hours had she wasted chasing her own tail down that damned hallway?

Every time she'd entered his mind before, he'd met her almost immediately. Now that she needed him to engage, he refused to give her the time of day.

Raven compressed the rumble of her temper into a tight ball before her, then shrank it smaller and smaller until the pressure made it glow.

As her frustration grew, so did the light, until a small sun floated up toward the ceiling, pushing the darkness into retreat.

Raven blinked. The same bed, the same luxurious crimson sheets. And there was the Shadow with his naked copy of her in his arms.

Only they weren't having wild, crazy sex anymore.

They were sleeping. Cuddled together with fake-Raven's arm around the Shadow's waist, her cheek pressed to his chest. And he held her so tight, his whole body curved around her, and his face was in her hair as if he couldn't get close enough.

He wasn't a copy. That was the real him lying there, conveniently unconscious for the first time since they'd put him in the detox tank.

Looking pretty peaceful, too.

He was about to get the awakening of his life.

Raven stomped around the bed to his side without making a sound on the thick carpet. Curling her hand into a fist, she raised it high and slammed it down on his shoulder.

In a flash of movement, he disappeared, and strong arms wrapped around her in a vise that would have cracked ribs and squeezed the life out of her in the physical world. Here, the hold locked her in one shape and one location. His newly built self-awareness lent him a strength he hadn't had before. He was far more solid in his identity. More in control of what he did and what he allowed to be done to him. A Shadow Hawk in full force, trying to kill her.

Raven was a master telepath. No matter how much resistance he'd managed to build up, she could still shatter him piece by piece until all that remained was an obedient automaton with a vault of memories for her to study as she pleased.

She should do it.

Except she couldn't. Because his manufactured copy of her was still there on that bed, still peacefully asleep.

Raven had startled a Shadow Hawk out of sleep next to his fake girlfriend. He was only fighting back to protect *her*.

Raven's unspent energy morphed into a wild scream.

The Shadow's murderous expression blanked out, and his hold loosened. "Raven?" He lowered her enough for her feet to touch the floor. "What are you doing here?" A separate version of his voice echoed across the room with a very different greeting: *I could have killed you!*

Raven shoved out of his hold, swaying as a strange dizzy spell overtook her. "Tell me everything you know about Sandoval."

"I already told you—"

"Now!" Something wasn't right. The unease she'd felt before was back, and now her stomach roiled, her mouth filling with saliva as if her physical self was about to throw up. "No more games. Tell me, show me, whatever it is you do here, but do it now."

Out past the ornate door, the Christmas tree shuddered, causing its many bells to screech in alarm. The Shadow didn't seem to notice. "What's going on?" he asked. "What did you do?"

Thousands of invisible wings beat at her face and neck. *Raven!*

She stumbled backward, shaking them off. "Enough!"

The Shadow frowned at her, his hands hovering between them in a gesture of peace. "Just tell me what you need."

The air was getting too thick to breathe. Her entire being felt constricted and trapped. Oh, but he wasn't getting rid of her that easily. "I saw Sandoval's files. As in *multiple*. And *active*. Tell me what you know!"

His presence froze as if time itself had stopped, and all she heard was the beat of his heart shuddering the walls around them. Fear snaked its way up her legs, demanding that she *runrunRUN!* But Raven stomped her heel into the thick carpet and held her ground.

"You didn't," his voice said a split second before his being unfroze to catch up to it. "Tell me you didn't."

She wasn't about to throw her seventeen-year-old boss into a pissed-off Shadow's crosshairs. Raven drew herself up, raised her chin in defiance, but her spine curved her forward again as if someone had just kicked her in the stomach.

Zach's hands curled around her shoulders, raising her up, shaking her. "Tell me you're lying!"

"I—"

The pain in her stomach looped around her spine and *yanked* her backward—

—straight out of his hold, out of his mind, and back into her body.

Raven blinked through the cloudy haze, winced through the ringing in her ears, but none of her senses made sense. What the hell was Ripley doing, screaming in her face? Why were the lights flashing red?

She wiped her running nose and stared at the blood smeared over the back of her hand.

Get up... run...

Raven tried to shake the dull thrum out of her head, but her neck was so stiff she could barely move. Her body felt utterly disconnected from her consciousness, as if she'd been out of it for hours longer than she'd planned.

The sharp sting across her cheek registered several seconds after the fact.

Raven squinted at Ripley's furious face, trying to make out their words. "*Get the fuck up! We have to run!*"

Run?

Raven blinked to clear the haze, but it wouldn't go away. Her eyes weren't the problem. Smoke filled the room. The red flash, the ringing in her ears—they were part of the building's emergency alert system. What the fuck was going on?

Ripley disappeared sideways, and Raven slowly turned to see them pressing a hand against the opaque glass partition separating the quarantine chamber from the rest of the med center. Whatever they attempted to do didn't seem to work. They swore and backed away, turning frantic circles, looking for something.

As if noticing her for the first time again, Ripley stomped over and grabbed Raven by the arm, dragging her toward the Shadow's detox tank. "Wake him."

Raven frowned, her mind refusing to translate the words into meaning.

Ripley slapped her across the face again, then grabbed her hand and forced her palm flat against the glass. "Wake him! You're the only one who can control him now. If we can't trade him for our lives, we can use him to fight our way out."

Fight?

Slowly, so very slowly, Raven fought the mental burnout and the fog of a forced disconnect to tune in to the real world. Through the din and chaos of Ripley's panic, she began to pick up on a whole lot more of it from the other side of the partition. The entire building was awash in it.

Terror.

Pain.

Rapid movement in the dark.

A spray of blood cutting off a high-pitched scream.

The scent of charred flesh.

Desperate feet sliding over bodies fallen on the staircase, trampling them into silence.

The SU was under attack.

The rational part of Raven's mind knew she had no time to waste, but it was so tired. She could barely maintain consciousness. Her body had been asleep for too long while her brain had worked overtime. She couldn't make either obey the simplest commands. Her mouth was parched, her tongue stuck to the roof of her mouth. Her legs were so numb they didn't feel connected to her anymore. When Ripley let go of her hand, it slid lifelessly down the detox tank, and her forehead thudded against it for support, amplifying her pounding migraine.

Ripley scream-roared in fury and whirled toward the control screens, stabbing and swiping through a menu of commands they weren't trained to understand.

Warnings flashed left and right. Tubes detached, spilling thick liquid all over the floor. It pooled around Raven, glittering like the

Shadow's Christmas tree.

She turned her head sideways. In the far corner of her peripheral vision, lights flashed beyond the opaque partition. The soundproofed barrier silenced the chorus of plasma shots, but it wouldn't hold up to direct weapons fire.

There was Ripley again, stepping in front of her, a gun in one hand, and a long piece of tubing in the other. They tore their gaze away from the partition long enough to cast her a look of utter disgust before taking a stand against a rising tide of violence.

So tired…

Raven let her neck relax back into a neutral position, which turned her toward the tank and the Shadow's feet floating before her. It took every last ounce of strength she possessed to lift her palm to the glass again. She closed her eyes, resisting the pull of sleep to spear her consciousness back into the Shadow's mind.

Her telepathic body crumpled and disintegrated as soon as she stepped out of the floor-length mirror of her gateway. She'd barely made it through.

It was far enough.

Before she could gather her strength to call out, Zach was there, his touch forcing her body to coalesce as he lifted her off the floor. "You're burned out, Blackbird," he said, holding her up with one arm and cupping her face to help her look at him.

"They're here," she forced out on an exhale. There one moment, gone the next. Flashing back and forth between Zach's mind and the chaos reigning around her body.

The shatter of glass dragged her out of Zach's hold.

Ripley's scream chased her back to him.

She fought the relentless force dragging her into darkness long enough to mumble, "You have to wake up."

The oppressive sense of several people crowding into the chamber threatened to yank her back, but she resisted.

"I can't," Zach told her. "I'm sedated, remember?"

Raven whimpered a helpless moan.

He pulled her tighter into him. "Stay with me. I'll keep you safe here. I'm sorry, Blackbird. Fuck, I'm so sorry."

Raven's focus shattered on an exhale. She faded back into herself in time to see Ripley hit the ground, blood matting their pale hair to their scalp.

Dark boots. Deep voices barking out words too muffled to make out.

Her vision swam. One soldier became two, then five, then eight. They weaved one in front of the other, and she couldn't tell how many of them were real.

Sedation slowed down neural functions. Telepathic activity ramped it up. That's what Dr. Zyxon had said. She didn't have the serum to counteract Zach's chemical coma. But maybe she didn't need it.

One of the soldiers crouched down in front of her. He was pale, his ashy brown hair cropped close to his scalp. She couldn't make out his features, but a little blue light flickered at his temple.

The light went out, and he fisted her hair, arching her neck and forcing her body out of balance so he could examine her left side. She saw him turn toward the others and heard him speak muffled words.

The response was just as incomprehensible. But she recognized the cadence as dark humor.

The Shadow dragged her by her hair to clear the path for the others.

They didn't approach. Just raised their guns, barrels pointed at the detox tank.

She felt the heated tip of one press against her cheek.

So tired…

Raven turned her hand palm out.

One deep breath. One final act of rebellion.

She gathered it all in her heart: anger, grief, shame, regret. Everything she'd spent the last three years shoving deep down where it couldn't hurt her anymore. Every last ounce of defiance she could muster to amplify it all into one solid telepathic blast.

It shot out of her, and her heart stuttered its next beat, lungs forgetting what it was to take a breath.

At least she wouldn't feel it.

At least she wouldn't have to watch them kill anyone else.

But death couldn't claim her fast enough. It stayed its skeletal hand for one more second. Long enough for her to see the flash of several plasma bolts shatter the detox tank.

Drowning. Burning. Falling.

Zach's body reacted before his mind had fully caught on to what was happening. Sliding along the slick, cold floor, he grabbed hold of the first sharp thing his hand encountered. A shard of glass from the shattered detox tank. The current of spilling liquid carried him right to a Shadow's booted feet.

He had seconds.

Zach didn't waste a single one staring down the barrel of a plasma gun. He grabbed for it and used its owner's resistance to pull himself up and slash at the Shadow's neck.

He missed the cut, but threw his opponent off balance enough that it didn't matter.

The soldier still had hold of his weapon when Zach turned it toward his companions and fired at their unprotected faces. The Hound fought Zach as they both went down, fucking up his aim. One Shadow lost his eye, the other half of his neck. Both were still alive when they dropped.

Zach, covered with the slick detox liquid, was now pinned beneath the gun's owner—and the Hound wasn't happy about his gun hand being held captive.

Then a series of plasma bolts slammed into the Shadow, courtesy of his two remaining friends. None of the shots bored through to Zach, but they did manage to kill the Hound.

He wrenched the gun free of the dead man and returned fire.

One down.

The other grabbed Zach by the ankle and dragged him sideways before Zach could get a clean shot. But he slipped in the liquid and went down on his ass. Zach shoved off the corpse and got up to his knees. Three shots to take out the active threat. Two more to finish off the ones still writhing on the floor.

Silence.

Zach swept the perimeter, seeing no other movement outside the shattered glass partition. The medical floor had already been swept, and the rest of the unit had moved on. Nothing left, just a few corpses on the ground—guards, by the looks of them.

Lowering the gun, Zach bent over and forced the rest of the oxygenated solution from his lungs, gagging and choking. It came out red with a substantial amount of blood. Lightheaded from the effort, he took quick stock of his physical condition.

Dull, hot aches bloomed across his body. One in his shoulder, one through the right side of his chest, two in his abdomen, and one more through the outside of his left thigh. He patted himself down, searching for open wounds, and found none in his torso. A pale pink scar the size of his hand marked his thigh, looking like a chunk of his muscle had been blown off. He watched the flesh fill back in beneath the scar before it, too, faded into nothing.

No time to think about it now.

Zach pushed to his feet and slid across the floor to the maintenance panel he'd spotted in the far corner when they'd brought him in. The functions he'd once contemplated hacking to attack the building's residents would only take out civilians and piss off the Shadows, but the console did provide real-time location data for everyone inside the building.

A swarm of dots representing fleeing civilians had bottlenecked on the second floor. Three teams of five converged on them. They would be dead within minutes.

On the roof, ten dots ambled back and forth. Shadow rear guard. There would be a concealed hover waiting above the building to retrieve the infiltration team and return them to base with whatever prisoners they'd decided to take.

No movement toward his position. The Shadows had to be aware that five of their buddies were dead. It appeared they were following protocol. Better to sacrifice one compromised team than risk them all. They would prioritize their own assignments and clear the building first. Bad for the telepaths. Good for him. Extra time to figure out how to get out of this in one piece.

The console located him on the forty-seventh floor. Unless he somehow managed to fashion a paraglider out of medical supplies—

"'scape pod."

Zach had to stop himself from pulling the trigger at the barely moving body in the middle of the chamber. Dark blood stained Ripley's pretty pale hair. Half of their face was swollen from a solid blow, and their arm was bent wrong, bone stabbing through the skin.

"'mergency exit," they mumbled. "For patients."

Escape pods were the equivalent of flight-enabled transports clinging to the building's outer walls. They were a safety requirement for any building taller than forty stories.

And they, along with any coms, would have been the first thing the Shadows disabled upon arrival. Couldn't have targets running off to warn others.

But *disabled* didn't mean *destroyed*.

He turned back to the console and brought up the emergency schematic. The medical floor had more escape pods than any other. Each window served as an exit, and all the pods outside of them registered as INOPERABLE.

They were also networked for a coordinated evacuation.

Perfect.

Zach marked the closest one to his current location, then stepped back and shot the console, ducking stray sparks. A few struck the custodial bot in the corner, waking it to life. The green light of its scanner swept over the room. "Spill detected," it declared, moving out. "Please watch your step."

Zach moved out of its way as it swept past him, sucking up the debris and spilled liquid. "Please watch your step. Please watch your step."

Its top light turned red as it maneuvered around Ripley and the dead Shadows, but it didn't stop.

Zach turned away from the Shadows and the clothes and gear he could have used. He nudged the bot out of his way and stepped over the bleeding Ripley to where Raven lay unmoving at the foot of the detox tank.

As gently as he could, he brushed her hair away from her face. He detected no significant injuries, only a few shallow cuts and scrapes on her hand, but blood had stained the corners of her eyes and still oozed from her nose. Her heartbeat fluttered fast and light in the side of her neck. Too erratic. Too weak. But she was still breathing. Barely.

Zach scooped her up. She was as light as a feather in his hold. So delicate.

"Please…" Ripley moaned, watching him. "Please…" they repeated a little louder as he stepped over them again on his way out.

Zach paused just long enough to cast them a glance over his shoulder. "Who are you?"

He didn't wait for a response.

The closest floor-to-ceiling window had an emergency open sensor next to it and a walkable ledge on the outside. The sensor was disabled. Good thing the Shadows had come armed. The gun he'd appropriated from them still had fourteen shots left. One was enough to shatter the glass into tiny, harmless pieces.

The night wind howled, mercilessly sharp and cold this far up. Naked and wet from the tank, Zach stepped into four inches of snow on the outer ledge, breathing through the bone-deep chill.

A neat row of escape pods formed a line all the way around the floor. The first one, right in front of the broken window, would have been an obvious target. Zach shuffled through the snow to the eighth one, then doubled two back, just to be safe. He had to put Raven down to manually wake the pod and open it. With his whole body shivering, it took longer than he would have liked to pry open the lock panel and reactivate the system.

But as soon as he did, all the other pods hummed to life, doors opening for patients who were long gone already. Zach gently laid Raven on the seat-gurney, grateful for the pod's automatic environmental controls. It might not have flown on its own, but its medical systems still functioned. The heat engaged immediately, and the gurney spat out a scan reading of Raven's condition.

Mild dehydration, partial shut-down due to telepathic burnout, minor bleeding in the brain, which had already drained and stopped on its own, and a collection of minor cuts and scrapes from flying glass shards that didn't pose a medical risk. The system recommended a nutritional IV drip and rest. A compartment underneath the gurney popped open onto a prepped IV set. All he had to do was place the red patch over the inside of Raven's arm and hang the bag from a small hook in the ceiling.

That done, he quickly turned his attention to the flight controls.

Movement in the sky above. The Shadows had deployed drones.

Zach rushed through the reprogram. He needed to disengage the autonav so he could fly the damned thing manually.

Six small drones descended on his side of the building.

Out of time.

Zach slammed the control panel shut with enough force to kick out the manual yoke. He pulled away from the ledge, and all the other pods followed suit. When he turned the vehicle to face out, all the others followed suit. Then he engaged the engine and gunned it as fast as he could.

The other pods took off in tandem. But unlike his, they didn't have anyone at the controls. They flew out in a straight line, some crashing into nearby buildings, others continuing for miles.

The Shadow drones followed. But there weren't enough to track them all.

Zach dove his pod as soon as he had a clear path and descended to street level, where he could hide among civilian transports. A few blocks later, he veered off the road into an underground speedway that spanned the desert and emerged in the next closest city, Kalchama.

The pod only had the most basic sensors to monitor the surrounding traffic and prevent collisions, and the speedway tunnel was almost pitch-black. If even one of the drones had tailed them, the Shadows would be waiting for them at the speedway exit. Zach had no way of knowing. Racing at double the permitted speed over the top of regular traffic, he only saw a line of lit-up transports in front and behind.

He pulled over on the emergency shelf, turned everything off, and waited.

Minutes ticked by without any sign of a Shadow drone—not that he would have noticed in the darkness. But he sure as shit would have noticed one opening fire on him.

After an hour, still unharmed, Zach let himself relax enough to search through the pod. Raven remained unconscious, but her IV was finished. The scan told him to replace it with a fresh one, so he did.

In another compartment, he found scrubs for medical staff and two sets of standard replacement patient outfits.

They couldn't keep going in a medical escape pod without drawing attention. The scrubs presented the same issue. He opted for the patient garments instead. The standard sizing fell an inch or two short in the sleeves and pant legs for him, but it would work fine until he could procure proper clothes. At least they'd fit Raven. Her black-on-black uniform was far too conspicuous, not to mention soaked through down the left side of her body.

"Not how I pictured peeling you naked for the first time," he said. "You'll have to give me a pass on this one. And I'm sorry for this next part, but it needs to be done."

The side wall compartment held suture kits and scalpels. He picked out the smallest one and a sterilizing light.

The scanner had located Raven's ID chip in the back of her arm, just above her wrist. Zach turned on the light and felt for the indentation in her skin. He made the smallest cut possible to dig the chip out. A drop of liquid bandage sealed the wound. He rubbed his thumb over it to ease the ache she likely couldn't feel.

The chip itself, Zach slipped into his pocket. Once they got somewhere safe, he would reprogram it for one of his backup identities. Until then, he just had to hope that Kalchama was a little less paranoid than Chairo.

Smoke in the air made breathing difficult. Raven couldn't see two feet in front of her nose. Everything ached. Her head was splitting open. She couldn't tell what was real and what wasn't.

One moment, bloodcurdling screams echoed from all sides. The next, her heart pounded like a drum in the sudden silence.

One moment, the floor was polished gray tile. With her next step, she tripped over something and went down hard, her hands and knees splashing into something wet and sticky. Blood. She'd fallen into a puddle of blood. She didn't turn around, didn't want to see the dead body that had tripped her. It didn't matter, anyway. A dozen more lay scattered right in front of her like discarded toys.

And she knew them.

Stars, she knew all of them. Darrow, Ripley, and the rest of the council, and Tessa a few feet beyond them, her sweet face contorted in a grimace of agony.

Raven turned away and came face to face with the one she'd tripped over. Eyes gone gray with death, skin turned green, bloated and cracking. Jaw unhinged and mouth open on a blue-black mess of decaying flesh.

Julian.

Raven screamed so hard her entire body shuddered, but no sound would come out. She tried again, screaming harder, hating the void in her throat where her voice should have been.

Bloody tears tracked down her face as she jerked herself away to escape somewhere—anywhere.

Her body pulled up short, her left arm pinned in the wreck of warped metal that tore through her flesh with every move. She couldn't stop *herself. Desperate to flee far, far away from there, she pulled and yanked, mutilating herself to gain an inch.*

Stars, it hurt. She couldn't take it anymore.

Raven braced her feet and pushed herself away from the wreck of her life. The shoulder joint held, but soft skin and muscle tore easily, stripping the last shard of her broken arm to the bone. Jarred free, she fell to her back, breathless, tired to her very soul. Pain had become a suffocating embrace, pinning her down.

But at least the floor had softened. At least her heart didn't feel so heavy anymore.

She blinked up into the bright light above her and imagined it was heaven opening its gates wide in welcome. All she had to do was get up and fly. But how could she, with only one wing?

She imagined voices calling her name.

And then those same voices wailed in agony.

Raven turned away, bracing herself for the sight of a shard of naked bone where an arm should have been.

Instead, she saw a person lying next to her, smiling as if they were old friends. But Rajeev Sandoval was no friend of hers. And that smile was nothing short of a threat.

She jerked away, but he caught the splintered end of her arm bone, and pure white agony shot straight into her brain. Raven screamed, finally hearing her own voice rip out of her throat.

In the next instant, a big hand pressed over her mouth, and Sandoval fell on top of her. "Shhh, Blackbird. Now is not the time for that."

And Raven knew she was about to die.

January 16, 3040 – Kalchama

No drones waited at the exit in Kalchama because, aside from a handful of buildings tall enough to break through the ceiling, the entire city had been built underground. It was nowhere near the scale of Chairo, but the gigantic cave cradling the city made it feel crowded with too many structures.

Along its edges and over the top, shimmering plasma shields kept people and vehicles at a safe distance from preserved natural rock formations. Massive floodlights embedded in the stone illuminated entire sections of the cave, while tiny little pinpricks in the ceiling simulated starlight.

Most of the streets only allowed one lane of traffic, and the buildings mimicked the underground environment, resembling primitive cave dwellings carved into massive stalagmites.

It had a profound effect on the residents. Where Chairo's vibrant architecture had fostered a lively, energetic atmosphere among its people, Kalchama's population reminded Zach of rats in a maze. With single-lane streets limiting the number of transport vehicles and aerial walkways crisscrossing among the tall buildings to encourage foot traffic, everywhere Zach looked, the people here *scurried*. Their movements were purposeful and quick. They didn't pause to catch up with a neighbor, or take leisurely strolls to window shop along the avenues. Dressed in shades of brown, red, and tan, they kept their heads down and walked quickly to their destination without any detours.

Zach could work with that.

He found a shadowed little corner on the outskirts to pull over on a residential street. Some of the windows were lit up, but he didn't see any people inside. Not a lot of movement outside, either. Impossible to tell what kind of security measures the city had.

He needed to find a community center. Every neighborhood had at least one to provide entertainment, and access to basic technologies and communications to the local residents. Zach only needed thirty minutes at a com station to reprogram the ID chip and get the lay of the land. Once he had a means to access and use the financial accounts he'd set up, he'd be unstoppable.

But he couldn't walk into a public space carrying an unconscious woman in his arms. And he couldn't leave Raven alone and unprotected in an emergency vehicle that stood out like a sore thumb.

She'd been quiet throughout the long drive, but her vitals had started to improve as they'd entered Kalchama. Her color was better, her heartbeat was steadier, and she seemed to be breathing deeper. More like she was sleeping now.

Zach gently lifted one of her eyelids, then the other. Her pupils were still blown, but reactive to the sudden flood of low light. "Raven, can you hear me?"

He didn't expect a response.

"You're safe now. I'll take care of you."

Her eyebrows twitched in a quick frown, and her next breath quivered.

"Would be easier if you were awake, but it's fine. You take all the time you need."

Zach could figure this out. He opened the pod doors on both sides to let in some fresh cave air. To his relief, the city smelled better than it looked. But he could definitely tell they were underground. Minerals from the rock mingled with ozone from the municipal air filters. Clean enough, but in the absence of natural wind currents, the cool humidity carried a hint of decomp, like dried autumn foliage left to rot in the mud.

"We won't stay long," he decided. Not that he had a problem with enclosed spaces, but he preferred having a clear sky above him whenever possible. If his life ever settled down long enough to have a home, Zach wanted it to have observation glass roofs so he could watch the clouds and the rain without any eyes in the sky peeking down on him.

Maybe one day.

Raven made a small sound, drawing him back to her. Her eyelids fluttered, and the scanner showed an elevated heart rate, indicating distress.

"Raven?"

Her face turned toward him. She looked like she was trying to wake up.

Zach's training hadn't included the care and maintenance of post-burnout telepaths. He had no idea if he should encourage her toward consciousness or if she needed to be sedated.

Then her eyes cracked open the slightest bit, and she let out a blood-curdling scream.

Zach covered her mouth. "Shhh, Blackbird. Now is not the time for that." The pod was open. They were exposed. Anyone within a hundred yards would have heard that scream.

Raven bucked on the gurney, arching and twisting to get away, but she had nowhere to escape in the cramped cabin. She'd end up hurting herself.

Zach shifted over her, using his weight to pin her down while the scanner flashed red with a whole slew of alarms. "Easy now. It's okay. You're safe."

It didn't work.

A compartment popped open on the pod's side panel, and a small glass shelf of colored patches slid out. Each color had a different purpose. The shelf's lights spotlighted the two that the system suggested he use. He peeled off the white patch first and applied it to Raven's right temple.

She settled immediately as the sedative took effect, and Zach hung his head. For all he knew, he'd just locked her into whatever nightmare she'd been fighting her way out of. "I'm sorry."

The second patch was blue. Pain relief. The screen told him to apply it to the back of her neck. Zach snaked an arm underneath her shoulders and raised her up to rest against him. He applied the pain patch to her nape and rubbed circles over it to help the medicine release faster.

It took three minutes for her vital signs to return to a normal rhythm. Zach waited five more minutes before he laid her back on the gurney.

"Did you just kill her?"

Zach didn't reach for his gun. He'd heard the woman creep up on the pod. She was alone and posed no threat. If she did, she would have attacked him already. "I'm trying to keep her alive."

"You don't belong here."

Zach chuckled bitterly. "Story of my life."

The woman frowned. She was the definition of average in this city. Skin a shade too deep to be pale, but too light to call tan, hair in an indeterminate shade of brown. Average height, average weight, coasting through a stage of life where she could have been twenty-five or fifty. Even her clothes were nondescript. Bland and simple, but not dirty or damaged. Not someone who liked to stand out in a crowd. Which made her the perfect lookout.

"I'm Zach," he said before she could ask. "This is Raven. We just escaped a Shadow attack in Chairo."

"Bullshit," she replied. "There hasn't been a Shadow attack on this moon in years. They forgot about us. Just like everyone else."

"They may have forgotten about *you*, but not the building full of people they just wiped out a few hours ago."

She didn't look convinced. "We didn't hear anything."

"And you probably won't."

"You one of 'em?"

Zach sighed. "Would I be here, in an emergency escape pod, dressed in hospital clothes, if I was?"

"You have a gun."

"So?"

"Why didn't you fight back?"

He liked this woman. She seemed like someone he would want in his corner. So he decided to lie. "I'm not much of a fighter. People were getting killed, Raven was hurt. I didn't think about anything other than getting us both out of there as fast as I could. I found the gun on the way. Someone must have dropped it."

She stared him down for a few unblinking moments, her face unreadable. "She your wife?"

"Not yet."

Her eyes narrowed.

"Listen, I'm happy to keep chatting, but can we maybe do it somewhere indoors? Maybe with a proper bed for Raven and some food for both of us?"

"Sure," she deadpanned. "Let me make a quick call to the police. They'll take real good care of you both."

"Go ahead," he invited. "I dare you."

She held his gaze for a second longer, then twisted her mouth with displeasure that he'd called her bluff.

"What's your name?" he asked.

"None of your damn business!"

Zach held up his hands. "Fair enough. I'm not asking for charity here. Just need a place to lie low for a few hours until Raven wakes up. If you can get me access to a com system, I can pay you back. You and the rest of your crew."

Not exactly a shot in the dark that she wasn't on her own. She had all the surly personality markers of someone in a street urchin gang. The war had forced a lot of people into poverty, and not all of them took it lying down. Those who didn't mind a bit of moral ambiguity tended to band together and wreak subtle havoc for local authorities. Sometimes, they became folk heroes, stealing and scavenging to provide for their communities. But mostly, they just concerned themselves with their own survival, where no one, be they friend or foe, could find them.

In either case, the one language they all spoke fluently was money.

This woman was no different. Her eyes sparked with pure avarice at his words, but she made him sweat a bit. "How much?"

"Four thousand credits. Each."

Her bold arrogance slipped just a little. It was probably more money than she'd seen in years. She looked over the pod and as much of Raven as she could see with Zach blocking her view, then gave him a shrewd once-over, clearly debating how much trouble she'd be buying for her crew if she let them in.

Zach figured he could afford to sweeten the deal a little. "Make it five."

The woman's chin jerked up. "If you can afford five, you can afford ten."

He firmly checked a smile and hid a chuckle behind a frustrated huff. "Six. I don't know how many of you there are."

"Nine," she countered, crossing her arms. She looked adamant, but her eyes danced. She was enjoying this.

"Eight. Final offer."

She chewed on the inside of her cheek for a moment. "Deal." Then she waved her arm high at someone across the street and jerked her head sideways at Zach. "Follow. My crew will take care of the pod."

Meaning, they'd squirrel away the medicines, strip down the console, and wreck the empty shell where no one would mind a little extra garbage.

Fair enough.

Zach scooped up Raven and climbed out of the pod.

The nameless woman immediately relieved him of the gun he'd tucked into the back of his waistband. With his arms full, he couldn't stop her, and he didn't bother trying. Let her feel in control for a while. She probably had little of it in life these days.

But her demeanor changed when she took a good look at Raven. Pity instantly dulled her sharp edges, and she hesitated.

"Don't fucking stare," Zach growled.

The woman flinched, her eyes going wide as they met his. She gulped and nodded, turning away to lead them across the street toward a group of four rough-looking men. Three others had already split off to start stripping the pod. The rest fell into step around them.

They led him in a couple of large circles through the abandoned neighborhood, thinking he wouldn't notice, then entered one of the giant stalagmite buildings. The staircase led down instead of up, taking them deeper underground until they emerged in a utility tunnel that had been converted into communal living spaces.

Zach couldn't remember if he'd ever seen poverty like this before. Nests of blankets and pillows on the floor served as beds and chairs. Ragged drapes hung between the pillars, creating crude walls. A series of semi-solid structures along one section were barely recognizable as portable sonic showers and waterless toilet stalls. Here and there, the flicker of small handheld holoscreens indicated at least some contact with the outside world, but their reach and access would be limited without a powerful booster.

And there were so many people, all of them sickly-looking and half-starved. They gazed up at him with bleary eyes utterly devoid of hope. Zach counted roughly two hundred people down there—that he could see.

The woman leading their group turned her head sideways as if she would look back at him, but stopped herself. She took them down to an intersection where the primary tunnel branched off into a smaller passage. They veered into it and followed the well-lit path to a hole someone had blasted through the wall, exposing a natural cavern with clusters of thick white crystals growing here and there like bouquets of icy flowers.

The space looked no better than the main tunnel outside, but at least here, the natural stone created a slightly warmer atmosphere, and the artificial candlelight was a little less harsh. A wooden plank of a table was set against the rocky shelf that provided seating for four solidly built men to eat their meager meals.

And at the far end, a large screen displayed the latest news. Weather reports, sports and entertainment, a schedule of upcoming events…

No mention of what had happened last night a few hundred miles across the desert in Chairo.

"We have guests," the woman announced.

A figure poked up from the recessed floor in front of the screen and turned to face them.

The man's thinning white hair, backlit by the screen, had a blue tinge to it. He wore glasses so thick that his rheumy eyes looked tiny behind them. His papery skin hung from his skull, short stubble covering his sagging jowls. "Do we now?" he rasped, pushing to his full height. He was skin and bones, his spine curving his shoulders inward, but Zach imagined he'd been a strong, handsome man in his youth.

The woman—a close relative of his, given their similar features— gestured for Zach to move forward. "He says his name is Zach, and that's Raven. He offered to pay us ten thousand credits each for a place to stay until she wakes up."

"Our deal was for eight each," Zach corrected.

She smirked at him. "That's not what I heard."

The patriarch clucked his tongue. "Manners, child. You know we don't discuss money before breakfast."

The woman flushed. "I apologize." She allowed him to give her an affectionate pat on the head, but made a face as if she didn't like it.

"You are, of course, welcome here," he said to Zach. "We share what we can. What little we have."

Behind them, the three who'd looted the pod carried in armfuls of supplies. They piled them on the floor to one side, then left again without a word.

"The people here call me Teacher," he said to the pile, rather than to Zach. "You already met my niece, Penelope. The others can introduce themselves as they will." With a skeletal hand, of twisted fingers and swollen joints, he gestured for Zach to come closer. "You can put her down here. It's the most comfortable bed we have."

"Thank you." Zach placed Raven on the worn mattress cradled in a rocky channel on the floor. "We'll be out of your hair later today." Hopefully, the entertainment unit had broad enough access for Zach to make the next leg of their trip more comfortable, whether she woke up by then or not.

"No rush," Teacher assured him. "I don't sleep much these days, anyway. Penelope, dear, why don't you go and fetch us something to eat and drink while I have a chat with our new friends?"

"I don't think—"

"There are eight strong men here to keep me safe. I promise I'll still be alive by the time you get back."

Penelope shot Zach a glare, but obeyed.

"She is the daughter I never knew I needed," Teacher said with a sigh. "I just hope she has what it takes to keep this place running when I'm gone. Our people will need someone to take care of them."

"She'll have the means to turn this place into a luxury resort," Zach promised, shifting to sit with his back to a broken stalagmite. From that position, he had an unobstructed view of the entire cavern and everyone in it, and was close enough to shield Raven if needed.

Teacher waved that away, returning to his seat in the curved pit.

Given its shape, Zach assumed it had once been a natural underground pool. Its layered shelves were lined with pillows for more comfortable seating, and grooves along the top offered practical handholds for an old man to get in and climb back out again.

With Zach sitting on the floor and Teacher in his pit, Zach had a significant elevation advantage, yet the weight of Teacher's gaze, amplified by his thick lenses, made him feel small. Teacher had a fatherly air about him, more caring than anything Zach had experienced before, and he had to remind himself that he wasn't a child anymore.

"What's your name?"

"Zach," he replied. "Zachary VanWarren."

By the way the men in the chamber shifted around and exchanged looks, they recognized the name.

Teacher just chuckled. "What is your real name?"

"What's yours, Teacher?"

He nodded sagely. "Right you are. Names don't matter much these days, do they? What a shame."

Penelope returned with a large bowl and a pitcher. She placed both on the floor between him and Teacher, then retrieved mugs and cutlery from a nearby nook. "Meal wasn't included in the price," she quietly murmured to Zach so her uncle wouldn't overhear.

Zach couldn't hold back a grin. "You drive a hard bargain. I can respect that."

The light was too soft to tell for sure, but he could have sworn she blushed as she left him to sit on Teacher's other side.

"Please, help yourself," Teacher invited. "It's not much, but it'll fill an empty stomach for a while."

Zach reached into the bowl and selected a small chewy ball he recognized as a nutritional pellet from a standard emergency survival pack. The ICG had airdropped hundreds of crates of them in war-torn regions. They were a faster and cheaper alternative to rebuilding infrastructure and subsidizing local food manufacturers.

"Thank you," he said graciously and popped it into his mouth. It tasted old and dusty, but it would keep his body functioning.

Teacher inclined his head. "Now, what brings you to our humble corner of the moon?"

"He says the Shadows attacked Chairo," Penelope answered for him. Her tone made it clear she still didn't believe him.

Teacher's face tensed. "How many dead?"

"I don't know," he admitted. But if the news hadn't picked it up, then the casualties hadn't extended beyond the SU. Therefore, it wasn't worth reporting.

"You were there, but you don't know how many died?" Penelope challenged.

"I was there for medical treatment. I woke up to dead guards on the floor and Raven barely breathing. There were emergency pods outside the window, so I took one and got us out of there as fast as I could."

"Pods don't take speedways across the desert."

Zach shrugged. "I'm good with machines."

Teacher and Penelope exchanged a long look.

He was losing their goodwill fast. "Look, I don't want to make trouble for anyone here. If you let me access your com, I can transfer you your money, and we can get out of your hair. It's probably better if we keep moving, anyway."

Teacher's gaze snapped back to him. "They came for *you*."

Shit. He'd said the exact wrong thing for Teacher to draw the right conclusion. The old man was a lot sharper than he looked. Lies would only complicate the situation further. Zach needed to present a solution Teacher would find acceptable and leave no room for negotiation.

Threatening these people didn't sit well with him, but intentionally or not, Zach had involved them in something they weren't equipped to handle. They already had the look of cornered animals prepared to go down fighting.

"The less you know, the safer you and your people will be."

Penelope swore and jumped to her feet, rushing out into the tunnel. Two of the men who'd brought them in followed her out. The rest conferred with the ones eating at the table, then all but three of them rushed out, too.

Those three pulled their knives and batons and formed a loose arc at Teacher's back, watching Zach in a way he didn't like one bit.

He shifted a few inches farther from the stalagmite to give himself room to move. Raven was cradled in the bed, tucked against the cave wall, and covered on two sides. If they wanted to get to her, they'd have to go through him first.

They wouldn't live long enough to try.

"There are more than five hundred people living in these tunnels," Teacher rasped.

"Then that's over five million credits I owe you for your hospitality. Let's call it an even six." Zach didn't think Penelope believed him about the money. She must have decided the pod's medical supplies would be payment enough. Given the state of this place and how intensely Teacher had looked at the pile of medicines, they likely would have been grateful to have that much. "I'll have it in your account in minutes if you let me use that com. As soon as I'm done, I'll take Raven and leave. You'll never see either of us again."

Teacher coughed a laugh. "That easy, is it?"

"I'll make it even easier. Get your people ready to move, and give me four pickup points. I'll have hovers waiting for them by the time they reach the street. Tell me where you want to go, and I'll get you there. All of you."

The prospect of getting out appeared to be enticing enough to make Teacher's guards consider his offer. How long had they been stuck down here, subsisting on stolen emergency supplies and not much else? Six million credits could pay for a lot of things. Not just transport, but food, clothes, and much-needed medical treatments. It might even be enough for them to establish a new home—above ground.

"I'm offering you a chance to start over."

Teacher stared at him, slack-jawed. He seemed to have been struck speechless. "Who are you, really?"

Zach smiled. "Someone even the Shadows never saw coming."

Teacher decided to discuss the situation with Penelope when she returned. The guards clearly had orders to prioritize keeping their leader safe over detaining Zach. When Teacher and Penelope slowly made their way out into the tunnel, the guards' attention shifted to them. Zach pulled out Raven's ID chip and the small scalpel he'd palmed from the emergency pod.

It took him three tries to insert the chip into his wrist. On the first two attempts, he made the cut too small and it healed shut before he got the chip anywhere near it.

Still made no sense.

But it worked in his favor, not having to conceal a bleeding wound when the guards turned their attention back to him and Raven. They appeared undecided about whether to take him out now or wait until he transferred the money to them.

Zach could tell by the animated gestures out in the tunnel that Teacher and Penelope were having a heated discussion on the same topic. But they kept their voices too low for him to hear, and he couldn't read their lips.

Zach decided to press his luck.

He stretched his legs and shifted to the edge of the sunken pit so he could dip his feet down to the first ledge.

The guards immediately straightened to attention, squaring off for a fight.

He ignored them, rolling his neck and shoulders, stretching his arms, and twisting his spine to work out the stiffness. It wasn't strictly for show, either. The detox tank had kept his muscles from atrophying, but it hadn't done much for his joints and ligaments. Sure, he had the *strength* to fight and run if he had to, but his body still felt the effects of being asleep for the last few days without proper movement. Stretching helped him recover his flexibility.

He took one more nutritional pellet from the bowl, then poured himself a mug of tepid water to wash it down.

When the guards relaxed just a little, Zach stretched to one side, then the other, snagging the com control pad in the process.

"Hey!" one of the guards snapped. Good eyesight.

"Mind if I change the feed?"

The second guard snorted. "We only got the one. Put that down. Teacher didn't say you could mess with the com." He sounded bored.

"He didn't say I couldn't, either." The screen was massive enough that even the half-blind Teacher would be able to see everything he did from out in the tunnel. Zach took a chance. "One feed, you say? Let's fix that, shall we?"

The outdated system had been improperly connected. It had minimal access, and the signal was so weak underground that everything took longer than it should. Zach accessed the utilities to bypass the com's paywall. Immediately, the screen split into multiple rectangles, each showing a different data source that they hadn't had access to before.

The first guard cursed.

The second snorted. "Shit, you got half the moon up there."

Zach grinned at him and rubbed his hands together. "What's your fancy, boys? A little action? Arts and leisure? Sports?"

They appeared to be overwhelmed by the options. No one said a word.

"How 'bout this one?" He selected one of the feeds and expanded it to half of the screen. It was a live broadcast of one of the more popular local sporting events.

He must have guessed right because the guard who'd shouted at him gaped. "That's my team."

Excellent.

Zach left the feed up and split the other half of the screen into four separate windows, each displaying what he needed. The system was registered to Teacher's ID, and when Zach prompted up the account, it instantly displayed his profile and financial information. He'd intended to close out of it right away to access his own, but the readout gave him pause.

Teacher, also known as Owen Jeremiah Laidley, had exactly four credits in his account, and the last transaction to withdraw funds was dated two years ago. He'd taken out everything except those four credits. Zach might not know what he'd used the withdrawn funds for, but he didn't need to. Four credits was a very precise amount to keep stashed away. It wouldn't buy a cup of coffee these days. But it was the base amount needed to make a call.

Teacher had saved himself a final goodbye.

Zach left the screen open and accessed a different database in a separate one. It required an ID scan, and the only one he had was Raven's. He passed his freshly healed wrist over the pad. Raven's ID popped up. In the other two screens, Zach multitasked a series of commands he'd used so many times they'd become muscle memory. Each ID chip was hardwired for one set of data, but you could overwrite it if you knew the security protocols. Except, without a new identity ready to go, doing so would only erase the original and destroy the chip.

Zach rushed through the first part of the process. The smaller screen flashed, and Raven's image and personal details disappeared.

Now came the hard part. He had ninety seconds to attach a new identity to the chip. If he missed that window, it would shut down and become inoperable.

The third screen displayed the public portal for the Census Department, which stored and maintained all records of births, deaths, and the personal identifiers associated with them. Zach accessed the staff portal, logged in with the credentials his pre-EMC-self had provided, then copied Raven's chip ID and searched it in the system. It had a thirty-nine-digit personal identifier number which now flashed an error, since Zach had removed it from the chip.

He quickly typed in his own. His image and a personal profile for a man named Jaxon Pluck filled the screen. Zach confirmed the sync and watched the details fill in for the chip's readout.

Hard part done.

He shut down the CD portal and accessed the banking institute, where Mr. Pluck had an account. It was one of four for this identity alone. The readout showed a staggering total balance and a history of three monthly interest payments that the institute had processed since the account's creation. One of those payments was more than enough to cover the debt he owed to Teacher.

He transferred the six million directly into Teacher's account, confirmed that it went through, and then shut down the portal.

"Did that just happen?"

Different guard. Apparently, not everyone liked the same team.

Zach winked at him, then closed Teacher's account to bring up a different set of consoles. It took some creative maneuvering to appropriate four municipal hovers from the fleet for his own purposes. He flagged them as out of service, then scheduled them for repairs. The last step was to hijack the delivery location so they would come to him, rather than their designated service centers.

Since Teacher hadn't bothered to give him his preferred locations, Zach selected the one they'd used to enter the tunnels, then three more where the city schematic indicated utility tunnel access points nearby.

And because the man hadn't told him where they all wanted to go, either, Zach programmed each one to take a different route to the same place: the nearest shuttleport.

By then, Teacher and Penelope had joined the three guards, staring at the screen with their mouths hanging open.

But Zach wasn't finished. The last and most important thing he needed to do was take care of himself and Raven. He hacked the Kalchama municipal agency and accessed the registrar, where transport manufacturers reported their inventory and every new owner. There weren't a lot of options to choose from, but Zach wasn't picky. He selected a standard model in gray that had been sitting in the database for several months and overwrote the record to show Jaxon Pluck as the new owner, with a home address in the city of Petrus, five hundred miles from Kalchama.

While working out the details for immediate delivery and reserving a hotel room in Petrus, Zach felt his audience regain their senses and turn their attention to him.

"The hovers will arrive in thirty-two hours," he told them while he worked. "That's how long you have to get your people together at the four pickup points. Hovers will be there on time, but they'll only wait for two hours before they take off again. Whoever isn't on board by then is getting left behind. I suggest you get moving."

"Bale. Quincy. Go," Penelope ordered.

The two guards she named took off running.

Good. It meant that Penelope wasn't just Teacher's right hand. She'd established enough authority with their people to keep them organized. Teacher had groomed her well. It might just save all their lives.

And he was done. The Starlight Hotel in Petrus would be expecting Mr. Pluck before midnight. His appropriated transport was on its way, and it was time for Zach to get going. He hopped out of the hole and put the console pad into Teacher's hands, making sure his twisted fingers were securely curled around it before he let go.

Then he turned to Raven. She hadn't moved a muscle the entire time. Zach wanted to tear the sedative patch off her and shake her awake, but he had no way of gauging her state of mind, and he needed them both to be in a secure location before he woke her into a potential meltdown.

Scooping her up into his arms, he turned to find his way blocked by the last guard and Penelope. She aimed his stolen Shadow gun at his face.

"Our bargain is finished," he told her.

"You're coming with us," she informed him.

"Penelope!" Teacher snapped.

"If the Shadows want him, they'll come for him! They'll find us, and if we can't hand him over, they'll kill us all."

So suicidally naïve. As if the Shadows didn't already have a well-established reputation of "shoot first and move on."

Zach sighed. "You now have thirty-one hours and fifty-five minutes to get your shit together so they *won't* find you. You'll need every second. Might wanna stop wasting them."

"Penelope," Teacher said, "put the gun down. He paid more than his fair share. We are people of our word. And we don't take hostages."

Penelope didn't hear him. Seeing Zach do his thing with the com so quickly had freaked her out in a bad way. He wasn't a mark to her anymore. He was a threat. Possibly a Shadow. And she'd brought him into their midst. Eyes wide, nostrils flared, she was a twitch away from squeezing the trigger on a gun that shook like a leaf in her grip. "It's not enough," she said. "Can't you see? He's put all of us in danger!"

"Let it go," Zach said gently. "It's done. I'm walking out of here—around you or through you. That's the only choice you have left."

"Yeah?" The gun's barrel tilted lower. "What if I choose to take out your not-yet-wife?"

Wrong thing to say.

Zach felt the familiar chill of absolute apathy settling over his brain. His vision tunneled until all he saw was Penelope and her gun. Not a person, not a victim, not a survivor. An active threat he needed to eliminate.

In a split second, he knew how this could play out. He'd have to absorb the first shot to keep Raven safe. But once he set her down, Penelope's arm would be forfeit. The last guard would drop immediately after her with a hole through his forehead. If Teacher didn't drop on his own by then, Zach wouldn't waste a shot on him. Easier to snap his neck.

No one out in the tunnel would notice a thing.

But Zach would likely need to shoot his way out past the other guards—

Who are you?

My name is Zachary VanWarren, he reminded himself. *I am not what I was made to be. I can choose what needs to be done.*

He fought back the Shadow instincts programmed into him since birth, grasping for anything he could to remember that these people were not his enemy. They were just desperate and scared, and needed help.

Four credits.

One last goodbye.

Zach latched onto that thought and held on for all he was worth. His body didn't throttle down, but at least his jaw unclenched enough to allow him to speak. "You harm one hair on her head, and I will rip out your spine with my bare hands and use your bones to tear your people into ribbons." He let her see the full weight of his wrath in his eyes as he stared her down, his lips curling away from his teeth in a feral snarl he couldn't hold back. His arms were full of precious cargo; he couldn't throttle the bitch. But he could trip her and crush her throat beneath his foot in an instant.

Penelope's pupils shot wide, and she whimpered, frozen in fear.

"*Move,*" he growled, barreling past her before she could comply.

The verbal vitriol she hurled at his back became warbled noise as Zach retraced their path back out into the main tunnel and to the staircase that marked his exit. He breathed down the rage, forcing his fingers to unclench from their bruising grip on Raven's sleeping form.

One breath at a time. One marching step at a time. He counted them to keep himself on track and on mission.

To keep the Shadow from breaking through and drenching their sorry little world in blood.

30

January 17, 3040 – Somewhere Else

Bright lights dragged him back to consciousness. His eyes kept want-ing to roll back in his skull, but the fingers prying open the right one refused to let him slip back into the void.

"Pupils responsive."

"*Mmph*," he groaned, straining away from the light. His limbs were too heavy to lift. His head ached like a son of a bitch and, even though he couldn't see much, he felt the whole world spinning and whirling beneath him.

Someone gripped him by the chin and angled his head in a different direction.

He squinted at the floating blur of color vaguely shaped like a hu-man being.

"Open your eyes, soldier."

He thought they already were…

"Do you understand me?"

He frowned, blinking hard to clear the fog and focus on the face in front of him. A hard face, with cold eyes and a burn scar marring the right side, melting the outer edge of her eye almost shut. He tried to nod, but her grip wouldn't let him. He moved his eyes up and down to confirm. The slight motion set the whole world atilt.

"Mental faculties appear functional," someone else said.

The hard woman released his face and straightened. "Do you know where you are?"

He gripped the armrests to steady himself. Why couldn't he get his bearings? Fuck, his head was killing him.

"Answer me," the woman demanded.

What was the question?

"Do you know where you are?"

His tongue stuck to the roof of his mouth. He shook his head in the negative.

"Do you know *who* you are?"

He opened his mouth to introduce himself and came up blank. The absence of an identity lodged in his throat and made his insides tingle in unpleasant, unnerving flutters. Something was wrong with him. He couldn't remember.

"Your name is Hansel Atwater."

"Hhh…Han…sel." That sounded right. It fit into the empty slot in his mind where a name should be. He unclenched with relief. Hansel Atwater. Yes, that was him. He was…

Who was he?

"You are a soldier in the Shadow army," the woman supplied. "You've been assigned to outpost Yellow Six. I am Commander Greives. You'll be reporting to me going forward. Is that understood?"

"Yes, M'm." She knew him. She could tell him why he was there, what'd happened to him. He appeared to be in a medical facility of some sort. Maybe he'd been injured in combat, being a soldier and all.

But that factoid didn't fit into the occupation void in his mind. He didn't feel like a soldier. Just the idea of soldiering sent a shiver down his spine. The thought of raising a weapon and taking someone's life…

Dead bodies tossed on a pile. People lining up to be next. Soldiers in dark blue uniforms shooting guns that burned holes through them…

The CO nodded to someone else. "Commence testing."

A sharp zing of sensation zapped through his brain and down his spine, snapping his body taut. It wasn't quite pain. It was so much worse than that.

"Initiating warm-up sequence."

Hansel's body sat up straight on the gurney. Despite the whole world still spinning out of control, his ass remained firmly planted, and his shoulders pulled back.

"What…?"

He hopped off the gurney, bare feet slapping against the cold ground.

Then his knees bent into a squat, followed by four more.

"The hell is this?"

Snapping upright, he spun sideways and dropped all the way forward into a pushup.

"Relax, soldier. Don't fight it."

Fight what? What the hell was happening to him? Why couldn't he stop?

After five pushups, his feet kicked up off the ground into a handstand, then his elbows bent and he tucked in his chin, rolling smoothly through the motion he had no control over. It kicked him upright and to his feet, pivoting back toward the scarred Commander Greives into a regulation-perfect salute he had no memory of ever performing before in his entire life.

And all the while, Hansel felt every stretch, flex, and impact, like an observer completely detached from inside his own physical shell.

"Test complete."

Whatever force had taken hold of him released, and Hansel slumped over sideways, catching himself against the gurney with arms as limp as overcooked noodles. His heart tried to beat its way out of his chest. His fingers and toes tingled with residual electricity. He couldn't feel his mouth, but his head continued to spin and spin, jumbling thoughts into each other until nothing made sense.

"Finally. I was starting to think this whole batch was defective."

"W-what's happening? What have you done to me?"

"We made you a soldier," Commander Greives snapped. "We gave you purpose."

His empty stomach clenched tight. "Purpose?"

"You will stand side by side with your brothers and sisters in arms against the greatest threat mankind has ever faced."

Hansel dragged his left foot closer, pressed the ball of it into the cold floor, reacquainting himself with his own body. It still felt disconnected, like the control he'd regained was a momentary illusion. He reached a numb hand to rub his vision straight again, and barked in pain as his fingers brushed against something hard embedded in his temple.

The other person in the room stepped around him into the light. A man with his head shaved bald and shiny, and a set of medical scanner specs perched on the tip of his wide nose. He tilted Hansel's face at an angle. "The application site will be sore for the next few days. Try not to touch it too much."

"You have until nineteen hundred hours tomorrow to rest up and get your effects in order," Commander Greives said.

Hansel made every effort to straighten and face her again. That's what soldiers were supposed to do, wasn't it? Face their CO when receiving orders. It embarrassed him how much he struggled to stand upright and keep still. It shamed him that he had to face Greives dressed in stained patient clothes instead of his uniform.

He shuddered at the thought of putting one on.

"I expect you to be in your assigned seat for take-off at twenty-two hundred. Do you understand?"

"Yes, Ma'am," he replied, fighting not to sway on his feet. Sleep. He needed sleep. A few hours of rest, and maybe a pain patch or two to get this damned headache under control so he could think again, and remember who the hell he was, and what mission he'd been assigned to. It would all fall into place eventually, Hansel was sure of it. He just needed to get some rest.

"Good." Commander Greives nodded to the medic. "Dismissed."

The unfamiliar force once again zapped through his limbs, taking over his body. It made him execute another salute, then marched him out of the tent and along the yellow line to his bunk in the barracks.

It wouldn't let him stray from his assigned path a single inch.

It wouldn't even let him turn his head to see the pile of corpses get scooped up by an excavator bot and carted out of the hangar.

But it couldn't stop his thoughts from churning. *Who am I? Who am I? Who am I?*

31

Consciousness crept in on the weight of air dragging into Raven's lungs. Each breath left her on an exhausted sigh, and she had to force herself to take the next one.

The dull ache in her head reminded her that she was not okay.

It wasn't until she tried to move that she remembered how badly she'd burned out.

That's when she noticed the silence in her mind.

Raven opened her eyes.

A mural of clouds across a cerulean sky adorned the ceiling above her. Recessed lighting strips on all sides showcased the tranquil artwork and illuminated the room.

"Hello, Blackbird."

Raven turned her head, and the whole world spun. She couldn't keep her moan in check if she tried.

Zach came to her immediately and snaked one strong arm beneath her shoulders. She didn't have the strength to fight him as he practically draped her over him like a doll. "Easy, I've got you."

She felt a sticky patch adhere to the back of her neck, and then he massaged her nape and shoulder, somehow knowing exactly where to dig his thumb to work out the aches.

Mercifully, the dizziness began to subside. "Where are we?" she tried to say, but it came out as, "Whrr'we?"

"Petrus," he said, rubbing down the sides of her spine, working sensation back into her sleeping body. "I got us a penthouse suite. Hundred and fiftieth floor. Figured you could use some distance when you woke up. How do you feel?"

"Mmph."

His chuckle nudged her a little closer to awareness. "You want to see something beautiful?"

She'd give her right arm to see something other than the memory of Ripley bleeding on the quarantine room floor. Raven nodded against his shoulder.

Zach abandoned his massage, and she instantly regretted her decision. The massive bed had a duvet just as big and very fluffy. Without releasing his hold on her, Zach yanked on it until something ripped. He folded it to double thickness and bundled her in it, then picked her up and carried her through a door from delicious heat to a freezing darkness.

"Look up," he said.

Raven turned her head to see.

Breath left her.

The sky was on fire with streams of color. Bright whites and gentle blues streaked through clouds of pink and orange. Curling curtains of shimmering light weaved through the air, and on the hundred and fiftieth floor, they had an unobstructed view. The entire sky from horizon to horizon domed above them, with the sleeping giant, Vesta, dominating its own corner.

They were still on Valhale 602.

"There were Shadows," she said.

"They're dead." Surely, not all of them.

But, "My people?"

Zach's long silence broke her heart before he even spoke the words. "Dead, too. I'm sorry, Blackbird."

Raven shook her head. She refused to accept that. Someone must have survived. There'd been alarms, and people running for their lives. At least some of them must have made it to the bunkers. And a good number of them had been evacuating already when Raven had gone to see Zach. They'd made it out. She was sure of it.

"I need to make a call." The SU had an emergency dispatch on every world. If she called them, they'd be able to connect her with Darrow. He had to be alive.

If not…

"Take a minute," Zach said softly. "Get your legs under you first before you get knocked down again."

So she did. She watched the sky perform its colorful dance and breathed the wintry chill into her lungs until it didn't take as much effort anymore. She allowed Zach to cradle her while she slowly worked out her limbs. Toes and fingers first, then wrist and ankles.

By the time she managed to straighten her knees with the thick duvet weighing down her legs, her face was numb from the cold.

Zach took her back inside and set her down on the edge of the bed. Crouching before her as he had done in his mind-world once, he studied her so intensely that Raven wanted to squirm. She was still too numb to do much more than meet his gaze, but she felt invaded by it as if he could read her down to her weary soul.

Then his hands cupped her face, long fingers brushing into her hair, and he closed the distance between them, pressing his mouth to hers. He didn't force it. Didn't demand anything. His lips massaged hers with a patience that bordered on reverence, and she knew that if she made the smallest move to retreat, he would stop immediately.

She didn't want him to.

Instead of pulling away, she leaned into him, parting her lips and holding her breath.

His sigh puffed across her mouth. The pressure of his kiss increased the slightest bit, and he caught her lower lip between his. But when she would have expected him to take her invitation and ravage her mouth until it bruised, Zach surprised her yet again. *He* pulled away, just enough to break the kiss. He nudged her nose with his, touching his forehead to hers in the process, then let her go and sat back on his heels in front of her.

"Why did you do that?" she asked, her lips still tingling for more.

"Because going through something bad doesn't hurt nearly as much as missing out on something good." He said it as a statement of absolute truth, but his eyebrows twitched just a little, as if he hadn't accepted it himself until he'd just said it.

Swaddled in her cocoon, Raven's fingers curled into the duvet until her nailbeds hurt. "I owe you a name."

Zach sighed. "Later. You must be starving." He pushed to his feet and turned away. "I ordered us room serv—"

"Geraldine VanWarren."

He stopped, his shoulders drooping. "I know. I found her while you were sleeping."

She fought her arm free of the covers. "And?"

"And nothing. She died, her family had her cremated, and shot the remains into space in some fucking PR spectacle for her fans." The tray cover he'd picked up slammed down on the table, rattling a lot of silverware. "And I still remember fuck-all about her. Except a whole lot of regret."

Geraldine VanWarren had died in the attack on the family's Ela estate just a few months ago. Whether he remembered or not, the wound of her passing was clearly still fresh.

"I'm sorry for your loss," she said, and meant it.

Zach dipped his chin as if to nod, but ended up hanging his head in silence.

Nothing Raven said or did right now would make him hurt less. Grief didn't work like that. No amount of other people's sympathy could make it go away. Sometimes, it just made things worse. Raven knew that all too well.

She untangled her legs from the covers, then carefully touched her bare feet to the floor and stood up. Her knees didn't buckle—progress—but she was as weak as a baby bird, and just staying upright took everything she had.

Zach crossed the room in a second, taking hold of her hips to keep her steady. "Where to?"

"Bathroom."

He grinned at her. "Need help in there?"

Raven glared. "No." Considering how not-dirty she felt, she suspected he'd already taken the liberty of bathing her at least once while she'd been unconscious. She must have needed it and should probably thank him for not leaving her to sleep in her own filth. But that didn't mean she wanted to get naked around him while conscious. The last thing she wanted right now was a visual comparison between his muscular perfection and her feeble, scarred body and missing limb.

He grinned wider and waggled an eyebrow. "How 'bout some company?"

"What is this?" she blurted out.

"What do you mean?"

"I mean, what are you after? It made sense in Chairo. The prisoner trying to seduce his captor—I got that. But you're free now. You don't need me anymore. Hell, you didn't even need to save me." Her voice wavered on the last part as she remembered that was exactly what he'd done. Raven should have been dead back there. Once he'd woken up, Zach had had no reason to take her. He'd compromised his own escape by taking the burden of her with him.

Knowing what he would have faced if the Shadows had captured him, it begged the question, "Why did you save me?"

He lowered his head to stare straight into her eyes. "I. Like. You."

"I'm your interrogator."

Zach rolled his eyes and turned her sideways, shifting behind her. Hands still on her hips, he ordered, "Left, right, left," as he walked her across the suite to the bathroom.

It had an actual bathtub, with spigots for running water. Senseless luxury for the ultra-rich on a moon with such water scarcity that ordinary people hoarded their drinking rations. He left her beside the hip-high vanity while he ran a hot bath for her and placed the largest towel on the warming shelf. Then he came back and grasped the hem of her top. "Arm up."

Raven slapped his hands away. "I can undress myself, thank you."

He *pouted* at her. "Killjoy." Instead of leaving, he turned his back. "Fine, go ahead. Deprive me of what little delight I still have in life."

"You're just gonna stand there?"

"The bathtub doesn't have handles, and you're still unsteady. I'm staying to make sure you don't slip and break your neck getting in and out."

"With your back turned," she deadpanned.

He looked at her over his shoulder. "I can turn around, if you want."

"You're trying to deflect your grief with humor. It won't—"

Zach threw his head back and growl-sighed in frustration. "You wanna talk about deflection? Look in the mirror, Blackbird. You're the only person I know who'd go playing hide-and-seek with the obvious. Woman, you've been inside my head."

"And we both know your head is nothing as it should be."

"Have you never heard of Occam's Razor before?"

"Disproven in the twenty-eight hundreds."

He stared at her.

Raven tipped her chin up. She could outstubborn a rock and, her minor slip of self-control aside, she wasn't about to let him through her defenses. They were up for a reason.

"I see. You still think I'm playing you."

"Aren't you?" Of course he was! The only question was, for what purpose? What more could he want from the SU? They'd already established they couldn't keep him safe from the Shadows. He was better off on his own.

And no, that didn't sting. At all.

"You still want something from us. You're still grieving. You still don't know me. Men like you—"

"There are no men like me. There's only me. And this should be the easiest thing in the world, but since you insist on making it difficult, let's do that. I still want something from the SU, I'm still grieving, I still don't know you—*I still like you.* What if all four are true at the same time?"

Raven opened her mouth to deliver a witty comeback, only to realize she didn't have one.

"Have a ponder on that while you bathe. I'll wait outside." But before he closed the door, he shot back, "By the way, the tub has massage jets. Do with that information what you will."

The soap bottle she threw at him thunked against the door as it clicked shut.

She heard him laughing on the other side.

32

It wasn't until Raven got out of the bath, feeling semi-human and hollow with hunger, that she remembered the concept of clothes. More specifically, the ones she'd woken up wearing, which she had no intention of putting on ever again.

The oversized bath towel would cover her from shoulder to knee, although, after Zach's last comment, she was tempted to walk out naked and dripping wet, to mess with his head the same way he'd been messing with hers this whole time.

Apparently, he wasn't finished, because he'd left a small stack of folded fabric sitting on the corner of the vanity closest to the door. Raven was pretty sure it hadn't been there when she'd walked into the bathroom. The deep, blood-red fabric on top of pale marble would have been hard to overlook.

She hooked her finger into a fold and tugged, unfolding barely a few inches of a silky, *sleeveless* camisole. Detailed stitching hemmed the bottom edge, and black, feather-shaped embroideries trimmed the neckline at the front in a dramatic accent.

Raven closed her eyes and reached deeper than she ever had for the last crumbs of patience she possessed. She draped the top over a towel rack and picked up the second part of the outfit, a pair of skintight pants in swirling shades of black and gray. No zippers, buttons, loops, or clasps. And no underwear.

Walk out naked and dripping wet, or let him dress her in an outfit that would leave her exposed and vulnerable?

Either way, he'd won this round.

Shaking her head, Raven stepped into the pants and pulled them up. Yep. Like a glove. The material felt like a second skin against her body, seamless and smooth from the high waist to the beaded bottom cuffs that hugged her ankles. She might as well have been naked. But they were so lusciously easy to put on with one hand.

The top was also skintight and soft enough to outline *everything* in detail, leaving far too much of her exposed. But now that it was on, the outfit felt more like a winter base layer than anything else. Harsh colors notwithstanding, the silken fabric hugged her form as if it had been made just for her, and Raven hated that she didn't hate it. Before the accident had left her mutilated, she might have even chosen to wear something like this herself.

But that had been another life.

She tugged a little here and there to align the seams along her ribs, keeping her gaze firmly down and away from the mirror. Without sleeves, the angry scars of her amputation were on full display, and the bold red top accentuated the jagged maroon ridges of her ruined flesh.

The surgeons had preserved as much of her anatomy as they could in preparation for what everyone had assumed would be Raven's eventual augmentation surgery. They hadn't done any cosmetic repairs. Why bother when they would all disappear once her bionic arm was properly grafted?

Pure agony shot down the limb no longer attached to her, phantom bone fragments grinding, stabbing into non-existent muscles. Fingers cramped into claws that had turned blue hours ago, blood trickling between the swollen knuckles.

Raven's head swam, and she fell against the vanity, bracing her hand on its surface as she forced air through her raw throat into her lungs. *Look up.*

Another grinding twist, a desperate, wrenching pull that popped the shoulder joint out of its socket.

Look up!

Raven gritted her teeth as a wretched scream shuddered through her mind. Her knees locked, keeping her upright, but her body shook so hard her hand began to slip.

LOOK UP!

With a whimper, she did, locking onto her own reflection, the dark shadows beneath her glistening eyes, the wet strands of black hair sticking to her green-tinged cheeks, the pained pinch of her mouth.

And the rough, scarred, bumpy skin where an arm should have been.

The pain abruptly ceased, and her throat opened, turning her wheeze into a sob.

Raven collapsed onto the covered toilet seat, bending to put her head between her knees as her body slowly remembered it wasn't pinned inside a shattered transport anymore.

Eventually, the shaking stopped, too, and her heartbeat slowed to a more reasonable rhythm. She raised herself in slow degrees, pausing every few inches to fight off the darkness of a headrush.

Deep breath in. Push up to stand.

Deep breath out. Unclench fist.

Deep breath in. Tuck stubborn strands of hair behind the ears.

Deep breath out. *And we move on.*

Raven shoved the memories back into the dark abyss where they belonged, schooled her face into a neutral mask, and walked out of the bathroom with her head held high.

"Thank you for the clothes," she said toward the entertainment area where Zach slouched on the couch. He was halfway melted down the seat, his legs spread wide, and his head against the backrest turned far to the side as he watched her emerge. "I will be discarding them at the earliest opportunity."

He winced. "Massage jets didn't work, huh?"

Raven pulled the blanket off an armchair to drape around herself. He might have bumped up the temperature inside the room to sweltering levels, but full winter still howled outside the glass doors, and every time she looked that way, it gave her chills. The hunger and residual flashback nausea didn't help, either.

"I'm ready to make that call now, if you don't mind." The sooner they returned and the SU replanted somewhere safe, the sooner they could start strategizing the rebuild.

Zach's expression shuttered as he stared at her for a moment longer than necessary. Taking it as a challenge, Raven held his gaze head-on. But it seemed he wasn't trying to intimidate her. After a tense moment, he sighed and dropped his chin forward. He took a breath to speak, then shook his head. "You should eat something. Plenty of food on the table."

What was it with him constantly trying to feed her? "Will you take the first bite?"

His mouth quirked. "If it'll get you to swallow, I'll even pre-digest it for you."

"Ew!"

Zach chuckled, but there was precious little humor in it. "You know, I don't know what you did to me back in Chairo, but I think it had some unintended side effects."

"What do you mean?"

He tapped the back of his head. "I felt you just now."

Her face went cold.

"Never happened before," he quickly amended. "But I could tell something happened to you. Felt like a bunch of insects scratching on the inside of my skull."

He'd felt her flashback in the bathroom.

There was no way this man didn't have some form of telepathy. Shielding him should have cut him off from other minds, not connected him...

Oh, damn, she'd fucked up.

She'd constructed a standard shield, but, on an unknown architecture, 'standard' didn't exist. A mind like Zach's could have incorporated it into his own framework in any number of different ways.

Raven's bare foot slid back an inch at the idea. The shield was her creation. It should have stayed *hers*. If he could sense her, it clearly hadn't. Would she even be able to dismantle it now? What if she ended up making it worse?

Words like *hive mind* and *subjugated will* stabbed cold terror all the way into her soul.

Zach shoved his fingers through his hair. "I know something's wrong. And I know you won't tell me what it is. But I'd consider it a kindness if you could calm down a bit so I can figure out a way to manage this."

Raven backed up another step, and Zach's expression skewed a little as if in pain. She turned her back on him and took a seat at the dining table, laid out with a feast fit for an army. The sight of it clenched her stomach tighter.

"Give me a minute." This was bad. She needed to get control of herself before she ended up irrevocably mind-melded.

Raven closed her eyes and set her breath to a meditative rhythm, focusing on the feel of air flowing in and out of her lungs, the sensation of her ribs expanding and contracting, her weight sinking through her hips into the cushy chair. Her mind was still raw from her burnout. Under normal circumstances, a telepath would be sequestered for days to allow their mind to recover in a safe environment. It was a mental equivalent of lounging around naked to heal from a sunburn before being forced to put on a scratchy uniform again.

Raven didn't have that luxury. If Zach could feel her, it wasn't safe for her to stay open anymore. It hurt to force herself back behind her shields, but she kept breathing, shrugging on layer after soft layer to rebuild her protections.

Zach's sigh told her she was on the right track. His palpable relief made her muscles loosen in response, even as a headache bloomed at the base of her neck despite the pain patch he'd put on her earlier.

She kept it up for a few more breaths, putting a little more mental distance between herself and the rest of the world.

Calm…

Calm…

Everything was fine. Nothing to worry about. Just a little wrinkle. No big deal. They were on the one hundred and fiftieth floor. Quick way out if she ended up needing one.

Another minute, and she felt almost back to herself. Raven took two more just to be sure. Then she braced herself, opened a small door in her mind, and reached out to Zach's. She latched onto her mental signature embedded in the shield she'd created and traced along its surface, checking its integrity.

No…

The smooth eggshell she'd constructed was shattered into pieces that had shrunk along the surface of Zach's mind. Something else filled the fissures. It was liquid and sharp at the same time. Just as strong, but more aggressive. It ate away at her shield, absorbed it, and turned it into something that more closely resembled spikes or briars.

Zach wasn't *connecting* to her. He was using her shield's structure and frequency to *tune in* to her. She'd never seen anything like it.

Raven pressed against a section of her shield—there wasn't much of it left—and traced the edge where it met with Zach's construct. The three closest spikes swiveled toward her, stabbing longer and forcing her into retreat. Figured that a soldier's best defense would be offensive.

A rustle of movement in the room pulled her partway into her physical self long enough to hear Zach say, "I felt that."

Her position was too precarious for distractions. Raven shut out the real world and focused on her shrinking shield. It felt safe enough in the center of the largest patch—for about five seconds until Zach's warped creation leaped toward her from all sides, shrinking the patch to half its size, the surrounding spikes all pointing directly at her.

She jerked back to her physical self, her eyes snapping open.

Zach was across from her, hands splayed between serving dishes as he leaned over the table, frowning. "What happened? You pulled away."

"I…" Where to even begin to explain? "I think you need to make a decision. And I think it needs to be quick."

A hard mask shuttered over his features, and he became a stranger. A Shadow in full battle mode. "Go on." It sounded like a warning, rather than an invitation.

"How badly do you want to be a mind reader?"

He drew back. "Pardon?"

"It's not a side effect, what you're feeling. I think you may be a latent telepath." And holy shit, did that throw her for a loop. "You may have been triggered when we started scanning you, but your brain couldn't fully activate the ability until the EMC chemicals got detoxed out of your system." It would explain his evolution of personhood and why it accelerated so rapidly once he went into the tank.

"The problem is, your mind doesn't have any instructions for what to do with it, so it's using what I gave you as a guide. And what I gave you is a shield. It feels like your mind is building over it and…making modifications." In a disturbingly Shadow way.

"Shields keep people out," he said. "So how come I can feel you?"

"My shield is embedded with my mental frequency, which could be why. In a way, it's still part of me and, since it's the only available signal you have, your mind automatically wants to seek it out. Telepathy is connection. Most of us don't work to create it; we struggle to set boundaries so we don't lose ourselves in it. Without the shield, you'd probably be picking up on a whole lot of noise from a whole lot of people right now."

"That doesn't sound pleasant."

"It's not. It can drive you insane if left untreated—un*trained*. But you have my shield, which is locked to keep others out and, by extension, it's keeping you in. If I unlock it, your potential will be limitless, except you'll already have the makings of some very aggressive protections."

A good telepath with solid shields could detect when someone tried to breach them. The stronger the shield, the better a telepath's ability to withstand an assault. If attacked, the standard strategy was to repel the attacker with a blunt force *shove*. At most, it could stun an intrusive telepath, maybe knock them out. But they would eventually recover.

But here, again, Zach just had to be different. When he'd sensed her telepathic touch, his shield had engaged not to remove the threat but to *destroy* it. Take no prisoners, leave no witnesses. Typical Shadow. He was turning his mind into a death trap.

"If I don't unlock it in time," she continued, "I don't know what will happen. It might end up being just you and me. To whatever extent you allow. You might never be able to read anyone else."

"And no one else would be able to read me."

She nodded once. "Correct."

"Can *you* still get in?"

"I don't know. While a piece of my architecture remains intact, maybe. Once it's gone…" She shrugged. Ultimately, it would be up to Zach. If he decided he didn't want her in his head, the lightest brush against those shields could leave her mentally maimed or worse.

"Try." His Shadow mask was still in place, his arms rigid, biceps twitching. He was tense, but not aggressive. It wasn't a warning. Not quite an invitation, either.

Raven closed her eyes and braced herself for a world of pain as she reached out to his mind again. The pieces of her shield had shrunk a little more, and now the liquid spikes stretched a lot longer, undulating like antennae seeking an intruder. *This is gonna hurt…*

She gave herself a few seconds to build up some courage. Then she reached out to the spikes.

And they *caught* her. Sharp spears turned into tentacles that curled around her and pulled her through to the firelit chamber she'd come to know as well as her own bedroom.

And there was Zach, standing just out of arm's reach, every line in his body rigid with tension, while a winter storm howled through the night outside. "You can get through," he said, some of the tension leaving his stance as the storm abruptly quieted.

Raven pulled out, returning to herself with a simple breath. Unharmed. "I can get through—for now," she said.

"How long before there's no going back?"

Raven split her focus to track the progression without leaving herself vulnerable. "Minutes," she reported. The spiked shield had consumed most of hers in the time it had taken her to make the trip in and out. "It's moving faster now." Almost as if his conscious knowledge of the shield sped up its evolution. "You need to make a choice, Zach. Once my shield goes, so does my key."

But he didn't. He stayed right where he was, those fathomless dark eyes watching her with a calm she didn't feel.

"Zach…"

The corner of his mouth twitched a little, the Shadow mask slipping just enough to soften his gaze. "I do like that name."

Slivers of her shield remained. "Seconds left."

Gone.

Raven exhaled a shuddering breath, blinked herself fully back into her body.

Zach hadn't moved an inch. But the Shadow was gone. "Try again."

The little she'd done so far had already taken a toll on her. It was dangerous to push so soon after a burnout. But, for both their sakes, Raven needed to know. If he'd wanted to kill her, he would have already, she reminded herself.

"I know your touch," Zach said. Was he trying to put her at ease? "I know *you.*"

Raven's mouth went dry. Deep breath in. Deep breath out. She closed her eyes.

Her shield was gone. Zach's mindscape had cocooned itself in a shimmery, quicksilver web of sharp blades. And he wanted her to fall on them.

If he wanted to kill me, he would have.

The thought reflected off his shield right back to her, multiplied by a dozen echoes.

"Down feathers," Zach said. "Blackbird, you don't need a key. You *are* the key."

Without meaning to, Raven drifted closer, sinking toward those deadly spikes faster and faster, as they pulled her in. At the last second, a breath before they touched her, the spikes *bent* the same way they had before, wrapping around her. She got lost in a thousand discordant reflections before the squeeze of Zach's shields turned into the solid brace of his arms around her. The slide of quicksilver over her telepathic self became a tangle of silken sheets.

He'd pulled her straight into his fantasy. Raven's world spun as he rolled them to put himself beneath her, one arm banding around her hips to hold her close, his free hand roaming over her back in long, reverent strokes. His mouth was on her shoulder, the side of her neck, her jaw.

His knees drew up, hitching her higher, spreading her legs wider—

Raven gasped and pulled out in a rush. She met no resistance, melting out of his arms and through his shields as if they weren't there at all.

"Never said I wouldn't play dirty," Zach said, his eyes dancing.

33

"One problem solved."

And her cheeks finally had some color in them. For a minute there, Zach had worried she'd collapse again.

Still too pale, though. She needed to eat something.

"Why did you do that?"

"To prove a point."

Raven gaped at him. "Are you insane? You just gave up one of the most effective weapons in the universe. To *prove a point*? What point? That you're an idiot?"

"First, words hurt, Blackbird. You wound me. Deeply. I may never recover. Second, I'm not going to miss what I never had." But all he really needed was the potential and a strong enough desire to make it work. It was *his* shield now, after all. "Third, I would think by now you know me well enough to understand that I don't do things on a whim. You said, 'just you and me,' and I took you at your word. I showed *trust*. That was the point. You and me. Starting to get it now?"

He chucked her under the chin to close her gaping mouth before he did something she wasn't ready for. Speechless Raven was adorable. But she still needed to eat.

Zach picked up a fork and speared a piece of juicy steak he'd cut up for her.

She stared at him, her eyes filled with too many emotions for him to sort through, but the crawling sensation in his mind had faded, so he figured she couldn't be too upset. Still, if he tried to hand-feed her, she'd hand him his ass. So instead, he took the bite for himself, enjoying her eyes on him while he chewed.

Then, just to mess with her, he leaned in to pass the masticated meat into her mouth.

He tried not to laugh when she slapped her hand over his face and pushed him away. "Not funny."

It was a little funny. Zach caught her wrist and nuzzled into her palm. "Will you eat by yourself?"

Raven scowled. "Not without my hand."

Zach debated his options for this scenario, not finding one he didn't like. "I can work with that."

"Let go of my hand!"

With great reluctance, he did. But only because he needed her to get some sustenance into her body. Her arm felt as delicate as a bird's wing. He'd break it if he squeezed too hard. "It's the eighteenth of January. You've been out for days with only IV nutrition to keep you functioning. You need to eat."

Raven reached for a half-gallon pitcher of juice. Zach slapped her hand away and poured her a glass. Watching the damned thing shake in her grip as she brought it to her lips, confirmed he'd made the right call. While she drank, he picked up a plate and piled it with a little bit of everything. Small pieces she wouldn't have to work too hard to chew. Simple foods that her body wouldn't have to struggle to digest. He'd hand-selected every dish, intimately familiar with how much starvation fucking sucked.

At least she didn't protest when he set the plate before her and took his seat with a glass of water for himself. A quick frown furrowed her brows before she picked up her fork.

"What?"

She shook her head. "Nothing."

"*What?*" he pushed. Something clearly bothered her. And it wasn't the *just you and me* thing.

The fork's tines pushed food around on her plate, not picking up a single piece. She had two minutes before he would take it out of her hand and feed her himself, whether she liked it or not. Her hunger clawed at *his* gut. He wasn't above tying her down and making shuttle noises if it got her to eat.

"It's just… The last time someone put this much effort into taking care of me, I was in a hospital bed, half dead and half out of my mind."

"Been there myself a few times." Though his medical team had mainly consisted of preprogrammed bots bringing him food and relaying the doctor's orders for PT. He hadn't been afforded the option of non-compliance.

Raven shrugged. "Feels weird."

Finally, she forked some food into her mouth, and Zach unclenched. He watched her take small bites and chew for ages before swallowing each one. Seemed she was no stranger to this, either. She went out of her way not to look at him while she ate, which allowed him to study her at his leisure.

Her hair was still wet from her bath, the spiky ends teasing just past the top of her shoulder. She looked exhausted, but her color improved with every sip and bite. In minutes, her lips returned to their natural raspberry red, and her cheeks flushed a little as her body began to regain enough energy to produce some heat of its own. The blanket she'd bundled around herself drooped in deference.

"Red suits you," he said, staring at the points of her nipples poking through the fabric of her top. "You should wear it more often." The outfit he'd chosen for her had all but short-circuited his brain when she'd come out of the bathroom. Clothes didn't *make* a person, but when worn well, they sure as shit did a fine job of accentuating one. Raven made him jealous of the scraps of fabric so lovingly wrapped around her. She was a work of art, finally peeled free of the confines of that godawful black uniform. Even the way she moved in it was different. Looser, more fluid. It made him want to play some music to see if she'd dance.

Raven pulled the blanket tighter around her left shoulder.

"Don't." The word was out before he could stop it. He understood why she hid her left side. The medics who'd amputated her arm had fucking butchered her. Her shoulder looked like it had been haphazardly treated with a field dressing in the middle of a warzone and left to heal that way. He'd be paying them a visit once all this was over. And he'd have a few choice words for her boss, too, for not only allowing, but approving this, and leaving her to suffer for years without even a temporary prosthesis.

But none of that had a damned thing to do with Raven. He'd chosen her outfit for a reason. He needed her to wake up and see herself the way he saw her. "Your scars are a badge of honor. You don't hide them. You wear them with pride, and make it known to anyone who looks at you that you are a force not to be fucked with."

"Right," she murmured into her juice. "Because, clearly, I am a fierce, battle-hardened warrior. One look from me and people cower everywhere I go."

"One look from you puts me on my knees."

Her flush deepened, and Zach barely restrained himself from leaping across the table to feel its warmth against his skin.

"You of all people should know that perception is everything. *You* decide how you let people see you. You are far from a shrinking violet, Blackbird. Own it."

She swallowed another bite and took a few breaths in the slow, deep rhythm she preferred as a calming technique. Setting down her fork, she raised her head and looked him dead in the eye.

And Zach's dick hardened to full attention so fast he almost flinched. Raven's eyes were pure fire and defiance. It scorched him to the bone. *More.* "Drop the blanket."

A flicker of uncertainty, the slightest tension in the closed press of her lips.

"Not to be fucked with, remember?"

Her throat worked on a swallow he wanted to trace with his tongue. It took her several eternities to shrug and let the blanket fall from her shoulders. Her pulse raced in the side of her neck. Her pupils spasmed, widening and narrowing in a rhythm he'd learned to associate with her switching focus between the outside world and her inner mindscape. He couldn't feel her mental touch; she kept her distance from his thoughts.

Was she tempted, though?

For all of two seconds, he regretted keeping his mind locked. Then he reminded himself of who he was: whoever the fuck he chose to be. Raven was his key. He knew her mind. He could train himself to find her thoughts. Maybe if he asked nicely, one day she'd let him in.

"You're staring," she bit out.

"I am in awe," he countered. Then he pushed to his feet and rounded the table to her side, not bothering to hide the effect she had on him. He wanted her to see. The catch of her breath was music to his ears. He felt her gaze as if she'd physically stroked him. His knees buckled and hit the floor on her left side.

Reaching up, desperate to feel her flush, he froze when she flinched. *Slow.* He needed to take his time, to get this *right.*

"Do you trust me?"

"You saved my life."

She'd saved his first. "Do you *trust* me?"

Down feathers brushed across the inside of his scalp. Tentative, hesitant, too cautious. He latched onto the sensation and dragged it deeper.

Raven gasped. "I need to teach you some telepath etiquette. You can't just pull people in like that when they knock."

"Fuck etiquette. Fuck knocking." He palmed her cheek and pulled her forehead down to his. "You've been in my thoughts since the moment you walked into my cell. Stop acting like you don't belong there." Soft. Warm. She smelled so damn good Zach's mouth watered for a taste. "Acknowledge." He had just enough self-control left to temper the order into a plea.

"No more knocking," she said. Not quite what he wanted to hear, but he'd take what he could get. The smallest victory felt monumental with her.

"Are you done eating?"

Raven nodded against him.

"Good. My turn."

He scooped her out of the chair in a harsh lurch that had her latching onto him for balance. In three strides, he had her on the couch, and Raven's argument disappeared down his throat as he sucked her tongue into his mouth, demanding equal participation.

There was the fury Zach's fantasies had conditioned her to expect. He didn't kiss; he devoured as if he'd been the one starving and she was his meal. His tongue swept against hers, sought every corner. He pulled away just enough to allow her a breath, and then he delved right back in again, as if the momentary pause had offended him. Like air was something he wouldn't tolerate coming between them.

Raven's head swam. She was sweltering in the heat, melting under his sensual assault. But while she clutched at his shirt over his shoulder, crushing the fabric in her fist for all she was worth, Zach's hands were braced on the couch. He didn't lay a finger on her.

He pulled away with a reluctant suck at her lower lip. "You say stop, I stop."

Don't stop.

Zach's eyelids drooped half-mast. "Heard that." His lips whispered across her cheek to just below her ear. "I think I like this thing between us." He swept his tongue over her pulse.

Raven's back arched, her hips curling as heat pooled between her legs. Stitches popped as her nails dug harder into his shirt.

Zach rumbled a satisfied growl against her pulse point. "I definitely like this."

He pressed a knee between hers on the couch, dragging his lips down the column of her neck to her shoulder.

Her *left* shoulder.

Raven tensed. "Stop."

Zach froze, his mouth in the hollow of her collarbone, one hand braced on the couch, the other partly beneath the bottom edge of her top, long fingers stroking her ribs. Everything stilled, even his thoughts. Every part of him zeroed in on her. He held still, matching his breath to hers—stopped, as he'd promised, but unwilling to retreat. Waiting for her to guide his next step.

Not to be fucked with.

It was her turn to choose. She could keep living the way she had been for the last three years, holding her breath and pretending life was just a temporary inconvenience…

…or she could choose to *live*. Own it—own herself—and decide to take whatever good life chose to send her way.

She had seconds before Zach read her hesitation as rejection and pulled away completely.

Deep breath in.

Deep breath out.

Not to be fucked with.

Raven let go; let herself relax back into the moment and—*gulp*—trust.

Deep breath in.

Deep breath out.

"Okay."

Zach nuzzled her shoulder, his thumb caressing the underside of her breast, and a powerful wave of relief swept over her. She couldn't tell if it was hers or his.

She closed her eyes as he brushed his parted lips along her shoulder to the joint. His hot breath against her worst scars made her flinch. The gentle kiss he pressed to the uneven ripples of her skin was the first touch she'd ever allowed outside of a medical exam. He knew. Whatever he felt through this strange bond between them, Zach could tell this wasn't just about her scars. It went beyond the physical, straight to the heart of her soul, and all the fear, pain, and heartache she carried there.

He didn't turn away from any of it, accepting every part of her with a reverence that melted her heart. Kiss after careful kiss, he worked every last bit of tension from her body, tracing the ragged surgical scar. His hand swept her top up over the swell of her breasts so he could follow the scar lower to where it faded into smooth skin once more.

—*Beautiful.*—

Zach's voice in her mind.

Or was she still in his?

Raven couldn't tell. Forgot why it should matter when his lips closed around her nipple.

"Zach!"

—*Yes!*— He speared his hands down the back of her pants, palming the curve of her ass, pulling her against the column of his thigh while he transferred his attention to her other breast. The thin fabric of her pants was already soaked through, and the sudden pressure against her clit made her inner muscles clench. She clamped her leg around his back, curling her hips, seeking friction. She was close. Stars, a few kisses, and she was ready to come apart.

Zach shuddered over her, mentally shaking himself as he released her breast to kiss a hot, moist path down her body, forcing her away from him so he could pull down her pants.

As soon as they hit the floor and he turned back to her, Zach froze again, staring at her splayed out like an offering before him.

Raven almost balked. Until she felt him rooting the sight into his core memories. Every detail meticulously preserved for all time, from the wild spread of her hair on the pillows to the shade of red in her kiss-stung lips, the camisole shoved up to her armpits, baring her modest breasts, which he thought were *perfect*. He followed the ridges of her ribs down to her stomach and documented in excruciating detail every inch of her leg rubbing against his hip, revealing the glistening wetness drenching her pussy.

Zach licked his lips, searing her to the bone with his dark gaze. "You say stop, I stop," he repeated. —*Don't say stop.*—

His mouth was on her a second later, strong hands clutching her hips to keep her still. He licked at her, into her, feasting on her without mercy. And all the while, those dark eyes watched her every reaction, learning her tells, adjusting the angle, the pressure, the rhythm to push her right to the edge.

He pulled her awareness into himself, taking her pleasure as his, showing her through his eyes and his body what it did to him. He soaked up her gasps, reveled in the twitch of her thighs. When she speared her hand through his hair, his mind *quivered* around her.

The game was everything, and he dragged it out, edging her, teasing her, promising relief right before he pulled away. The torment was as much his as it was hers—he made it so.

"Zach… Oh, stars… Please…"

Triumph rang through his mind and echoed back to her. This was what he'd been waiting for; dying for. His name on her lips. He wanted to hear her scream it as she came apart.

Stars, he was killing her.

"Please," she begged, "please…"

—*Soon,*— he promised. —*Bear it with me a little longer. Just a little more.*—

Raven sobbed out a curse. It *hurt!* Riding so close to the edge for so long—and she knew he felt it, too. Why was he torturing them both like this?

Before you and I are through, you're going to beg me to fuck you.

That's what he'd told her the first time they'd met in his cell.

That's what he was waiting for.

A man of his word, he wouldn't let up until she submitted completely, and he would drag this out as long as it took until he heard those words. He *couldn't* go any further until he heard them.

His tongue speared into her, curling up as he pulled back and dragged it flat and hard across her clit. Just enough for her to feel the first hint of pleasure, a split-second relief from the ache, but not enough to send her over the edge.

Raven thrashed, yanking on his hair, playing right into his hand. "Fuck! Fine, I'll say it."

He paused, breath puffing against her oversensitized flesh.

Raven was shaking, but she met his burning gaze, hoping her voice didn't come out as desperate as she felt. "Fuck me, Zach. Make me come. Please. I'm begging you."

Victory had never felt so much like relief.

Zach opened his mouth around her clit and pressed his tongue against it hard.

Raven cried out as she went off in a full-body orgasm that shook her from head to toe. And the whole time, she felt Zach right there with her, riding it out, guiding her through it with his mouth, feeling exactly when and how to touch her to keep the pleasure rolling through her body in waves until all she could do was take it.

Keep it together!

Holy fucking shit…

Zach turned his foot sideways into the couch, using the pain in his twisted ankle to anchor him through the storm. He'd played with fire, and now he was burning, drowning in Raven's pleasure that his brain couldn't distinguish from his own. If he came in his pants, still fully dressed, he'd never live it down.

Fuck, was this what sex was like for telepaths? Endless echo chambers of pleasure? He'd thought he'd had some damn good sex before, but nothing in his remembered experience had ever come close to anything like this.

This was…

It was…

Life-changing.

He felt Raven coming down to something a little too sharp and acute to be called a plateau. He could work her up to another orgasm in seconds—and he wanted to so badly it hurt.

But he wanted to feel her coming on his cock. Just the thought of it made his balls pull up tight, and he shoved his ankle into a harder twist, breathing it down.

Raven's soft thighs relaxed as she sighed. He kissed her hip before extricating himself from her hold. His shirt went sailing, followed a second later by his pants. He was painfully hard, his mind still floating in Raven's afterglow, and he wanted to luxuriate in it for the rest of time.

But they were far from finished.

Zach crawled over her, savoring the sleepy, satisfied smile playing along her lips. He couldn't help himself. He took her mouth again, letting her taste herself on his tongue. "You say stop, I stop." *Please God, don't say stop.*

Raven looped her arm around his neck, her legs locking around him. *Caught.*

About damn time.

"Are you waiting for me to beg again?" She curled her hips up, dragging the wet heat of her delicious pussy up the length of his cock.

Breathe it down!

Zach gritted his teeth and clamped one hand on her hip. "I don't think I'd survive it."

She laughed, flooding his mind with sparkling, giddy joy. "Then I suggest you hurry up."

Yes, ma'am.

He palmed himself and shoved his foot back against the couch. He got the tip of his cock right to the seam of her pussy and almost lost his shit. He gasped for breath when he gave her the whole head and felt her muscles contract around him.

She echoed the squeeze with a feeling of stretching, the slight burn of invasion, and a frenzied need for more.

"*Fffffuck!*" Raven hadn't done this in too long. She needed time; he didn't want to hurt her. *Breathe, motherfucker.* Zach's ankle was about to sprain.

Better than embarrassing himself like a virgin schoolboy.

Raven tilted her hips up again, and he slid in deep, feeling the hairs all over his body stand on end. Too good. Too much, too soon. Too *perfect.*

Raven's nails dug into his back, and he groaned, hanging on by a frayed thread.

"Stop," he bit out. "Just…wait."

The brush of down feathers slipped across his scalp as she pulled away, leaving him completely. His gaze snapped to hers. "The fuck are you doing?"

She blinked. "You said stop."

"Not *that.* Get back here. *Now.*"

She responded with that tentative brush again.

Zach growled and stamped his mouth over hers, shoving balls-deep into her.

There she was. A sweet moan on her lips, a scalding quiver through his mind, and an unspoken plea to move. She was fully in the moment with him, not an ounce of doubt left in any part of her.

As it should be. Always.

Zach rewarded her with a hard thrust that pulled a gasp from her lips. He did it again, relishing the flare of budding pleasure in her body and mind. He had her now. And he wasn't letting go.

He set a steady driving rhythm, delighting in how responsive she was. Her every twitch and breath told him exactly what she liked without her needing to think a word.

Oh, but her thoughts…

Zach dived into the sweet, heady fog of pure feeling, rocking with her, into her, minds and bodies melting together until he couldn't tell where he ended and she began.

A thread of unease snaked through their joined consciousness, something about going too far. Zach brushed it away with a kiss, fucked her harder. He felt her body winding tighter; sensed her thoughts spiraling toward that one sweet moment of culmination, and he was right there with her.

And when she went, she took him, too, their combined pleasure cascading over him so hard, all he could do was hold on and ride it out.

And it went on…

And on…

And on…

35

Valhale 602 marked two sunrise times on clocks and calendars. The first was when the sun cleared the horizon. The second was when it cleared Vesta. The time in between painted the sky in dark grays, pinks, and violets. Deep in its wet season, every night since Kalchama had blown in heavy clouds and deposited a fresh layer of frosty snow. But the winds always died down with the first sunrise, as if by magic. Daytime raised the temperature to just around freezing—comfortable, but not high enough to melt the city's white frost cover.

The penthouse had an unobstructed view to the east from all across the unit, but it was most beautiful from the massive bed. When the city lights went dark and the sky brightened, the floor-to-ceiling window framed a stark masterpiece of skyscrapers spearing up like pillars of salt as far as the eye could see. They were built so tightly together that not a single roadway broke up the landscape from this far up. But as the sun rose, the buildings melted and absorbed their frosty shells, revealing the city to be a geode of faceted crystals in shades ranging from dark teal to bright emerald green. It had quickly become Zach's favorite time of day on Valhale 602.

He'd been too busy with more pleasurable pursuits to enjoy it the day before, and slept through it today.

Poor Raven was beginning to understand that Zach was very much a man of his word. By the end of round two, she'd lost the last of her inhibitions. After round three, she'd barely murmured a weak protest as he'd carried her to the bathroom and showed her where the massage jets were—and why she'd never need them while he was around.

Round four had left both of them so spent his legs had been shaking as he'd made the exhausting trip from bed to table to get them some more food. He'd rewarded Raven with a kiss after every bite she let him feed her.

Now, well past noon, he was alone in his thoughts, with Raven still asleep, sprawled half over him, her face tucked beneath his chin and her hand curled at his ear. Hands-down his new favorite position to sleep in.

The silence, though, he could do without.

After spending hours with her mind tangled up in his, disconnecting had scared the shit out of him at first. Raven had faded away from sheer exhaustion, falling into a deep sleep, and he'd spent the next hour watching her every breath to make sure they didn't stop coming.

Telepathy is connection. Most of us don't work to create it; we struggle to set boundaries so we don't lose ourselves in it.

Zach got it now. The sense of oneness had felt so natural, so right, he might have let himself stay there if Raven hadn't pulled back. Now that he was alone in his thoughts, he recognized it would have been the end of both of them.

Raven sighed against him, her body tensing in a stretch that had him rubbing his hands all over her again to feel it. "Wha'time'sit?" She sounded like she'd been screaming for hours.

Oh, wait…

He grinned. "Late. Might as well go back to sleep."

She groaned.

"Are you hungry?"

Raven half nodded, half nuzzled into him. He couldn't even tell if her eyes were open.

Five more minutes, he told himself. It wasn't wise to stay in one place for so long; they should have moved locations the moment Raven had woken up from her burnout. But he'd been monitoring the news and the law enforcement channels, and the moon appeared to be calm. There'd been no more Shadow sightings or attacks. The one in Chairo had been hastily swept under the dunes with some bullshit about a mechanical malfunction that had caused the emergency pods in one of the buildings to trigger spontaneously. Clean-up crews had contained and repaired any damage within hours, and life had moved on in blissful ignorance.

Just to be safe, though, he'd done some creative shuffling to move his stolen loot around to different accounts and identities, and he'd switched his ID chip to one that wasn't directly connected to the fattest balances. Jaxon Pluck had checked out days ago and booked a shuttle flight to Earth. Mr. Vincent Goff now had the penthouse suite. A down-on-his-luck finance officer who'd been unexpectedly upgraded because the cheap room his company had reserved for him had malfunctioned.

"I don't want to get up," Raven said. "I don't want to leave the bed."

Zach chuckled. "Are you proposing, Blackbird? Because my answer is yes."

She tugged on his hair in retaliation.

"I mean it." He did. "Say the word, and we're gone. Somewhere no one will ever find us. Let the galaxy sort itself out. I'll build you a house in the mountains… Okay, I'll *have* a house *built* for you in the mountains, and we'll never have to see another Shadow as long as we live. Just you and me. And whatever piece of furniture is sturdy enough to handle us."

He savored her huff of silent laughter and the sweet flare of humor that was there one moment and gone the next. "I can't just disappear. We need everyone on the front lines, fighting back. It's the only way we'll get through this."

Zach heaved a long-suffering sigh. "Maybe later, then."

Neither of them made a move to get up. For the next few minutes, Zach basked in the extravagant pleasure of a simple life. Fancy bed, stunning woman, and not a care in the world.

But the silence in his mind got to him. "You had a timer when you worked on me in the detox tank. How did you do that?"

Raven raised her head to frown at him. "Why do you ask?"

Because if he wanted to spend telepathic happy time with Raven, which he did—a *lot*—he needed to make damn sure they both had a way out. He might be new to this mind-melding thing, but he refused to let his ignorance become a liability. "I'll also need you to teach me how to initiate."

The logical assumption was that it took more effort to enter someone's mind than to have one's mind entered. Zach taking the lead would keep Raven from depleting herself unnecessarily. He had a shield. She had an arsenal. If the situation arose, they would both need her at full strength.

Raven pulled away from him to sit up. "The time for experiments is over. I told you, your mind is locked down now."

He was too comfortable to move. Giving her the high ground presented him with a glorious view of her body bathed in the pink afternoon light. For a second, he lost his train of thought, tracing the plump swell of her breasts down the flat planes of her stomach to the juncture of her thighs. It would take so little to tug her back and sit her on his face.

"You can still get in," he said to distract himself back to the conversation. "And I still have your… frequency, you called it. So tell me what I need to do to trace it back to you."

"Your self-assurance is truly astonishing. You really think you can break every established protocol and be the exception to every rule, don't you?"

Zach grinned. "Try me."

"Do I have a choice?"

"Of course you do. You can let me stumble through it on my own, and then deal with the consequences."

"So, no."

"Now you're getting it."

Raven rubbed her forehead. "Fine. Close your eyes."

And give up this view? "I'd rather keep my eyes on you."

"The whole point is for you to *not* see me. It forces you to focus on your other senses. It would be better if I wasn't in the room."

He clamped a hand on her inner thigh before she'd finished the sentence. It put his fingertips inches from her pussy. "Don't you dare leave this bed."

She raised an eyebrow in challenge. "Then do as I say, and close your eyes."

"Fine. But just so you know, that still leaves four other senses to distract me." The feel of her skin alone was enough to keep his thoughts on things he shouldn't be thinking about. Inches away. He obediently closed his eyes, but slid his hand a little farther.

Raven caught it. "Concentrate."

Oh, he was. Fully on target. But, to keep things fair, he tucked his free hand behind his head.

"I want you to think about how I feel—"

Zach groaned, fingers curling into the supple leg he had no intention of releasing.

"—in your head!"

Right. "Down feathers." She was the softest, warmest thing his mind had ever felt. No wonder he craved it so.

"Okay, sure. Now look for the memory of it. Lock it in your mind."

Her grip on his wrist prevented him from going any further. But Zach could still do plenty from his current position. He brushed his thumb back and forth across her skin, picturing his mouth there. Her taste was addicting. Who needed food, anyway? Zach could break-fast on her every morning and count himself sated. Raven's breath hitched a little, her nails digging into him in a warning that he chose to interpret as a dare.

Down feathers. "Got it."

"Now comes the tricky part. Let the feeling drift away, and try to follow it."

With muted light still filtering through his eyelids, his vision wasn't entirely black. But he blanked his mind to darkness, where all he felt was Raven's leg, and the brush of down feathers over his entire body. He didn't want to let go of either.

"If it helps, pretend the feathers are a bird in your hand. Let it fly."

Zach condensed the full-body sensation to just his palm.

Fuck, he'd have to release his physical hold to make this work. The heated self-debate didn't go well. Zach liked touching Raven.

But he'd asked for this lesson.

Linking the physical sensation to the mental one was easier than he expected. As soon as he made his fingers let go, the feather touch slipped from his mind, black wings flapping through the dark void away from him.

Zach followed, but the bird was too fast and, within seconds, even the sound of its wings disappeared. He lost the trail.

He'd failed.

Again.

"What's option B?" He needed an alternate approach.

"Try picturing yourself in the room you made for me in your mind."

"Done." Before she'd voiced the next instruction, he was already at the floor-length mirror she'd used as her pathway into his thoughts. All he had to do was step through its liquid surface. So he did.

And found himself right back in the black void, without even a whisper of a wingbeat to be heard. "Nope. Not working."

"It's okay," Raven said softly. "We can figure out another strategy and try again later."

Again.

"We're not done until I get it right." That's how it worked. The lesson repeated until it was learned. Or until he dropped.

"Again," Sandoval's voice barked across the darkness, mocking him with his failure, and the old, familiar chill seeped across his entire being. The mission objective was to find Raven's mind. Until he accomplished that, nothing else mattered.

"Whatever you're thinking, stop it."

Zach had tensed up so hard his face ached.

"Again." Muscles cramping. Teeth grinding together. His lungs seized, throat working to breathe, but his ribs wouldn't expand to accept it.

"Again!"

Do something, even if it's the wrong thing. Inaction costs lives.

Zach lurched through the dark mindscape, running full sprint at nothing. Straight line—without a path. A single degree of deviation could mean the difference between locating his target and getting lost in the void. But which way?

Which fucking way?

"Again!"

Keep going. Giving up was not an option. He'd get this right if it killed him.

"Again!"

It just might…

Soft, giving flesh met his palm as Raven pressed his hand back to her inner thigh. "Zach… come back to me."

The darkness begot texture. Soft feathers brushed across the mental equivalent of his face, turning him in a different direction. He sucked in a breath, reaching ahead. Couldn't grip the feathers without crushing them. But he maintained contact, following along as they slipped away, tracing a path.

Black gave way to a dark gray mist.

The mist turned into white smoke.

And between one step and the next, his mindscape filled with context once more.

He found himself back in Raven's room, with Raven looking at him through the rippling floor-length mirror. She was just on the other side, and an impossibility away.

Zach opened his eyes to Raven watching him, her brows furrowed with concern. It felt so much worse than a CO's disappointment. He couldn't stomach it. "Let's try again."

"You should take a break."

"I'm fine. I want to try again."

"Neither of us are in a good condition to continue. We can—"

"Now!"

"No!" she barked back, shoving his hand away from her.

Zach sat up, ready to go a round or two.

Raven met him glare for glare for all of ten seconds before her expression shuttered with what he could only interpret as disgust. "I have no interest in dealing with Operative M right now," she hissed, knocking the breath out of him without raising a finger. "Let me know when Zach comes back."

She climbed out of bed and closed herself in the bathroom, leaving Zach reeling.

36

The most frigid ice plunge wouldn't have been as effective as watching Zach fall back into his Shadow self. He exuded so much warmth and easy charm most of the time, she'd almost let herself forget who and what he really was.

Who he'd consciously chosen to be.

It hadn't slipped her mind that Zach had chosen to preserve them memory of his Shadow training. Worse, he seemed to have latched on to the brutality of it the hardest. He hadn't internalized the pain of those lessons, but the relentless drive to succeed, no matter the consequences.

The Shadows had taught him from birth that the individual was expendable. Didn't matter how many died in pursuit of an objective, as long as the objective was achieved in the end.

But Zach wasn't a soldier anymore, and he didn't have an army of expendable assets to waste. And Raven didn't know how to redirect him—if that was even possible.

There had to be telepaths better suited to teaching him the skills he wanted to learn, but with his shields, she couldn't think of a single one who'd be willing to try.

Well, hiding out in the bathroom wouldn't solve anything.

Raven took some time to calm herself, wash up, and perform an internal diagnosis. Her shields were intact, but she wasn't at full strength yet. It would take a few more days of complete rest to recover—unlikely to happen if Zach continued to push. She needed to get them back to the SU. She needed a second opinion and possibly some time away from Zach.

That would go over well.

Wrapped in a clean, oversized bath towel, she emerged from her hiding space, bracing herself for round two.

It didn't come.

Zach stood outside on the balcony, his hands braced against the raised barrier, and his head bowed. He was shirtless and barefoot out there, and the weak afternoon sun didn't make full winter on the hundred and fiftieth floor any warmer.

He'd left a new stack of clothes for her on the bed, complete with socks and underwear this time, and a flower resting on top. Apparently, he didn't lack all common sense. He'd chosen a much more practical outfit this time and included several weather-appropriate layers.

She was fully dressed, shrugging on a sweater with a thick cowl neck, when the balcony door opened. Zach stepped through and closed it behind him, leaning back against the glass. Shoulders hunched, hands shoved into his pants pockets. "I'm sorry," he said in contrition, but his posture was tense, as if braced for a physical blow.

"Who's apologizing?"

He flinched. "Me. Zach. And I promise you, it won't happen again."

"It will." He couldn't avoid it.

Zach pushed away from the door, reaching for her. "No, I would never—"

Raven raised her hand to stop him. "I don't think I was clear enough about this the other day. There wasn't time to explain before your shield fully formed, so let me give you the most important lesson you'll need to learn about telepathy."

Pain flashed across his features before he blanked his face and backtracked, stepping his feet apart. Chest out, hands clasped behind him, he nodded mutely for her to go on.

"Your body has a self-preservation mechanism. It has your mind to tell it when it's time to stop. Your mind doesn't have that. Mental connections between telepaths create a positive feedback loop that is addictive. If you don't set limits for yourself, no one else will do it for you. You won't just lose the identity you put so much effort into forming, you'll willfully throw it away. And once you cross that line, *there is no going back.* There is no treatment or recovery. You will be gone, along with whoever else you happened to drag along. So, for your sake and mine, when I say stop, you *stop*. Or I will make you. Permanently."

Some of the tension leaked from his posture. "Acknowledged." He sounded relieved. "Permission to approach?"

Raven rolled her eyes. "Knock it off with the soldier shit."

Zach crossed the suite in three ground-eating strides, squeezing her up off her feet. He was chilled through and through, his cold nose in her neck sending shivers down her entire body. "You say stop, I stop," he said against her shoulder.

Raven sighed and put her arm around him, relaxing into his hold. "You can't Shadow your way through this."

"Soft touch. Down feathers. Got it."

At least he didn't argue the point. After his outburst earlier, Raven had expected him to put up more of a fight. And yet not once during the altercation had it entered her mind to fear for her physical safety.

Somewhere up there in the sky, Tessa's spirit was laughing and doing her *I told you so* dance.

The thought almost made her smile, despite the sharp pang of heartache.

"So, uh… Are you gonna let me down now?"

"Nope."

"I meant literally."

If anything, his arms around her tightened more. "Didn't stutter."

"Okay then."

They stayed there, with Zach holding her up, until the chill of his self-imposed time-out on the balcony had faded in the heat of the suite. Eventually, he let her feet touch the floor again, and they shared a meal while he caught her up on what had happened on the moon since Chairo. She got a little lost in the part about a bunch of refugees escaping to some backwoods planet, her no longer having an ID chip, and her identity needing to be rewritten for the new one he'd had delivered to their penthouse suite.

Raven sported a good number of cuts and scratches all over her arm. It had never occurred to her that one of them might be the result of his surgically extracting her chip.

"I have a new identity?"

"Not yet. But you will need one. I wanted you to have a say in what it is."

"My ID is on file with the SU. You can't hack them like you did the registry."

"Then I guess we have a problem, because Raven Dello Russo was reported as deceased in an accidental pod collision in Chairo."

Shit. "I need to make that call."

"You need a new name first. You can check in with the SU and let them know you're alive, but the second they flag you as not dead, you'll be a target. No one wants that. So think of a new name to give them."

She scowled at him. "You're betting on Blackbird, aren't you?" Raven Blackbird. Not in a million years.

He grinned. "Zachary Blackbird does have a nice ring to it."

"And why would you be changing your name?"

"Married couples are less conspicuous as travelers. If the Shadows are still looking for me, they'll expect me to fly solo, like they trained me to do."

"Bennett," she said.

"Raven and Zachary Bennett. Nice. Where'd it come from?"

"It was my maiden name."

Something flashed across his expression, and his easy smile turned wan. "You kept your husband's name."

It seemed like the least she could do to honor his memory. And she hadn't exactly been in a state of mind to think about changing it after he…

"Pick something else," Zach said kindly, but firmly. "We want to stay away from any connection to your past life. Maiden name, mother's maiden name, fourth cousin twice removed—family names of any kind are off the table."

"Very well, how about Sinclair?"

"Connection?"

"Indirect. And no longer living."

"Works for me. With a minor modification, to be safe."

He took over the entertainment console and broke it.

At least that's how it looked to her when a whole lot of random text and scary warnings started flashing all over the screen. None of it appeared to faze Zach as his fingers flew over the control tablet with enviable speed. Within minutes, he'd changed his name and ID, then registered a whole new persona for Raven under the name St. Clare. He marked her home address on Mai, of all places, with her current age and biometrics, but a different ID code.

A few more minutes, and Raven St. Clare had her own bank account, a contact ID, a medical history of a boating accident, of all things, and a marriage certificate with Zach's new name and ID marked down in the Spouse section.

"Hand me that box over there, will you?" He never once looked away from the screen, still typing up a storm.

Raven picked up the flat white parcel that barely had any weight to it and held it out to him.

Instead of taking it, he passed the control tablet over, triggering a new window with more random characters scrolling through it at a frightening speed.

Distracted by the mess scrolling across the screen, she almost jumped out of her skin when Zach caught her arm in one hand and opened the box with the other. A second later, he had a tiny injector shoved against the inside of her wrist.

"Ow!"

"Sorry," he said, rubbing his thumb over the puncture wound. "It hurts less when you don't see it coming."

A tiny red light blinked twice underneath her skin as the chip settled into position. Then all that remained was a growing bruise.

Zach pressed a kiss to it before turning back to the control tablet.

Two minutes of digital pandemonium later, the screen cleared back to normal, as if he hadn't just shaken everything Raven thought she knew about universal security protocols.

With a lot more leisure, he brought up the communications console. "Who're we calling first?"

It took her a second to realize Zach was talking to her.

The screen displayed a contact ID prompt. The system was voice-operated, so she only had to say a name and ID, but the prompt icon looked to be *jittering,* and she knew Zach wasn't done with whatever he'd been doing. She just couldn't see it anymore. Raven perched herself on the couch armrest and, in as steady a voice as she could muster, said, "Shining Star Pizza Palace."

The system chirped to confirm, and a few moments later, a young man with bright blue eyebrows appeared on the screen while a graphic menu scrolled by on his left. "Pizza Palace, how may I help you?"

Zach took up typing again, the control tablet now a screen of its own, with a jumbled mess of codes scrolling through it.

"Hello?"

Raven shook herself and faced the boy. "I'd like two medium hand-tossed pizzas, please. Plain cheese."

The young man's smile froze. "No toppings?"

"Not today."

"Okay, and where would you like that delivered?"

"Chairo Visitor Center." A fallback location for emergencies. If anyone had made it out of Hilder & Pine, they'd have regrouped at the Visitor Center before evacuating the city.

The young man looked away as he entered her request into his system. "I'm sorry, that address was blacklisted a few days ago."

Raven's gut clenched. "Where is the closest you can deliver for pickup in the area?"

"One moment, please."

Raven spared a glance toward Zach as he swiped through window after window of stars-knew-what. It made the Pizza Palace menu flash and flicker, as if in a system malfunction. The dispatch operator didn't appear to notice.

"The closest we can deliver is Questa Major."

That made no sense. Questa Major was about sixteen hundred miles outside of Chairo and had no SU facilities as far as Raven knew. Why would they evacuate the city but not the moon? "Let's do that."

"All right, that'll be eighty-seven credits."

Raven reached for the control tablet to scan her new chip, but Zach batted her hand away, still typing. She tried again, and he caught her wrist to hold her back, typing one-handed.

"Thank you so much!" the young man said just as she was about to kick Zach. "Your pizza is in the oven. Have a wonderful day!"

The call ended, and a silver icon appeared on the screen, rotating against a black background.

"We do not spend money needlessly," Zach lectured, releasing her wrist.

The icon flickered once.

Twice.

Then the screen flashed white, chirping another alert as a new connection opened.

Zach shoved to his feet, the control tablet dropping to the thick carpet as he shifted to put himself in front of Raven, blocking her view.

She had to lean out sideways to see Ripley's mouth pull into an arrogant smirk on the screen, their cold eyes locked on Zach. "Look who's not dead."

"I can fix that," Zach said. "Let's meet up. I'll even let you choose the place."

The telepath he'd thought he'd left to die looked too alive for his peace of mind. They'd dyed their hair a russet brown and adopted a more masculine look, but nothing could disguise the animosity that practically radiated out of them through the com screen. Most of their injuries had been treated enough that whatever bruising remained almost disappeared beneath their make-up—definitely something Zach would need to rectify.

"What the hell is going on, Ripley?"

Shit. Raven. Zach tried to pull her back, but she'd pushed to her feet beside him, frowning at the screen, her hand fisted. Didn't need to read her mind to know this was not who she'd expected to pick up the call.

"Where's Darrow?"

Ripley never took their eyes off Zach. "Who are you?" they demanded, the same way they had in Chairo. And it still raised his hackles, the way they watched him so calmly, as if they expected him to answer without delay.

"Raven asked you a question." And he'd be damned if this piece of shit made her repeat herself.

Ripley's mouth twisted with displeasure. "I see we may have a problem."

Oh, they very much did. But Zach could solve it in seconds. "Raven, hand me the tablet."

Ripley looked sideways for a moment. "Good thing I prepared for this."

The com console popped up a new window in the lower right quadrant. Ripley had decided to share something through the call.

He recognized the voice before his mind registered what he saw. *"You're talking like this is a negotiation."* It looked like him and sounded like him, but Zach was ninety-nine point nine-nine-seven percent certain he'd never said those words. *"I told you what I'm bringing to the table, and I told you what I want in return. Only thing you get to say is yes or no. And make it quick, will you? I'm due in medbay in twenty minutes."*

The response came from none other than Ripley, back in their feminine energy, with platinum hair draping in a silky-smooth curtain past their shoulders. As if he'd ever lower himself to making deals with them, no matter what they looked like. *"You talk like you can actually deliver. How do I know you won't come to us as blank as all the rest of you?"*

The other Zach grinned. *"You want a preview? Sending now."*

"What is this?" Raven demanded.

"Hush, sweetie," Ripley crooned, "the adults are talking now."

Zach was going to tear that reptile's throat out.

"How reliable is this?" past-Ripley asked.

"That report is from two weeks ago. Assume they'll make significant progress toward roll-out in the next month. And then decide how badly you want to keep breathing."

"And in return for everything we discussed, you just want the serum?"

Past-Zach raised an eyebrow. *"To be specific, I want what Quinn got—as a start. I'll also be expecting a reasonable level of autonomy."*

"Meaning, command," they retorted dryly.

Past-Zach shrugged a humble shoulder. *"I can take orders under the right circumstances."* He was *flirting* with them? The fuck that would ever happen. *"But I work best on my own. Oh, and since we're restating the obvious, let's also put my last condition on the books, shall we? Go on. You can say it. In fact, I'm going to need you to verbalize it for me."*

"No matter the outcome, you get immunity after the fact," past-Ripley said, then smiled that cold little smile of theirs. *"If you survive."*

"Do we have a deal?"

"Zach?" Raven didn't like this.

Yeah, he wasn't exactly jumping for joy, either. He caught her hand in his and held on, watching the farce play out. Because that's all it was. "A clever farce to throw us off." It wouldn't work.

"Not yet. We still haven't addressed your potential uselessness upon arrival."

"You'll get what you need, whether I know who I am or not."

"Not good enough. I need to know you'll be the right *person when you arrive."*

Past-Zach turned up the charm, turning his stomach. *"Baby, I can be whoever you want me to be."*

Raven made a sound of disgust and pulled to get free of him. He held on tighter. It was the only way he could keep watching. Something told him he'd better watch this through to the end.

"Come on, tell me. Whisper in my ear, and it shall be done. Who do you want me to be?"

Ripley didn't thaw a single degree. *"Someone you can live with."*

The request set both versions of him on his heels. A second later, past-Zach became all business. *"You'll get what you need. And you'll have my cooperation, whether I remember or not."*

"And I will confirm this how?"

"All it takes is three questions…"

"Oh, fuck."

The screen disappeared, leaving current-Ripley watching him with those icy blue eyes. "Who are you?" they demanded.

Fuck!

Who are you? Where do you reside? What do you do?

It was real. The only way Ripley could know about the questions was if he'd told them. They were specific to *his* Shadow training, a failsafe Sandoval used to ensure Zach's slate remained blank.

Who are you? No one.

Where do you reside? Nowhere.

What do you do? What needs to be done.

Two of those were a lie. The recording he'd left for himself had made that painfully clear, and Zach had been operating this whole time on the assumption that past-him had put all this in place to keep present-him safe—because what sane person wouldn't?

But this…

Raven sank to the couch, her hand limp in his. "You betrayed us," she said numbly.

Ripley ignored her, their unwavering focus on Zach. "Who are you?"

Get it together. The mission parameters might have changed, but he still had a choice and, as far as he was concerned, the deal Ripley counted on had been made with a dead man. Zach was not that guy anymore.

"Come on, you know this one. Who—are—you?"

There was only one response he could live with. "Zachary St. Clare."

Ripley tilted their head slightly as if the answer had surprised them. "Where do you reside?"

He hated the knee-jerk impulse to pull back his shoulders and respond like a good little soldier. But he took savage satisfaction in giving them an answer of his choosing. "Monte Erebus, Mai." To Raven, he added, "It's beautiful. You'll love it there, I promise."

She huffed a baffled breath.

"What do you do?" Ripley asked.

And Zach's shoulders went back of their own accord as he stepped up in front of Raven, still holding her hand. "What needs to be done."

Ripley's eyes narrowed. "Including stepping *over* me on your way out of a hostile situation?"

"Agreed, that was my mistake. I should have killed you on the spot."

"Well, you had your hands full."

Was that supposed to be humor?

"At ease," Ripley said. "You did exactly what you were supposed to do. And you're going to keep doing so. Sending you an address. Meet me there tomorrow. And bring Raven."

"No."

"Yes," they insisted. "There's something there she'll want to see."

"*She* is still right here," Raven grated.

Ripley finally deigned to look at her, their expression softening into something resembling earnestness. "*I* didn't betray you."

But someone else had?

Before Zach could lean into them, the screen went blank. Ripley had ended the call.

January 21, 3040 – Lavari Dolmi, Valhale 602

Zach checked them out of the hotel as Mr. Vinci, and the valet called up their shining silver transport. Luggage had already been packed and stored inside it for them, and a box of light snacks and beverages had been included, courtesy of Mr. Vinci's diamond membership.

Raven barely registered any of it as they got into the transport and Zach turned off the autonav to manually drive them out of the city. The address Ripley had provided was on the other side of a dry, grassy plain that spanned thousands of square miles. At the transport's legal speed limit, it took them two and a half hours to cross.

And neither of them spoke a word the entire time.

Ripley knew Zach. Or rather, knew the Shadow he'd been before.

Bile rose in her throat again at the memory of him shamelessly flirting during their illicit negotiations.

What do you do?

What needs to be done.

Including leaving his partner in crime to die.

Including turning himself into someone who could get through every last one of Raven's walls and make her feel like—

Her stomach clenched, and she pressed her hand over her mouth, swallowing back a wave of nausea.

I didn't betray you.

No, Zach had done that.

She'd fallen for a con. A masterful one, but a con nonetheless.

And the worst part was, she couldn't even confront him about it, because *he didn't remember*! He'd thought of absolutely everything.

No one could pry answers out of his mind when he didn't have any left to hide. He hadn't just played Raven; he'd played the Shadows into wiping his memories for plausible deniability, and he'd likely played Ripley, too.

Stars, she was in way over her head here.

She couldn't even run.

Forget about any guilt at abandoning her people or duties. Zach had erased her identity once already—with a terrifying quickness. What would stop him from doing it again, rendering her new chip defunct and leaving her stranded?

They slowed to a more reasonable speed as the city of Lavari Dolmi rose along the horizon. If memory served, the colony was about a tenth the size of Chairo, built out along the banks of a river that only filled for two weeks of every year. The short, broad buildings had roofs painted a deep blue to mimic a real river. Wide avenues snaked between them, lined with stalky trees, presently covered with a protective sheet in deference to the winter freeze.

Zach pulled over in front of a squat little building that had an ice cream parlor tucked into one street-level corner, and a community center in the other. Between them, almost blending in with the vibrant mural of a tropical scene, a glass door marked their destination.

He turned off the engine, and the transport lowered to rest on the ground. "Nothing I say right now is gonna make a difference, is it?"

Raven clenched her teeth, breathing through her nose.

"You talk, then. Tell me how to fix this. Say the word and I'll—"

Raven forced open the transport door and stumbled out onto the sidewalk. The cold air slapped her in the face and provided some much-needed clarity.

This wasn't about her anymore. It was about Ripley, and Darrow, and everyone else who'd survived the Chairo attack.

It was about getting their shit together so they could *keep* surviving.

And if Raven wanted to be something other than a burden, she needed to focus on what was right in front of her: Ripley, with their arm in a sling, opening the glass door for her to walk through.

They hadn't bothered to put too much effort into their appearance today. Their face was clean of makeup, striking in its nakedness, with faint bruises and scabs still mottling their forehead and jaw. Instead of their usual high-fashion outfits, today Ripley wore a pair of wide lounge pants and a thick sweatshirt that fell to their knees. The only remarkable part of their appearance was that they'd dyed their hair a rich brown and cropped it even shorter.

They looked like an entirely different person. More human somehow, with their elaborate masks finally stripped away.

"You look like shit," she muttered to them as she stepped into the lobby.

"Looked in the mirror lately?" they returned without missing a beat, making the insult almost friendly. Ripley, of course, was too closed off for anything of the sort. Still, now that all their cards were on the table, it seemed to have relieved some of the tension between them and Raven.

They'd never be friends, but at least now Raven understood why Ripley had tried so hard to elbow in on her case back in Chairo.

They'd wanted to get whatever Zach had promised them.

"Where's Darrow?" If she kept her eye on Ripley, the Shadow conman stalking up to them and taking a stand behind Raven's left shoulder as if he belonged there didn't exist. She only had to dig her nails into her palm hard enough and ignore the static of his closeness raising her hackles all over her left side.

"Busy," Ripley said shortly. "It's better that way. Come with me."

Why the hell not?

She followed them to the farthest elevator that looked a little too new to fit in with the rest.

The cramped cabin forced her into closer proximity with the Shadow. She refused to acknowledge the tension radiating off him when she shifted a step away.

Ripley scanned their ID. No command to indicate the floor. The elevator just dropped, the overhead screen scrolling rapidly through five floors, pausing on the sixth while the cabin continued to descend.

"I want you to know that I didn't know about this until it slipped out during the Chairo attack," Ripley said. "No one did."

The Shadow's animosity bristled against Raven's nerve endings.

She kept her gaze on the frozen number screen. "What are you talking about?"

"You'll see. And…" Ripley took a deeper breath. "I'm sorry. I truly am." Their remorse was genuine, and their confession rang with an awful truth.

Raven dug her nails harder into her palm, breathing through a deep sense of dread that her rock bottom was about to open a trap door beneath her.

The elevator came to a stop at least five floors lower with the screen still displaying the number six.

Ripley stepped out first.

Raven balked, already sensing the faint buzz of a Faraday cage. It extended past the elevator, which meant her telepathy, as well as Ripley's and anyone else's, was effectively null down here.

"Say the word," Zach murmured.

It propelled her forward, away from him.

At the end of the short hallway, Ripley scanned their ID again at a metal sliding door, similar to the elevator. As soon as it opened, the buzzing in Raven's brain intensified tenfold. What the hell was this?

Again, Ripley stepped through first without hesitation. They knew exactly where they were going and what they would find at the end.

Raven followed, her nausea kicking up a notch, and finding a new friend in the migraine blooming at the base of her skull. She squinted in pain by the time they reached another door, but Ripley bypassed it, leading them farther down and around a corner to a different one.

This time, when they opened the door, Raven stopped in her tracks. A moan fought its way past her throat as the buzzing turned into a roar that made her eyes water. She swayed on her feet, barely feeling big hands clamp down on her hips to keep her upright.

Raven gripped the doorframe to pull herself through.

"Almost there," Ripley said, more to themself than to Raven or Zach.

The last door took them into a control station with several screens showing live feeds of various parts of the facility. As soon as it closed behind them, the roar quieted into a more manageable hum.

Raven's spine sagged, her knees turning weak.

Four people manned the controls. Ripley dismissed them with a wave. To the last, they obediently got up and marched out without a word in protest, and none of them even glanced Raven's way.

"When I was a kid," Ripley said, "I spent a lot of time with a cousin of mine. His parents were…uninterested, so he became more of a brother. His name was Michael."

They had to come all the way down here to have this chat?

"Michael wasn't like the other kids in our neighborhood. We would play, and he would sit back and watch. And sometimes, his eyes would go blank, and I knew he was seeing something else. And then, on my fifteenth birthday, he just disappeared. We contacted the police, reported him as a missing person, but they suspended the search two years later. No leads. It was like he never existed."

Beneath their conversational tone, Raven picked up on a pain that went deep. Both of them had seen it before. It still happened far too often—kids and young adults manifesting new abilities they couldn't control. Their onset was unpredictable, and it could be terrifying.

"Imagine my surprise when I got my SU acceptance letter, and five minutes later, a call. My favorite cousin, alive and looking haggard. And boy, did he have a tale to tell."

"Was that when you turned traitor?"

Ripley speared her with a cold glare. "That was when my eyes were opened to the inevitability of our defeat. See, Michael was a precog. I didn't believe him, at first, which, of course, he anticipated. He gave me a list of specific dates and events to look for over the next six months, and I didn't hear from him again until after all of them had come to pass. Every single one. Forty-seven things he couldn't have known about, unless he'd already seen them happen."

"And yet he didn't feel it necessary to warn anyone about the last three years?"

Ripley sneered. "He died the day the SU officially took up the fight. The instructions he sent me before his own brain killed him are the reason all of us are still alive. He sent me to the Evolutionaries so I could see for myself how ill-prepared the SU was for war. And, before you start accusing me again, my involvement with them was never a secret. It's why the acting director endorsed me for the council seat in the first place. She wants us to work together. According to Michael, it's the only way we'll win." Their gaze slipped away to one of the screens. "But he wasn't infallible. At a certain point, he could only estimate the future, not predict it."

Zach stepped around her to take a closer look at the feeds. "The fuck is this?"

"What happens when you put true power into the hands of a naïve, inexperienced child."

Frowning, Raven edged closer.

At first, her mind refused to comprehend what she saw.

Then, the horror of it sank in, and she braced herself on the edge of the console to keep from crumpling to the floor.

The circular room housed what appeared to be a massive flower in its center with five petals shaped like a curved troughs or caskets, each one filled with a liquid similar to the one used in detox tanks. In the center, a thick tangle of wires and tubes connected the pods to the ceiling.

And inside each pod was a person.

"That's…"

"A hive mind," Ripley confirmed.

That's why they were so deep underground. That's why the entire level had layers of Faraday protection. Two telepaths together could sway a crowd. Five could change the population of an entire planet—unless they were securely contained.

"You're thinking this can't be happening. And you're right. It *shouldn't* be happening."

They had protocols for this sort of thing. Telepaths didn't merge minds unless the threat was catastrophic and unavoidable. And they did so with the knowledge that, once they were finished, their lives would be forfeit.

"A hive mind is too dangerous to allow to persist," Ripley continued. "And yet, here we are."

"Are they…?"

"Four of the five show no cognitive function," Ripley answered. "They were fully subsumed into the dominant mind within weeks—as Michael predicted would happen. Unfortunately for all of us, the dominant mind had a little trouble letting go. And what Michael failed to foresee was the person left in charge deciding to allow it.

For the sake of hope."

The naïve, inexperienced *child* in charge…

"*Darrow.*"

Darrow had stepped up to oversee the SU's day to day operation while the rest of them, the adults, had worked 'round the clock to restore order and function back into the moon. At that point, they'd all been so busy surviving and so grateful that someone had willingly taken charge that they hadn't thought about it twice. And it wasn't as if Darrow hadn't been fully capable. With support from his sister, the SU's chief of medicine, and no objection from the acting director, he'd held them all together so well he'd earned everyone's confidence. They'd had no qualms at all about leaving him in charge until someone else took over.

And no one ever had.

"Darrow," Ripley confirmed. "I think he would have kept this secret for the rest of his life, if not for the Shadows storming Hilder & Pine. The moment he saw them, he panicked and it all came rushing back—and out. I sent him off with the rest of the council and went back myself to find you."

"Why?" she grated. What the hell did any of this have to do with her?

Did you notice our acting director turned to you *for an explanation? Maybe she knows things would have turned out differently if* you *were the one to call the shots. Maybe she's wondering why you aren't.*

Raven felt sick.

"Look closer." Ripley zoomed in on the flower's center, where the telepaths' heads clustered as close together as they could get.

Their features were almost alien after such a long time suspended in the tank, but Raven recognized every one of them. Including…

The world fell out from beneath her.

"Julian."

Zach's sharp inhale was right at her ear. He'd crossed to her without her noticing. His arm around her waist held her up. His strength kept her from falling apart where she stood. She couldn't look away, even as her vision tunneled and her mind screamed that this was wrong, this couldn't be real.

Darrow would never…

"It should have been you," Ripley said.

"I will fucking end you," Zach snarled, clutching Raven tighter, tugging her sideways away from Ripley.

They ignored him. "Michael predicted you would be the one to lead the merge. You would have broken Benna Havely in half before you let her absorb you. But you were fighting for your life, so Julian took your place. He was always everyone's favorite. Everyone's best friend. A true hero, all kindness and warmth. He didn't have it in him to fight back. When Benna decided she didn't want to give up on life, that was that. None of the others were strong enough to resist."

"Raven, look at me."

She couldn't.

"It broke Darrow just as much as you, you know. He loved Julian like a brother. Standing witness at your wedding was the proudest day of Darrow's life. And then his chosen brother sacrificed himself to save everyone else and left his mutilated wife all alone in a world on fire.

"You were supposed to be the strongest of us. Even after the accident, you had more talent in your right arm than the rest of us combined. Everyone expected you to step up and pull us all together, but you just…fell apart. You couldn't even get out of bed, let alone lead us. Your pain ran so deep it started to affect the trainees.

"And Darrow couldn't take it. The helplessness drove him crazy. He *needed* to take a stand and make a difference. He couldn't fight the whole Shadow army on his own. But saving his brother and reuniting him with his pretty, broken doll of a wife to fix her, too? That was almost easy in comparison. Achievable, one might say."

Raven whimpered. Her vision blurred, concealing Julian's bloated face, but some perverse, masochistic impulse prevented her from closing her eyes, from telling Ripley to shut their fucking mouth and stop this.

"All he had to do was protect you and contain the most dangerous secret in the universe. He knew it was wrong. But he loved Julian too much to let him die. I imagine that watching you struggle must have felt validating in some way. He wasn't being selfish—he was doing it for *you. You* needed your husband back. He convinced himself that it had to be possible to separate the hive. So he hired experts to study how telepathy functioned on the most physical level, how to map the frequencies so they could eventually be restored to themselves."

Oh, stars. Vernon and Zyxon's research. They knew.

"Blackbird, I need you to breathe."

"Truth is, it was too late for them the minute Benna panicked. She took everything from the others to make herself inviolate. Their individual minds are gone. They're just extensions of her now. Batteries amplifying her will. Even inside the strongest Faraday shield around that room, she can still read anyone who crosses the threshold. And if she senses a threat, they don't make it two steps."

Raven was *gone*. If she registered anything happening around her, Zach couldn't tell. She was slumped in his hold, her face filled with horror as she watched that fucking feed while tears silently ran down her cheeks.

It should have been you.

Ripley was fucking dead.

So was Darrow, whoever the fuck he was.

Whatever genius had decided to put him in charge would be next in line.

But he needed to address the biggest issue first.

Careful not to set her off, Zach moved Raven to sit in one of the chairs the henchmen had vacated. Her only reaction was to turn her head to keep the feed in sight. "Blackbird, come back to me."

No response.

Cold rage gripped him by the gut. "Where is that room?"

Ripley shook their head. "It's no use. And we can't afford to lose you."

It should have been you.

"Where?" he growled.

The soulless asshole deigned to look at Raven and what they'd done to her. They frowned. "You'll die."

"Make me ask again. See what happens."

Finally, some semblance of rational fear seeped into those cold eyes. "Through the door, to the right, all the way to the end. There's no lock. Think happy thoughts."

Zach cupped Raven's cheek, turning her face toward him. She blinked, unseeing. And the tears kept coming. There would be no getting through to her until he fixed this. Zach pressed a kiss to her forehead. "Don't watch."

As soon as he let her go, she turned right back to the feed.

"Wait until you see me go in, and then get her out of this room," he instructed Ripley. "I don't need to tell you to keep her safe while I'm gone, do I?"

"Fuck you," they muttered, but there was no bite to it. "Better hope that serum worked."

He stalked out the door, a cheap throwing knife in hand. The metal buzzed in his grip like an antenna picking up on whatever the fuck made his brain crawl with static electricity. At the end of the hall, the glass door slid open at his approach.

The room was bigger than it had looked on the feed. It smelled like bleach and oil. The structure at the center took up most of the available space, but half of the perimeter wall was covered with equipment. Five screens mapped the telepaths' vitals. Four of the 3D brain models looked like empty glass vessels spinning in holographic space. Despite their hearts beating and their lungs breathing, there was no life in any part of those telepaths' brains.

In contrast, the fifth tracked a storm of activity that spiked way off the charts. The 3D brain scan glowed so bright it whited out the entire screen, while the numeric measurements read ERROR in every box.

A sudden pressure squeezed Zach's skull seconds before the far pod erupted in splashing movement. "Benna Havely, I presume."

He rolled his shoulders, pushing the sensation out of his thoughts so he could focus. Four pods remained still, the telepaths inside unresponsive. One woman and three men. Zach rounded the perimeter, putting himself at the same angle as the feed view to locate the pod that had broken Raven.

Julian Dello Russo was a shell of the man she'd shown him through her memories. His brown hair had mostly fallen out, leaving tufts of white here and there. He'd paled in the absence of sunlight, and his body had deteriorated after years of convalescence. While he'd retained most of his mass, his body had lost its muscular structure. He looked rubbery, like a chubby-cheeked blow-up version of his former self. Eyes closed, face slack. A corpse powering a coward.

It should have been you.

A drop of crimson fell into Julian's pod, spreading through the life-sustaining fluid in a small ripple that faded almost instantly. Zach wiped the trickle from his nose. His hand came away bloody. He spared it half a thought before turning his attention back to Raven's husband. "Thank you," he whispered. For taking Raven's place. For giving Zach time to find her.

Benna Havely emitted a sound he'd never heard a human make before. Her body thrashed in the pod, limp limbs slamming weakly against its walls. Liquid splashed and spilled over the edges, but the squeeze on Zach's brain had eased the slightest bit.

It was enough to get him moving again.

The pressure pulsed the closer he got to Benna's pod. It clenched until his eyeballs threatened to pop out, then released just as quickly. His ears felt wet, blood still dripped from his nose, but Zach didn't stop until he reached the monster made flesh.

Benna's body hadn't fared any better than Julian's. What little he could see of her in the murky water was bloated and limp, but her face was contorted, animalistic, with a fury that didn't stop the blood leaking from her eyes, nose, and ears. Even in this state, so far removed from any semblance of a normal life, locked underground and cut off from the world at large, Benna still fought with everything she had to hold on to her pathetic existence.

Zach watched her struggle, savoring her obvious torment, while enduring his own, muted version of it. He felt her trying to get into his thoughts. But it seemed the harder she attacked, the more she hurt herself.

"Very aggressive protections." That's what Raven had called his shield. "Keep going. It gets worse." Pain was an old lesson his mentor had drilled into him since birth. It didn't stop him; it made him fight back that much harder. So every time he felt that squeeze, he made himself a blade and stabbed through it. "That's it. Hurts so good, doesn't it?"

Benna's mouth opened, expelling more blood on a choked whimper. Her eyes raced behind eyelids that looked glued shut. Sausage-like fingers emerged from the mess of her pod, almost curling, but not quite.

Zach leaned lower, putting his neck an inch away from her reach.

"Beg me to end it, bitch."

Benna arched, her torso rising as her face submerged with a soundless scream that he felt like pinpricks against his forehead.

When he buried the knife in her proffered heart, the force of it drove her beneath the surface, soaking him up to his shoulder. He held her down for the three seconds it took her to stop moving.

The instruments beeped a short alert, and then, one after the other, the remaining four echoed it. Without Benna to keep their hearts beating, the other telepaths simply…stopped.

Zach didn't take the blade with him. He stripped off his jacket and used it to wipe off Benna's blood and his own, then tossed it over her head in the pod on his way out.

That annoying static feeling had disappeared, probably turned off after Benna kicked it. It was so quiet and *open,* Zach's inhale felt like the first one in fifteen minutes.

Ripley gaped at him. "Holy shit."

Sitting at their feet with her back to the wall and her forehead resting on her updrawn knees, Raven looked shattered, lost to the world.

Ripley backed away from Zach's approach.

Good.

"You'll be wanting to contact Darrow now," he said.

Then he sat down beside Raven and counted her shaky breaths to make sure they kept coming.

THE EVOLUTIONARY GOSPEL OF MICHAEL

Abridged transcript, dated February 14, 3036

Hey Lee-Lee. I know, I know. I look like hell chewed me up and spat me back out. Yes, I'm eating. Most days. Yes, I'm drinking. Most days, it even helps. Don't worry about me. We're getting to the finish line now.

I don't know if I'll be able to get in touch again after this, so I need to tell you as much as I can fit into one message. I hope you get it in time. But don't worry if you don't. It'll be years before the wheels turn in your direction. You'll be ready by then. You'll be just fine.

As long as you remember this one thing: You can **never** trust a soldier. But you **have to** trust the warrior. Pause and take notes if you need to. You'll want to make copies, too. Just to be safe.

So, bad news first: I'm not gonna make it, Leels. But it's okay. You know me, I'm gonna go out with a bang that'll shake those fuckers for years to come. It'll be quick, and I'll be gone before I feel any pain. I'd tell you not to mourn me, but we both know you will, so I'll just say this: Don't mourn me too long. There's too much work to do. There will be too many more people to bury along the way. Mourning can come after we win.

The good news is that we still have a chance to win. And it won't be in space battles of exploding warships. We're playing chess on a whole nother scale here, cuz, and every piece counts. Collect them like your life depends on it.

That gets us through the first three years. Now, this is going to be the tricky part. There are events set in stone, but where the current moves from there isn't clear. Too many equally possible scenarios, and too many decisions still to be made between now and then.

But remember what I told you? It's the pieces on the board that will make the difference.

Look for a catastrophe in the Karos system. Something that makes all the news across the galaxy, and they will not shut the fuck up about it. You'll want to scoff—correct reaction, by the way—but that event will be the catalyst.

You will be contacted by a soldier from their side. He will tell you things you won't want to believe. Believe him. He will ask you for something you won't understand at first, and then won't want to give. But, Leels, you have to. As soon as you get your hands on that soldier, give him what he asked for. Sneak it through his initial treatment. Make sure no one sees. He won't make it otherwise.

When he wakes up, he won't know you, and you won't trust him. But he won't be a soldier anymore. And you **have to** trust the warrior. Otherwise, you'll all be fucked.

And, just because I know you, try to resist the temptation of taking some of that serum for yourself. It changes the timeline to a place you really, really don't want to go...

40

The solid rook, the faithful bishop, and the steadfast knight wielding a mace. But it's the poisoned pawn who will take out the true enemy. The scorpion who absorbed several deaths-worth of venom and made it its own.

- The Evolutionary Gospel of Michael

January 28, 3040 – Lavari Dolmi, Valhale 602

Darrow, the coward, never made an appearance. But other people came to clean up the mess. Raven recovered her senses enough to stand when prompted, walk when prompted, and sit when she got tired. But she never acknowledged Zach or anyone else. She never spoke a word, and when others tried to reach her telepathically, they only found a thick, cold fog.

The two of them were given adjoining rooms in one of the neighboring buildings because, as it turned out, the entire city of Lavari Dolmi was a telepath sanctuary. Raven went into her room, closed the door behind her, and Zach didn't see her come out again. Every time he tried to go in, he hit a solid wall of resistance. His feet refused to approach the threshold. His hand refused to knock. His throat locked up when he tried to talk.

I say stop, you stop.

Message received.

So he parked his ass on the floor outside her door and waited.

For seven days, only the kitchen staff were allowed to enter to bring her meals. At least she was eating.

Ripley stopped by once to tell him that Darrow had been removed from Valhale 602. The SU didn't have the equivalent of a dishonorable discharge, but they did have something like a court-martial. Ripley assured him that the kid's actions had earned him a severe punishment. But apparently, he was still breathing, which meant it wasn't good enough. Zach figured he'd give the kid three years to grow up. The same three that Darrow had kept Raven, her husband, and the rest of the hive in torment. Then they'd see. Zach could track anyone anywhere. Finding one terrified kid wouldn't be a problem. And three years was a long time to contemplate all the ways to make him pay.

Of course, Raven could still decide to forgive him. Zach didn't like that option, but it was her pain, so her choice. She could get into Zach's head; she could erase Darrow's name and identity from his memories. She'd have to, for him to let this go.

Ripley had also provided him with a heavily redacted copy of *The Evolutionary Gospel of Michael*, which turned out to be hours upon hours of some guy talking into a recorder. Weirdest thing Zach had ever seen. There were times when he was fully lucid and focused, spelling out exact dates and times with detailed descriptions of each event—months before they actually occurred. Down to the color of someone's T-shirt as they got shot down in the street outside a government building on Earth.

But those were interspersed with long stretches of trance-like stares when he monotonously delivered cryptic prophecy bullshit like, "You can never trust a soldier, but you have to trust the warrior," and, "The father will never know the friends his son plays with." Or, Zach's absolute favorite, "Only when the prodigal returns will the black bird fly again."

Safe to assume Raven was the black bird. But a prodigal didn't sound like his idea of a trustworthy individual.

Eighteen hours of this.

With nothing better to do, Zach had watched it four times over, confirmed the events that had already happened, and tried to make sense of the *approximations* of what Michael had predicted was still to come. Some of those dots almost connected in his mind. Most of it sounded like the unhinged ramblings of a man with a massive aneurysm pressing on his brain.

But they called it gospel for a reason.

At the end of the week, a windstorm kicked up outside. It howled relentlessly for two days straight, and blew in some new faces. Through the third-floor hallway window, Zach watched a swarm of customized transports fly in from multiple directions and descend in a tight formation on the street below. Ripley and a few others met them outside and quickly dispersed them to take shelter in nearby buildings. But a small handful came straight into Zach's.

Raven hadn't made a sound inside her room.

He didn't want to leave her door unprotected, but it was best to meet a potential threat where he had room to maneuver. Plus, he preferred to make his own introductions over Ripley feeding the newcomers more bullshit.

By the time he made it down the stairs to the lobby, only Ripley remained, speaking to a couple. The red-haired woman looked none too pleased. She had the air of someone who routinely made decisions she didn't want to have to make.

The man beside her was a Shadow, if Zach had ever seen one. He sported a short, non-regulation beard and a seashell necklace, but he spotted Zach the second he appeared, and his posture shifted to guard the redhead.

Zach felt like he should know the man. Something about his eyes sparked a memory fragment. But he didn't have enough context to put a name to his face.

Might as well say hello. It was the polite thing to do.

Ten feet out, the redhead suddenly gasped and gripped her head.

And, with a vicious snarl, her Shadow charged Zach.

He didn't make it two steps before the redhead caught him by the sleeve and said, "Wait! It's not his fault."

The man stopped in his tracks, an attack dog pulled up short by his leash. Good to know Zach wasn't the only Shadow who had that kind of weakness.

Ripley shrugged. "Tried to warn you."

The redhead winced and tugged on her Shadow. "I'm not broken."

Zach raised his hands. "I didn't do anything."

"He didn't," the redhead confirmed. "Stop it, Seashell."

The Shadow backed a step toward her, his eyes never leaving Zach.

Squinting in obvious pain, the redhead looked Zach over. "What did you do to yourself?"

"I worked with what I had."

She nodded, sniffled, then wiped her nose, checking for blood. Thankfully, there wasn't any, or Zach was pretty sure her Shadow would try to tear his head off.

"Zach…we still going with St. Clare?" Ripley asked.

He nodded. "For the moment." Until they beat the Shadows. He still intended to recover his VanWarren identity eventually.

"Meet Acting Director Emma Wayland. She's our version of a commander-in-chief. The man currently contemplating your eventual evisceration is her husband, John Wayland."

Oh…

Oh, this was an interesting development. "I thought I recognized you. The first Hawk to fly the Shadow nest. An honor." His name had been briefly mentioned in the file attached to Zach's pre-EMC recording as a potentially valuable contact, considering the Shadows still had a standing kill-on-sight order out on him across all databases. Although even past-Zach hadn't been quite sure whether Wayland was still alive.

"I'm sure you two will have loads to talk about," Ripley deadpanned. Not a fan of Wayland's, apparently. Zach would love to know what that was about. "We were just catching up on the Raven problem."

"Only problem Raven has is that you're still here, and that can easily be remedied. Watch your mouth," Zach warned.

Something shifted in Wayland's expression, and his posture loosened the slightest bit. From a Hawk, it was as good as a peace offering.

Zach still wouldn't turn his back on the man. That would be a quick way to an early grave.

"This isn't fit," Emma Wayland said. "We need to nest. Then we can chirp."

"I want to scope the bird first," her husband replied.

"I hear there's a conference room on the fifth floor," Zach offered. "Let's go squawk."

Ripley stared at him. "You understood that?"

"You didn't?"

John Wayland cracked half a smile. "Let's go squawk."

"I'll call the others to roost," Emma relented on a long-suffering sigh.

"Not necessary."

She scowled at her husband. "They'll want a piece of the worm, and you want your wingman, and he wants his. Don't make me catch the dominoes."

"Might as well make it a group lunch to break the ice," Zach said. "Ripley, make yourself useful and let the kitchen know, will you?" He waved Wayland ahead. "Elevator's this way."

"Five minutes out," Emma said to the other Hawk, then speared Zach with a glare. "You and I will bump heads later."

"How 'bout a friendly chat instead? Hurting women doesn't do it for me."

She appeared to consider this, then nodded. "Fair."

41

When they fail to destroy us, they will try to become us,
and that will be the beginning of the end.

- The Evolutionary Gospel of Michael

Zach had to give it to the telepaths—they knew how to decorate. His room was a riot of colors and textures, and the conference room was no different. A bright tile mosaic with abstract shapes outlined in shiny gold and silver covered one wall. The table was a massive slab of rough-hewn wood, grooved and uneven around the edges, and probably weighing a ton. Every chair around it was different from the rest. Some of them weren't even chairs, but padded perches, or massive pillows stuffed into a frame to keep their shape. The windows had lacy draperies, the floors were covered in dozens of mismatched rugs, and the ceiling looked like an upside-down 3D aerial map.

Color, upon texture, upon pattern, every part of the chaos designed to keep the senses from turning inward. The polar opposite of everything Zach had known with the Shadows.

Wayland didn't appear bothered by any of it. If he'd been with the SU all this time, he was probably used to the sensory overload. He didn't let it distract him. Crossing the room, the former Shadow pulled back the edge of a drape to scan the street below.

It felt weird, being in the presence of someone who'd been trained almost the same as Zach. Outside of his CO, he'd never personally met another Hawk—that he remembered, anyway. Always wanted to, though.

"They call me The Wall," Wayland said.

"You don't look like one."

He was about to respond when the rest of the company filed in, led by a fearsome-looking giant who fit through the door with only a few inches of clearance around his muscular shoulders.

"That's what a wall looks like."

The giant scowled. "Now, is that any way to talk to your favorite cousin?"

"I don't have any family."

The dark-haired woman coming up behind the giant snorted as she flipped a shining knife in her hand. "That's new."

"Hello, gorgeous." Zach rounded the table between them, ignoring the giant's warning glare and the way the woman's razor-sharp gaze tracked him. When he reached, she snarled, shifting her left foot forward, fisting the knife handle in readiness.

Zach caught her by the wrist and pried the knife from her grip. "Alloy, through and through. Flawless construction. Perfectly balanced." He tested the edge with the lightest brush of his thumb and immediately drew blood. "Oh, I know this blade." He still remembered how it felt, twisting in his gut.

While he was distracted by the knife, the woman watched him warily, waiting for him to make a move. Poised to put him in the ground if he made the wrong one.

The rest of their company—nine total—was just as tense. They weren't quite a cohesive unit, but they had each other's backs. Better, they trusted each other to hold their own.

Zach grinned, flipped the knife, and spun it this way and that. "Nice to put a face to the pain."

The woman caught her weapon when he tossed it up an inch higher. "Don't. Ever. Touch my knives."

"Acknowledged," he said, grinning. "I'm Zach."

"I know," she retorted, removing herself to the far corner. There, she perched in the widest armchair and pulled a whetstone from her pocket. She applied it to the blade as if to make sure he hadn't dulled it with his rough handling. Each stroke would sharpen the edge and strengthen the alloy. Knives like that were hard to come by. And only an expert or a connoisseur would willingly spend what they cost. The woman appeared to be both.

Heavily muscled arms the size of tree trunks locked around him and squeezed so hard his ribs groaned. His feet left the floor as the giant muttered, "Glad to see you alive, cousin."

"Thanks," Zach managed to squeak out. If this was his idea of affection, he didn't want to know what it felt like when he got mad.

"They blanked him," Wayland informed the others.

The giant set Zach down and offered his massive hand. "Quinn VanWarren. That there is my wife, Vega. You saved our lives last year—"

"No, he didn't," Vega, the blade master, cut in.

"—we're grateful," Quinn finished pointedly.

Zach braced to have his bones crushed, but, for wielding so much muscle, Quinn had remarkable control over his strength. They shook hands without incident. "I don't remember any of that."

"That's fine," Quinn assured him. When he smiled, his face became almost friendly. "Some of it you probably won't want to, anyway. We can talk about the rest later."

He'd take it.

From there, Quinn introduced him to the rest of the company. Brent Catton was a Hound who didn't seem to like Zach very much. Non-starter, as far as Zach was concerned. Somewhere during the introduction, Catton let slip that he'd known Vega back in their Talon days, whatever that meant. The insinuation being that Vega was also a Hound. Somehow, Zach doubted that.

The Shadow missing a digit on his left hand presented a bigger threat. Finnegan Rowe, whose name Zach knew as well as Wayland's.

Two Hawks, good friends, by the looks of them, and a potential problem if they decided to turn on him. Even if they didn't, Hawks were notorious for not playing well with others. The way Vega and Catton seemed to defer to Rowe, they'd appointed him as the de facto leader, which could be an issue if the Hawk tried to throw his weight around.

A short barrel of a woman with spiky blond hair and a scar through her left eyebrow stepped up next to introduce herself. "Sadie. Former Hound. I will be commanding the Evolutionary forces. This is Alec, my right hand and strategist."

Alec looked like he could handle himself in a fight, but he wasn't a Shadow, as evidenced by the lines and musical notes tattooed around his bicep. He kept his arms crossed as he nodded a wordless greeting, then followed his commander to the table.

After the fighters had marked their turf, a tall woman with short brown hair stepped out from behind Quinn. She took one look at Zach, shook her head, and backed out the door. "Sorry. Can't." Rowe frowned and made to follow her, but she held up her hand. "You stay. I just…need to be somewhere else."

"Laura McNally," Quinn explained after she closed the door behind her. "Telepath."

"Yep." Zach figured.

"She's really good at what she does."

Zach nodded. "Safer for her to be somewhere else, then."

It seemed there were certain types of telepaths whose brains couldn't shut off. They left themselves open, passively picking up on things around them. Unfortunately, what they picked up from Zach was telepathic damage. His shields reacted to their mere presence, regardless of whether they were actively trying to connect or not. Zach had no more control over it than they did.

Eskel Andersson filled the gap after Laura made her exit. "I've been drafted as a field medic," he said by way of introduction. He was as much a stranger to Zach as Zach appeared to be to him. He definitely would have remembered the chin tattoo. "If you're open to it, I'd like to put you through a scanner and do some tests later."

"Hey! No more poaching." The last member of their company, a woman with hair as white as snow, shouldered the medic aside. "Bad enough you stole my formula. If anyone's dissecting him, it's me."

Quinn groaned.

"And you are…?"

"The reason you're still breathing," she said cheerfully. "Also, the interim chief of medicine, now that the Brain is on leave to deal with her brother."

"Zach, this is Hailey Chase-Calen," Quinn supplied. "She and her sister developed the healing serum they gave us."

"Which Eskel here decided to test on himself, replicate on an industrial scale, and then distribute among his favorites on Mai—without authorization."

Eskel didn't balk from her glare. "Don't know if anyone told you, but that's what healers are supposed to do: keep their patients healthy."

"You don't look like a telepath," Zach said to break up the pissing contest.

"Oh, no, babe. I'm something worse." Right in front of him, her face began to change. Thick black outlined her eyes and faint panther rosettes bloomed like faded tattoos across her forehead and cheeks. Her hand, shaking Zach's, tightened, and black, pointed claws poked into his skin before she retracted them again.

"That's...different."

When she grinned, her nose flattened and her upper lip split. A few seconds later, she was human again, winking at him. "Eat your heart out."

"No, thanks."

One of the others snorted.

Hailey sobered enough for the wild humor to temper into something like sympathy. "Emma filled us in on what happened. Your girl doing okay?"

"Not really, no."

She nodded. "Eskel, maybe you should check on her first. She'll probably respond to your bedside manner better than mine."

Zach looked Eskel over again. "You a prodigal?"

The man frowned. "Uh, can't say I've ever been accused of that."

"Then stay away from Raven."

"I'm just here to help," he said.

"We all are," Quinn added. "You can trust Eskel. He's kept me and my family alive for years. He won't mind adding a couple more relatives to his patient list."

"I—don't—have—family."

From her corner seat, Vega chimed in with a dry, "Would you be willing to reconsider if I stabbed you again?"

Zach took a breath for patience. "Possibly."

"I demand this to be noted for the record," Hailey announced, "I am no longer the freak of the company. I have officially been outfreaked. Thank you very much." She whirled away, her white hair whipping around, and took the most practical seat at the table.

Everyone stared at her.

She growled in warning, and it was far from a human sound.

"I guess we sit," Rowe muttered.

Everyone else followed his lead, congregating around the table. Zach was the last one to join the group, taking a padded perch closest to the door. Vega didn't deign it necessary to leave her station by the window. Despite her apparent focus on honing her knife, Zach could tell she didn't miss a single word or gesture. She was as much a Hound as Zach was a ballet dancer.

"First order of business," Rowe said, already taking the lead, "we lost contact with Earth. Mars 2 reported Shadow sightings right before we left Mai. They were ordered to evacuate. Jericho is still recovering from last month's strike. And Persephone 5 is…"

"Fucked," Wayland supplied.

Rowe nodded.

All of those were massive, densely populated hubs. They'd been among the first to be hit at the beginning of the war because of it. Yet none of the attacks had made the news. The closest Zach recalled seeing was a volcanic eruption on Persephone 5—clearly a cover-up. He recognized Sandoval's brand all over it. With his connections in the ICG and every major news network, the only Shadow activity civilians knew about anymore were the ones Sandoval chose to publicize.

"They appear to be hit-and-run attacks. No tactical advantage to any of the targets, other than to sow panic. It's working. St. Clare, Councilor Parecourte said you had intel on what's driving this. Care to share with the class?"

This was a war council.

Zach looked around the table and saw the faces of a coalition. As he understood it, the Special Unit and the Evolutionaries operated as separate entities. Michael's Gospel had portrayed them as adversaries before the war. Since the fight began, they'd adopted an "enemy of my enemy is a neutral player" philosophy. They didn't team up, didn't freely share intel, but didn't get in each other's way, either.

Wayland and Chase-Calen sat in for the SU. Wayland's Hawk training made him the ideal general for their forces, and it probably didn't hurt that he was married to their acting director. Chase-Calen was the secret weapon that gave them an edge in battle. A soldier who could survive a fatal wound and keep fighting could sway the outcome of this war.

Sadie and Alec represented the Evolutionaries. Zach didn't know enough about them, and that made him wary. Ripley was the bridge between the two organizations, a double-agent in as cooperative a sense as they could be. It offered little comfort if the two factions couldn't reconcile the differences that had kept them apart this long.

But whom did Rowe represent?

He had Catton, Vega, and, by extension, Quinn, in his pocket, which gave him a majority advantage. Zach would expect them to have each other's backs over anyone else's. If something didn't sit right with them, they'd go rogue.

As far as councils went, Zach supposed he should be grateful they were all willing to sit at the same table. If the situation out there was as bad as Rowe said, they didn't have much time to waste.

This was what he'd been looking for. A sign that they were ready to fight back, that what he had to share wouldn't fall on deaf ears. That they would rally together, not scatter apart.

Raven should have been there.

Zach took up the control tablet and turned on the 3D holoprojector embedded in the ceiling. The windows blacked out automatically, and the lights dimmed. He hacked into the network, used it to connect with his encrypted server, and pulled up a schematic.

A 3D model of a metal node trailing two long wires hovered above the center of the table.

"Raise your hand if you don't know what EMC is."

No one did.

"Count the Shadows around the table and raise your hand if you think it's still working."

Someone swore.

"Wait, isn't that a good thing?" That, from the heretofore silent Alec. Didn't bode well for his role as a strategist.

"Not if this is their solution," Zach said. "Almost got my brains fried to get this out, so pay attention. What you're looking at is a neural networking node. When applied successfully, it eliminates free will on command. No more repeated chair treatments that put soldiers out of commission for hours every few weeks. No more wasting time re-briefing them on mission parameters. They wipe a soldier once, and then shove those wires straight into their brain right through the temple.

"When it's in sleep mode, the node is dark, and the soldier goes about his business. When it's activated, a blue light goes on, the signal overrides conscious decision-making and turns the soldier into a sophisticated puppet. They can talk, they can understand what's happening to them, but their bodies will only obey one set of orders. Try to disable it in active mode and it fries the brain. Try to remove it in sleep mode, the internal structure shreds brain tissue on the way out."

"They spent years killing telepaths, just to become them in the end?" Hailey shook her head in disbelief.

If only it were that simple. "The nodes don't network with each other. It's a hub-and-spoke model. To reduce communication delays, each region has a local processing unit, which connects back to the central AI system. The processing units collect sensory inputs from the nodes for the central AI. The AI then calculates the most efficient path of attack, and relays commands back through the processing units to each individual node."

Wayland shook his head. "A fucking hive mind."

Benna Havely's savage, bloodied face flashed across Zach's memory. "Worse. AI doesn't get scared. It doesn't panic or make mistakes. You can't appeal to its conscience because it doesn't have one. All it cares about is the mission. And it will sacrifice as many nodes as it takes to ensure its completion. The best part: while it's active, no amount of telepathic persuasion can alter its course. You can scramble the host's brain into soup, and it would keep their body moving. As long as the host has a pulse and a solid nervous system, the node can make them do anything the AI wants."

Sadie swore a vicious streak. "This is…"

"The end of the line," Zach said. "Initial rollout has already begun. The attacks you've seen were test missions. They haven't *networked* everyone yet, but they will ramp up the conversion now that the tech is proven to be effective. I estimate three months before total coverage of existing Shadows. Eighteen percent won't survive the initial implant. Post-implant failure rate is three to seven percent over two weeks. But the nodes are recyclable. And, now that they don't need to *train* soldiers, they can build entire armies in a fraction of the time."

Rowe rubbed his face.

Wayland appeared stunned.

Quinn watched Vega, who had abandoned her perch to take a closer look. The way she studied the model slowly spinning in space suggested she had some experience with a similar technology. Which made her the most likely of all of them to hear and understand the full implications of what he was telling them.

"You see one or two of them coming at you with a blue light embedded in their temple," he said to her, "take the quickest kill shot. Any more than that, you abort and run. If you're lucky, the AI will deem the risk of you too low to pursue."

42

It should have been you.

Every time Raven thought she was making progress back to herself, those words sent her spiraling again. She couldn't stop picturing those pods. Julian's bloated face haunted her every time she closed her eyes. She threw up most of what she ate, but the food kept coming, so she kept forcing herself to eat.

It was purely out of spite. Keeping herself alive was the only way she had to get back at Ripley. Everything else took too much energy. But as long as she kept breathing, Ripley couldn't win.

Except they'd already won.

Save his brother and reunite him with his pretty, broken doll of a wife to fix her, too...

Broken. That was exactly how she felt. A broken marionette with its strings cut.

It should have been you.

Yes. As one of the most skilled telepaths on the moon, it should have been Raven. At the very least, it shouldn't have been *Julian.*

After three years of therapy, she'd almost convinced herself that was her grief talking.

Apparently not.

Precogs were rare. They varied in the way they predicted the future and to what extent, but they were generally considered highly reliable.

And one of them had predicted that Raven would step up to the merge. Ripley seemed to believe the outcome would have been different if she had, and Raven couldn't stop thinking about it.

What if it had been her? What if her participation was the thing that would have prevented Benna from taking over the others? What if she'd managed to break the rest of them apart before the merge became irreversible?

What if...?

It should have been you.

Julian might have been alive. The two of them might have been across the galaxy, touring the stars the way he'd always wanted. They might have had their first child.

Raven was ambivalent toward the notion of procreation, but Julian had always loved children. He would have made such an amazing father.

But you were fighting for your life.

Maybe she couldn't have stopped Julian from falling into the merge, but what if instead of sinking into grief after her surgery, she'd stepped up and taken over from Darrow? She might not have been able to save Julian even then, but she never would have left him like that. She *would* have broken Benna Havely in half to get him out of there.

He wasn't being selfish—he was doing it for you. You *needed your husband back...*

Raven swept the food tray off the coffee table, making a mess all over the floor.

No matter how she spun it, the arrow of blame always came back to point at her. Raven had been trained to excel, taught that she had a duty to protect and defend, and when it had really counted, she'd let herself fall apart instead.

What a disappointment you turned out to be...

She should have known when the doubt refused to go away. On some level, Raven had always felt like Julian wasn't fully gone. She should have trusted her instincts. Julian had given up his life to ensure Raven got to live hers, and in return, she'd completely given up and left him...

She should have done better.

It should have been you.

Raven curled up on the couch, hiding her face in the cushions until she couldn't breathe anymore. She pressed her face in harder, fighting for an inhale, grateful when she ran out of air to scream.

Just as the clawing need for oxygen became unbearable and Raven felt the boundary of no return, she sat up and gasped for breath, her heart racing and her face burning.

Why couldn't she make up her damned mind? Live or don't live? It was a simple decision.

Tessa would have known what to do to break the cycle.

Tessa…

What if Raven had fought harder for her friend? Would she be alive now?

What would Tessa say if she saw Raven wallowing like this again?

Stars, she missed her friend. She missed having someone to talk to.

Suddenly, the com control was in her hand, and the call prompt blinked across the far wall.

Raven stared at it for so long that it chirped to remind her it was still active and waiting for a command. "Tessa Sinclair, 447832 Chairo."

The system beeped, and the symbol changed, flickering rapidly. It wouldn't connect. Tessa was dead. Her account would have been disabled—

CONNECTED.

RECORD MESSAGE...

"Hey," Raven said. "It's me." And that was as far as she got before her voice dissolved into sobs. She cried until her whole body ached, and the entire time, the message kept recording. "I miss you so much it hurts." Tessa couldn't hear her. She would never get the message. But pretending otherwise at least made Raven feel a little less alone. "I can't believe you left me in this shitshow. But I'm so grateful that you weren't there when…"

Flashes of plasma fire. Shattered glass. Blood on the floor.

Raven squeezed her eyes shut against the memories.

She stopped the recording and ended the call.

Two hours later, she was speaking Tessa's name into the command again.

RECORD MESSAGE...

"I saw Julian. All this time… Darrow lied to me, Tess. How could he do that? How could he…"

She ended the call again.

It was pointless, anyway. Not like Tessa could answer. And even if someone found the messages one day, what would they care about Raven's issues? They wouldn't. Because it was all Raven's fault, anyway. She was supposed to have mastered extracting the truth, and for years—*years*—she'd chosen to accept Darrow's lies blindly.

It should have been you.

Raven stumbled into the bathroom and dry-heaved over the toilet, but her stomach had nothing left to expel. She passed out there, too tired to even make it back to her bed.

When she woke up, her mouth was dried shut. Someone had cleaned up the mess in her room and left a new food tray with a fresh, hot meal and cold herbal tea. Raven chugged it straight from the jug.

Then she called Tessa again. "I slept with the Shadow." She tried to say more, but words failed her. The hours they'd spent tangled with each other had been amazing. But everything that had come after... "I don't know what to do, Tess."

And 'round, and 'round she went, cycling through her grief, and shame, and anger. She choked on betrayal one minute, then drowned in the hollow pit of despair the next. She ate cake, remembering the last time she'd had it—the night of Tessa's farewell. She drank juice, remembering Zach hand-feeding her after their marathon of sex.

And back she went to the toilet, emptying it all out at the memory of Julian's face on a surveillance feed. Physically alive, mentally gone. Hidden away from her for *three fucking years*.

RECORD MESSAGE...

"It's me again..."

Only in sleep did Raven find some respite from her looping thoughts. But even in her dreams, she always wandered, lost and adrift. Sometimes, the streets were filled with massive crowds that jostled her along, and the only way out was up. But as she rose above the mob, she saw them heading straight for a cliff, and the street behind them was painted with countless bloody footprints all blending into a field of solid crimson.

Other times, she ran through a dark maze where every dead end had a person chained to the wall. Bloated, pale, and limp. Their hands were swollen and blue above the shackles that held them up. Their feet buried in the ground. They never moved, yet she still heard them breathing. And every exhale was a plea for help.

But then there were times, like now, when everything was mired in a fog…

She sensed things around her, like walls and furniture. She even heard people walking around. But she didn't see anyone past clouds of smoky gray.

Raven weaved her hand through it, creating a current that cleared her view for all of two feet, just in time to keep her from walking into a closed door. The ornate door handle beckoned to be pulled, but Raven didn't want to go through it. The buzzing was too loud beyond it.

She turned back and felt her way to the other side of the room, where muffled voices murmured behind a wall. Raven pressed her ear to the aged, peeling wallpaper, but no matter how hard she tried, she couldn't make out what they were saying. It felt imperative that she find them and join the conversation. But this part of the room didn't have any doors or windows. No way to get through.

Raven thumped on the wall without making a sound.

She called out without a voice.

She traced the wall sideways, looking for a crack, a break in the pattern—anything to give her a starting point.

The wall just kept going.

And the fog got darker.

Soon, there was no furniture left to trip her. A little after that, the solid wall became as soft as a curtain. Between one step and the next, it disappeared, and she found herself in total darkness.

Raven turned circles left and right, shouting into the void, hearing only silence. She was fading. Losing herself little by little. Soon, there'd be nothing left of her.

A guttural croak of a birdcall behind her.

Raven froze. Sensation returned just enough for her to feel her heart for a beat. Breath didn't exist, but she held it anyway, straining to hear something other than that deafening silence.

The call came again, a rough caw in the distance. Raven ran for it headlong. Her essence stretched, straining the anchor keeping her teth-

ered. If it snapped, she'd be lost forever in the darkness. But what was there left for her in the light?

The tether frayed, each broken filament lashing at her. Raven ought to go back.

The bird cawed again.

She didn't go back. She ran harder, leaving her feet behind, letting her arm fade away, until she unraveled into a streak of consciousness holding on by a single thread.

The darkness thickened, slowing her progress. Squeezing her back together. It stopped her with a soft, unyielding impact when it enclosed her in a full-body prison and shoved.

Raven was forcibly thrust back the way she'd come, tracing her tether to where she belonged, leaving the darkness behind.

But the shadow around her remained. It coalesced the same way she did, until she was whole again, and it wasn't a shadow banding around her but strong arms clutching her to a solid body.

"I missed you, Blackbird."

Raven knew that voice. Why couldn't she see his face?

"I need you to listen to me," he said urgently. "It was never going to be you."

The words stabbed ice into her, and she flinched, pulling away. She didn't want to hear this. It hurt too much.

But though she couldn't see him, he refused to let go. The mist around them brightened and cleared in patches, echoing with voices. Floating, uniform shapes of smooth white circled around her, fading in and out of the gray.

It should have been you…

"No," her Shadow snarled, and the insidious voice faded back into the mist. "Accident or not, they never would have let you merge," he said.

The shapes rotated to face inward, clearing to reveal a person inside each one. But they raced around the circle so fast their features blurred.

Until they came to a dead stop, with that one pod right in front of her. That painfully familiar face, devoid of expression, yet still somehow screaming at her.

It should have been you…

"You don't waste your most effective weapon on a miss."

It should have been you...

"They would have held you back, the same way they've been doing ever since. Blackbird, they need you too much to lose you. But I need you more. Come back to me."

But that wasn't right. They were the ones who'd been with her for years, holding her up when she couldn't do it herself; drying her tears when they wouldn't stop coming; giving her purpose when everything had felt meaningless.

Except it had all been a lie.

Reunite him with his pretty, broken doll of a wife to fix her, too...

The Shadow was supposed to be the enemy, manipulating her, using her...

Not saving her life. Not cradling her grief. Not mending her soul.

He'd warned her about them.

He'd asked her not to watch.

Whom was she supposed to trust?

No one.

Raven didn't fight her way free of his hold. She let herself fade through him. He was just a shadow on the periphery of her consciousness, a figment of her imagination. But his pain cut as sharp as a razor blade down her throat.

If she couldn't trust her own people, how could she ever trust him? How could she trust anyone again?

"Please," he begged.

But the fog had already closed in around her, and she sank into its cool embrace, grateful for its buffer against the relentless misery of everything outside of it. She welcomed the familiar numbness and let it carry her away...

43

Five will stand, four will fall. The monolith will only be brought down by talons.

                                    - The Evolutionary Gospel of Michael

February 6, 3040 – Lavari Dolmi, Valhale 602

Zach sat up and hurled his pillow across the room. So close. He'd been so fucking close to getting through to her. And she'd faded away like it had all been just a dream.

It was still progress, he tried to tell himself. After days of pushing his mind to find some direction to trace, he'd finally made contact. For those few moments, air had returned, and he could breathe again.

He shouldn't have said what he had. She clearly wasn't ready to hear it. But the fragile link he'd managed to build had been too weak to sustain, and he'd needed her to understand. No matter what bullshit Ripley spewed, Michael's prediction wasn't clear enough to point a finger at Raven.

While the war council had kept busy with gathering intel, warning their most vulnerable outlier colonies, and strategizing potential counter-offensives, Zach had occupied himself hacking into the SU's databases to do a little homework.

Turned out, Raven had been a star pupil since she'd been identi-fied as a telepath at age four. They'd invested a lot of resources into sharpening her mind to its full potential, even going so far as to fly in tutors from all over the galaxy because her skills had surpassed the local telepaths by age fourteen.

Her most prestigious tutor had been the SU's former director, who'd disappeared without a trace four years ago.

According to Raven's extensive file, she was rated a master in three distinct disciplines, placing her in the top five percent of all registered telepaths, ranked by ability. She wasn't just the lead interrogator. Her duties extended to *reprogramming* problematic subjects—entirely rewriting their brains to erase their old identities and create new ones.

Only five other telepaths in the entire SU database had those abilities, and of all of them, only Raven had ever worked on Shadows. As such, she was classified as a 'tactical asset'—one of the few instances where any SU language incorporated military terminology.

They might not have been trained in the ways of war, but the SU had enough brain power among its ranks to more than make up for it. Between precogs, strategists, readers, and *neural engineers*, they had enough smarts to know when to hide, when to strike, and when to retreat.

The telepath encyclopedia said that merging telepathic abilities had an amplifying effect. If that was true, then it would make more strategic sense to sacrifice a larger number of weaker players than a smaller number of stronger ones. The end result would essentially be the same.

Which meant that, no matter what, it never would have been Raven breaking Benna Havely's chokehold on the hive. One moon wouldn't have been a significant enough loss to risk their big guns. Even if Raven had been at full strength, they would have found a way to keep her out of the fight. You didn't waste tactical assets to hold a minor defensive line. Those were reserved for when they would count.

The SU was saving Raven and others like her for a direct attack at the heart of the Shadow military complex.

Zach's Shadow training agreed with the strategy wholeheartedly. He knew enough about Sandoval's plans and ambitions to understand that it would take a truly extraordinary and unexpected weapon to take him down, and stars knew Raven qualified. But the thought of her going anywhere near his CO had him in his boots and storming out the door to the gym.

Water scarcity meant no exercise pools, but the gym still had enough equipment to help Zach temper at least some of his excess energy. He sprinted until his knees started to buckle. He pulled himself up and over the bar, forward and backward, until his fingers cramped on it. Then he laid into the composite boxing column until his knuckles split.

"Damn. You good, bro?"

Zach stumbled a step away from the column and swiveled around.

Brent Catton stared at him like he felt bad, a sixty-pound dumbbell frozen halfway into a bicep curl.

Across from him, Vega VanWarren had paused her sit-ups to watch—displaying considerably less concern.

On the other side of the gym, the rest of his audience stared at him in various degrees of alarm, half of them twitching to bolt, the rest tensed at the ready, just in case.

He hadn't noticed any of them on his way in.

A glass bottle entered his field of vision.

Zach blinked at it, then followed the arm to its owner. "Hydrate," Eskel said. "It'll help with the recovery."

He took the bottle and downed half of the water in three gulps. Almost immediately, his heart rate leveled out, and his muscles loosened. The ache he'd built up disappeared, and his knuckles looked like he'd never bruised or split them. Zach finished the water, then handed the bottle back to Eskel. "How many of your people got the serum?"

"As many as I could identify," he answered readily. "It only works on chem-resistants, and there aren't as many of those as we'd like. Not for the front lines, at least. Wayland has it. So does Catton. Sadie and Alec had it before I met them. Finn's and Vega's DNA are incompatible. Ripley refused the injection, but a few other telepaths here specifically requested it. I had a heart-to-heart with Dr. Chase-Calen and the acting director, and it was decided that we won't be hoarding it anymore. We can't afford to."

"Agreed." As soon as Raven felt better, Zach would get her a dose, too.

"Dr. Chase-Calen insists that everyone who received the serum report to the hospital down the street for a comprehensive physical as a precaution." Eskel looked Zach up and down. "But I think it's safe to say you're doing just fine."

Zach liked this guy. Seemed like the type who didn't waste time on bullshit. He'd do what needed to be done and move on to the next. No wonder they pulled him in for field triage.

"Regeneration burns a lot of energy. You'll need to up your caloric intake. You missed lunch by about an hour, but they have ready meals set out 'round the clock."

"Is that an order?"

Eskel shrugged. "Not your mother. Don't care either way."

If that were true, he wouldn't have bothered saying anything at all.

The medic went from Zach straight to pointing an accusing finger at Vega. "Did you do your stretches today?"

"Fuck off, you're not my mother, either."

Eskel crossed his arms. "Get your ass up off the floor, or I'm calling Quinn to make you." His courage bordered on suicidal.

But shockingly, Vega made a petulant face and got up as instructed, muttering something unflattering under her breath. Zach caught "prick" and "serve him his balls one day" as he passed.

To which Catton said, "I think you meant to say, 'Yes, Mother.'"

Zach took a quick sonic shower to wash off and put on a clean set of clothes. Ever since Petrus, he'd fallen back into the habit of wearing his uniform. Except these days, it was black and silver nanofiber with two weapons holsters and a brace of knife sheaths.

Every time he saw the other Hawks, he envied their wrist units. He missed his like a phantom limb and, unfortunately, there were no more to be had. Sandoval had ordered all of their emergency caches shut down. Weapons and supplies had been relocated, and the cuff-and-lens sets had been destroyed. No need for infiltration specialist gear now that the gloves were off. It would be pure brute force going forward.

As Eskel had promised, the dining hall was mostly empty, except for a couple of faces he didn't recognize and the kitchen staff prepping for the dinner rush. Racks of meals filled the warming hutch beside the closed serving window. Zach selected a couple of plates, added an apple and two bottles of enriched water, and took a seat by the window so he could keep an eye on the street below.

It had been suspiciously quiet the last couple of weeks. Aside from a steady traffic of incoming guests, the streets had been empty for the most part. It made his scalp itch. The entire town resembled a giant art exhibit more than an active community. Even if it was by design, it felt too open and vulnerable for his peace of mind.

He'd need to have a talk with the Waylands about the town's defenses and evacuation strategy—

"You must be Zach."

A stranger sat down across from him and put a plate of fresh-baked chocolate cookies in the middle of the table. Their sweet aroma filled his nose and made his mouth water.

Chocolate had always been his biggest weakness. In the early years, Sandoval had used brownies as an incentive for Zach to complete his assignment, then yanked them away to teach him not to expect rewards.

A time or two, Zach's rebellious streak had won out, and he'd managed to snatch one first and stuff it into his mouth. Sandoval had broken his fingers for insubordination.

And Zach had spent the next two days in medbay, purging a bite's-worth of poisoned brownie.

"My name is John," the stranger said. He looked like a stereotypical grandpa, complete with more-salt-than-pepper hair, crinkles around his eyes, and a you-can-tell-me-anything smile.

It immediately put Zach on alert, and he fisted his steak knife. "New here?"

Grandpa John didn't telegraph an ounce of fear, as if Zach posed no threat whatsoever. "Recently arrived. But not new." He took his eyes off Zach to look out the window with something like pride. "This place was my idea, you know. It looks good, doesn't it? Pretty impressive, considering they only had two years to put it together."

Zach released the steak knife and sat back for better access to his more effective weapons.

"I have no desire to hurt you," John said. "I just want to talk."

"About?"

"Life. Yours, specifically."

"Because I'm such a fascinating specimen?"

"Yes," he said plainly. "And also because I want to make sure you're good enough for Raven."

And they were done. "You can walk away now."

"I'm sorry, that didn't come out the way I intended. Who Raven chooses to associate with is truly none of my business. She is more than capable of making her own choices. But I happen to know a few things that make me a little apprehensive about what's to come. I need to make sure she is…tethered."

Zach's favorite thing about his gun holsters: magnetic clasps that opened easily and quietly. "Consider your next words very, very carefully."

The bastard grinned. "You've seen Michael's predictions, I take it? At least some of them."

Zach nodded.

"They show you the one about the queen's gambit?"

The whole damned recording was full of chess metaphors. Rooks, and knights, and poisoned pawns. He'd seen several references to queens, sometimes in the singular, other times plural. Nothing specific enough to draw any conclusions about the future. "Doesn't ring a bell."

John shook his head. "I was afraid of that. None of the Evolutionaries have ever seen the full message. For whatever reason, Ripley took liberties with the edits. They only doled out the parts they deemed relevant. They still think they're the only one Michael contacted before he died."

"I take it you got a message of your own."

He winced, his shoulders bowing inward as he said, "I did. It… changed everything. It broke my heart and hurt a lot of people. But trusting Michael was the right thing to do." He spoke like someone who carried several lifetimes of regret. The kind that broke a person.

Looking at him, Zach had a hard time reconciling the kindly grandpa mask with someone who might or might not have a lot of blood on his hands. Which made him suspicious like nothing else could. In his experience, the appearance of innocence was all but a confirmation of guilt. "Who the hell are you?"

"Back before this all started, I was a collector of lost souls. In the early days when chem-resistance was still being swept under the rug, I used to look for people whose minds had turned on them. I took them in, taught them how to control it, and trained them to recognize it. I provided them with a safe haven, a purpose, and a support system so that they could thrive. I built a family. And that family steadily grew into a community, and eventually an organized movement."

Zach's eyebrows rose. "You're saying you founded the Special Unit."

"Well, we didn't call ourselves that at first, but yes, I suppose I did. Once my little community was established, others took up the cause and began doing the same throughout the galaxy. It built on itself out of necessity. We had a council to address any big issues that came up, but, for the most part, we really were just one big family, checking in on each other, trading stories, helping relatives get the support they needed."

"You're the reason Emma Wayland is the *acting* director." The woman was an excellent leader, but she behaved like a placeholder, a substitute who filled in and kept the house in order for someone else—John MacMurphy. She still referenced him on occasion when mumbling herself through a situation.

He would have been her mentor, after all, just as he'd been Raven's and, Zach assumed, many others' over the years.

For some reason, he'd pictured the man differently.

"I left Emma in charge for a reason. A lot of the children I took in had been abandoned by their own parents. Most of them adopted me as a surrogate father figure. They wouldn't understand that sometimes, people leave because they have to. I would never insult them by pretending I could pick up where I left off. They have Emma now. That's how it has to stay."

Oh, he was laying it on thick. The only thing missing was a misty eye and a lip quiver. Humoring him for no reason other than gathering some potentially valuable intel, Zach asked, "Why did you *have to* leave?"

Grandpa John heaved a big, long sigh. "Because I realized I was wrong. I was hand-picking people *I* thought needed help the most, and inadvertently left many others out in the cold. The ones I didn't help—"

"Decided they were better off without you and became the Evolutionaries," Zach finished.

That part, he'd sussed out all on his own. Every Evolutionary he'd met so far had a chip on their shoulder about the SU. They kept interactions civil, but minimal. No love lost for the SU's chosen elite.

Their resentment was palpable, but so was the ignorance on the SU side. Very few telepaths seemed to understand *why* these people hated them, thoroughly ignorant of their own history. It would have been fun to watch, except the fate of humanity literally depended on them working together now.

"Yes," John confirmed.

According to the SU registry, which had next to no encryption within the network, their members were ninety percent telepaths. While the ratio had recently started to shift at a much faster rate, non-mind-reader classifications hadn't even existed within the registry prior to four years ago. Right around the beginning of the war, when Emma Wayland had taken over.

Zach had studied those early days quite a bit recently. Despite widespread propaganda, the Shadows hadn't been the first to open fire. Up until early 3036, they'd mainly operated in secret, relying more on Hawks than Hounds to get what they wanted. A senator here, a telepath or two there… Small, tactical missions.

And then the antichem riots had turned into a revolution.

But even then, the first public strike hadn't been a Shadow bomb dropping on a rioting mob, but a recorded message broadcast on every screen across the galaxy: *"Nature always prevails. Broken and bloody, it will yet rise to turn on its oppressors. Stand with us or stand aside."*

The Evolutionaries had been the ones who'd pulled back the curtain, forcing both the Shadows and the SU into the spotlight and direct, full-scale conflict.

Zach imagined their revenge must have tasted so very sweet. For about two months, until they saw the merciless destruction the Shadows had rained down on every major world, and realized they'd started something the SU wasn't equipped to handle.

"So," Zach mused, "the enemy tips his hand, you get smacked in the face by your biggest failure, and immediately abandon your people right when they need you the most."

John flinched.

"Because an Evolutionary precog told you it was the right thing to do."

"Yes," he grated with complete, unwavering conviction.

"And now you've come back, having completed your epic journey of self-discovery and learned the error of your ways. *After* over half of the SU's original members have been buried."

He frowned. "You won't ask me where I've been?"

"Don't really care."

"You should. It concerns you, too."

"I sincerely doubt that."

There it was. The grandpa mask finally fell away. The man who sat back, mirroring Zach's loose pose, was suddenly shrewd and self-assured enough to look down on Zach. "How many Shadows are with the SU?"

At least he didn't insult Zach by asking if he knew. "Four thousand two hundred and eighteen, give or take." He wasn't naïve enough to assume they kept accurate records. Sometimes, it was better to keep your assets off the books, so to speak.

"And given what you know about failing EMC and the rate of Shadow soldiers going MIA, how many more do you estimate to have deserted?"

Zach shrugged. Accounting for about sixty percent of MIAs, "Best guess, hundreds of thousands."

He'd known what he'd be signing up for when he threw himself at the SU's mercy. Defecting to the enemy wasn't a ticket to retirement. It just meant trading one uniform for another. Most soldiers who'd been drafted, brainwashed, and sent to their deaths against their will wouldn't be looking for another fight, but a way out of it. Whether that meant disappearing into the uncharted wilderness or punching their own ticket.

"Over five hundred thousand ended up with the Evolutionaries."

Zach's mind blanked.

"I'm sure it felt like an easier option, considering a lot of them still harbored strong feelings when it came to the SU being the enemy. The Evolutionaries have managed to fly low enough under the Shadows' radar to avoid being grouped in with the SU. And they are a lot more inclusive. Whatever your physical or mental difference, they'll find a place for you."

Holy shit…

MacMurphy pushed his plate closer toward Zach. "Have a cookie. It helps with the cognitive dissonance."

"They have an army."

"They *are* an army," MacMurphy corrected. "The deserted Shadows are only one part of their combined power. While I was busy sticking my head in the sand and doing my best to insulate and protect my chosen ones from the truth, *they* trained theirs to stand up and fight back. But they needed someone to give them a purpose other than hate and resentment, so I stepped up. To make up for not seeing them sooner. Not giving them a chance. I left the SU in Emma's hands because I knew she'd do right by them while I took care of the forgotten ones. And I have never been prouder of one of my kids than when she started opening the doors to anyone and everyone willing to join. Shadows and all."

He looked like he meant that.

"Un-fucking-believable."

"I know, it's a lot to take in."

"The sheer audacity of you waltzing back in here after you set your beloved *family* up for wholesale slaughter. You abandoned them in favor of the side that had given *themselves* the best chance of survival. And now you have the gall to sit there and puff out your chest like it was the best thing you could have done, to force your young, traumatized protégé to pick up the pieces and fight a whole-ass war all on her own."

Must have struck a nerve, because John MacMurphy, the benevolent father turned deadbeat rat went so rigid his jowls quivered. "I am—"

"A coward? A traitor. A filthy, back-stabbing, double-crossing piece of shit *parasite*. You think coming back with the big, shiny army you had *no* hand in building will make you a hero? You think the helpless kids you left in the crosshairs without any guidance will thank you for it?" Zach spread his arms and looked around the empty dining room. "Where is the protégé you're so damn proud of? She doesn't even know you're here yet, does she? You're terrified of her judgment—and you should be. Haven't known her for very long, but Emma Wayland doesn't strike me as the type to take betrayal lightly. And her husband…" He wanted to laugh. "I just hope I'm there to see it when one of them decides to tear you the fuck apart."

MacMurphy's expression shuttered. He dropped the cold stare and reached for a cookie from the plate. "Emma knows exactly where I've been and why. I've been in direct contact with her for months now. She's not here because she has more important things to do than trumpet my return. She has an army to consolidate. And I have a broken Raven to heal."

Dig as deep as you want to find a different answer, but
you already know the truth.

- The Evolutionary Gospel of Michael

"Over my dead fucking body."

Zach knew the second the vindictive smirk appeared on the bastard's face that he'd missed something. He braced for a verbal attack, hoping for a telepathic one so he could watch—

"Uncle John?"

Everything stopped.

MacMurphy's grandpa mask snapped back into place as he pushed to his feet and opened his arms in welcome. "My sweet little Raven." But his signature patronizing smile slipped as he took his first good look at her.

Raven's mentor would have gone MIA about a year before her accident. That look said he hadn't bothered keeping tabs on her in the meantime, and whoever had caught him up on the current state of affairs had clearly failed to mention her amputation.

Zach wanted more than anything to turn around and see Raven, but he didn't dare take his eyes off MacMurphy.

"You're alive." He'd never heard her sound so small. That MacMurphy didn't appear to notice made Zach seriously weigh the pros and cons of slicing the man's face into ribbons.

"Yes. I came back." The words were right. The tone was off. And his arms were still empty. He lowered them awkwardly to his sides. "They told me about Julian. I am so sorry, Raven."

The lightest down feather brush skimmed Zach's mind. Not a direct touch. More like a reflexive reach, pulled back before it could connect. Zach hated how much uncertainty he felt in the small action. He hated that she was in the same room with MacMurphy, and that it wasn't his place to do or say anything about it.

More than anything, he hated the long silence of her non-response.

MacMurphy frowned. "Raven?"

She left as quietly as she'd entered.

Zach pushed to his feet. "I'm guessing that didn't go the way you thought it would."

"What did you do to her?"

"What needed to be done," he said, turning his back on the man who wasn't worth another minute of his time. "I showed her what it really looks like to have someone on her side."

He caught up with Raven halfway up the stairs to the third floor. She was flushed, panting as she leaned on the handrail for support. He braced her against his side, took her weight, and kept them moving. "Where to?"

"Roof."

Zach took the stairs two at a time.

The late afternoon was freezing, with the sun and Vesta occupying opposite halves of the sky. The roof's miniature park had a paved path looping through artificial foliage. Here and there, he saw small statues of animals and abstract shapes, but not a single bench or chair.

Raven pushed out of his hold and put a few feet of distance between them. She wouldn't look at him, still breathing hard, but that was from shock, more than physical exertion. He took the opportunity to look her over. Still pale, with patches of bright red across her cheeks. Still too thin, swallowed up in oversized lounge clothes someone other than Zach had provided for her. Still visibly shaken by what'd happened.

But she was on her feet, outside, and talking. Sort of.

"What do I do?" she asked so softly he almost missed it.

"What do you mean?"

"Everything I knew, my life the last three years…" Her face tilted up toward the sky. "How did you do it? How do you pick and choose which parts are true and which ones aren't?"

Ah. "It's not about truth. Truth is what you make of it. If you want to believe there's a rainbow-colored gnome in the sky who pisses down diamonds when you're really, really good, then that's your truth."

She huffed, and he couldn't tell if it was a laugh or a sob.

"Truth is subjective, which makes it irrelevant. What matters is what you can live with. You choose the parts that make you stronger, and build on them until you're standing on solid ground again. You can choose to remember Julian in that pod and let it break you, or you can choose to remember the life you had together, and that you were loved—fiercely—to the end.

"You can choose to remember how the people in your life failed you, or you can acknowledge that they just did what they had to, to keep themselves upright. And then take a look in the mirror and acknowledge that you're still standing, too. All on your own. You're not a broken doll, Raven. You're not weak. And you're not alone."

Raven dropped her chin to her chest, eyes closed. "I didn't want to be here," she said, as if confessing some grave sin. "After the accident, and Julian… It was like I dropped through a wormhole into a different world. Nothing felt right. I didn't belong anymore. I didn't want to be there."

A breeze tugged her hair to hide her face from him. He didn't dare move a muscle or make a sound.

"Darrow did try to do right by me. He and Tessa literally kept me alive. And for the longest time, I felt like the worst kind of parasite for how hard I made it on them. But part of me resented them, too, for caring so much they refused to let go. Now I question everything."

For a moment, only her ragged breaths punctuated the silence. Then she frowned. "He kept bringing up Julian, almost like he wanted me to catch on."

"Maybe he did. It would have been a heavy secret to carry alone. You're the only one who might have understood."

"No," Raven bit out. "I wouldn't have—I *don't*. But…"

Zach shifted a little closer. "But?"

"Ever since you showed up, the way Darrow talked about him… Even after three years, he still believed Julian would come back. And I…" She breathed down a shuddering sob. "Was it just denial, or did he have a real reason to hope?"

The naked pain of uncertainty in her eyes, twisted something inside Zach. His voice broke low and hoarse when he said, "Blackbird, don't do this to yourself. You were there with me. You saw the same thing I did. You know there was no hope."

Her shoulders sagged. "I don't know where to go from here."

"That's always the hard part, isn't it? Deciding which path to take. For what it's worth, my offer stands. Just say the word, and I'll take you anywhere you wish."

She fell silent, so still he couldn't tell if she was breathing. If she told him to take her away from here, they'd be gone within the hour. If she asked him to raze the entire town, he'd turn it to ash in minutes. As long as she was still there with him afterward.

"I'm not a broken doll," she finally said.

Zach almost fell over in relief. He caught himself on a step in her direction. "No, you're not."

"I won't be a tool—for them, or you, or anyone. Ever again."

"I never—"

"Stop." She turned to him, and her down feather touch didn't just brush across him; it gripped him tight, forcing his mouth shut and his hands to his sides. "I'll beg forgiveness later if you let me, but right now I just need to know the truth."

Zach lost sight of her as his vision turned inward and what felt like the sum total of his life flashed past his mind's eye. It came on too fast, the scenes cycling through too quickly for him to stop it. He didn't even try. No more locked doors, no more secrets. No more fantasies masquerading as memories. He let go and gave her free rein to do what she needed to do.

Drab walls. Hard faces.

"Who are you?"

A kick to the ribs sent him sprawling. "Again!"

"Where do you reside?"

Electricity fried through his cranium, leaving him boneless and drooling.

A plasma blast to his lower back numbed his legs, and he fell face-first to the blood-stained gray floor. "Again!"

"What do you do?"

People laughing at a party. A man's tongue in Zach's ear; his hand on Zach's crotch. Sweet guy, so full of life, joy, and laughter. It didn't seem possible that a person could exist that way. But the injection had already started to take effect. His lover was falling asleep. All that joy, all that life, fading gently into silence. No witnesses.

Explosions rattled the city. Fire consumed entire buildings. Panicked crowds trampled each other.

Running down a narrow alley toward his extraction point. Mission accomplished. Seemed so pointless now.

Drab walls. The pool's current picked up, forcing his head under water. A brief moment of panic as he neared his limit. But he had to hold out a second longer. One second could make all the difference one day...

A sweet voice sang the refrain of her new song. The scene was too blurred, but that voice hit him straight in the chest. And on its heels came the pain, and a soundless scream into the void. That it was his fault. That he should have been there.

But he'd been kneeling over a wild-eyed stranger, cutting into his neck to pull out a small, metal device.

Too late. "I can't do CPR without crushing her..."

"What does a soldier trained to destroy and kill do when he wakes up from the nightmare long enough to ask questions, and no one can tell him what he's supposed to dream next?"

A smoky hallway and a woman's bloodied face snarling at him as her knife twisted in his gut. "I knew you liked me."

"Who are you? Where do you reside? What do you do? Two of those are a lie... Run."

Staring up at the sky as his vision blurred. The knowledge that his next breath was about to be the last.

Raven introducing herself to him for the first time.

Raven in his mind for the first time.

Raven's unexpected down feather touch sending him over the edge in the most intense orgasm he'd ever experienced, rocking his entire universe on its axis. Convincing him that she would beg for him one day—because he'd get on his knees over and over again to make her.

"Well, you have been a good boy. So far."

The chaotic replay stopped there on the sound of his laughter, so achingly carefree, as if nothing else mattered, except the woman smiling back at him.

The rush resumed in a flood of detox fluid and dead Shadows littering the floor.

Watching Raven in the back of the emergency pod.

The cold weight of murderous rage as he marched out of the utility tunnel, carrying her sleeping weight in his arms past a blur of war refugees.

"Woman, you've been inside my head!"

The carefree laughter again. She hadn't heard it that time, but Zach had. It meant everything.

"Married couples are less conspicuous as travelers." But that wasn't the reason.

"Don't watch…"

"Beg me to end it, bitch."

Four thousand eight hundred fifty-six breaths until the door closed between them.

"I'm not gonna make it, Leels…"

"Would you be willing to reconsider if I stabbed you again?"

"This is…" "The end of the line."

"It was never going to be you…"

"Only when the prodigal returns will the black bird fly again."

"Over my dead fucking body."

Raven sobbed, and her telepathic grip released him in a rush, leaving him dizzy. He braced his hands on his knees and breathed in deep as his mouth flooded with saliva.

"I'm sorry," she gasped. "I'm sorry. I'm sorry…"

She sat on her heels, rocking back and forth, apologizing over and over as she cried.

Zach let his ass hit the ground and spat sideways, sucking dry winter air deep into his lungs. The whole world rocked underneath him, and

Raven had just yanked back her anchor like he didn't need it anymore.

Two weeks of living in close proximity with a lot of telepaths had taught him that they didn't usually take liberties with other people's minds this way. They would classify what Raven had just done as an invasion. A gross violation, subject to severe punishment.

Based on her reaction, that thought now repeated in her mind every time she said, "I'm sorry."

Zach was just glad she wasn't running away. He'd happily cool his heels on the roof with her for as long as she needed.

It took a while for everything to settle. Eventually, Raven grew quiet. A bit later, she stopped crying. Then her rocking turned into hard shivers. She hugged herself and finally braved a glance his way.

Fearful.

He quirked an eyebrow in question. "So are we still dating?"

45

Some of us are so used to the concept of ***sacrifice*** that we don't know another way to live. And we can't comprehend someone incapable of comprehending it.

- The Evolutionary Gospel of Michael

February 8, 3040 – Lavari Dolmi, Valhale 602

"I told you, *I don't know*."

"You must have some clue. You knew the guy your whole life."

One day very soon, Zach and Rowe would come to blows. And it wouldn't end well for Rowe. "Do you remember the details of your CO's personal life?"

"No," Rowe snapped back. "I was wiped, same as you. But I do remember some things, like the fact that our base had training circuits, gyms, and hundreds of soldiers. You make it sound like you were raised in an empty lab all by yourself."

Vega's whetstone came to a stop halfway up the blade.

Quinn shifted in his seat, causing the chair to creak ominously.

As if he just realized what he'd said, the former Hawk swore under his breath.

"Give it a sleep," Wayland said, rubbing his forehead. "You're cracking my egg."

"I second that," Quinn said. "We could all use a break."

They could all use a beating. This was the fifth time in as many days that they'd tried to pry answers out of him. Zach had run out of ways to tell them he didn't have the information they were asking for. He didn't know where Sandoval had built his factories. He didn't know where the AI hub was housed. He didn't have a fucking clue about how many additional soldiers they'd already drafted, or if there were more babies getting snatched from delivery rooms, or whether Sandoval's scientists had managed to reverse engineer the regenerative serum.

Did they really think he'd have put himself through all this shit to hold back the most crucial information at crunch time? Their heads couldn't possibly be that far up their asses. Some of them were Hawks, for fuck's sake.

"Has he been scanned?"

The sound of MacMurphy's voice set Zach's teeth on edge. He refused to acknowledge the whoreson as a matter of principle. But the old man wasn't talking to him.

"Yes," Raven replied shortly. She didn't appear to be a fan of his, either. From what little she'd told Zach, MacMurphy had been her mentor the longest back in the day. His specialty was similar to one of hers, which had made him the most qualified person to teach her. They'd gotten close enough for her to start calling him 'uncle', yet he hadn't attended her wedding feast, and he hadn't deemed her important enough to come back when she'd had her accident.

"By someone else?" MacMurphy pushed. He hadn't taken Raven's rejection well at all.

Raven glared at him. She wore her black suit again, but as a subtle fuck-you, she'd swapped the black shirt for the silky, deep red camisole he'd bought for her. She'd never answered him about them still dating, and she still slept in her own room, but Zach took her wearing his clothes as a good sign. He could wait her out. At least she was sitting next to him.

And he had to admit, her obvious grudge against MacMurphy made him irrationally happy. "You want to give it a try?" he offered.

MacMurphy looked ready to launch himself across the table. It had to rankle that he couldn't bend Zach to his liking.

"Is there a point to this discussion, other than wasting more time?" Sweet Sadie, the 'shoot first and think later' Hound didn't have a lot of patience for these strategy councils. She kept talking about mobilizing the troops as if they already had a target. The more agitated she got, the worse she fidgeted. Zach himself had taken to squeezing a stress ball at these meetings lately, and he had to stop himself multiple times a day from throwing it out the window and telling her to go fetch. Clearly, the pup had too much energy to burn.

"Sandoval doesn't have an outpost of his own," Raven said. "He's too smart for that. Whatever he has going on, he would have had it assigned to someone else, who has no clue what they're overseeing."

"I do love a smart woman."

He clocked Quinn's raised eyebrow, Vega's smirk, and MacMurphy's death stare. But all he cared about was Raven's faint blush.

"The point is," she said, "Sandoval is too active to track. He's a distraction. If we want to find the right targets to strike, we have to look somewhere else."

"And what do you suggest?" Rowe asked, his tone bordering on sarcastic.

Raven noticed. "Are all the Shadows we have from the same out-post?"

"No," Sadie answered. "Ours came from thousands of different ones."

"Then I guess you know what to do," Zach told her. "Start asking questions. That should keep you busy for a while."

The Hound blinked at him. "Questions…?"

Zach squeezed the stress ball tighter. "Yes. Ask them where their outpost was, and what they did there. Were they guarding something? Did they have a science team on base? Did they have telepath hold-ing cells? Were there telepaths in them? For how long? Do I need to keep going?"

Sadie's eye twitched, but she shook her head and wordlessly left the room, the faithfully quiet Alec hot on her heels.

Rowe and Wayland exchanged a long, speaking look.

"What?" Zach growled.

"Our old outpost had holding cells," Rowe said.

"And labs," Wayland added. "But that's not where we finished."

"Which one are you thinking?"

Wayland rubbed his bearded jaw in thought. "We torched Green 24 when we extracted Emma and the other telepaths."

"Yeah, that place got torched a few times," Rowe returned. "And they keep going back there. Why?"

Zach sat forward. "Tell me everything you remember."

It turned out, Wayland, Rowe, and cousin-in-law Vega had all come from the same outpost—Blue 56. They described a standard layout and population, everything by the book, down to the last detail. Except for the prisoner holding cells. And the fact that Senator Griffith had visited it on several occasions. That was where they'd originally held Emma Wayland prisoner. Telepath holding cells weren't standard across all outposts. Of the sixty-seven included in Zach's post-treatment notes, only three had had them. At least one of those he could confirm had been destroyed: Orange 18 on Karem Shem.

Green 24 was infamous enough for every single Shadow to know about it. It was a case study they still taught to keep soldiers motivated in their fear and hate of telepaths. Green 24 was where someone had fucked up big time by drafting a telepath into the Shadow ranks. Said telepath had then gone nuclear and leveled the place. Hundreds of soldiers dead or wishing they were in a matter of hours.

A good number of them, he'd killed seemingly with his bare hands. The rest—the ones who hadn't been reduced to vegetables—had been psychologically destroyed. Raving lunatics screaming at shadows and pissing themselves at the sound of marching footsteps. One's heart had literally exploded in his chest when they'd turned off the lights his first night in a holding cell.

Every single one of those Shadows had been rendered useless. Not even EMC could put them back together again. Most of them had had to be put down. A few had been left alive for study and ended up bashing their own brains out—the hard way, by slamming their heads against the closest available solid surface over and over again.

What Zach wouldn't give to have that telepath on their team.

Wait… "He's not one of yours, is he?" he asked Wayland.

"No," She-of-the-snow-white-hair answered. "Not anymore."

"Dead?"

"Gone," Dr. Chase-Calen said. "He… He's not coming back. For anything. Jer already tried, but Tristan Hunt is very, very good at disappearing. If he doesn't want to be found, he won't be. And no," she said to MacMurphy, "my sister and her four-legged companion won't be partaking in this exercise either. She doesn't even want me involved."

"Which is why you're here in the first place," MacMurphy retorted with something like an affectionate grin.

She grinned back. "Exactly!"

"You're weird," Zach decided.

"Look who's talking," she shot back.

He shrugged. "Didn't say it was a bad thing."

"Can we get back on topic here?" Rowe's patience looked to be on its very last little thread. "Green 24 is our primary target. We can get to the solar system, but the second we breach the star's orbit, they'll know, so direct recon will be a no-go."

"Why would we orbit?"

Everyone at the table turned to find Emma Wayland leaning against the doorframe. Zach hadn't heard her open the door. Apparently, no one else had noticed her arrival, either. He was impressed.

MacMurphy shifted his seat, presumably to make room for her, but Emma didn't move from her spot.

It was awkward as fuck.

Luckily, they had Vega to break the ice. "How close would you need to be to get into someone's head there?"

"By myself? Two lighthours. With help? From right here. Without a grappling hook? Wiped."

"You need a specific person to tap," Zach translated for Rowe, who looked very confused. "Which means we need a roster and a target who's susceptible, but also has high enough clearance to get us the intel we want."

"Too risky," Wayland declared. "On all fronts. We can get the lay from space."

"Not if the facilities are underground," Zach returned. "You can get the surface schematics from their satellite surveillance, if you're feeling suicidal. But, given that the outpost has been bombed to shit several times already, odds are the important bits will be deep underground and camouflaged. Satellite scans will give us fuckall."

"They'll give us aboveground numbers," Rowe argued. "It's a start."

Zach crushed the stress ball in his fist. "Did they fry all common sense out of your head the last time they zapped you? You don't tap Shadow resources unless you want them to tap back. The second you connect, they'll trace it. We'll have bombs dropping on this cutesy little town within hours. Minutes, if they're already in the neighborhood. You ready for that?"

"Yes," Emma said from the doorway. "But we don't tap from here."

"Gray Dublin," MacMurphy said to the table. "It has to be from there."

Emma shook her head. "Too many bodies."

"That's why it'll work. We reestablished contact yesterday. They're ready to do their part."

Raven shivered. "What? What are you talking about?"

"He wants to use Gray Dublin as a decoy," Zach guessed. "Relays alone won't work. The Shadows can trace them back to the source. We can't risk the people here because they know too much. But if we hack them from a location that's too remote and isolated, they'll know it's a setup, and they'll strike the most densely populated target they can find instead, to teach us a lesson. If we want intel, we'll need a blood sacrifice big enough to satisfy them."

"Gray Dublin still has a population of five million people," Vega said. "Civilians."

Quinn blanched, looking back and forth among all of them, probably waiting for someone to tell him they were joking.

But they weren't.

"The city is still in ruin from the initial attacks," Rowe said.

"We're talking *people* here," Quinn growled. "*Lives.* Five-fucking-million of them."

"Welcome to war," MacMurphy said.

Emma turned on her heels and left without another word.

Raven shook her head, staring at the old man in disbelief.

But every Shadow around the table wore the same expression.

Weary acceptance. They all knew what this war would cost. They were prepared to accept the consequences and make the hard choices.

Someone had to.

"A war to end all future conflicts," Quinn said to Zach. "Was this what you meant?"

Zach didn't recall saying anything like that. Didn't matter, anyway. "If we do this, it better be fucking worth it."

Quinn shoved away from the table and stomped off after Emma.

Dr. Chase-Calen followed slower, quiet as a ghost slipping out the door.

Raven was still shaking her head. "We can't do this."

MacMurphy looked like he'd aged another ten years in the last two minutes. "If we don't, we've already lost. Michael—"

Raven exploded out of her seat. "Fuck Michael! Fuck all of this! We don't kill innocent people, John. At least we didn't use to. Weren't you the biggest champion of the little guys once upon a time? Weren't you the one drilling into my head every single day that we have a responsibility to protect those under our care?"

Her mentor flinched, but didn't say a word.

The backs of her legs bumped into her chair as she retreated a step, and Zach reached out instinctively to keep her from falling over. She took a half-hearted swat at his arm, but he kept his hand firmly on her hip while she stared at MacMurphy like he'd grown a second head. "Who are you?"

"Morgues," Vega said, digging the tip of her throwing knife into her thumb. A thin trickle of blood painted its way down to her wrist, dripping onto the fluffy white rug beneath her booted feet. "Evac the civilians. Warm up some corpses and tie them to bots so they can move."

"Do you have any idea how long that would take?"

Her jaw twitched. "With enough telepaths pulling the strings, I'm thinking a couple of days."

Raven collapsed back into her seat. "Three lives, instead of five million. It's never going to end, is it? Us throwing ourselves on the blade."

"It'll be more than three," Zach said, because no one else was going to. "We get one shot. We have to make it count. We need to get everything we can from the Shadow databases. Every roster, every map, every classified document—all of it. And that will take people. Even with an automated worm to get us inside, it'll take at least five people at the controls to scrape the data and route it through the relays to a secure server. We'll need at least two to encrypt the attack and buy them time. Four would be better. And if you have two or three decent hackers who can fuck up their shit and cripple them from the inside while the others work, we might even have a fighting chance." With the three telepaths merging to work the corpses and evac, that totaled… "Fifteen. Fifteen people to save an entire city."

And possibly win them the war.

MacMurphy raised his head, just barely, to look at Zach. "As I said. Gray Dublin is ready."

46

They didn't get fifteen. They got twenty in Gray Dublin, and five more remotely working the relays on uninhabited moons and space stations.

And those were just on their side.

The Evolutionaries mobilized seven battle-ready shuttles to strike at known Shadow targets to create a diversion and buy them more time. Each one required a skeleton crew of four people at the controls and seven on the weapons. Using the Gray Dublin strategy, they also filled the empty hulls with as many corpses as they could get. That way, when the Shadows scanned them, they would find the appropriate number of bodies on board.

Raven didn't talk to anyone for the whole three days it took to organize.

Welcome to war.

She hadn't expected the conflict to end without bloodshed. Well, that was a lie. In her deepest fantasies, she had hoped that if they could take out Sandoval, all of this would be over. A fool's hope. If it were that easy, the war would have ended when they'd brought down Senator Griffith.

The only people who seemed to understand were Emma and the giant Cousin Quinn, who now carried his own chair around, having crushed four already just by sitting in them. Raven liked him. His natural glower was terrifying, but she never sensed anything other than kindness and warmth from him. Any time she went up to the roof for fresh air, she always found him already there, staring off into the distance. He didn't seem to need coats or blankets, but he always had one to share with her.

She sat with him in silence for hours, trying to absorb some of his strength by osmosis. It didn't work, but at least in his company, she didn't feel so completely out of place.

Today, after an hour of watching the storms on Vesta's surface, he suddenly broke the silence with a quiet declaration. "They're not heartless."

"I know that."

Quinn shook his head. "No, I mean… The people in that room, the ones I know, would throw themselves on grenades if it meant saving just one life."

She tried to smile. "I know. You'd do the same." And so would she.

He grunted. "I still hate it."

"Me too. At least the soldiers have some battle training. The telepaths are just lambs to slaughter."

They'd briefly discussed shipping batches of the regenerative serum to Gray Dublin to give the team there a fighting chance, but it would have been too risky. Now that they'd started mobilizing forces, their efforts would be visible, if someone knew what to look for—and the Shadows always did. The serum would take days to reach Earth and longer to take full effect. Given the level of destruction the Shadows were known to inflict, no one was expected to make it out of there alive.

"Lambs to fucking slaughter," Quinn agreed grimly.

Raven kept flashing back to her wreck and the hours she'd spent screaming in agony. She imagined the people in Gray Dublin waking up after the attack, torn to shreds but still alive thanks to the serum, buried in the wreckage with help too far to reach them.

No one deserved that.

They'd agreed. Instead of the serum, they'd asked for something to send them to sleep in seconds so they didn't feel any pain. The SU had obliged.

That was the problem. They had too many people willing to die for the cause. It was a weakness the Shadows had exploited for years, causing just enough chaos to force them into merge after merge, thinning their ranks and making them easier to wipe out. And the telepaths kept doing it—because what else could they do?

That night, when Zach knocked softly at her door, hair tousled and deep shadows under his haunted eyes, she let him in. They curled up together on the bed and wrapped themselves around each other. Zach put his forehead to hers, nudging at her until she relented and let herself sink into his mind. His shield sucked her in so quickly, almost desperately.

Only when he could feel her in his thoughts did Zach unclench against her. His breathing turned deep as he drifted off, but his dreams were faint and misty. He woke out of them any time she shifted an inch in his hold.

"Sleep," she whispered the command, but imbued it with unyielding will.

Already exhausted, Zach didn't have the power to fight her. His mind sank into a dark fog of deep sleep, and the protective weight of his arm around her settled even heavier as he finally relaxed.

Raven stayed awake a while longer, floating aimlessly through the hallways of his mind. There were no more infinite loops or locked doors growing roots. The pieces he'd valued most had already been slotted into place, and he'd discarded everything else like so much garbage.

She faded out to the periphery of his being.

The galaxy of his self-actualization was gone. Zach's genesis was complete. He had a solid core now anchoring his identity in a way that left no unanswered questions. The abstract pattern she'd witnessed taking shape was as unique as his shields. A complex structure of layers that had layers of their own.

Raven traced one to its tapered end, then drifted farther to take in the whole from a distance.

There, in the darkness of space and random particles of light floating in its orbit, Zach's essence pulsed from within with a warm glow, casting beams of light and long shadows through the void.

It was a hawk with a sharp silver beak, silver talons, and bright white eyes that seemed to stare right at her.

But its feathers were black as pitch, through and through.

47

As is tradition, on Valentine's Day, people will die. A lot. Make sure they're not ours.

- The Evolutionary Gospel of Michael

February 14, 3040 – Lavari Dolmi, Valhale 602

In the morning, the war council convened in a different room, with sound partitions between multiple consoles. The Shadows wore full black uniforms with silver trimming, armed with weapons and knives. The effect was harrowing, to say the least.

Finnegan Rowe took the far console. His job was to monitor the attacking shuttles. Their targets were so far that they would have a two-minute transmission delay. A lot could go wrong in two minutes. Receiving the right order at the wrong time could be disastrous. Rowe was there to give direction only when necessary. He had Vega standing at ease behind him to back him up.

Across from them, Ripley had a console of their own. Their job was to help the relay team bounce the signal through as many different contact points as possible to scramble their trail. They'd chosen one hundred and twenty of the newest and therefore fastest relay points for the data transfer, and eighty-five of the oldest ones to connect

Lavari Dolmi with Gray Dublin, and the shuttles. Each relay had a small delay of its own, which would compound the time needed to access the Shadow systems and retrieve their data.

Emma stood nearby to monitor the situation. She couldn't do anything if something went wrong, but as the one who'd authorized all of this, she felt obligated to be there and see it through. Her ever-present Shadow husband kept an eye on all of them from the middle of the room. John Wayland was supposed to be watching the skies above them to make sure they didn't get ambushed, but his sharp eyes missed nothing. Raven couldn't read him, but his grave expression and rigid posture spoke volumes. She was glad to have him on their side.

And in the corner closest to the door, Zach sat at the only console that had multiple interactive controls. His job would be to verbally guide the Gray Dublin team and ensure the data got delivered where it was supposed to go. Rowe was the only other Shadow who might have enough technical knowledge hidden inside his brain to help. But since he was about to get busy with other things, Zach didn't have a backup.

He didn't seem to mind Raven hanging around, keeping to one side so she wouldn't be in the way. When he saw her plucking at the seam of her pantsuit, he caught her hand and pressed a kiss to the back of her wrist. "You don't have to be here."

"Yes, I do."

It was just the seven of them. Everyone else was considered non-essential and therefore not allowed in. She felt them out in the hallway, though. Quinn, John MacMurphy, and Rowe's wife, Laura, paced back and forth. Their nervous energy already drove her up the wall. Dr. Chase-Calen's presence rumbled low and dangerous in Raven's mind. Any second now, she would snap at the others to knock it off with the pacing. Only Eskel seemed to be holding steady. Although how he did it was beyond Raven. The rest of them, at least six more spread out down the hallway, were so tense it made Raven's shoulders ache.

If she went out there to join them, she'd go insane.

"Strike force in position," Rowe announced.

"Signal is bouncing," Ripley responded.

"All right, nerds," Zach said into his com piece, "get those fingers warmed up."

"*Ready to rock and roll*," responded a female voice from Gray Dublin. Soulful, but raspy. Raven didn't know her, but she imagined a woman in her fifties, with a mean look and a sharp tongue.

"Move on my mark," Rowe said, watching the cuff on his wrist. "Go!"

The room fell silent as they waited for the troops to receive the order.

Raven's heart pounded in her ears. Everyone held their breath, waiting for a response.

"*Moving in.*"

"*Copy.*"

"*Here we go, boys and girls!*"

"*Yee-haw!*"

The seven shuttle pilots sounded off almost in unison, and then the sound became a jumble of multiple voices speaking and shouting at the same time. The partitions dulled the noise but didn't completely block it out. Everyone in the room could hear it. John Wayland drifted over to Rowe's side, his hand raised, finger pointing up.

"Get ready," Zach said to his team, watching Wayland. His jaw clenched as he listened to the chaos.

"Six, break off," Rowe ordered. His fingers flew over the controls as he switched from channel to channel. "Four, keep an eye on your horizon. Three—"

"Fuck," Wayland muttered as one of the feeds cut off.

Rowe's face blanked, but he didn't falter. "One, watch out for the launchers."

"*Keep the channel clear for when we actually need you,*" came the response. Raven recognized the voice—Brent Catton, one of Vega's friends.

Vega snorted. "Saw that coming."

Wayland's hand moved down, pointing at Zach.

He turned to his console, and everything else ceased to matter. "Go," he snapped. "Let's get that worm wriggling. You got the signatures—"

"*I'm in,*" someone said. Raven didn't recognize him, but he sounded like he knew what he was doing.

"Good job. You'll have to break the maze before you even get to the firewall. Track your moves, and don't double back. It'll fuck you up faster than you think."

"*I need that third relay!*"

"Ripley," Zach snapped over his shoulder, "what the fuck are you doing over there?"

"Keep your shirt on," they replied calmly. "Or don't. Some eye candy wouldn't hurt. Got your relay."

"*Got it!*" the man confirmed.

A different person whistled. "*Holy fuck, this is…a lot.*"

"So get moving," Zach ordered. "Hackers, you're up. As soon as they get one part, send in the bug. *Communicate* before you do."

Things were not going well in Rowe's corner. "Five, abort! *Abort!*"

Vega had now taken over one of the controls. "Catton, the fuck are you doing over there?"

Raven's fist clenched so tight it hurt as screaming filled the com feed, and then abruptly cut off. They'd lost another shuttle. She couldn't tell which one. Vega and Rowe talked over each other, somehow managing to make sense of everything at the same time, but it didn't sound good.

"*Got sections C through H. Bug 'em.*"

"*Yeah, buddy, how you like them anties?*"

"Keep the chatter down," Zach said, but he watched four different screens as data began to stream across them.

"Fuck!" Ripley snapped at the same time as the raspy voice said, "*We lost a relay!*"

Wayland went back over to Ripley's side to check on the situation. The look on his face said he didn't like what he saw. "They went fishing. We gotta swim harder."

"*Relay two is gone.*"

"Four, I want you out of there *now!* One—status report."

"Seven, where the fuck are you?"

"*Shit, guys, I have some big things incoming, and I don't think they're clouds.*"

Zach froze for a second, and Raven went cold all over. "Pick it up, people. Let's move. You're over halfway there."

"We lost two more relays," Ripley reported. "They're picking them off."

"Fishing," Wayland confirmed darkly. "Our decoy wasn't enough.

Get them out of there, Finn."

"All shuttles—abort, abort, abort!"

"Catton, get your ass out of there—Owens, don't you *fucking dare!*"

"Seventy percent."

Someone sobbed on the Gray Dublin side. People hyperventilated into their coms, their voices quivering as they tried to keep it down. Their overwhelming fear tasted bitter in the back of her mind. Raven started shaking.

"I can't get through the last firewall. It's locked down. I don't recognize the codes."

"They're within range. We're out of time!"

"Read them out," Zach snapped.

The man rattled off some stuff, correcting himself here and there.

"I repeat, all teams *abort!*" Rowe snapped. "Get the fuck out of there!"

In Gray Dublin, the person reporting on movement said, *"We need to stop them."*

"Yeah? You got a spare nuke shoved up your ass that I don't know about?"

Zach spoke over them. "Use this sequence exactly as I say it to you."

He didn't get a chance to walk them through it as more voices rose in the background.

"We can do it if we merge."

"Keep working!" Zach snapped. "You're almost there."

"I don't want to die like this," a woman whimpered. *"I'm sorry."*

There was a commotion, as several people shouted in unison, then the com went silent.

"She's dead," a new voice reported. *"I guess we know it works."*

"We need to merge!" the same person insisted. *"Ain't none of us getting out of this, anyway, so what the fuck are we waiting for?"*

"Come on, guys, you can do this," Zach said. "We're at eighty-seven percent. Someone get back to the keyboard."

"Relay five out. So is three."

"Essie, take my hand."

"Oh, god, I can feel them—"

"Take my fucking hand!"

Whimpers.

A brief scuffle broke out, ending in the thud of a soft weight dropping.

"Someone talk to me," Zach said.

More noises. *"Taking over,"* this one was new. A woman who seemed to be holding it somewhat together.

"We're out of time!"

"Get over here—move!"

Raven shot away from the wall. "Darrow?"

"One last firewall… Whoever has the codes, I need them now."

Rowe and Vega had abandoned their station—there was nothing more they could do. "This is gibberish," Rowe said, leaning over Zach's shoulder.

Zach elbowed him back—hard. "Do exactly what I say as I say it…"

"…this is what we signed up for…"

Raven's heart jumped into her throat. "Darrow, is that you?"

A big hand came down on her shoulder, pulling her away from the console. She'd drifted into Zach's space, and he stared at her while reciting the code sequences to the person who'd taken over the hack.

A smaller hand caught Raven's. "He was given a choice," Emma said softly, her voice full of grief—for far more than just the people screaming their panic through the com as the woman hacking into the Shadows' system repeated everything after Zach. "What he did was unforgivable. He knew the cost. He chose to pay it back in kind."

"Breathe through your nose," Darrow said. *"Let your mind float and let go of the anchor. I'll catch you."* He was taking over the same way Benna Havely had.

"What is he doing?"

"They will expect…resistance," Emma's husband replied, struggling to find the right words. "He's going to bring them down on top of the center." Killing himself and everyone in the building in the process. "Make it look like a failed takeover."

He could do it. As a lance, all he needed was a good boost, and he could stop the heart of every single Shadow above them. Their crafts would fall out of the sky and bury what remained of the first official facility the Special Unit had ever built.

"Got it," the woman said. *"Tell me you're receiving."*

Data resumed streaming over the last screen. The rest of the room had gone quiet. Five bodies now crowded at Raven's back, but she didn't see or hear any of them.

"Receiving," Zach confirmed. "Good job. You may have just helped us win the whole damn war. I'm proud of you."

Aside from a few soft sobs and a chorus of whispered prayers, the com had gone silent.

"It's on you now. Do me a favor, will you? Take those fuckers down."

"Copy that."

Sigh. *"I think I'll go hang with the cool kids for a bit."*

"We're right here with you," Zach said. "Not going anywhere."

Her voice grew more distant and indistinct as she walked away from the console. *"Come on, girl. Can't let those assholes have all the fun."*

More whimpers, answers that were impossible to make out.

"It's okay. I got you. I'm right here. It'll be over in a minute."

The data stopped streaming.

"We got it," Zach said. "All of it. Thank you. It won't be long now."

The woman in Gray Dublin hummed a soft lullaby. No one around Raven breathed a word.

Raven's eyes fogged over as a vision invaded her mind—Emma's doing. She saw the small room in Gray Dublin, with windows looking out onto the night. It was so dark without the city's vibrant lighting. A soft hiss of rain filled her ears, accompanying the mournful song. It came from the woman whose mind they currently occupied. Nell. Her name was Nell, and every single person in the room with her felt like her child.

She sensed Emma, and her mind calmed with a maternal warmth. —*You deserved so much better, Pixie girl. You all did. A better world than this.*—

—*Then I'll make one,*— Emma replied fiercely.

A soft chuckle. —*I guess you were right after all.*—

—*About what?*—

—*It's Valentine's Day. Tradition for people to die. A lot.*— There was a bittersweet note of nostalgic humor in the strange comment, but it came with a memory of Emma in the early days after her rescue from the Shadows. "Confused with prose, but muse operational," as she'd called it, making an anachronistic connection between the annual celebration of love and the Valentine's Day Massacre from Earth's medieval times. It was filled with so much emotion. Love, pain, regret, guilt—the tumult of a parent who'd failed to protect their child.

Emma delivered the equivalent of a telepathic embrace of forgiveness and a final goodbye, and gently nudged Nell's focus to the others. Eight bodies lay across the floor, side by side, their faces relaxed as if in sleep. Four more slumped in their seats at consoles similar to Zach's.

The girl in Nell's arms was in her early twenties. Through Nell's fingers pressed to the side of her neck, Raven felt the girl's pulse slow…slow…

At the far end of the room, the remaining six sat in a circle on the floor, their eyes closed, their hands clutched tight together in the center.

Raven whimpered, seeing Darrow among them. Blood dripped from his nose, but his voice was calm and steady, so grown up as he guided the others through the merge. She saw the moment when each of them gave in. One by one, their shoulders slumped, their heads dipping a little lower.

A loud noise outside drew Nell's gaze back to the window, where a brief flash of blue lightning illuminated a massive dark shape in the sky. The rumble of its rapid descent became a quake she felt in her bones. Fear spiked a disconcerting tickle throughout her entire body, her hands losing their dexterity despite her determination to hold strong, be brave in the face of her coming death.

Behind her, Darrow sighed. *"Bye, Rae. I'm sorry."*

Nell squeezed her eyes shut.

Raven did, too.

It was over in an instant.

The father will never know the friends his son plays with.

- The Evolutionary Gospel of Michael

February 21, 3040 – Lavari Dolmi, Valhale 602

They lost five out of their seven shuttles and every last relay. Gray Dublin had a new, two-mile crater with the former SU facility at its center. Three Shadow vessels had engaged there; they must have been waiting for the SU to make a move. Public media reported that the city had suffered total destruction with no survivors. The zone had been declared uninhabitable and quarantined due to high radiation levels. By the time they found their balls and sent in response teams, no one would be able to tell that the corpses that hadn't been vaporized on impact had been dead long before the attack.

Catton didn't come back to Valhale 602. His shuttle's controls shut down as he brought it out of subspace near Torrey. He and his crew evacuated to the planet's surface, where they would remain until further notice. The shuttle was out of commission, but no one on board had gotten hurt. Small miracles.

The other shuttle made it back to the Evolutionaries unscathed. Survivors were being debriefed and reassigned to other duties.

And then there was the asset.

The sum total of everything they'd extracted from the enemy now resided within the SU's servers. The hackers had infected a good sixty percent of the Shadow servers, which would keep them busy for a while, but there hadn't been time to corrupt the rest. And Zach still didn't know what that rest was.

"All of that…for *this*?" Rowe had been throwing hissy fits since they'd received the complete transmission and he'd realized it was all encrypted.

"Did you expect it to be easy?" Zach asked, only half paying attention to the former Hawk as he worked on his section of the data. "The fuck did you think we were here for, sitting pretty and sending other people to die?"

The two of them were the only ones who had at least some knowledge of Shadow encryption. In *someone's* case, probably scrambled beyond recognition. But they were still the best hope anyone had of making sense of the gibberish they'd acquired. Zach had been chipping away at it for three days now, trying every trick he remembered to unravel the code and make the content coherent.

Rowe, meanwhile, shook his head at the mess, typed a few sequences, hit a wall, and threw another fit. His leg hadn't stopped bouncing since he'd sat down. It annoyed the shit out of Zach.

Apparently, Hawks came in two flavors: combative and infiltrative. Rowe was the former. He knew how to take control of a situation and take action, but he seemed to have little experience with long-term strategies. Patience was not his strong suit. He looked at the daunting task before them, and all he saw was mission failure. Lives wasted for something they couldn't even use. He seemed to be taking it personally, and it impaired his ability to focus and get shit done.

To be fair, time wasn't exactly on their side, which did add a little extra pressure. The longer they spent trying to make sense of this mess, the longer the Shadows had to augment, strategize, and mobilize.

The problem was that, without intel, the combined Evolutionary-SU forces had nothing to work with, other than Prophet Michael's very vague predictions, which even Ripley and MacMurphy couldn't vouch for anymore. Unless they figured out exactly where to strike the

Shadows to bring them down, they would keep trading blows until one side ran out of fighters—and that side wouldn't be the Shadows.

"We should have hit Green 24." This from Sadie, who'd volunteered Alec to take a crack at the encryption and decided to stick around to oversee his work.

"Your mouth is moving," Zach told her. "Might want to look into that."

"If Green 24 is a primary target," Alec said to his screen, shocking Zach out of his temper. "It's the last place we want to hit as a decoy. Our strike force wasn't sufficient to destroy the outpost. At best, we would have wasted resources. At worst, they would have retaliated with mass attacks, reinforced the outpost, or moved the assets to a new location, which would have left us all up a massive river of shit."

Zach raised an eyebrow, impressed. "Any other asinine comments from the audience?"

Sadie grunted.

Alec admitted utter defeat after five hours. He dragged Sadie out of their hair, leaving Zach alone with Rowe and his bouncing leg.

And so they kept trying.

Hour after hour.

Day after day.

Zach stared at the mess of shifting numbers and symbols until his eyes crossed and everything blurred. He fell asleep at his station, only to wake up a few hours later with a raging headache and no progress.

Emma Wayland looked in on them every so often, taking a quick peek from around the doorjamb and then disappearing again. She tried to stay unobtrusive, but Zach always noticed. He just kept expecting to see someone else.

Darrow's death had rattled Raven, but instead of shutting her down, it seemed to get her moving. She'd been meeting with Ripley, Mac-Murphy, and Laura McNally to analyze Michael's prophecies, compare notes, and attempt to make some sense of them.

She reached out once or twice a day, her down feather presence brushing away the burnout fog, letting him know she was there, holding it together, and doing what she could to keep them moving forward. It was going about as well for her as Zach's attempts to decrypt the Shadows' data.

Still the highlight of his days.

The nights, the few when they both managed to make it to the same bed at the same time, they spent wrapped up in each other, sleeping. Zach cursed the alarm that always woke him when it felt like he'd just closed his eyes five minutes ago. They got up, shared a quick sonic shower, and went their separate ways.

The absolute worst part of his days.

By the end of the first week, the pressure started to get to him almost as badly as Rowe. None of them had made any progress, and with every hour that passed, Zach felt the Shadows closing in around them. He began to feel paranoid about being in one place for so long, about the lack of any visible defenses or escape routes from the community.

And then the questions got so loud he couldn't shake them.

Why was everyone else so complacent?

Why weren't they moving to throw the Shadows off their trail?

How had the Shadows not found them yet?

"How's it going?"

Zach shook his head. He'd dozed off in his seat again; he hadn't even heard Vega come in—and she was right behind him.

"Fan-fucking-tastic," Rowe deadpanned.

Vega leaned over Zach's shoulder. "Is it me, or does the pattern keep changing?"

"It's not you," Zach said. He'd been trying to predict the scramble, but even an AI trawl couldn't tell him anything. It happened at seemingly random intervals and didn't follow any patterns that the AI could discern. Maybe if they had a month or two to extrapolate, they might be able to catch a scramble before it happened, but until then, Zach was throwing figurative shit at a wall and hoping some of it stuck. And most of the time, the pattern changed long before anything could hit in the first place.

She pointed to a side window. "That an AI thing?"

"Yeah, it's tracking the changes as they happen."

"How long has it been running?"

"About a week." He pulled up the results, which looked like more of the same numbers and symbols, except these were organized into tables. The AI had attempted to map the pattern in a scatter chart underneath it, only there wasn't one.

"That's a lot of numbers," she said.

"Never figured you for wasting breath on the obvious."

She smiled. "Looks to me like you could use a numbers guy."

"And, let me guess, you happen to know one."

Ten minutes later, Zach moved himself and his chair out of the way to make room for his self-proclaimed cousin Quinn. The guy was so big that the span of his shoulders blocked out most of the screen. "How long has this been tracking?" he asked, deep voice rumbling.

"'Bout a week," Vega told him. She leaned against the far wall, flipping her knife and half-smirking at them.

Quinn grunted to acknowledge, then spent the next fifteen minutes quietly watching the AI do its thing. Sure. Why not? Not like Zach had made any progress whatsoever.

He was zoning out, half asleep, when Quinn spoke again, startling him awake. "I don't know how to work this stuff. Can you recover a snapshot from this timestamp?"

Zach nudged him out of the way to bring up the console and retrieve the snapshot.

"Can you crack that?" Quinn asked.

"Sure, but it won't do jack shit, now that the pattern's scrambled to something else." No pattern ever persisted longer than a handful of minutes. Zach didn't even have time to analyze it, much less begin to decode before it scrambled again.

"Can you preprogram the decode for faster delivery?"

"Yyyeeaah…?"

"I suggest you do that. The pattern will repeat in… two hours, twenty-one minutes, and ten seconds."

Zach did a double-take. "Say what now?"

"Chop-chop, cousin," Vega crowed. "Time's a-wasting."

Zach met eyes with Rowe, who only shrugged. "Worth a shot."

"Worth a shot," Zach agreed. He brought up a new window and got to work. Decoding the snapshot wasn't a matter of typing in the correct password; it required a specific sequence of code that would actively rearrange the data to decrypt it. Meaning, he needed to identify the lock (a specific location in the snapshot to apply the decryption), the key (a translation pattern to make the data readable), and the combination (a sequence of functions to move the key across the snapshot to unlock it quickly).

With a steady pattern as his reference, Zach assembled the decoder in an hour and ten minutes.

And then they waited.

The AI kept working, but now it had a timer in the lower right corner counting down. If Quinn was right, then the decoder Zach had created would unlock the bulk of the data they'd scraped. But he couldn't tell Zach how much time they'd have to deploy it once the pattern appeared. The way their luck had been lately, Zach figured five seconds at most.

He watched the timer tick down to ten minutes, then five, then three.

At ninety seconds, he brought up the prompt and shook out his hands to stop the annoying nervous quiver. One typo, and they could start this shitshow all over again.

Vega put away her knife and joined the row behind Zach. He felt all three of them breathing down his neck, but he was too busy watching the timer tick down the last few seconds to bother snapping at them.

Three…

Two…

One.

Zach typed in an activation sequence and then swiped the whole window over the main screen to apply the decoder. A status bar swept across it to mark the progress.

Done.

Zach held his breath, waiting for something to happen.

A second later, the pattern on the screen flickered, and the chaos of random characters reorganized itself into a graphic dashboard filled with icons and readable text.

Silence.

"Holy shit," Rowe whispered.

"*Yes!*" Zach shot out of his seat and launched himself at his cousin. He grabbed Quinn's face and planted a loud, smacking kiss on his mouth. "Damn, I love you, cuz."

Quinn's shock made Vega burst out laughing.

Zach grinned, winking at the big guy before he shook Rowe's offered hand. "Nicely done," the former Hawk praised.

"Am I interrupting something?"

Of course, Ripley would choose that exact moment to ruin Zach's good mood by still existing. "Get your analysts and what-have-you," he told them. "See what they can pull out of there. Rowe, you saw how I set up the AI? Do the same thing for the other two batches and let it run. Let's give it a few hours and see if my favorite cousin can spot a pattern quicker."

His favorite cousin was a lot more receptive to Vega's kisses than he'd been to Zach's. He chose not to take it personally.

"Looks like things are going well," Ripley said, nowhere near as impressed as they should be, considering the monumental miracle Quinn had just performed. "They're about to go less well. You got mail."

They brought forth a small package marked with shipping codes. It was addressed to Zachary VanWarren, care of the Lavari Dolmi post office.

"Congratulations, you're the first official mail recipient of the Hallowed Plains."

The good mood shattered. Quinn shoved the cursing Vega behind him, and both he and Rowe stared at the package like it was a bomb that would go off the second Zach opened it.

"Do you know where it came from?" he asked Ripley.

"No. But I can make an educated guess."

Yeah.

"The roof is clear," Ripley said. "But if you'd like some privacy, I suggest the museum across the street. There's a shielded holding cell down on Sublevel C."

Rowe ordered Vega and Quinn to stay behind as he followed Zach to the holding cell, three floors underground. It looked like an exact replica of his cell in Chairo, which momentarily threw Zach for a loop.

"What are you thinking?" Rowe asked, following him inside. He left the door open, in case it had an automatic lock. The walls appeared to be reinforced, and they were a safe enough distance from other people that if the damned thing did explode, it wouldn't hurt anyone else.

"You should go back," Zach told him.

"Not happening."

"They'll need every Hawk they have."

"Yeah, that includes you."

Zach swore.

"So? Are you gonna open it or what?"

He set the box on a replica of the table where he'd shared his lunch with Raven weeks ago.

Someone had packed something and shipped it to a city that had all the standard infrastructure, but little to no human activity. And they'd addressed it to Zach.

The contents didn't even matter. "They know we're here."

"They know *you're* here," Rowe corrected.

"We need to evac."

"And confirm their hunch? Hand-feed them our exact numbers and location? You're smarter than that. Think like your CO. What does he want?"

"We fucked up their shit," Zach said. "They might suspect we stole their data, but they won't know until they clean up their servers—which they might have done already. They know we have battle-ready shuttles, but not how many. Our hit-and-run strategy will have clued them in that we have at least some defected Shadows on our side."

"And they went full-force after those relays to cripple us," Rowe added.

Zach frowned. "But only the ones we were actively using." All other communications had shut down for the duration of the mission to keep them hidden, and none of the other SU bases had reported communication issues or any equipment damage since the attack.

"Which means they don't know everything."

As if that was a good thing. "Just enough to put them on high alert." And that was when Shadows were at their most dangerous.

"So what do they need?" Rowe prompted.

The SU was a known target for the Shadows, but they had precious little information about the organization or its members. It was not a military institution. Most of their people were civilians living normal lives among the general population with no intention of ever confronting the Shadows. The one perk of John MacMurphy's hide-first strategy: as long as they blended in, they couldn't be targeted.

The Shadows could only strike at the SU when a telepath became too obvious in their community or when they deliberately stepped out of hiding to strike at the Shadows. And then the Shadows' penchant for total destruction meant there was little left for them to learn from the resulting wreckage.

What did they need?

The same thing the SU was after: "Intel."

Zach pinned down the box and pulled the tab to rip open the seam. He met eyes with Rowe, who nodded, and they both braced for the worst.

Zach lifted the top flap, then opened the two below.

Nestled inside the box was a Hawk wrist unit cuff, wrapped neatly around its paired lens. And beside them, the sender had tucked in a small white card with three words written across it in a heavy hand.

Griffith may be gone, but he's still a chess player. Don't think he didn't plan fifty moves ahead...

- The Evolutionary Gospel of Michael

Same time – Lavari Dolmi, Valhale 602

"...and he's not just playing against you."

Stars, this guy and his chess metaphors. He'd chosen them for a reason, and it clearly had something to do with Griffith, but after a week of replaying the recordings over and over, Raven now had a visceral reaction each time one came up.

She rolled her shoulders to work out the soreness in her upper back. It didn't help much while her eye still twitched. "Do we know what happened to Griffith?"

"He's gone," said her former tutor. He'd brought several more excerpts of Michael's prophecies that weren't in Ripley's collection to share with the group. That had been the extent of his assistance so far. He didn't pay attention when they played, didn't offer any explanations, and in general didn't do much aside from take up space and waste fresh air.

She was sick of his non-answers. "Gone *how*? Is he dead?"

"If not, he dearly wishes he was."

Laura McNally raised her head from the table's surface to meet eyes with Raven, devoid of any kindness. She was at the end of her patience with John, too. Whatever she'd just picked up from him made her shake her head no.

"Talk," Raven gritted out.

John had the audacity to say, "I told you everything you need to know."

"You don't get to make that call," Laura said.

John glared at her. "Pretending a lack of control is a crime in our ranks."

Laura didn't bat an eyelash. "I am not in your ranks. You have no authority here. And if you make Raven ask again, I'll be happy to give you a comprehensive demonstration of how much *control* I really have."

John's temper snapped cold across Raven's mind. It didn't feel intentional, but it didn't matter. Raven shoved back, anyway.

He flinched as if she'd hit him.

"Talk," she said again.

He tried to stare her down, but when Laura straightened in her seat as if to stand and physically confront him, he dropped his shoulders and took a chair at their table. Laura wasn't a Shadow, but she'd been trained to fight like there was no tomorrow. And her unique flavor of telepathy was more of an art form than a weapon. She could see and manipulate someone's intent. Where Raven felt the pathways of truth in someone's mind, Laura saw the lie and a person's need to hide something manifesting as different colors in their aura.

John fisted his hands on top of the table. "What I have to say doesn't leave this room."

"No deal," Laura said.

Raven agreed. "Whatever you say will be evaluated. If I deem it relevant to our efforts, we will be sharing with the others." She'd had it up to her eyeballs with people lying and hiding things that had the potential to change everything multiple times over. No more.

"This is playing with fire, Raven."

She leaned forward. "Then—fucking—burn."

Laura whistled. "I'd start talking if I were you. She's ready to literally set your ass on fire."

"I'm getting that," he retorted. And still, he dragged it out a whole minute before he unclenched his jaw to speak. "I went to see Griffith after Green 24."

Raven reeled.

Laura shook her head. "Wait, what? You just…went to see him? Like, for a cup of tea?"

John sighed. "Matthew and I worked together decades ago. Before he became radicalized, we used to be colleagues. Maybe even friends. We fell out when I caught wind of him building out a mercenary force behind the ICG's backs and accused him of treason. He deduced that I would never support any form of violent action against chem-resistants, and that made me an active threat.

"He became a lot more secretive about his pet project after that. I tried to expose him, but it backfired. I suspected that he'd made deals with other high-ranking politicians to cover for him and put me in a vulnerable position. I was forced to resign my post at the ICG. His mercenaries became the Shadow army, I built out the Special Unit to protect the most vulnerable, and we never spoke again. Except when he sent his minions to deliver a message."

"The missing telepaths," Raven said.

"Yes. Griffith knew that those who could read and alter thoughts would be the greatest threat to his bid for power. He needed subjects to study so he could manufacture defenses against our abilities."

"How many did he take?" Laura asked.

"Over the span of three decades, hundreds," Raven answered. "That we know of, anyway." Given how selective John had been with the ones he'd taken under his wing, there would have been many more left to fend for themselves. People driven into seclusion, cut off from family and friends—people who could disappear in the night and no one would ever notice.

John nodded. "Yes, he would have needed as many subjects as he could find. But what he wanted was to get to me. What he did to Emma was a direct attack on me. He chose her *because* of me. When we got her back—"

"When the *Evolutionaries* got her back," Raven corrected. The Green 24 rescue team had also included SU telepaths, but none of them had been fighters. The Evolutionaries had been the ones who set the course, led the charge, and fought their way through to Emma and four other telepaths. The deserted Shadow, John Wayland, had been the decoy. The official report said they'd carried him back, comatose and circling the drain.

Raven still remembered the uproar as the news had rippled across the SU networks weeks later. The Shadows were real. The war had begun. And their director was gone.

"When they came back," John said, "they had a data crystal for me. Michael's very long farewell. It told me when and where I'd find Matthew, and made it clear that, for the good of everyone I cared about, he needed to be neutralized."

"So you killed him. Right?" Laura prompted.

John winced.

Raven deflated. "Dammit, John."

"I destroyed his mind and rendered him incapable of any form of communication. He can't see, hear, or speak in any comprehensible language. For all intents and purposes, he *is* neutralized."

"Unless they have a way to fix him."

"They don't," John insisted. "They can't. No one else can do what I can do."

Lie. Raven's ability to rearrange memories mimicked John's ability to rearrange sensory and cognitive functions. It was very possible that others like them existed. And if Zach could have spent his entire life among the Shadows as a latent telepath, they likely had others in their ranks, too.

Whether or not they knew about them was a separate, more concerning matter.

"That you know of," Laura snapped.

"We can't map telepathic work yet," Raven added. "We have no way of knowing how EMC might affect it. What if they put him in the chair and reset his brain to make him functional again?"

John shook his head. "If they did, it would render him obsolete."

"You don't know that."

"Without his memories, Matthew Griffith is—"

"Still a functioning precog," Raven finished.

The former senator shared Michael's gift of prophecy. The only reason they'd been able to strike such an effective blow at Green 24 had been because of Griffith's arrogance. He hadn't seen them coming because he hadn't thought anyone else like him existed, much less chose to play for the other side.

"He wouldn't need his memories. In fact, he'd be more useful to someone like Sandoval without them. A powerful precog stripped of any delusions of authority, just doing whatever his CO told him to do… The perfect tool for winning a war."

Laura swore and pushed away from the table. She ran out the door before anyone could stop her. Neither Raven nor John tried.

Raven didn't need to read John's mind to see he'd already considered the possibility. He knew how badly he'd miscalculated. He just couldn't accept it. After all the time he'd spent with the Evolutionaries, watching from their secret lair as worlds burned around them and the people he'd proclaimed to love died, he still couldn't stomach the thought that at least some of it might have been prevented if only he'd been willing to get his own hands dirty.

His internal conflict would ultimately tear his soul apart. It would break him in ways no one would be able to heal. And he would find no sympathy anywhere among his own.

"When this is finished," Raven said, a strange calm settling over her. "I never want to see you or hear from you again."

"I'm only human, Raven."

"So was Michael. And Julian. And Nell. And Darrow. The difference is, in the end, every single one of them had the guts to step up and do what had to be done. All you did was let them."

February 21, 3040 – Yellow 6

The barracks were arranged like college dorm rooms, with four soldiers to a room. Each room featured two bunk beds against opposite walls, a desk with two chairs positioned by the window, and a retractable closet on either side of the entry door.

As the last to arrive, Hansel got a bottom bunk on the right, currently blocked by a leg hanging from the top one.

It was late into the night, but both his top bunkmate and the soldier on the bottom bunk opposite him sat up when Hansel walked through the door, and the night light automatically turned on.

"Fresh meat?"

Hansel nodded at the man to his left. He had the same kind of device on his temple and the same haunted look in his eyes that Hansel saw every time he looked in the mirror. "Hansel. Atwater."

"Victor James Mesler. Or so they tell me."

Who am I?

"Gibbs, don't be rude. Say hello."

Gibbs flipped them off with both hands, rolled toward the wall, and started snoring.

"Don't mind him. He's just an asshole. Thinks he's better than us 'cause they haven't stuck anything in his brain yet. Get yourself situated. He won't bite. He's been ordered not to."

Hansel set his duffel down at the foot of his bunk and sat. At least he had enough headroom to straighten his back.

The night light dimmed further, but didn't turn off completely.

"Mika Mayer's got the last bunk. She's on watch tonight, but you'll probably see her in here a lot. Kinda shy. Doesn't talk much. Easy on the eye, though."

"Will you shut the fuck up already?" Gibbs muttered. "Trying to sleep here."

Mesler rolled his eyes and made a dismissive gesture. He was a dense shadow across the room now, his dark skin blending in with the night.

"I saw that," Gibbs said.

Hansel felt like he should at least crack a smile at the obvious joke, but he couldn't seem to dredge up much emotion these days. The shuttle flight to get this far had been worse than anything he'd experienced before. Days on end closed inside a metal hull with narrow beds, buzzing lights, and three identical squares a day. Oh, and about two hundred men and women walking around like zombies, with their hollow eyes and monotone greetings.

A lot of time to freak out over how much Hansel didn't know about himself, and how much it concerned him. It was always there at the back of his mind, like a word he'd used a million times before but couldn't quite recall on the spot. Something he should be doing. Something important.

But how important could it be if he couldn't remember?

"So, you lost your memories, too?" he asked Mesler.

The soldier snorted. "Yeah, you could say that. But some of the others say they come back eventually. Maybe not all, but enough, y'know?"

Yeah. Enough to stop spiraling through the void in his head so he could focus on something other than that nagging sense of despair licking at the backs of his eyeballs. Like the mission.

Gibbs growled and rolled over again. "You didn't lose 'em. They took 'em. You get 'em back, they'll take 'em again. Do yourself a favor. Don't try to get 'em back."

The way he said it made Hansel's skin crawl from the base of his spine all the way to the top of his head.

"Now shut the fuck up. I got first watch in the AM."

Mesler sighed loudly and stretched back out. Conversation over.

Hansel wouldn't be on watch for the next two days. CO Greives had informed him that the newbies would spend tomorrow getting acquainted with the outpost, and training with the other 'pinheads' as she called them. Hansel had noticed that everyone on his shuttle flight had had the same device implanted in their temple. But not everyone here had them. In fact, other than his shuttlemates, he hadn't seen many at all.

He had noticed that those without devices had a pin on their collars instead. Weird shape. Like a dog, but not anatomical. One woman he'd passed had one shaped like wings. Hansel figured that meant they outranked him. But everyone who'd crossed paths with the CO had saluted her.

Maybe they would explain that during orientation tomorrow. It was bad enough not knowing who he was. Not knowing where he fit in was somehow almost worse.

You get 'em back, they'll take 'em again.

Gibbs' warning repeated in Hansel's head as he reached to untie his boots. His hands shook so badly he couldn't grasp the laces. The shivers crawled up his arms and across his chest, and by the time he'd removed his shoes and shrugged out of his jacket to hunker beneath his blanket, Hansel shook all over.

He hugged himself and squeezed tight to hold still. It didn't work. His arms felt empty.

When the exhaustion finally became too much, Hansel dropped headlong into darkness, and strange, disorienting nightmares of exploding hovers, and children's laughter, and a soft, somber voice saying, "I should have died with them. Everything would have been easier if I'd just died with them."

51

Run, run as fast as you can... Where was I? Where are you? Who are you? Who are you? Who are you?

- The Evolutionary Gospel of Michael

February 22, 3040 – Lavari Dolmi, Valhale 602

Zach didn't come back to their room that night.

Rowe, Quinn, and Vega were still working on decryption.

Ripley had called in six of their top researchers to review everything Quinn had managed to unlock so far. They'd taken one look at it and requested ten more people for their team.

Emma and her husband were now dealing with John MacMurphy, and whatever else he'd been keeping from them. The Griffith bombshell had shaken everyone, and now the people who'd held the line against the Shadows for years questioned every choice they'd made in the war so far.

And Zach didn't come back to the room.

Midnight blew in a massive wind storm that kicked up sand and ice crystals into swirling vortices all over town. Raven listened to the hiss and howl, watching the particles slam against her window in pulsing waves. Her eyes hurt as she tried to see through them to the street below.

An hour before sunrise, the winds shifted and calmed enough to no longer be a health hazard. Raven put on her thick boots, bundled up in a long coat, wrapped a shawl around her head and neck, and crossed the street to the museum building.

As with all others, it was unlocked and accessible, but no one operated it. Her footsteps echoed eerily on the smooth marble floors. 3D art pieces depicting mythical creatures and figures from ancient history books hung suspended above her. Glittering crystals and thin lines of silver in their bodies mapped out constellations that no longer looked like that, even from Earth.

She took the elevator down to Sublevel C and stepped out onto a too-familiar floor, except there was only one holding room, and the lights were on inside. Raven knocked before walking through the door that had been left ajar.

Zach didn't look up. He sat at the table, staring through the open package before him, his face void of expression.

"Good morning, Mr. VanWarren," she said, hoping to break him out of the daze.

He blinked awake, frowned at her, then rubbed his face and stretched his arms up. "Is it morning already?"

He hadn't commented on the name. "What's wrong?"

"For starters, you're way over there, for some reason." He shifted in his chair. "Get that sweet ass over here."

Opening the front of her coat in deference to the heat, Raven complied, but his playful tone didn't fool her. His eyes looked haunted, his face ashen. "What's wrong?" she asked again.

Zach pulled her in tight and pressed his forehead against her. It had become his way of demanding telepathic intimacy. These days, both of them were too tired to practice him looking for her mind, but he always craved her in his. She'd be lying if she said she didn't enjoy it.

She'd also be lying if she said it didn't concern her.

When she didn't immediately fall into his thoughts, Zach deflated on a sigh. "I got a birthday present."

Raven drew back. "It's your birthday?"

"Not the point, Blackbird."

Like hell it wasn't. "Your ID file says your birthday is in August."

He gave her a look.

"You kept your first name, but not your birthday?"

"Names matter," he said, hitching up a careless shoulder. Then he twitched his chin toward the table behind her. "Which, as it turns out, is the problem here."

Raven twisted in his lap to look. "What is it?"

"It's a Hawk wrist unit. A special weapon only for my rank. Got lots of nifty features like a shield and a pulse grenade. And the ability to interface with any technology nearby."

"Is that why you're holed up three floors underground?"

"It doesn't work until you put it on, but yeah. Can't risk it picking up anything we don't want them to know."

"But you're not wearing it."

She felt him wince where his mouth brushed against her jaw. "It can also explode pretty spectacularly. I'm a little hesitant."

"Then we should destroy it."

He chuckled, nuzzling into the thick material of her shawl to get to her neck. "I need to know what it's about. Sandoval never does things just for kicks. Every action, every mission always has multiple objectives, and they're always geared toward getting everything he can possibly get."

"Greedy bastard."

"That, he is."

"So what do you think his objective is with this?"

"I'm afraid to find out."

Raven twisted back to face him. The words were flippant, but she sensed genuine fear beneath them. From the man who hadn't shown an ounce of it since she'd met him.

"What if I'm a sleeper?" he said on a whisper, as if even giving it voice was too dangerous. "What if I put it on, and it triggers something in my head to make me…"

Raven brushed her fingers through his hair once, twice, until his eyes grew heavy-lidded and some of the haunting uncertainty melted. She brushed a kiss over his lips, intending to reassure him, but got lost in it when he followed her retreat. He pulled her back, his mouth clashing into hers, his fingers curling into the material of her coat as he squeezed her to him as hard as he could without hurting her.

She hummed, trying to temper the devouring fury, but Zach was beyond rational thought. Fear still dominated his mind, spilling over her, drowning her.

No, not drowning. Drawing her in.

Raven let herself sink through his shields like mist, hoping her ephemeral presence would calm him. Instead, she found herself straddling him on the couch of his mindscape den, still clutched just as tightly, only this time, they were both naked, and Zach's hands roamed anxiously over her back as if he couldn't get close enough.

The fluffy red blanket was draped over the back of the couch. Raven raised herself just enough to reach for it and pull it over the top of them. The thick material shaded them from the rest of the room, but, in the way of dream magic, they still had enough light to see. "There," she said. "Now no one can find us. We're invisible."

He cracked a smile, and the blanket grew to stretch over them all the way to the floor. In the soft hiss of its motion, she almost made out a voice. Secret words whispered across the silky fuzz of faux fur. Three of them.

"Blanket fort," Zach said with a lightness that felt a little too forced. "The most effective of all defenses. Can't believe I didn't think of it myself."

A deflection. He didn't want to acknowledge what she'd heard. "Well, I suppose that's understandable," she said, playing along, for once in her life not chasing down the truth that wasn't trying very hard to run away in the first place. "One can hardly expect you to think straight with a sexy naked woman in your lap."

He hummed in agreement. His fingers trailed abstract patterns along her spine. "Every man has his limits."

She played with his hair, enjoying the way he melted into the simple gesture, the way he drifted into her, his mouth on her neck, her shoulder… But those three words refused to leave her. They seeped into her through the light brush of his fingers and covered her skin like invisible tattoos with every breath he puffed against her. He might have silenced them, but he couldn't make them leave. He did everything he could to distract her instead.

"Sandoval can't have you back," she told him, because acknowledging those words was too dangerous. But going through something bad didn't hurt nearly as much as the idea of missing out on something good. She couldn't stomach the thought of letting Zach go out there to fight for her without knowing she would fight for him just as hard. "You're ours now. Mine. And I don't share."

He pulled back, searching her gaze.

"Shall we call Sandoval's bluff?" She shifted her focus enough to retrieve the package and hand it to him.

"Blackbird…"

"I'm right here with you."

"That's what scares me."

Raven didn't budge.

Zach looked like he might want to say something, but stopped himself and took out the wrist unit instead. He strapped it to his left wrist, then put the lens in his left eye.

Immediately, the wrist unit lit up, and Zach went rigid.

Raven tuned in to his senses, to his left eye specifically, where a ghostly hologram of Rajeev Sandoval's upper body floated in the space above the table. He was a coldly handsome man with even features, a no-nonsense expression, and cruel, calculating eyes. Streaks of gray snaked through his short dark hair, and a wicked scar cut from under his right ear across his neck, disappearing beneath the edge of his uniform collar.

"*Who are you?*" he demanded. Without an earpiece, the recording didn't come with sound, only captions that scrolled across the space in front of him. But Zach's mind, still so entrenched in the horrific life his CO had created, supplied his voice all on its own to go with the visuals.

Zach's thoughts churned rapidly over all possible points of vulnerability around him. The wrist unit was active, but too far from any systems it could hack. It kept searching, though, scanning and mapping Zach's immediate vicinity. It would pick up the layout of the room, and everyone in it, including Raven sitting on his lap.

He deliberately averted his gaze to keep her identity hidden.

Raven leaned more into him, putting her cheek to his so he wouldn't have to strain so hard.

"Who are you?" Sandoval repeated the same way, like a recording on loop that demanded a response to continue.

Zach's throat worked on a dry swallow. He knew who he was, but that wasn't who Sandoval wanted him to be. "No one," he said out loud.

The hologram flickered, and Sandoval smiled like a predator who'd just caught his prey by the tail. *"Where do you reside?"*

"Nowhere," Zach answered.

"And what do you do?"

Zach's eyes flickered sideways, seeking her, but unwilling to put her at risk.

Raven put her arm around him and hugged him tight. —*I'm right here with you.—*

"What do you do, Hawk?"

"What needs to be done."

The hollow words shuddered through her as his arms fell loose to his sides. She refused to let go. When he drifted through her in his mind, floating away like a ghost, she put herself in his path and forced him to stop. She held him tethered to the place where his identity was strongest. Right there in front of the fireplace, with a winter storm howling outside, and hundreds of tiny bells tinkling on the Christmas tree.

She rooted his bare feet to the coarse wooden floor and pulled the fluffy blanket over him. "I am right here with you."

But Sandoval was talking now, addressing a soldier under his command whose obedience had never been in question. Zach imagined his voice cracking across the space like lightning, each word curt and precise, speaking to a side of Zach he knew still existed within him.

"Well done, son. You have successfully infiltrated the stronghold of our enemy. The orchestrated attack was a brilliant strategy and worked exactly as planned. I am proud of you."

Zach shuddered, his mindscape wavering like a mirage, disrupted by shame and a wave of raging denial.

"Now it's time. This is what you've trained for all your life. You know what to do. What needs to be done. Find a weak spot and take them

down. Finish it. When you do, send a signal for immediate extraction. I'll be waiting at Green 24. Dismissed!"

Something snapped. Raven's stomach did a cartwheel as Zach shoved to his feet, dislodging her from his lap and from his mind. He tore the cuff off his wrist, eyes wild as he roughly plucked out the lens and threw it across the room.

"Zach?"

"Stay away," he snapped, backing himself toward the wall and shoving the heels of his palms against his eyes hard enough to make her wince. "Just…give me a minute."

Raven shrugged off her coat and scarf, then pulled out the other chair and quietly took a seat at the table. Zach's mental shields flared in chaotic waves, the sharp points seeking a target to sink into. His body shuddered on every deep breath, physical evidence of how hard he fought to recenter himself.

Watching him struggle and not doing anything to help hurt Raven in ways she hadn't thought possible, but she owed it to him to give him the space he asked for. Rather than push, she stayed silent and set her breathing to a deep, steady rhythm, counting off in her mind.

Eventually, Zach caught on to the sound and made an effort to match her breath for breath. The tension slowly eased out of his shoulders, and his arms lowered, but his face remained set, his eyes closed.

Raven felt the tight chokehold of his panic give way as the spikes of his shield receded to their normal size and pliable shape, but she didn't try to force a connection. Instead, keeping her voice low and even, she said, "It's not real."

"Oh, it's real, all right," he retorted. "Exactly the kind of sick mind-fuck Sandoval enjoys the most. You heard him: Find a weak spot, and take them down."

"Then he's way off his game."

Zach pried open one bloodshot eye to glare at her.

She shrugged. "Just saying. He's poking at a weak spot you don't have anymore."

"Don't I?"

Raven gestured at the room around them. "Room's still in one piece. I'm still breathing. The cuff is way over there. And you're still here."

"Means nothing."

"It means *everything*."

"If Sandoval knew about the attack—"

"You and I both know that's bullshit."

"Is it? What if it was all a setup? What if everything I've done played right into his hand?"

Yeah, she couldn't dispute that when she'd thought pretty much the same thing not too long ago. Wiping Zach's memories created the perfect alibi. He wouldn't risk betraying himself if he didn't know anything outside of what had been fed to him. Sandoval had groomed Zach from childhood; he had to know how his mind operated, what breadcrumbs to sprinkle into his path to lead him exactly where he wanted.

But even as she considered the possibility, Raven found herself smiling.

"Care to let me in on the joke here, Blackbird?"

She fucking hated Michael and all his stupid chess prophecies. But right now, she could have kissed his four-year-dead corpse. "The father will never know the friends his son plays with."

Zach groaned, thumping his head back against the wall. "I am too tired for this."

"Then allow me to do the math for you." She nudged the chair across from her with her foot, inviting him to sit. He wasn't kidding—she felt his exhaustion like lead in her bones. That wall wouldn't hold him up for much longer.

He looked at the chair, then at her.

Raven raised an eyebrow.

Zach rolled his eyes and dropped into the seat.

"Good boy," she praised, earning herself a quicksilver grin. "Sandoval doesn't know anything about you because he doesn't know *you*."

"He raised me."

"He raised *Operative M.* An obedient, blank soldier. But that's not you anymore. And, if I had to guess, it hasn't been for quite some time. Possibly long before the quote-unquote *terrorist attack* on Ela last year." The disaster that Michael had predicted the media wouldn't shut up about. The catalyst that had set all the wheels in motion. "You were there. Quinn said you helped save him and Vega. But you weren't able to save Geraldine. I think you took that personally. I think it's why you turned on the Shadows. And, yes. Had you been nothing else outside of Operative M, then Sandoval would have clocked your every move since your desertion. You would've been caught within a week, and we wouldn't be sitting here, having this conversation right now."

Zach frowned. "I'm getting a weird sense of déjà vu."

"Remember when you told me that married couples are less conspicuous travelers? You knew it then, that Sandoval expected you to have no one to turn to. He didn't anticipate that you'd make personal connections at all, much less make them part of your escape strategy. He didn't notice when Operative M stopped being who you were and turned into who you pretended to be."

Zach shook his head.

"Who are you?" she asked gently.

His jaw twitched, shoulders hunching against the conditioned reflex to straighten to attention at the question.

"Zachary VanWarren, I'm asking you to tell me who you are."

His gaze met hers, swimming with so many unspoken words.

"You are my husband. You have a very large, scary-looking teddy bear of a cousin. You have friends who'll watch your back, and allies who'll fight at your side. Sandoval knows none of this. He still talks like you're playing a part, because that's the only way he has to get under your skin—by making you believe it's all pretend. He's counting on your own doubt to drive you away from us, and our prejudice to let you." She scoffed. "He's missing a crucial bit of intel there, too."

Zach swallowed hard and, in a rough voice, asked, "What's that?"

"You don't remember? I told you just a few minutes ago."

"Tell me again."

Raven sat forward and leaned her elbow on the table. "You're mine. And I will personally reduce Sandoval's mind to soup before I let him take you from me."

52

Some of the things I see, I wish I didn't. Some would have been better enjoyed with snacks.

- The Evolutionary Gospel of Michael

The table between them went flying.

In the next instant, Zach had scooped Raven out of her seat and tossed her onto the narrow bunk. His mouth stole her breath along with every last remnant of a rational thought, and her mind tumbled into his on a vortex of pure feeling.

His heart hammered rapidly against hers.

Hot chills raised goose bumps all over his skin as he tore off his shirt and peeled her out of her sweater.

His weight sank them both into the mattress before he rolled to bring her up over him.

Only then did his fervid press slow. His kiss became almost languid, his hands massaging her as far as he could reach, from her shoulder, down to her thighs. His fingers speared down into the back of her waistband, cupping her between her legs, teasing at her pussy.

Raven braced her hand to push up, only for him to grip her back down to him.

She felt how much he needed the contact, the intimacy. But she also felt his exhaustion. The things he wanted to do with her—*to* her—could wait.

Raven broke their kiss, leaned away when he tried to follow her, earning herself a disgruntled growl and a hard squeeze of her buttock in punishment. "Whom do you answer to?"

Zach frowned. "No one."

She nipped his lower lip, grinding her hips down over his erection. "Whom do you obey?"

Comprehension bloomed, sending a wave of unbridled lust across both their minds. "You," he said, clutching her down toward his thrust.

"I don't think I believe you," she teased.

He grinned. "Try me."

"Sit up against the wall."

With a flex of his abs, he raised them both upright and turned sideways on the bunk.

Raven rewarded him by kissing and nipping her way across his jaw to his ear. "Hands behind your back," she whispered.

His displeasure at being forced to stop touching her was deep and instantaneous. In a petulant refusal, he gripped her hips tighter, rocking up against her.

"I promise you'll like it."

"And I promise I'll be paying you back in kind."

"Sounds like a date."

Delight and reluctance washed across their connection. He took the slow path of rubbing his hands up and down her thighs, then trailing his fingertips across the seams of her knees, before he tucked his arms behind his lower back.

"That's my good boy," she purred, trailing kisses down the column of his neck.

She had to shift farther across his lap to keep going lower, earning herself another growl. In retaliation, she closed her teeth around his nipple a little harder than she'd intended. Zach swore, his head thumping against the wall, but he straightened immediately, watching her slow, teasing progress down, and down.

At the edge of the bunk, she climbed fully off his lap, kneeling on the floor before him. "Spread your legs for me."

He was flushed, his pupils blown so wide they made his eyes look black rather than brown, and the pure fire in them scorched across her body and mind, making her heart pound and her mouth water. But she sensed a faint thread of hesitation in him. He knew what she was after, and it wasn't as if he'd never done this before. But every other time, regardless of his partner's gender, the act had been just that—an act. A lie and a manipulation with the end goal of furthering the Shadows' agenda.

Raven licked her lips as she nudged his knees farther apart to get closer. He dropped them wide, but hooked his ankles together behind her, and issued a wordless challenge in the quirk of his eyebrow. She'd only ordered him to put his hands behind his back, not to stop touching her so, technically, he wasn't cheating.

But the position did make his pants more difficult to undo one-handed. Good thing Raven was a resourceful woman. She used her teeth as well, slipping her fingers into the slit to ease it open across the bulge of his erection.

Just as it began to slip free, almost as if he couldn't help himself, Zach's mind filled with images and fantasies of her going down on him. He wanted her to take him deep, all the way into her throat. He wanted his hands in her hair, holding her still as he pumped into her.

He wanted things that were physically impossible—Raven stroking him while also fingering herself. He craved her pleasure as much as his own. For Zach, they existed in tandem.

She'd never been more motivated to get that damned surgery.

"Changed your mind?" he taunted, his heart beating so hard she heard it. "Too much for you to handle?" His shoulders twitched as if he could barely hold still. But he kept his hands behind his back like she'd told him to.

She curled her fingers around his base. "Are you complaining about my technique?"

He shrugged, but his jaw had gone tight. "Just saying it's getting kind of cold, Blackbird."

"Hmm. I'm told friction creates heat. Maybe I can try that?"

An eager nod. A drop of precum just for her. "Yeah. Try that."

Squeezing just enough, she stroked up the length of his cock, milking that drop a little bigger. She kissed the bead off and met her hand with her mouth as she sucked herself down the head to her fingers, then letting him pop out like a popsicle. "Mmm, delicious."

Zach cursed, legs locking around her, hips thrusting up. "More," he demanded.

Gathering saliva in her mouth, she closed her lips around him and took him all the way to the back of her throat. Her eyes watered as she gagged a little, drenching him with more saliva. She spread it up and down his length with her hand while her mouth and tongue lavished attention on the tip, sucking, swirling, teasing with shallow bobs.

"Fuck, that feels good."

More fantasies spread heat all over her body, pooling between her legs. Images of her straddling his face while she went down on him, of him bending her over the table to fuck her from behind, his hand wrapped around her throat to arch her up into his kiss. He wanted everything. Every inch of her, in every way he could get her. Marathon nights and quick, covert detours into utility closets.

But between each fantasy, he snapped back to right here and right now—her taking him balls-deep, and sucking him all the way dry so he could make her dripping wet to make up for it.

Teetering on the sharp edge of her own release, Raven moaned and took him deep, loving the rumble of his pleasured groan, the tight, almost painful grip he had on the covers bunched behind his back to keep himself from touching her. When his legs tightened around her back and his hips curled up, Raven gave him what he craved, swallowing him all the way down past her gag reflex until her nose met his groin.

"*Raven!*"

She let him slip out slowly, following up with her hand all the way to his tip, twisting her fist over him while she caught her breath.

Then down she went again, and again, each time holding him in her throat as long as she could. Zach's groans turned into a long string of mumbled words, praising her, begging her, and cursing creative streaks in turn. His fantasies drifted away as his entire focus centered on her mouth. She felt his pleasure build, his body tensing, fabric ripping where he clutched it behind his back.

"Fuck, I'm gonna *come!*"

Raven swallowed him down, choking on him, but she took every-thing as he pulsed over her tongue and spurted down her throat. His pleasure washed over her, setting off her own, and she knew he felt it, too. The telepathic orgasm echo chamber heightened every sensation to a sharp peak that bordered on agony.

It left them both boneless, exhausted, and covered in Zach's spend.

She didn't even realize she was still connected with him until the pins and needles of his arms falling asleep stabbed at her shoulders. His exhaustion became almost unbearable as he extricated himself and pulled her up onto the cot with him.

Raven had just enough energy left to wipe away the mess before her limbs stopped cooperating. The last thing she remembered before sinking into a deep, dreamless sleep was Zach tucking her against him under the torn covers.

53

You will be visited by the ghosts of gods long dead.

- The Evolutionary Gospel of Michael

February 22, 3040 – Lavari Dolmi, Valhale 602

"Ahem!"

Raven woke with a startled squeak as the world jerked sideways and she found herself sandwiched between the hard wall at her back and Zach's big body in the front.

"I did knock."

Ripley.

Raven groaned. With her arm pinned beneath her, she couldn't even flip them off.

But her irritation paled in comparison to the tense vibration of Zach's entire body. He'd braced for impact, his instinct to tear into the enemy warring with his need to protect Raven. Barely halfway awake, he'd reverted to full Shadow mode, more dangerous than she'd ever felt him.

"…still hasn't repeated, but the team thinks they found something in—"

"Get out," Raven said. "Give us a minute."

"We don't have time for—"

"If you don't leave," Raven said slowly, measuring each syllable and keeping her voice low, "I can't vouch for your safety."

Silence.

"Twenty minutes. Conference room across the street." Their clomping, high-heeled footsteps trailed off down the hallway.

Raven nudged Zach with her nose, the only movement his tight squeeze allowed, unless she wanted to knee him in the groin. His mental shields were fully engaged again, almost as bad as they'd been after Sandoval's message.

"Hey," she whispered to redirect his focus.

His breathing was ragged, his muscles tense from head to toe.

"Are you hungry?" she tried again. "I don't think there's any food down here. We'll have to go get something from the dining room."

Nothing.

Raven made herself relax, as if they were just snuggling in bed together. "I don't want to leave the bed, though. Comfy." She took a chance and mentally brushed the very sharp tip of one of his shield spikes.

It lashed out, snatching around the part of her it could reach. This time, it didn't pull her in. Instead, she felt it crawl and extend over her, a cool liquid sensation that lapped across her scalp and made her shiver.

"Zach?"

He tucked in his chin to blink at her. The confusion in his dark eyes almost broke her heart. She couldn't tell if he was fully back, whether he even recognized her in that moment. But that cool liquid shield still shivered across her head, keeping her mind as safe as the rest of her.

I love you.

It wasn't a thought or an emotion, so much as a solid conviction deep in her core. Raw, possessive, and utterly overwhelming. And it couldn't have chosen a worse time to take root. Raven swallowed back the ridiculous tears stinging at the corners of her eyes and attempted a smile. "Do you want to shower before we leave?"

Zach gave no indication that he heard her voice or sensed any of her inner turmoil. His expression never changed, his shield didn't slip, and his body didn't relax. He didn't say a word as he stared, but his pupils pulsed wide for a second. Then his hand claimed the base of her skull, nudging her upward, and he curled down to meet her.

He kissed her long and deep, with languorous laps of his tongue against hers.

They didn't make Ripley's twenty-minute window. They didn't even leave the bed for another thirty. Logic suggested that the holding cell had the same kind of security features as those in Chairo, and whoever controlled the feeds was likely getting a hell of a show.

For the next hour and a half, neither Zach nor Raven gave a damn.

~

Wearing a wrist unit primed to automatically hack anything and everything was out of the question. But leaving it behind would have been a stupid move. It was still a weapon, fully armed and primed for action; Zach could still use it once he got his boots on the ground in battle. For now, he had the cuff and lens safely tucked into a sealed pocket, and Raven safely tucked against his side as they took the elevator up to the conference room.

The floor was busier than usual, with people rushing in and out of rooms on either side of the hallway. Zach peeked into them as they passed. In one, a bunch of teenagers argued loudly and all at the same time across a table covered with paper sketches. In the next, two women had some sort of mechanical gizmo split open, its wiry guts spilling out over the floor.

A loud shouting match between familiar voices sparked his interest as they neared the third room on the left. He slowed and stopped at the edge of the doorjamb.

"—like hell I'm letting you—"

"—think you're going to do, aside from get yourself blown up—"

"—out there when you can't even sprint for ten minutes before you start to limp—"

"—and I'm not using you as a human body shield!"

Vega stormed out, shoving past Zach, a murderous calm over her face.

Zach leaned out to look into the room, raising an eyebrow at the man she'd left behind. "You okay, cuz?"

Quinn stared up at the ceiling, his jaw twitching as he grappled for control. Then he dragged his feet out after Vega, barely sparing Zach a look. "Do yourself a favor. Don't ever get married."

Zach winced after him in sympathy.

"He's worried," Raven said. "Vega is set on leading the front lines, but she won't take Quinn with her, and he doesn't want to let her go alone."

"Oh…" He shuddered. "*Damn*, that was ice cold with the human shield thing."

Raven nodded. "But, unfortunately, accurate."

Zach agreed. Quinn's heart was as big as the rest of him, and it hummed for his wife above all else. The problem was, he wasn't a fighter. Superhuman strength notwithstanding, he had no training and no business in any battle. But he did have one thing his wife didn't and could never get: the freakish healing abilities Dr. Chase-Calen's serum had given him. And he absolutely wouldn't hesitate to turn himself into a human shield to protect Vega. "If I asked you to—"

"Don't even finish that sentence."

"Yep. Got it. No sitting out any big fights." But they would definitely be going to see Dr. Chase-Calen later today.

Ripley was still waiting for them in the conference room, along with Rowe, the Waylands, and a few others.

To Zach's surprise, Laura McNally had also put in an appearance, looking uneasy, but determined. She spared Zach a glance and nodded in greeting, but quickly averted her gaze.

Someone had set out food trays, but holoprojections of other people glowed along the table's surface, and it seemed impolite to reach through them.

Sadie didn't look happy about whatever bug had crawled up her ass wherever she was at Evolutionary Central. Brent Catton appeared to have come out of the attack unscathed, physically and mentally. He tossed grapes into the air and caught them in his mouth, flickering over the top of a steaming coffee pot.

A man Zach didn't recognize hovered in the middle. Almost too pretty to be real, with his perfectly disheveled hair and his shirt collar open, he looked like a model posing for a fashion photographer. "I want you back on Torrey," he said to Dr. Chase-Calen.

"They need me here," she argued back.

"They have Eskel."

"You think they'll be able to manage with one medic for eighteen hundred people?"

"And how many medics are we going to need here in the infirmaries when the casualties start flying in?"

Dr. Chase-Calen snarled, dark rosettes blooming along her hairline. "Don't make me choose, Jer."

"I'm not," the stranger said. "Neither you nor Pixie have any business in this fight."

Wayland cracked his knuckles and his neck, looking anywhere other than at his redhead wife.

Rowe stared hard at Laura, who glared back and shook her head, forestalling any arguments.

Zach leaned into Raven. "I feel like we missed something important."

Sadie straightened from her slouch. "They're here. Take your domestic squabbles offline."

Catton missed a catch, the grape rolling off his chin to somewhere unseen. He cleared his throat and tuned in. "S'up."

Ripley waved a hand, and the holo-people shifted aside to make room for a detailed 3D schematic map. "We finally caught a break," they said, turning the model around with a pinch-and-twist of their fingers. "This came out of the first batch of data we decrypted. At the top, there is outpost Green 24. You see the craters here and here—remnants of previous explosions. It looks like the river gorge was the result of a bomb that set off a tectonic shift at the gulf."

"Fascinating," Zach muttered.

Ripley ignored his sarcasm. "It is, because it turns out the Shadows used that damage to expand the outpost downward. See here? Sublevels A through D are original to the first construction. This portion right here collapsed during the first attack, some ten years ago. They left it like that as a decoy, and then tunneled down lower here."

A web of utility tunnels lit up bright red, then flooded the area underneath a massive, pill-shaped submarine on stilts. According to the scale, that thing had a capacity of four thousand bodies, plus whatever personal vehicles, weapons, and equipment they brought with them, and they'd still have plenty of room left over.

"There are architectural failsafes all around this thing," Ripley continued. "Security is so tight, if they don't want you down there, you're not getting anywhere near it. And those pillars are rigged with explosives. If the system detects an invasion attempt, bombs go off everywhere. The pillars give out, and the rock ceiling collapses. River floods in and flushes the whole thing down this tunnel all the way out to sea. It'll be gone before you can say, 'Oh, shit, we fucked up.'"

"Unless we have a force waiting for it where it washes out," Rowe offered.

"Yeah, except they thought of that, too." Ripley swiped their hand across the projection to shift the aerial map to the gulf. "See all these cute little houses along the coast? They're barrel covers. See those hills and dips in the ocean floor right here? Those are mines. If we attack the base, they'll wash out. If we try to follow, they can shoot down entire shuttles before they break atmo. If we take out their defenses along the gulf first, they'll see us coming and launch an offensive."

"The right person could get in," Rowe said to Wayland. "You did it before."

"No," Emma snapped with a force that had all eyes turning to her, expecting an explanation, but she didn't give them one. Her word was final.

"She's right," Laura said. "It wouldn't work—*because* it's been done before. We're not going to give them any more willing sacrifices."

Probably not a good time to tell them they'd have to give up at least one more. Zach was the only one who might be allowed close enough to Sandoval to take him out. And, to do that, he'd have to walk in unarmed, and singing the tune his CO expected him to sing.

"We think this is where they're manufacturing the nodes," Ripley offered into the awkward silence. "There are permanent landing marks around the facility and enough energy usage to power a massive factory. I suggested taking out the whole planet—"

"No!" four different voices shouted at the same time.

"—but it's been pointed out to me that this would result in too many civilian casualties," they finished dryly.

"Any progress on locating the AI hub or the regional whatevers?" Raven asked.

"The regional ones won't be identifiable," Zach said. "They're just slightly more sophisticated coms. They could be literally anywhere. Built into an outpost, or carried in someone's supply pack. It's unlikely any of them even know it's there, let alone what it looks like. Too many needles in too many haystacks. The central hub is the only real target we have."

"And we have breadcrumbs," Wayland said, taking over the controls from Ripley. He brought up a grid of relays spanning the width of the galaxy. Over fourteen thousand Shadow devices that formed their own private channels of communication. "The hub has to have other spokes to sprint the race, so we put out trackers to sniff the trail, but a lot of it's gone cold."

"They're using the known grid to locate remnant echoes of any signals that might have passed through the relays leading up to the test missions the last few months," Zach translated for Raven. "The more recent ones might still have measurable levels of radiation on them, but the older ones would have dissipated too much. And there's no telling how many other communiques have passed through in the meantime, diluting the trail."

Wayland nodded. "They bounced all over before hitting, so the spawning grounds could be anywhere. We got a leash on three possibilities."

"Show me," Zach said.

The web lit up with tiny lights bouncing back and forth. As Wayland had said, the signal hadn't been sent in a straight line. But as the sequence sped up, turning points of light into continuous lines, three areas brightened significantly more than the rest, suggesting those relays received a heavier workload than the others.

Wayland zoomed in on each in turn. One was in the middle of an empty patch of space. Likely an unmanned satellite installed there as a signal booster. The second was on a small moon that didn't have a proper name. Chemical readings suggested it had been terraformed, but showed no active signs of life on the surface.

Zach pointed to the third spot. "Where is that one?"

Wayland added labels to the projection to reveal the planet's name. Loki, the scorched behemoth with fourteen broken rings, orbited the Goldilocks zone of a blue giant star. The planet itself had lost its atmosphere and burned to a crisp eons ago, but it had six moons, four of them habitable, but uninhabited. As far as the general public was aware.

Narfi and Vali were dead rocks, rigged with enough firepower to take out all of Loki.

Sigyn had a breathable atmosphere, but its surface was still churning with continuous volcanic activity which set off lightning storms, making it less than ideal.

That left Loki's three best-known children: Jormugandr, Hel, and Fenris. All terraformed, all deadly, and all perfectly in line with Sandoval's love of misdirection and treachery.

"Get everything you can on those three moons," Zach said. "One of them will be the hub."

"Are you sure?" Rowe pressed. "If we shoot and miss…"

"Then we're all dead," Zach finished with a shrug. "There is no being *sure* of anything. But if I had to guess…"

Brownies. Three perfectly equal cubes sitting on a plate, waiting for Zach to complete the impossible assignment so he could claim one. Just one. "There will be shuttle breakers on the planet's surface, and booby traps around each of the moons. They will have boots on the ground, fully stocked outposts, and decoy coms to dilute the signal from the primary hub. They will all look identical at first glance and second. And third."

"Shell game," Wayland said.

"So how do we pick the right one?" Dr. Chase-Calen asked.

"Easy. Take a bite, and see which one's poisoned."

If Sandoval's tactics held consistent, they all would be.

54

The queen's gambit is going to fuck you up. Hell, it's going to fuck a lot of shit up. But don't worry, it'll go a lot better the second time around. And, once you get the hang of it... Well, how many times can a soul die, anyway?

- The Evolutionary Gospel of Michael

February 26, 3040 – Lavari Dolmi, Valhale 602

The queen's gambit, as defined by the official Interplanetary Chess Player's Manual, was an opening move in which a white pawn got offered up as a sacrifice. It was a trap, since black couldn't take it without giving up a pawn in exchange. One of the oldest tricks in the book, apparently.

Zach kept thinking back to Gray Dublin, and everyone they'd sacrificed to get the smallest step ahead in the game.

And then he looked over at Raven, sleeping soundly in his bed, and couldn't take it anymore.

He shut down all systems and quietly let himself out of the room to wander through the empty hallway. A few of the other residents seemed to have similar issues with sleeping through the night. He heard voices drifting from floors above and below through the open staircase. Zach pretended they were young lovers sneaking out from beneath the watchful eye of their chaperone to spend their last night together.

He was a romantic like that.

It didn't lighten his mood at all.

Raven had refused to take the healing serum.

She'd talked to Dr. Chase-Calen for over two hours yesterday and left the meeting with too many doubts to go through with it. If the situation were different, if they had more time…

But not even the woman who'd invented the formula could give Raven the guarantees she needed. If Raven took the serum now, there was a chance that it would cause her body to reject any future augmentation procedures. She might never be able to get her bionic arm. Raven considered this too great a cost for the privilege of *not dying in battle*. And there was nothing Zach could say to change her mind.

Tomorrow afternoon, Zach would put on the wrist unit out in the open, sending an unmistakable signal to Sandoval that he was ready to play along and give up the major SU players. If his suspicions were correct, an attack would follow shortly after, wiping Lavari Dolmi off the map with the swift, uncompromising totality only the Shadows could espouse.

Another pawn offered up as a sacrifice.

It wouldn't be the last.

Zach had reviewed the plan a hundred times in the last few days. He'd discussed it with the other ex-Shadows and, with only a few minor adjustments—which Zach had magnanimously accepted as a compromise—they'd all agreed on the what, how, when, and where.

They'd then presented the plan to the rest of the council.

And watched it all fall apart.

Emma trusted her husband with her life, but she refused to be benched on the sidelines, even though she, as the acting director, literally held the entire collective together right now.

Laura had, of course, backed her and attempted to reassign herself to Vega's team, away from Rowe, and to a mission that would put her in direct conflict with the most vicious of Shadow defenses. Her reasoning: "The AI subverts free will. That's *my* deal. If anyone has a chance to turn the tide, it's me." She wasn't wrong, either. Which meant that Rowe was now reassigned to *her* team, with Catton taking his original place, and a guy named Mass stepping in for Catton.

John MacMurphy wasn't even supposed to be involved in the meeting, let alone the war. Yet somehow, not only did he get a seat at the table, he also put himself on Vega's team, tasked with locating and disabling the AI hub.

Vega seemed to respect Laura enough to tolerate her as an additional body. Getting saddled with MacMurphy, though, did not make her happy, to say the least. She kept staring him down as if marking targets for her blades all over his face and neck.

And then Ripley opened their mouth after everyone else had run out of steam to calmly inform the collective that they would be tagging along with Zach and Raven to confront Sandoval.

Poof went their meticulous plan of attack.

Good thing the rest of their leaders were scattered across the galaxy. Zach shuddered to imagine the clusterfuck of Catton throwing his sharpshooter weight around, and Sadie trying and failing to pull rank. Not to mention the pretty boy organizing their forces on Torrey. Turned out, he was Dr. Chase-Calen's husband and Emma Wayland's older brother. He'd probably had some choice words to say about the plan for *both* women, and Zach had a feeling it hadn't gone well for him. The whole damned collective was just one big feral family, all in one another's business, no boundaries to speak of, and no shortage of opinions to go around.

Never before had he been so grateful to be an orphaned only child. As far as he knew.

The small library at the end of the hallway was open, and the lights were on inside. Zach's curiosity got the best of him, and he decided to investigate.

As soon as he recognized Laura McNally sitting on the floor beneath the window, he spun right back around.

"Can't sleep either, huh?" she said, stopping him in his tracks. "It's okay. You don't have to run off. I don't mind the company."

He looked her over and made a loopy motion with his finger around his head. "What about your…?"

She graced him with a grin. "I can shut it down when I need to. I did it for years once. It's kind of like putting on a straitjacket. Not my favorite outfit, but it won't kill me." She sighed. "And I need to practice more, anyway."

Zach took a seat on the floor beside her, his back against the perpendicular wall. "Rowe still giving you a hard time about going into battle?"

"I caught him planning to tranq me tomorrow. Took that impulse right out of his head and put him to sleep for the night."

Zach burst out laughing.

Laura straightened from her slouch. "Not that I… I mean it's not like I make a habit out of taking away his free will. It's just—"

"Oh, I get it. Believe me, there are days when I wouldn't mind being able to do that to a few people around here."

"But I just—"

"You defended yourself with the best weapon available to you. As you should have." He shrugged. "Personally, I think it's suicide for anyone outside of the rogue Shadows to be involved in this at all. But you mind scramblers have borne the brunt of the death toll for longer than most people know. An opportunity to take revenge and defend your future is the least of what you're owed. If you're willing to fight, it's your choice." He raised an eyebrow. "Plus, I wouldn't mind having an ace up our sleeve against the AI."

Laura deflated, all of her confidence from yesterday drained away. "To be honest, I'm not even sure I can do it. You might be right. I might end up being just another body on the ground by the end of this. But I never could sit out a fight when it mattered."

"That's what makes you one of us."

She harrumphed. "And still, I'm pretty sure I have the better end of the deal. I *might* die. You're planning to walk straight into certain death."

"Nah. I'll have my Blackbird watching over me." Zach blinked at her. "How did you know? I thought you couldn't read me."

Her face burned bright red. "I mean, it's not comfortable. But sometimes when you're focused on other things, your intentions scrape against me. Everyone else's are clouds of colors, but you… You, my friend, are nails on a chalkboard. There is no softness to you, and your intentions have no give. I couldn't bend you if I tried."

"I'll take that as a compliment."

"It's really not."

Zach shrugged. "It's worked well for me in the past."

She hummed thoughtfully. "I wonder if that's true."

He didn't like the way she studied him, as if she could read his face and body better than his mind.

"Finn tells me one of the first things the Shadows teach you is that inaction gets people killed faster than doing the wrong thing."

"That's true enough."

"It's not," she countered softly, but with total conviction. "They tell you that because they consider you expendable. Even if the action is wrong, the mayhem it yields still benefits their cause, and they can replace dead soldiers much faster than we can."

"I do love a smart woman."

She didn't seem flattered. "I know you're used to being on your own, but you'll be going into this with a whole lot of other people who'll be depending on you and each other to survive. Raven among them. So when that impulse to do the wrong thing comes up—because it will, probably at the worst possible time—I need you to take a second and pause. Can you do that for me?"

"Been doing this a lot longer than you, you know."

"And you're very good at keeping yourself alive as a result. It's different when you have other people to look after." Her eyes went unfocused, and she paled a little. "Something happens to you when you see a loved one lie there like a broken doll. It changes you. Changes your priorities. You've never had to face that before. For your sake, I hope you never do."

February 26, 3040 – Outpost Yellow 6

Hansel's first day-watch ended after an hour when he got sent to medbay for second-degree burns all over his face and hands. He hadn't even done anything to them, other than forget to apply UV protectant to his exposed skin. Apparently, the sunlight here was three times as sharp as back home, which no one had bothered to tell him.

He hated this place. Inside the base, everything looked gray. All the rooms and hallways echoed, and no one except Mesler would talk to him. Outside, all he saw was dry, greenish-gray earth as far as the horizon stretched. His watches lasted for ten hours, and he was always on his own. The last man on this barren hell of a planet, until the thing in his head forced him to walk the perimeter and cross paths with one of the other soldiers on watch.

They weren't allowed to stop and talk to each other. The devices only allowed them to turn their heads and nod, maybe throw out a casual, "Hey, man" in passing to acknowledge the other's existence.

There were times out there when Hansel felt surrounded by ghosts. Creepy child ghosts who whisked past him at the edge of his periphery and giggled when he tried to find them. He'd yelled out for them a time or two, prompting the coms Hound to tell him over the earpiece that there was no one around, and if he didn't knock it the fuck off, they'd send him to the chair again.

Hansel only had a vague memory of the chair, but it was enough to shut him up.

But being quiet about it didn't make the ghosts go away. They were always with him, their voices filling his head with nonsense until he had goose bumps all over his body. They had names, too. Figured he'd get haunted by all girl ghosts. Ophie was the most mischievous, always trying to sneak up on him. But Issa could never keep her giggles under control and gave her away every time. Those two rarely stopped playing, but they were harmless. Just kids having fun. Once he got used to it, it almost made Hansel smile.

But then they'd go quiet, and instead of laughter, Hansel heard whispers and soft sobbing from someone trying very hard to keep their sadness secret.

He didn't have a name for this third ghost haunting him, but it ripped at his heart every time he heard her. *I should have died with them… I should have died…*

The outpost had entertainment consoles with connections to every database within range. Hansel had considered searching for the ghosts by name, but every time he started to, he remembered Gibbs' warning.

What if the girls weren't ghosts but memories?

What if he looked them up, and the CO found out?

Safer not to risk it.

For three hours every day, everyone who wasn't on watch duty had to participate in PT and sparring.

Hansel hated that even more than solitary watch assignments. During those sessions, he hardly ever had control over his own body. The thing in his head made him go through the motions of each exercise, strike, and counterstrike, and there was nothing Hansel could do about it. He tried. He tried so damn hard to stop himself from stabbing the knife into his opponent, just as the guy tried to block him. He tried to twist out of the way of a staff strike instead of raising his arm to counter. It never worked. In the end, there was always blood. His, or someone else's.

Between sparring and the ghosts, his nights were filled with a harrowing mashup of both. He dreamed about smoke grenades going off in his bedroom, and the girls screaming for him in pure terror. He dreamed himself into endless gray hallways, chasing after the sobbing girl, yelling for her to follow his voice. When she cried back, "I can't!" his chest panged so hard it woke him up in a cold sweat.

A month after they'd stolen his past, Hansel remembered Gemma.

And, like a cascade of falling dominoes, the rest of them followed. Issa and Ophie, and their parents, Karsson and Gretta Atwater. The accident. Gemma's surgeries. Their parents' funeral.

Needle after needle stabbing memories into his brain.

During his morning sparring session, he remembered Gemma breaking down after waking up in the hospital, and he couldn't stop the tears from coming. If it weren't for the device in his head keeping his body moving and his jaw locked shut, he would have given himself away then and there.

That night on watch duty, he took out his com earpiece and bought himself a whole five minutes to sob in total solitude before the device took over and forced him to put it back in. He still shook as he marched around the perimeter, but at least it was too dark for the soldiers he passed to notice his tear-stained face.

There was no escape. No way back home to his sisters.

No way to defy the implant; no way to get it out of his head.

No way out.

Except maybe in a body bag.

56

"Sir, we have a signal!"

The nav Hound flinched at her controls. Guiding a shuttle out of subspace was the trickiest and most dangerous part of a cross-galactic flight. One tiny miscalculation and the shuttle could end up way off mark. Like inside a planet. Or scattered into its molecular components, along with everyone onboard. Naturally, it would make the nav team a tad twitchy. Yelling at the top of one's lungs just as they emerged from a skip—not the smartest thing to do.

Commander Sandoval remained unfazed. "Where?"

Willow's nav screen disappeared as the coms Hound fumbled his controls and took over every display in the cockpit. She gritted her teeth and swiped it away, bouncing her foot. The incompetent asshole needed to have some sense knocked into him. But that would have to wait until they were safely landed and away from the commander's watchful eye.

"Valhale 602, sir. Looks like a small colony in the middle of no-where."

"Interesting," the commander mused, then stared at the map in silence for a good four minutes without speaking another word.

Willow needed to announce their ETA for landing, but she didn't dare disturb his thought process. The last Hound who'd done that had been assigned to watch duty on the outside of the shuttle right before a skip.

"Why are you still there?" the commander asked. From his tone, it was clear he wasn't addressing anyone in the cockpit.

"Sir, the fleet is still in place on the other side of Vesta. They are waiting for your orders."

Their usually decisive and forceful commander took another pause before responding. It wasn't like him, and Willow exchanged a covert look with her copilot, who shrugged in response.

"Raze it. No hostages. Track the signal for asset extraction. I want—"

The main screen flashed with an incoming transmission, tagged with a code they all recognized. It had an ID lock on it and wouldn't open for anyone other than Commander Sandoval. The coms Hound immediately swiped the message over to the commander's personal screen.

The simplest of actions, and he still managed to fuck it up and send it to the entire array of screens on the level beneath the commander's station. Everyone else dutifully swiped it away to resume their work, but Willow hesitated.

Just long enough for the commander to unlock the transmission and stream the message. Willow couldn't read as fast as he did, but she caught the gist of it before the commander closed it down again. The message had come from the Networked Automated Reconnaissance and Assault Engine, NARAE for short. It had identified four possible scenarios for the Valhale 602 maneuver and ranked them by predicted success rate. The commander's wasn't on the list.

Willow risked a glance over her shoulder to see his mouth briefly tighten into a thin line. The highest rated scenario specifically excluded any asset extractions.

The coms Hound was getting nervous. "Sir?"

"Vesta team is to proceed with asset extraction and demolition. What's our ETA for landing?"

Willow's spine straightened so fast it popped. "Two hours and fifteen minutes 'til touchdown, sir!" *Phew!* Close one.

"Alert the outpost and get me an updated duty roster."

"Yessir! On your screen, sir."

As Willow reached to switch to a different nav screen, a big hand closed on her right shoulder. She just about jumped out of her skin, tracing it up the uniformed arm to Commander Sandoval's face above it, looking down at her. "Follow me."

Oh, shit. Willow's stomach dived toward the floor, and then rocketed up into her throat. She swallowed down a wave of nausea as her entire body broke out in a cold sweat. "Y-yes, sir." She handed control over to her copilot and followed the commander out of the cockpit on rubbery legs.

The flight crew was already prepping the shuttle for landing. They passed three groups of techs who nodded at the commander while ignoring Willow completely, and several Hounds who stopped what they were doing to salute their CO.

Keeping a respectful three steps behind, Willow trailed the commander to an officer's conference room down the hall. It was locked to rank and fully sealed for maximum privacy. When it closed behind her, it felt like a tomb sealing shut. She almost pissed herself.

The room had a round table and several chairs, but Commander Sandoval remained standing, forcing her to lock her wobbly knees and pull her shoulders back to attention. "At ease, Hound."

Willow stepped her feet apart.

"So. Read anything interesting in my brief?" he inquired calmly.

Double shit, and holy fuck. She was so, so dead! "Sir?"

"You know better than to stall me, Hound."

"I... No, sir. I mean, it was an accident. I didn't mean to—"

"Perkins will be dealt with for his incompetence. I did not pull you away from your post to answer for him. What did you read before I closed down the message?"

Lying would only make her situation worse. Willow's throat suddenly felt too tight, but she licked some moisture into her lips and forced air through her vocal cords. "Not very much, sir. It scrolled by too fast. I only caught a few words here and there. But..."

"But...?"

"I did see that you made the decision not to follow any of NARAE's primary recommendations. Sir."

"And you have some thoughts on the matter?"

"No, sir! I trust your judgment. We all do. If anything... Perhaps I was a little curious about your reasoning behind the decision and what you saw in the situation that NARAE missed. Obviously, it missed something."

"Hmm. How long have you been with us, Hound?"

Willow raised her chin proudly. "Two years and eleven months, sir."

"You must have built up quite a resume for your CO to assign you to helm my shuttle."

"Yes, sir." Willow was the best pilot they had—and that said something, considering her unit consisted of nav experts and fleet pilots only. They were trained not just to fly shuttles, but to maneuver groups of five to ten of them through active battles. Willow had a ninety-nine-point-nine-eight percent success rate. She'd only ever lost partial control of one single shuttle over the course of sixty-two active engagements in the last two years. She was a goddamn legend.

"I suppose I can afford to take you into my confidence this once. You understand that what I'm about to tell you *will not* leave this room."

Willow almost smiled. "Yes, sir. Absolutely." A Hound was only ever as good as their superior decided. Willow planned to make herself invaluable. She had the rep, she had the chops, and now she had Commander Sandoval's confidence. This time next month, she'd be the one he called on when he needed a job done right. Guaranteed.

"What's on Valhale 602 is something of a pet project of mine. A unique asset we've never been able to replicate since the program's inception. Operative M has served our cause faithfully for over twenty-five years. He is cunning, resourceful, and effective, if a little reckless at times. His objective is, and always has been, to bring down the beating heart of the telepath resistance by any means necessary. NARAE scanned M's dossier and recent activity, and concluded that he is a traitor."

Willow bit the inside of her cheek to stop her jaw from going slack. A traitor? Commander Sandoval sent a retrieval team for a traitor?

"But I raised that boy," he said. "I know him better than he knows himself. He and I both speak the same language of necessity." He cocked his head and pointed to the prominent ridge of his scar. "Do you know how I got this?"

She'd heard rumors, but, "No, sir."

"My purpose among the Shadows is to find the strongest, most worthy warriors to bring into our cause. The most effective way I have to test them is through combat. Years ago, a potential candidate started to make a name for himself across university-run fighting competitions and illegal, back-alley brawls. He even got head-hunted by Rome. Have you heard of it?"

"Yes, sir." Everyone knew of Rome, the fabled privately-owned planet, where the galaxy's elites got to play pretend with other people's lives. They put on silky togas and partied through the night while indentured servants waited on them hand and foot, died of hunger and disease out on the streets, and fought to the death in the grand Colosseum for their entertainment. Because it wouldn't count if it wasn't authentic.

"I decided to attack him at night after one of his brawls. He'd gone twelve rounds with two opponents, one of them a weight class higher than him. When he faced me, he was bruised, exhausted, and unarmed, fighting for his life. And I still lost. I'd call it luck, but I think being disarmed and having your own knife to your throat goes a little way beyond that. He had the makings of a legend."

"Sounds like it, sir." Anyone who could defeat someone with the commander's experience and years of training was someone Willow wouldn't want to face on a battlefield. "So, what happened?"

"I waited to see whether he'd turn himself in to the police. When he didn't, I waited for his next university competition to see what kind of effect our little exchange would have on him. And when he won, I sent a Hound to deliver our congratulations and make him an offer. He refused. And my messenger was later returned to our shuttle in pieces, clutching a papyrus scroll in his severed hand."

What?

"That's how Rome's Caesar opens negotiations. A clever woman, the Caesar. She had big plans for our boy, and she was willing to go to great lengths to secure him. She opened with brutality to show her willingness to meet us at our level, but she knew she couldn't beat us, so she bargained. In the end, I let her keep her champion. But it cost her fifty of her strongest, most capable bodyguards, hand-picked by me." He traced the long scar from end to end. "I keep this as a reminder that sometimes, to get what you need, you have to sacrifice something you want badly enough to hurt."

Fifty lives, in exchange for one.

"So, does that mean Operative M is worth fifty lives?"

"He is worth every last credit he appropriated from our coffers to establish his credibility with the mind readers, and every casualty he claimed in the service of that mission parameter. What he now possesses is worth *everything*."

"What's that, sir?"

"Their trust. Operative M has accomplished what no other Hawk ever has before. He has infiltrated the highest echelons of the so-called Special Unit. In doing so, he would have uncovered all of their secrets. And I *need* them. Whether NARAE agrees or not."

"But if Operative M has been working for us this whole time, why would NARAE determine him to be a traitor? I guess I just don't get it."

Commander Sandoval smiled. "Of course, you don't. You're not supposed to. You're here to do one thing: pilot. Anything beyond that is none of your concern."

"Understood, sir. It won't happen again."

"I know."

Willow blinked. That was all. A split second. Not enough time for her mind to process Commander Sandoval unholstering his sidearm and pulling the trigger.

There was only a flash of blinding light, and then darkness.

57

I hate to see a pretty thing go to waste... But death births new life, as they say.

- The Evolutionary Gospel of Michael

February 27, 3040 – Lavari Dolmi, Valhale 602

This time, they didn't have any corpses to hide behind. Everything had to be real. And everything depended on the plan going exactly right, to the last detail. Over four hundred souls in Lavari Dolmi, eighty-two of them under the age of twenty, all trembling with nerves, waited for the signal to move out.

Quinn watched Vega sharpen her knives by the window and didn't envy her outward calm. He knew what it cost her to pretend she had it all under control. That was the thing about people like her, and Laura, and everyone else who'd spent the last twenty-four hours living as if they wouldn't get another. They *had to* be strong because everyone expected them to be.

"I hate this," he said for what felt like the thousandth time.

"I know," she replied, as she always did. She wore her black fatigues, her favorite boots, and a dozen throwing knives strapped all over her body. As ready as she could be. "Remember what I told you?"

"That you love me?" His wife was a woman of action, not words. The sentiment had never actually passed through her lips. But he felt it. Every time he found another gizmo in their house that he didn't recognize, every time she greeted a delivery person by name because she'd checked the day's roster and vetted them before they'd even left their station.

When a nightmare woke her in the middle of the night and she pressed herself into him instead of running away, he felt like the only living being that mattered in the universe. Two months ago, she'd given him a rare, 21st century edition Charles Dickens novel that Quinn was pretty sure she'd either stolen or bought on the black market for an astronomical sum.

No, Vega didn't bother with words. Words could be taken back.

She twitched a half-smile. "That, and don't fall behind, no matter what. Stick with the group, get on that shuttle, and get yourself out."

"Yes, ma'am."

Vega glared at him. She knew him as well as he knew her. Quinn would be grouped with the youngest kids. If even one of them happened to trip and fall, there was no way in heaven or hell that he wouldn't go back for them. He'd never left a kid behind, and he wasn't about to start now.

"I can take care of myself," he said as a compromise. "You just make sure you come back to me in one piece. And with a pulse," he added. This was Vega, after all.

She sheathed her knife and came to perch on his lap. "Want me to bring you back a souvenir?"

"This the part where you swear to rip out hearts and throats to lay at my feet, wife?"

She grinned, her eyes shining with so much love and humor it made his chest squeeze tight. "I can do that."

"Yeah, but where would we put them all?"

Her easy smile froze, and her eyes turned hard. She extricated herself from Quinn's hold, knife in one hand, sidearm in the other, and pressed herself against the wall to peek out sideways through the window. "It's time."

"The signal didn't—"

"It's time," she insisted, and his body went cold all over.

Quinn pushed to his feet slowly, his artificial heart whirring like mad, making his face burn and his back sweat. "How long?"

Another careful peek. "Minutes. But we can't move until they're more noticeable."

Right. Because if everyone started running now, the Shadows would know they knew, and no one would make it out alive.

"You know which elevator to take?"

He nodded, unable to find his voice as he stared at his brave, reckless wife for perhaps the last time. He didn't want to leave her. But she had to send him away. Quinn was one massive liability in a fight.

Vega raised an expectant eyebrow at him. "Words, Quinn."

"Yes," he rasped, his throat tight.

"Don't. Fall. Behind." *I love you.*

"I won't." *I love you more.*

She dipped her chin in a nod. "Get ready."

~

If the Shadows were to attack them anywhere, Lavari Dolmi was probably the best place in the galaxy for it. It had been designed with the worst-case scenario in mind. On the surface, the city lay wide open, an artistic collection of buildings meant to catch the eye and distract it.

Underneath, each building had a series of dedicated elevator chutes that dropped people fifty stories deep, straight into a subterranean tunnel and a small shuttle. The tunnel itself served as a barrel to propel the shuttle fifty thousand miles, mirroring the curvature of the moon, and then shoot it out into the sky from the other end.

In theory.

Being a secret escape hatch, the system had never been tested, and only the terminals were periodically maintained. For all they knew, the tunnels had collapsed in the middle, and take-off would boost them straight into a head-on collision, pulverizing them on impact without even the chance of taking the Shadows with them.

"Could be a short swim," Emma murmured with her ear pressed to her husband's chest, and her cold finger drawing shapes on his stomach. They'd gotten up and ready hours ago, and then quietly got back in bed, boots, weapons, and all. The sound of John's steady breath whooshing in and out of his lungs was the only thing keeping her tethered at the moment.

He tickled her neck with the end of her braid. "Pixies and seashells don't drown. They don't know how to."

Except, she wasn't going to be a Pixie today. Today, Emma was bait. A tiny red herring, wriggling on the end of the hook, waiting for the big fish to see her and come take a bite. They even had a special shuttle prepped just for her. It would launch a short two hundred miles away in the plains, where the Shadows would spot it right away.

Emma raised herself on her elbow to look, really look at her husband. He'd cut his hair and trimmed his beard. It made him seem younger, but harder somehow. The warmth she was used to seeing in his eyes only appeared when he looked at her, as if he had to switch from soldier boy to seashell mode to engage with her. Soldier boy knew how to kill and die. But he didn't know how to love. So he protected that precious side of himself and saved it just for her.

"What's churning in that well of yours?" he asked.

"I won't hear you. When we go, I'll only have this little cup to hear your voice." The plan was for Emma to draw the Shadows, so that John's team could fire their one and only weapon at the Shadow flanks. He would have one shot. If he missed, they'd take down Emma's shuttle. But as soon as he fired it, he himself would be exposed. He might have seconds to get out. Minutes if he was lucky. If the weapon was even still accessible, let alone functional, by the time Emma launched.

"That string goes straight to my heart, you know," he said.

"But not your head." He couldn't talk to her the way the others could. She'd only have an ugly little com earpiece to keep in touch with him. If she lost it or it stopped working, she'd be cut off completely. That, more than anything else, scared the red out of her hair. The very real possibility that one of them would die today, alone, without an anchor, and no way to find their way back together.

John mirrored her pose and nudged her nose with his. "You just remember you can always ring the bell. And keep swimming. No matter what. Okay?"

"You'll find me?"

"You're the flame to my Shadow, Emma. I'd find you deaf and blind, feeling your warmth."

She touched her forehead to his, wishing she could burrow through his shiny skull into his thoughts and stay there forever.

She felt the moment Zach put on the cuff.

She felt it when, minutes later, Vega noticed the disturbance in the sky.

The alert system didn't pick up on it. It remained dormant, oblivious to the threat bearing down on them. And it never set off the alarm.

So, Emma did it herself.

"Love you, Seashell. Please don't break."

"Love you, Pixie girl. Fly fast."

~

"You stick by me and Danvers. We'll clear the way for you. Anything feels off, you tell us. Don't play hero, understand?"

Laura nodded along with Finn's instructions. They'd been over this a hundred times. And he still thought he could choreograph the mission step by step. As if the bad guys would fall in line and follow his lead, the way everyone else did.

He knew better, of course. But it eased him to have this momentary illusion of control. Laura didn't want to take it away from him.

"If you can't do it, don't burn yourself out trying. Abort and get the hell out of there."

"I can still fight, Finn."

"No." No arguments on that point. Regardless of how good a shot she was, or how many times she'd kicked his ass during sparring, in Finn's eyes, she wasn't a fighter. She was the sixteen-year-old girl he'd left behind to join up with the people who'd ended up destroying their childhood home and making her life a living hell for years after.

The Shadows had manipulated him into it, then burned her out of his mind again and again because he'd refused to let go of her memory. He knew all that. He'd known it since the day he got free of them—and he'd been fighting for her every day since. But Finn still carried the guilt of his mistake in pulsing, dark blue threads that choked his aura every time he remembered another little piece of his past.

"Fine." Laura didn't want him worrying about her; she needed him to look out for himself.

"You checked your gear?"

"Twice."

"Check it again."

"Finn—"

He pulled her out of her seat and did it for her, running his hands all over her. It would have been nice if he wasn't so soldierly about it. He adjusted her collar, tugged her seams into better alignment, and yanked at her harness straps, loosening and tightening them for a snugger fit. He pulled out each of her weapons and checked the charge and setting, looking down the barrel even though none of them had a scope. She had a knife tucked into each boot. He wrapped her pant legs tighter so the loose fabric wouldn't block her reach and made sure each knife handle was accessible before retying her laces exactly as they'd been before, only with tighter knots.

"How are the boots?"

"They're fine."

On his knees before her, with his hands wrapped around her calves, he looked up. "No chafing?"

Laura's heart had never felt fuller. "None whatsoever."

He slid his hands higher and pressed a kiss above her right knee. "I'd feel a lot better if you were leaving with Quinn and the kids."

She ran her fingers through his hair. "Back at you."

That was the biggest tragedy of all. Both of them would rather die than be the last one standing. They haven't said it in so many words, but there was a quiet understanding between them that they would live through this or die together. Laura took comfort in that, if nothing else.

A mental *tap-tap-tap* jerked her out of the moment. She recognized the touch and the signal. "They're coming."

Finn shoved to his feet and hauled her into his arms, kissing her hard. "If you get killed saving someone else, we will have a discussion," he warned. "With visuals and possibly spankings. Don't be a martyr."

Then he took her by the hand and dragged her out the door.

~

Hailey didn't usually let herself feel things like regret. Life was one great river, sweeping you along in its wake. Didn't matter if you missed one stop or another, there were always more of them to come.

Until there weren't.

By unanimous agreement, no one in Lavari Dolmi had made or accepted any calls with loved ones in the last week. It was for everyone's safety. Of course, that went out the window when your husband needed to be kept in the loop because he was in charge of organizing an entire planet into an infirmary and safe haven. No one knew how this would end, but almost everyone expected it to, sooner rather than later. When it did, an awful lot of traumatized telepaths would need a quiet place to heal.

No better place for it than Torrey, with its rustic charm and limited technology.

So, yeah. Jeremy had been in everyone's ear nonstop for days. And every time Hailey spoke to him, he tried to get her to bow out of the fight. Relentless son of a bitch. She'd cut him off mid-sentence and ended the call when he'd tried that shit two days ago, and she hadn't spoken to him since.

Now she regretted it.

Her sister, Amelia, had already received Hailey's big speech about how she'd make a name for both of them and, if she went down fighting, to make sure no one used her pelt for a rug. She was a wall-hanging kind of gal.

Jeremy should have gotten one, too. She'd had it all planned out, with jokes that he would have hated and promises to turn his world upside down again when she came back. But somehow, given the circumstances, her usual humor felt a little too crass, even to her.

Her husband deserved better. Heartfelt words of love, and sentimental memories of good times to hold onto when she was gone, and assurances that she wouldn't be gone for long, that they'd meet again, and create the life he'd envisioned for them.

And for the last two days, Hailey had been trying to give that to him. Only, she couldn't.

She'd been staring at the com for hours now, Jeremy's name on the tip of her tongue, but every time she tried to speak it, nothing came out.

And now it was too late.

The signal had gone out. Shadows were coming to swallow them, and she'd run out of time for calls or regrets.

Hailey joined the crowd rushing out into the hallways in a well-orchestrated performance of anarchy. Too many familiar faces. Too much fear thick in the air, choking her.

Her inner Hellcat sharpened her claws on the inside of Hailey's skin, demanding to be let out. She wanted to take a chunk out of someone's flesh. She wanted to run away and hide somewhere cold and quiet. Way to inspire confidence.

At the edge of the landing, Eskel pretended to herd people down the stairs. Annoying as she found him, the guy was steady in a crisis. She smelled no fear on him whatsoever. As if he'd been through worse before.

"You know where to go and what to do?" she asked on approach.

"Better than you," he replied as she passed.

"And yet I'm still going to win."

The acrid scent of his anger was just what she needed to firm up her knees and march on. They weren't taking the same shuttle. Eskel would be stationed at a midway point to hover in space between their two target systems, serving as their coms relay and field triage center. Not that he'd be able to do much more than coordinate evac, but it was better than sending a skilled healer into battle to die.

Hailey was headed to Green 24. Paws on the ground—that's where she belonged. Tearing throats and sowing chaos. The Shadows would never see her coming. And so she'd proposed a contest to see if she could kill more people than Eskel could save.

Whatever it took to keep them going.

Forty people crammed into the elevator with her. She did a quick head count to make sure they were all in there, then nodded to Oliver at the controls to hit the button. She saw Eskel out there, waving her off before running to his own elevator as the door closed.

Then the damned thing dropped.

Straight down, so fast all of their feet left the ground, and Hailey's ears popped as the pressure changed. She tried not to breathe—there wasn't enough air, anyway—but the ride down took so long, she eventually had to. The oppressive fear almost made her throw up. Even Hellcat panicked, shrinking back into a dark corner of her mind.

The deceleration was as quick as the take-off, but softened enough to keep their legs and spines intact. The elevator let them out straight into a long hallway inside the escape shuttle. "Let's move it," Hailey ordered, shoving at the people closest to her. She needed to get out of this body-crunch. She needed space before she lost her goddamn mind. "Get to your stations and strap in. Go!"

They'd each been given a map of the shuttle and where they were supposed to go. Hailey sprinted ahead, following her memory and a deep sense of knowing that was probably one of the telepaths guiding her. She took one of the three seats in the cockpit, then waited two agonizing minutes for the other two people to join her.

"All set," Oliver reported. "Everyone's in place and strapped in."

Right after him came Deanna, their kind-of-sort-of pilot. The shuttle was self-guided, but they still needed a backup in case something went wrong.

Deanna closed the cockpit cabin behind her, took her seat, and initiated the launch sequence. "Let's see if the Reaper's taking walk-ins today."

The launch slammed Hailey hard into the back of her seat. She stayed there, glued in place by their rapid acceleration, for so long she almost screamed.

She kept thinking it should be louder. A massive vehicle hurtling through an enclosed space at the speed they were going should create a lot of noise. Air friction, engine sounds—something. But it was all so eerily quiet that she heard every breath and rapid heartbeat from both of her companions.

A closed metal shell, no windows, no way out. Hailey's claws came out in sheer panic, digging into the armrests as if she could claw her way to freedom.

She felt the others watching her. If they started pissing themselves, Hailey might eat them out of spite. Too bad her jaw was currently locked with fangs trying to tear their way out of her gums, and it wouldn't open enough for her to tell them so.

Deanna exchanged a look with Oliver, who grunted with effort and reached for the console.

A few seconds later, music blasted through the speakers. Heavy drum beats, a driving rhythm—a fight song if she'd ever heard one. It thrummed through Hailey's blood and set the pace for her heartbeat. She took a breath, then another.

Little by little, her claws retracted, and the ache in her jaw eased enough for her to say, "Thanks."

"Like my pulse," Deanna replied. "Wanna keep it."

"So do we all."

58

I want to tell you that you can sit this one out. You have no idea how much I want to tell you that. But the way I see it, they'll need you more than they care to admit. I can't tell what your job will be. That part, you'll have to figure out on your own. I just know that without you, shit goes sideways a whole lot quicker. [long pause] I'm... I'm sorry, Leels.

- The Evolutionary Gospel of Michael

Meanwhile, on the rooftop

The Shadows opened fire as soon as they came within range, blowing up the town's perimeter to cut off all paths of retreat and working their way inward. Automated transports took off into the sky the way they'd been programmed to do, only to be shot down before they'd cleared the rooflines.

The noise was deafening. Within seconds, the freezing winter winds filled with thick plumes of dust, smoke, and heat, and the building shook beneath Zach. He kept his knees soft for balance as he watched hell rain down around him.

The escape shuttles should be long gone by now. If all went well, they would erupt from their end terminals and launch into space within about two hours.

Zach's lens flashed an alert of a vessel ascending behind his back. He ignored it. The Shadows would notice on their own, without him pointing it out.

He had other problems to deal with.

Raven was already sound asleep on the ground in front of him. She hadn't put on her coat; her lips were pale, and the tips of her fingers were starting to turn blue. Ripley had offered to knock her out earlier, and almost earned themself a hole in the head. Seriously, how were they still intact?

"Remember," they shouted over the wind, "I'm more useful to you alive than dead."

Oh, right. That's how. They kept insisting that he would need them in this fight if he wanted Raven to live through it. "Alive, maybe," he agreed. "But I'm pretty sure I don't need you walking. Or talking."

Movement alert. Fourteen Shadows on foot converged on his location. Disappointing. He'd expected at least fifty. Maybe they thought he'd be more docile because he had company.

Time to rectify that.

Zach tapped a code into his wrist unit, then punched his fist out toward Ripley. The tranq dart hit them square in the two inches of uncovered neck and dropped them like a rock. He thought they muttered, "Fucker," as they went down, but there was too much ambient noise to hear.

A minute later, six soldiers with active AI nodes encircled him, weapons pointed at all available targets, including the unconscious ones.

This was where things would get dicey. Zach's lens had already calculated his odds of surviving this confrontation, and they were not good. The wrist unit had synced with the Shadow operating system and displayed a readout of their directive. The AI's orders were to shoot him dead if he so much as twitched his wrist unit hand. They would do it, too. Whether they wanted to or not.

Zach didn't move or bother speaking. Nothing he said would influence their actions—they weren't in control of them at the moment.

Then a command override flashed across his left field of vision, and, as one, the soldiers relaxed. Their nodes remained active, but the AI appeared to have either relinquished control or switched to a different strategy.

Emma's shuttle had reached fifteen thousand feet. High enough for the Shadow vessels to notice the tiny blip on their horizon.

Zach squinted up at the massive shapes blocking out Vesta to watch one of them slowly turn toward the tiny target. *Come on, Wayland. Time to shine.*

The Shadow vessel's biggest weapon began priming. Each battle shuttle had only one like it, used solely for targets they wanted to obliterate in one shot. It took too long to recharge otherwise. A high-pitched whirring sound and a pulsing light indicated the plasma cannon would be ready to fire in about three seconds.

The pavement exploded one street over, shooting rubble high into the sky, and, as one, the soldiers around Zach all turned toward it. Shame they couldn't do anything about it with their tiny sidearms. Zach closed his eyes and turned away a heartbeat before the shuttlebreaker fired a blinding beam of a plasma bolt into the Shadow vessel targeting Emma.

Hairs rising all over his body, Zach swore and dropped himself over Raven, grabbing for the roof hatch cover to use as a shield while his lens flashed an impact warning. A massive pressure wave rolled over them, throwing Shadows off their feet, nearly breaking Zach's arm as it flattened the makeshift shield and him right along with it.

The psychotic son of a bitch Wayland had hit the bull's eye—the fully primed plasma cannon. The blow-back tore the Shadow vessel apart from the inside, reducing it to transport-sized pieces of shrapnel that exploded outward at incredible speeds. One shot, and the Shadows were down a full third of their forces.

Zach's wrist unit calculated the shrapnel trajectories in an instant and the lens showed him the safest place to be to avoid impact.

He took hold of Raven and rolled them both toward Ripley—because, of course, it would be there.

They'd barely cleared their original spot when a shard of metal sliced clean through it and the five levels below. The next piece hit flat, and its impact cracked the building's roof like an eggshell.

The closest of the two remaining vessels had already fired at Wayland, turning the shuttlebreaker into a crater, and Zach hoped to hell Wayland hadn't stuck around to see his handiwork.

It took another five minutes for the debris rain to ease enough for Zach to look up and take stock of the situation.

Emma's shuttle had made it out of orbit and out of range.

No directives to pursue were issued—she was too small a target.

Raven was unharmed. Ripley looked intact from the outside, but the lens indicated some minor internal injuries from the pressure wave. They'd live.

Of the six Shadow foot soldiers, two were no longer a problem. The remaining four's AI nodes had gone dark, and they struggled to get up. One ripped a jagged piece of metal from his shoulder, opening a significant wound. Another limped, his right arm hanging too low from its shoulder socket.

He could take these guys so easily if he wanted to.

But there were more down on the street, and plenty more in the shuttles above. He'd never make it off the roof alive.

Case in point: the three new faces who dropped out of the sky in addition to the five who were already on their way up the staircase.

Zach got back up to his feet with a groan, tossed his warped hatch shield, and raised his hands in surrender.

Two soldiers lowered their weapons as they approached, while the others covered them.

His non-confrontation appeared to be enough to earn a smidgen of courtesy. "We have orders to bring you in, sir."

"Why do you think I'm still here, soldier?" The man didn't have any insignia on his uniform. Neither Hound nor Hawk. Newbie, then. One of the legions of bodies snatched into the Shadows to play puppet to the AI. They didn't warrant a rank. They hadn't earned one.

The two in front of him lowered their weapons, one aiming at Raven, the other at Ripley.

Zach took one step, and instantly, all weapons turned back on him. "Hold your fire," he said.

"We have orders to clear the area, sir. Commander Sandoval said no hostages."

"They're my assets, not his hostages, and Commander Sandoval will want to meet them before he makes that decision. Stand down."

They exchanged looks among themselves.

Zero-point-fuckall chance of Zach and his group making it out alive if he attacked the Shadows. He could only feign authority and hope to hell it worked long enough to get them off the moon in one piece. He drew his shoulders back and looked one of them right in the eye, holding his gaze. The soldier was a bug for Zach to squash beneath his boot. Insignificant. Nothing. And he would fucking feel it. "Stand—the fuck—down."

The soldier nodded. No one opened fire.

Zach didn't allow himself an instant of relief. This was very far from over. They'd just defied a direct order from a commanding officer. All of them would have to answer for it, including Zach.

He didn't fight them when they bound Ripley and Raven in cuffs. He was proud of himself for not breaking any heads for their rough handling.

Someone behind him relieved Zach of his wrist unit cuff, then turned him around and reached for his face. He knocked the woman's filthy hand aside, and eight weapons primed to fire. "If you don't mind." He removed the lens himself and handed it over.

They bound his hands behind his back. "Just a precaution," the woman explained. As if she really believed that restraints would save them if Zach decided to stop playing nice. He might not be able to take out all of them, or even most of them, but the two or three closest to him would be high-fiving the Reaper before Zach's ghost got evicted.

"All clear," someone else announced, and the shuttle that had returned Wayland's fire moved into position above them, birthing pods to scoop them up and lift them all into the belly of the beast.

The bay door hadn't fully closed underneath them when the shuttle blasted the building into a half-mile-deep crater.

And Lavari Dolmi was no more.

59

How do you play Find The Lady? Do you look at the cards being moved on the table? Or do you watch the hands moving them? The best hustlers always know the lady is never in play at all. But we're not playing Find The Lady, are we? We're playing chess. Take the queen. The king's nothing without his most effective weapon. Take it, and be done with it.

- The Evolutionary Gospel of Michael

March 4, 3040 – Outer edge of the Edda solar system

From a distance, planet Loki looked just like the hologram model. Charred black, with veins of white ice running through its surface, and a mess of moons and satellites in its orbit.

All three of their potential targets appeared to be orbiting in tandem. All three were the same color, as if they'd come from the same larger whole. All three had approximately the same layout of buildings on the surface, the same number of vehicles, and the same number of warm bodies walking around.

Except for size and some fluctuations in signal emissions, the three moons were practically identical.

Vega kept switching between the different scan readouts and comparing them to find the one they needed to hit before the Shadows on the surface noticed a fleet of unauthorized crafts in their sky. It wouldn't be long; they'd come out of subspace well beyond their scanner range, but they were coming up on that boundary pretty fast. Another few minutes, maybe an hour, before they were spotted. If they didn't have a target by then, the Shadows would scramble, and Vega's people would lose their very small, very short window of opportunity to make a difference.

"What are you thinking?" Laura asked. The two of them had worked pretty well together so far, all things considered. They didn't always agree, but they had enough respect between them to keep things civil.

"I'm thinking that a whole lot of lives are hanging on our choosing the right moon, and right now it's an even one-in-three." It wasn't just the fleet they'd brought with them. As soon as the AI detected an attack, all of the Shadow forces would be notified within the hour, and everyone Vega had ever cared about would become a target without knowing it.

"Any word from Rowe?" He'd taken command of one of the Evolutionary vessels, which had been a Shadow vessel once upon a time. Lucky him, he might get to fly in undetected—for a while, anyway. He might even be able to get close enough to do some damage.

"No," Laura said. "They're as lost as we are."

They were fucked.

"He still pissed about you splitting up?"

Laura grunted. "First and last thing I hear about every time we talk."

Vega chuckled, but a dark kind of envy gripped her tight around the stomach. At least Laura got to speak to her husband. Vega hadn't heard from Quinn since they'd parted ways back on Valhale 602. And she wouldn't unless and until they finished the job here and got out safely. There could be no chance of any surviving Shadows following them back to their most vulnerable.

She didn't even know if he'd made it off the moon.

"They're all right," Laura said. "We would have known if something happened."

Vega nodded in acknowledgment, if not acceptance, and changed the topic. "What's your bet, then?"

Laura studied the readouts. "What about this? Hel has a higher subterranean temperature reading. That could be something."

"Fenris has more carbon dioxide. And Jormugandr has a higher electrical output." All equal factors in determining a world's occupancy and activity.

Laura slumped. "So we're fucked."

"That's how I feel."

"What do we do? Toss a coin? Eeny-meeny-miny-mo? Split up our forces and hit them all at once?"

"We'd be hobbling our primary unit if we did that." They'd need a distraction for sure. As soon as they hit one target, the other two would mobilize. They'd need a line of defense to cover their flank—that was supposed to be Rowe's job. But the bulk of their forces would need to focus on the AI hub.

While Laura still insisted that she could get the AI-controlled soldiers out of their way, neither Rowe nor Vega planned to take any chances. Fourteen lance telepaths on this shuttle supposedly had the ability to make people's brains stop telling their hearts to keep beating. If Laura failed to redirect the AI forces, the lances would drop them dead in their tracks.

Hopefully.

Their range wasn't very wide, and, once the fighting started, they couldn't team up and take out every Shadow in bulk without killing their own as well. They'd have to get into the thick of it to do their thing, and none of them, as far as Vega could tell, was a trained fighter.

"What about the duty rosters?" Laura suggested. "Maybe there's a difference in who's assigned where. We could have someone try to read them."

"Eight hundred and seventeen brains per moon. You got someone who can read them all at this distance? In the next thirty minutes?"

The cockpit door swished open, admitting everyone's least favorite person alive.

John MacMurphy was an enigma to Vega. He had the arrogance of a leader, but it was weighed down with the guilt of his failures.

He acted like every person on board was related to him, but the way he spoke to them suggested he wouldn't bat an eye if all of them fell dead around him.

He wore a uniform like the rest of them, but instead of black, his was a shade of deep red that resembled Talon's old rebel uniforms a little too closely for Vega's comfort. Every time she saw him in it, she had to tamp down a powerful urge to turn him into a pincushion for her knives. He knew it, too, and he always avoided her gaze almost like he felt bad about it, but not enough to change clothes.

"What are you doing here?" Laura asked.

MacMurphy ignored her, staring out the front window at the tiny blue sun and an even tinier black dot that was the planet Loki. "How long until we reach eight hundred thousand miles?"

"At our current speed, about three hours," Vega said, making an effort not to grind her teeth. "I figure they'll spot us in the next forty-five minutes or less."

"Then we should speed things up."

"If you're that eager to die, I can make it real quick."

He looked at her then, and Vega knew in her gut that he was still hiding something from them. It was right there in his eyes and the subtle twitch of his mouth. His body wanted to spill his secrets, even with his mind telling it not to. "Eight hundred thousand miles is my maximum range," he said. "Get me there, and I might be able to locate our target."

Vega exchanged a long, speaking look with Laura. "Call Rowe." While Laura did that, Vega turned her attention back to MacMurphy. "How exactly do you plan to find our target?"

With another liar's twitch, he turned his gaze back toward Loki and its moons. "Call it a hunch."

A man can walk the breadth and depth of the world
and, when he comes back, a different man will look
out across a different world.

- The Evolutionary Gospel of Michael

March 4, 3040 – Green 24

They gave him a fresh uniform with a Hawk pin, a pair of throwing knives, and a standard sidearm—disabled, of course, and purely for show. Until Sandoval said otherwise, Zach was still a suspect, and arming him would be detrimental to a lot of people. Which was also why they hadn't returned his wrist unit. The shuttle remained in orbit while a smaller pod took Zach and an escort of six Hounds down to the surface. Raven and Ripley would be transported separately, sedated for the transfer. He hadn't seen them during transit, but the Hounds in charge of prisoner security had provided him with regular updates and a live visual feed from outside their cells. They'd gotten food and clean clothes and, on Zach's order, remained unmolested for the duration of the flight. But they'd remained in telepath quarantine, isolated and far away from anyone they might corrupt.

Zach would have gone to see them, except there'd been another

Hawk onboard the shuttle. He only knew because he'd hacked the roster. The name Iliana Yerranos didn't ring any bells. Her service record was clean, but otherwise unremarkable. Her file wasn't flagged for an active assignment, so she might have just hitched a ride, but he hadn't crossed paths with her a single time during the flight.

Hawks being as rare as they were, Zach figured they might be as curious to meet each other as he was to meet them if the opportunity presented itself.

But Yerranos had actively avoided him. He couldn't be sure she hadn't been sent to check him in case he went rogue.

For Raven's safety, he didn't take any unnecessary risks.

"Touchdown in T minus three…two…one."

The pod slowed to a smooth stop on the landing pad right outside Green 24.

"We have landed, sir. Local time is eleven hundred hours. Commander Sandoval is waiting for you on Sublevel G. Take the red hallway on your left, then turn right into the black corridor, and go all the way to the end."

Zach unstrapped himself from his seat. "And my assets?"

"We've been instructed to put them into holding cells until further notice."

"Understood."

In every outpost that had them, telepath holding cells were situated on the ground level to minimize transit time into and out of them. They needed to be easily reachable by those who required access, but away from potentially hazardous sections of the outpost. Like armories, or subterranean manufacturing facilities with highly sensitive instruments at work twenty-four-seven.

Once they were deposited, Zach would be separated from Raven and Ripley by a Faraday field and several floors. If anything went wrong, if anything happened to Raven, Zach wouldn't even know. He wouldn't be able to help her.

The pod doors opened, flooding the cabin with fresh, icy air. The temperature was a few degrees above freezing, and a five-foot layer of fresh snow covered everything outside the heated areas. Normally, Zach liked winter. He liked the biting cold and the quiet beauty of snowfall. But this place gave him chills.

Time and again, this outpost had been razed. And time and again, they kept bringing it back. Shadows weren't wanted here. The ground was soaked in their blood and madness. It haunted the air with silent screams, making Zach feel watched.

Then again, he was.

He delayed going in just long enough to see the second pod land. From this distance, he couldn't make out faces, but he recognized another Hawk uniform among the Hounds. Yerranos had taken charge of the prisoners.

Zach maintained a neutral mask, turned his back, and followed the Hound's directions through the facility, taking note of every minute detail along the way.

The elevator stopped twice before it reached his floor. The first time, it opened on Sublevel E, giving him a brief view of a sprawling lab with automated machine arms working over at least fifty tables behind a hermetic glass wall. They were as quiet as modern technology could be, but in the cavernous space, their combined hum rattled the glass. The lab techs were all covered from head to toe in suits designed to protect the delicate instruments.

Two got into Zach's elevator. They took one glance at his Hawk pin and averted their eyes, remaining silent until they got off on Sublevel F. Nothing there to spark Zach's interest, just a hallway with closed doors.

On Sublevel G, the two Hounds with dormant neural nodes guarding the elevator nodded to him in silent greeting. He was expected.

Zach didn't return the gesture. He turned left into the red hallway, then right into the black one, following it all the way to the end. Instead of terminating at an office door, the corridor spat him out into a vast open space. A shuttle landing platform, currently empty. Behind him, the gorge wall stretched up several levels where loading docks extended and retracted automatically. A shimmer against the gray sky suggested concealment shields. The open platform wouldn't be visible from above.

Along the sides, Shadows in uniform manually moved boxes from pallets to levpads for transport. All armed, with one guard on alert for each group of four workers.

At the drop-off edge, a series of droning speakers muffled the sound of rushing water.

And smack dab in the middle, Commander Rajeev Sandoval ignored the Hound requesting his approval on a digital pad as he watched Zach approach, a small, disingenuous smile playing across his mouth.

"I see you upgraded your office space," Zach said by way of greeting.

"You know me. Never one for four walls and a desk."

"Hmm." Zach stopped four feet away, just out of arm's reach, and focused on his breathing to keep his body loose and his expression neutral.

"That the way you greet your CO, soldier?"

Zach raised an eyebrow and waited.

Sandoval stared him down, stern-faced, then laughed and crossed the distance to throw his arms around Zach. "It's good to have you back, son. Your wrist unit was already downloaded. We have the full SU roster and a list of their safe houses. Finally, we can cleanse their corruption for good."

Zach didn't return the gesture.

Sandoval noticed. He stepped back to appraise him, some of his good mood sliding into cautious attention. "They tell me you brought back some specimens. Explain."

"You put me in the chair," Zach said.

"Of course we did. So what?"

"You—put—*me*—in the chair."

Sandoval scowled with impatience. "Yes, and you turned around and robbed us blind. By the way, I expect to have control of those accounts restored to us by tomorrow."

Not a word about the SU's brute force hack. Either he didn't know, or he was pretending it never happened to see if Zach would bring it up and implicate himself. He held steady.

"Now, if your little tantrum is finished, I asked you a question, Hawk."

Zach had a lot of leeway with Sandoval, but not when he pulled rank. "One of them contacted me before my wipe. Potential double agent for an offshoot group that we haven't tracked yet."

The news was not well-received. "Who?"

"They call themselves Evolutionaries."

Sandoval scoffed. "The terrorists from four years ago? They're a joke! They stirred up trouble and burned out in a month."

"More like went into hiding to build up their forces in secret. From what I've seen, they're not friendly with the SU, but they are substantially more combative."

Sandoval's jaw twitched. "That information wasn't included on your wrist unit."

"They weren't part of my mission. You wiped my memory of our previous interactions, and I didn't have enough time—or leverage—to alter course before you forced my extraction."

The commander sucked in a sharp breath at the reprimand, but didn't acknowledge his mistakes. "And the other one?"

"Telepath. Trained interrogator."

"Were you compromised?"

Zach felt a wicked grin coming on, and he allowed it. "On the contrary. You're looking at the first Shadow with impenetrable, *offensive* telepathic protections."

"Bullshit!" Sandoval snapped. "You're good, but you're not that good. *No one* is that good."

Zach shrugged.

"And so you, what? Convinced her to do the same for the rest of our troops?" The words were threaded with suspicion.

"I had two shuttle tickets booked out of Petrus before you interfered. One for me, and one for my *wife* under the names Zachary and Raven St. Clare. You can verify the marriage license if you want."

"You conned your way into the SU…with love."

"That's what you trained me for, isn't it?"

"And you have done so, so well." Sandoval grinned, waiting for more, eager to crow over what he would see as *his* victory. Zach had no recollection of his CO ever showing this much enthusiasm over anything. In the memories he'd preserved, Sandoval was a hard-faced tyrant for whom good enough was never enough. He demanded perfection and punished anything less with debilitating pain.

Something was different. This wasn't just about Zach coming back with a trove of intel. It was personal. He needed more time to investigate.

"I think I'd like to meet this blushing bride of yours." Sandoval reached for his com.

"My bride wasn't the only one I charmed."

It worked. Sandoval paused, raising an expectant eyebrow. "Oh?"

"The people who harbored me were very open about accepting me into their little family. They see me as one of them and will interpret my extraction as an act of war. They'll be coming for me."

As if on cue, the com pin on Sandoval's collar buzzed against his neck, and out of the corner of his eye, Zach saw the worker Shadows burst into action.

Sandoval accepted the incoming message, glaring daggers at Zach. "Not coming," he growled. "Arrived."

61

Once the fighting starts, it'll spiral fast. Brace for impact, but keep your eye on what's behind you.

- The Evolutionary Gospel of Michael

Beyond the Fenris Orbit

"Incoming!" The announcement sent the entire cockpit into a frenzy of activity. The nav team sat up to attention, coms team opened all channels to chatter from the rest of their fleet, filtering through what needed to be addressed.

Their primary nav tech was a young twenty-something Finn had named Blue for his crazy hair. "Fourteen vessels on approach, weapons hot," he reported.

Finn swore. "Where are they coming from?"

Blue fiddled with the controls, hands shaking. "I'm tracking movement on all three moons."

"Sir! Detecting plasma build-up on the surface of Hel and Fenris." Blue's partner was an ex-Shadow and a little more grounded in the face of battle. He called her Left Eye. She had a bionic eye that functioned similarly to a wrist unit scanner. "Looks like shuttlebreakers."

Nothing they hadn't expected. "Alert the rest of the fleet," Finn ordered on the off-chance someone out there was sleeping at the helm. Damned if he'd let a single one of them get caught with their pants down. "Keep your good eye on the surface weapons. Weapons teams to battle stations—now! Get every last cannon charged and ready."

Finn switched to a com on his wrist unit. Thank you, Operative M, for rigging their gear so it wouldn't get picked up by the Shadows. "Vega, tell me you got something."

His left ear filled with a lot of voices from her end before she filtered them out. "Negative. We're still too far out. Are you seeing this shit?"

"Oh, I see it, all right." Looked like the moons had mobilized every single shuttle they had available to stop their advance. "There's still significant movement on the surface. They must have deployed with skeleton crews only."

Vega scoffed. "I'll take comfort in that when they blow us out of the sky."

"Let's keep the channel sarcasm-free, shall we?" He switched back to general coms and addressed every vessel in their fleet. "Attention, all forces. We're about to be hit with a whole lot of firepower. There are fourteen of them, and nine of us. I don't need to tell you that now is not the time to be shy with firepower. Charge your cannons and sound off."

Eight shuttle commanders acknowledged his orders.

"Remember your mission and act accordingly."

"Sir, the shuttles will be within firing range in ten minutes."

"What's their status?"

"Systems read twenty to forty-five bodies onboard each one. Weapons are standard for Shadow vessels. Their long-range plasma cannons are all primed. Short-range weapons won't come into play for twenty more minutes."

"Any drones?"

"Unclear, sir."

Vega pinged him over the wrist unit.

He opened her channel. "Go."

"MacMurphy just collapsed on the bridge. He said 'Hel' before he passed out. How much do we wanna trust him?"

"How bad does he look?"

"Bleeding from the nose. He was twitching when they carried him out of the cockpit. Laura says he's not planning to die any time soon, but there's some damage."

Could be a trick. No one knew what the fuck MacMurphy was after, because he refused to tell anyone, and most of the SU was still in too much awe of their original director to force the issue. Finn didn't care about the man's personal mission, as long as it didn't endanger Laura. "How far out are you?"

"Coming up on eight hundred K in about five minutes."

"All right, we're going to play this hard and fast. Ulster, Hayashi, and I will clear the path for you. Keep up, but don't engage unless you have to. When we pass two hundred K, you're going to go dark and coast until Hel's gravity catches you. Got it?"

"Last time someone tried that, I ended up shot down and stranded on Anamtaigh."

"Well, you've got backup now. We'll watch your six."

She grunted in response and relayed the orders to her crew.

Fiddler, the Evolutionary woman on Blue's nav team, pulled up a schematic of Loki's orbit and the shuttles heading their way. "Two of the Shadow vessels have opened fire, sir."

"The fuck are they shooting at?" Blue's voice broke high with naked fear. "We're still out of range." He was an SU tech. Good with machines, but inexperienced with battle.

"They're laying down interference fields," Finn explained for the benefit of everyone else who hadn't served as a Shadow. "It'll fuck with our coms as we get closer." He addressed the fleet. "Commanders, pick your targets and communicate them now. Once we open fire, we may lose coms. Stay on mission and keep your eyes open. Roll through cannon fire. I want at least two charged and ready at all times. No mercy. They'll have none for us."

He relayed separate orders to Ulster, Hayashi, and Vega.

Vega and Hayashi responded right away. The coms failed before Ulster could reply.

"Give me some speed! Hot as you can. Hold formation until I say otherwise. *Go!*"

62

My one regret in all of this is that I never got to meet
the cats.

- The Evolutionary Gospel of Michael

Green 24

They were spotted the second the shuttle came within range, but,
by some techno-magic from the mind reader guild, they managed
to deploy decoy signals, abandon ship, and land six escape pods on
the surface of the planet in total lights-out. Systems down, no nav—
nothing. Just a few random globs of metal amid the shuttle remains
raining down until their parachutes opened at the last possible moment to slow their mad descent while the Shadows attacked a bunch
of blinking metal boxes out beyond the orbit.

The brains seemed to think this meant their landing hadn't been
detected.

How adorable.

But as soon as the windows cleared and Hailey saw the expanse
of pure white and gray below them, she lost interest in anything
else. The outpost stood out a few miles away across a jagged, rocky
terrain that ended at the river gorge. And it was all covered in snow.

She could barely keep her claws sheathed while she waited for the damned doors to open.

Stepping out into the cold, she got goose bumps all over her body and shivered with pure, unadulterated pleasure.

"Any movement?" The unwelcome vocal intrusion was called Massimino, a surly ex-Shadow friend of Finnegan Rowe. She called him Captain Ahab. The nickname made his left eye twitch in the most adorable way.

"Singh is getting some echoes off their satellites," his little henchman answered. Another surly ex-Shadow, except this one was an Evolutionary who carried a serious torch for Ahab. "The transmissions are incomplete, but from what we can tell, they're mobilizing the outpost."

"The other shuttles?"

"In position behind the nearest moon and ready to engage."

Hailey's fur itched the underside of her skin. She felt overheated in her clothes. When a fluffy snowflake wafted down onto the tip of her nose, she reached her limit.

"Make sure the rest of the pods landed safely. I want a full head count and all landing site coordinates in ten. Establish a base and—the fuck are you doing?"

Shoes off, jacket discarded, and her shirt halfway up over her head, Hailey winked at him before adding the garment to the pile. "The plan is to sneak up on them across eight miles of jagged rock and ice while they're busy chasing stray signals in the sky, right?"

"Yeah…?"

Hailey grinned, shucking out of her pants, taking her socks and underwear with them. "Then, baby, you better hope you all can keep up. 'Cause I'm going hunting."

Rolling her shoulders, she let her head drop back to catch more snow as her inner Hellcat stretched, sinking into physical form. Joints popped, bones realigned, her spine extended out into a tail. The white-hot agony bordered on ecstasy. Her hands were paws before they dropped to the ground with a predator's silence. She shook herself off, rolled onto her back to squirm in the snow for a second, and then got to her paws, lashing her thick tail as she looked far up at Captain Ahab and his secret admirer.

Both of them had gone a little green. She smelled fear seeping into every stitch of their clothing and contorted her muzzle into stink-face, sticking her tongue out to better taste it. How long had it been since the last time she'd worn fur?

Too damn long.

With a series of quick chuffs in challenge, Hailey the snow leopard took off across an environment she'd been built for. Her paws ate up the miles, finding traction where human shoes would have twisted knees and broken ankles. The cold wind smoothed her thick fur; the mineral taste of snow and ozone coated her tongue.

She heard the others running to catch up behind her, but Hailey was long gone, her senses leading her true toward a sentry on patrol well beyond the outpost walls. She slowed, belly to the ground. His sensors would spot her heat signature, but he wouldn't waste shots on an animal.

Hailey circled wide to get to his blind side, slinking along the rough gray rock, patched with snow here and there—perfect camouflage. The soldier spun around, searching, searching…

He spotted her.

Hand on his sidearm, he stared her down, waiting to see what she'd do next.

Hailey held perfectly still, slitting her eyes to disguise the direction of her gaze. She was too far to jump him, but close enough for him to shoot her if he thought she was a threat.

Hailey took advantage of his indecision and shot up from the ground, sprinting off to his right.

By the time she skidded to a halt and reversed course at full speed, he'd already turned back onto the path of his patrol.

He never saw her coming. With one powerful leap, she bore him to the ground and closed her jaws around the back of his neck. She didn't even have to strain herself to snap it. His blood coated her fangs, rich and hot, but she didn't let her beastly side indulge. Cannibalism was still gross, no matter what Hellcat thought.

One down, so many more to go.

Hailey stuck her nose in the air and picked her next victim.

~

"Twelve outposts are reporting hostile activity," Sandoval growled, marching past Zach into another corridor. "Six shuttles stationed around strategic targets have been destroyed, and three surveillance assets were expelled from their assigned locations. Hawks. *My* Hawks."

Zach followed, keeping pace a step and a half behind the commanding officer on a tear. Soldiers leaped out of his way or got shoved into walls as he passed. Silent alarms flashed overhead and random chatter filtered down the halls as Shadows scrambled to their battle stations.

"The body count's already in the six digits, and now we have shuttle fragments raining down on us here! You wouldn't know anything about that, would you?"

"I told you they'd come for me," Zach replied, unfazed.

They got into an elevator, and everyone else quickly got out.

"This is not a rescue mission," Sandoval snapped, his face darkening with a fury that made the pale scar on his neck stand out almost silver in contrast. "It's an orchestrated attack."

"I told you the Evolutionaries are combative."

Sandoval shoved his forearm against Zach's neck, flattening him against the wall. "What is this? What did you do?"

Zach swallowed down the impulse to break free. But damned if he wasn't going to enjoy this, just a little. "What needed to be done. You gave me a mission. I completed the mission and reported back to you as ordered. *Sir.*"

His mouth twisting with disgust, Sandoval shoved off Zach just as the elevator opened again.

They weren't topside. He'd taken them lower.

Above Zach's head, the undercut rock was still bare and jagged. Beneath his feet, a metal grate leveled the walking surface across the open space. Where the grate ended, the curve of a massive hull hovered several feet from the edge.

"Report," Sandoval barked into his com, then listened to the response, tensing more. "Monitor the skies, I want to know the second another shuttle comes within range. No, we don't evacuate. Double the guard and get that last batch of nodes finished and out of the lab. We don't leave until the shipment is complete. Get everything loaded onto the sub."

Noticing Zach's steady regard, Sandoval's jaw twitched. "You have three minutes until my personal guard fetches your telepath friends, and I make you watch as I cut them open. Let's see you talk your way out of this one."

Zach smiled.

And then he attacked.

63

We're playing chess on a whole nother scale here, cuz, and every piece counts. Collect them like your life depends on it.

- The Evolutionary Gospel of Michael

Hel

The shuttle crash-landed with enough force to tear the landing gear clear off and scrape the hull beyond salvaging. But the surface shuttlebreaker was disabled, and their troops had only sustained minor injuries.

"Systems are down," the pilot reported. "Auxiliary backups are at a minimum."

"Where's the other shuttle?" Two of them had made it through the barricade into orbit. Vega had seen the other one veer off the projected flight path, trailing thick plumes of smoke, before her shuttle got engulfed by flames as they entered the atmosphere.

"Unknown, Ma'am. We lost their signal over the deadlands. Some kind of interference."

Fuck. "Do we have shields?"

"Negative. Life support only. Portside escape pods are crushed. We still have five operational on the starboard side and eight in the aft."

Those pods weren't designed for launching out of atmo. At best, they'd get survivors to safety somewhere else on the moon's surface, but they'd need one of the other shuttles to extract them.

Assuming there were any survivors left in the next few hours.

"I feel a lot of fear coming our way," Laura said, staring off into space. "A tidal wave of it."

"Foot soldiers," Vega confirmed. Her wrist unit indicated several dozen bodies in transports. It attempted to connect with them but was prevented by whatever smart hack surgery Zach had performed on it. "How's that 'intent takeover' thing going for ya?"

Laura shook her head. "I'm too far. I need to be out there in the open."

Vega didn't bother rolling her eyes. Of-fucking-course, she did. "Let's go, then. Sigma Team"—the SU geeks who'd never held a gun before last week, plus six lances for security—"You're in charge of systems until we get back. You hear from Rowe, relay to me STAT. Otherwise, keep the channels clear unless you're about to die. Gamma Team"—the Evolutionary rebels who didn't take orders from anyone else, but were psychotic enough to go down in blood and take a dozen Shadows with them—"Hold the line and keep the pods operational. Shit starts to turn bad, you run, and you better fucking not leave a single person behind." She aimed the last at a guy who had tattooed half his face in curling calligraphy of swear words and long strings of imaginative curses. She called him Asshole.

"Yes, Ma'am," he crooned, treating her to a bloodshot leer. No one liked that guy. He ran on caffeine and a bad attitude, but he could take down a fully-trained Shadow hand-to-hand.

Marching Laura out of the cockpit, she said into her com, "Alpha Team, on me. Bravo Team, you're backup." The two teams were an eclectic mix of Evolutionaries and ex-Shadows Vega had deemed good enough for this mission, and every lance they could spare. Four per team. It would have to be enough. She didn't trust any of these people as far as she could throw them, but they were eager for a fight. She could work with that. "If anyone's not in formation by the time I get down there, I'll shoot you myself."

The bay doors didn't open so much as fall off. Outside, smoke and kicked-up dust thickened the air. They'd landed on the day side, but the sky was dark, and the ground looked like a cracked, deep green eggshell. Visibility ended at about twelve yards, but her lens had already mapped the landscape, including the Shadow forces coming at them.

Her teams were already mounted on their fast, short-range transports, with Vega and Laura taking the lead inside a larger, cabin model. "Five minutes out," Laura said.

"Lances, on me. I move, you move."

They sounded off. At least they knew what they were getting into. Unlike the rest of the telepaths, their unique gift was only useful for one thing. They'd been stopping life functions for about as long as Vega.

By the looks of them, it hadn't come without a cost.

They'd have to manage a little longer.

Vega turned her attention to the problem at hand. "We're over two hundred miles from the outpost." With about a hundred vehicles hurtling toward them, it'd be a battle to get that far.

"You heard the lady," Asshole rumbled through the coms. "Let's clear the way!"

"What the—"

Six unauthorized mounts zipped out over Vega's roof, disappearing almost immediately behind a veil of thick smoke. She'd bet Quinn's last credit it was Asshole out there, leading the charge.

"Vega, go," Laura said tightly, gripping the edge of her seat.

Vega grabbed the yoke and shoved it forward. The transport shot out, a mount on either side, followed by her Alpha Team, with Bravo bringing up the rear.

Weapons fire lit up the darkness. Transports dropped out of the sky in flames. Vega dodged exploding debris, swerving around plasma bolts as Asshole and his people tore a hole through the Shadow formation. "I'm gonna kill that guy."

Her lens view displayed a sea of red dots in a well-organized, tight formation that held and reformed wherever Asshole disrupted the pattern. The AI had structured them to mow her people down like grass.

Too bad it hadn't counted on their lances.

With Asshole and his team wreaking chaos in their midst, Vega watched the formation, tapping her foot and gritting her teeth. *Come on.*

A handful of Shadows dropped off. Impossible to tell whose handiwork that was. But the lances said she'd definitely know when they got to work. *Come on!*

"I can't get hold of them," Laura gritted out. Vega spared her a glance to see the telepath squinting like she had a spotlight pointed straight at her retinas.

Possibly the lances were having the same problem. Too many bodies moving too quickly to target. "Come the fuck on!"

A clean, defined circle of eighteen Shadows surrounding them winked out at the same time.

"*Yes!*"

The gap filled again with backup, which didn't last more than a few seconds before it winked out, too. The lances had created an unbreachable perimeter. For the moment.

The rest of the Shadow formation split into three, with two groups flanking Vega's forces, and the third bypassing them, heading for the downed shuttle.

"Fuck!" They were already twenty-eight miles away from that shuttle, and those left onboard only had a few lances for protection now, thanks to Asshole.

"I can do it," Laura insisted. "I know I can."

"You better, 'cause we're about to be sitting ducks. Alpha lances, abort. Protect the shuttle."

Her escort split off and raced back, chasing the Shadows.

Vega forgot about them as soon as they were gone, needing to keep her focus on the shitshow going on around her. "If that asshole survives, I'm going to pull out his entrails with a spoon."

A Shadow transport spun out of control into their path. Vega swore and swerved up over it. Bravo Team behind her wasn't as quick at the controls. The transport collided with one of them head-on, and their light winked out in Vega's lens.

Someone shouted across the coms, and a mount transport went up in smoke. Its rider threw his weight to the side while turning the controls in the other direction. With his whole weight throwing off the vehicle's equilibrium, the damned thing turned into a spinning projectile on a collision course with a tight grouping of Shadows. At the last second, Vega saw his body get thrown. The transport took out two Shadows. His dead weight downed a third.

Above and ahead, another of Asshole's group dropped down in a barely controlled descent, turning the nose up. As it coasted forward, the rider opened fire and gutted six Shadow transports from underneath. But she lost control and slammed into the ground, crushed beneath the machine's weight. Its explosion sent up a plume of thick smoke and plasma sparks that obscured Vega's sensors—which meant it would do the same to the Shadows.

She gunned it, fighting the forces of acceleration to maintain control.

Asshole had turned her scalpel incision into a bulldozer blast. Twenty-one minutes in, and they were already down three people.

But they were also well ahead of schedule, fifty-seven miles out from their target.

Alpha Team flanked her on either side, two of them pulling ahead to bolster Asshole's frontline assault.

"Ma'am, we have a problem."

Vega growled. "What?"

"John MacMurphy is gone. He disappeared from the infirmary."

"Is anyone tracking him?"

"No, Ma'am. He left his com piece on the bunk."

Laura gasped. "I got him!" She pointed up ahead into a cloud of nothing.

Vega winked through the lens settings to catch an oncoming transport just as it swiveled on a dime and opened fire on its friends. It took down four and almost collided with Asshole at the front of the charge before one of the others took it down.

"Well, I had him…"

"Good job. Now do it forty-three more times."

64

And, just because I know you, try to resist the temptation of taking some of that serum for yourself. It changes the timeline to a place you really, really don't want to go.

- The Evolutionary Gospel of Michael

Green 24

Raven opened her eyes and immediately squeezed them shut against the bright white light. The second time, she did it by slow degrees, taking careful stock of her situation while she checked the integrity of her telepathic shields.

Could never be too careful. Especially with Ripley in the mix.

It was all blank. Bright white all around her—walls, ceiling, even the floor. She was inside a seamless void. Not a soul in sight. No sign of a door or even a shadow. But the hum was so loud it rattled her brain inside her skull.

They must have landed by now. On the shuttle, her prison cell had been similar, but not quite as bad. Its walls had been gray compared to this brightness, and the lights had come from above, casting her shadow across the floor. Some sense of the outside had still managed to slip through the inconsistent coverage of the Faraday cage. She'd been able to pick up on the guards coming with her meals and random soldiers passing by. Brief, vague impressions, but still something. She might have managed to snare one of them if she'd tried, but to what end?

Here, the flawless design isolated her completely. She felt nothing. She heard nothing, except the incessant hum all around her, punctuated by the beat of her heart.

This was a standard Shadow outpost holding cell. It looked and felt exactly as Emma Calen's account had described it: a perfectly blank torture chamber built to shred the mind and break the soul of a telepath.

Raven's stomach was in so many knots she couldn't tell whether it was from hunger or the effects of sensory deprivation. How long could she endure it in here?

"Come on, Zach."

He'd come for her soon. Raven knew he would. She held on to that knowledge as the hum invaded her bones and began to crack her resolve.

He *would* come. She just had to hold herself together until he did.

Raven counted her heartbeats until a full-body shudder made her lose count. It wasn't cold or hot in the cell, but her skin felt like it wasn't fully attached. She broke out in a sweat, which caused shivers to run up her spine, and within moments, she was crawling along the floor looking for a tight corner to squeeze herself into.

"Come on, Z-Zach." Teeth chattering. Well, this wouldn't take long.

No. He would come for her. He'd get her out of this white hell, and then they'd bring it all down—for good this time. They could do it, too. Together, they could do anything. They just needed an access point and proper leverage. Easy.

Zach would come for her.

When the door opened, she was dead sure he had.

But it wasn't Zach standing in the shadows across the threshold, flanked by two armed soldiers in uniform.

Raven pushed to her feet, locking her knees to stay upright as the narrow, lanky figure stepped into the light. "If you try to bend me, my men will shoot you dead." Light voice. Feminine. "Acknowledge."

Raven managed a nod, staring into a pair of eyes that shone with too much familiar disdain despite the dark lenses.

Buttoned up tight in a dark blue uniform with a silver set of wings pinned to the collar, the dark-haired femme stepped forward. "Face the wall."

She did.

Rough hands snapped a belt around her waist, then wrenched her arm and cuffed her wrist to the small of her back. The physical touch should have opened a direct link between them, but Raven didn't hear anything over the hum. A helmet settled over her head, and then Raven's captor spun her away from the wall and shoved her out the door into the hallway. The visor formed a pale veil over her vision. The hum muted, but didn't go away as she looked around as best as she could, with her arm held in a tight vise.

Another prisoner, wearing the same type of loose clothing and a white helmet covering their whole head, waited a few feet away, their hands tied behind their back. Two more soldiers flanked them. Five total to control two disabled telepaths—three of them with dormant neural nodes in their temples.

"Move!" her captor snapped, and Raven just barely resisted the urge to snap back.

They moved. The other prisoner first, followed by Raven and her guards.

Seven bodies crammed into an elevator built for five at most. Her stomach flipped as the floor fell out from beneath her, the elevator descending rapidly through several levels.

Rough fingers gripped her wrist. Something scraped over her skin, and suddenly the cuff expanded enough for her to slip her hand free. But when she tried, nails dug into her skin in a silent warning. *Not yet.*

Raven's heart hammered as the elevator slowed to a stop.

The door didn't open.

One of the soldiers cleared his throat. Then again.

"Problem?"

Four pairs of eyes turned toward the person crowding Raven's back.

"Door won't open without authorization, ma'am. We don't have clearance."

Meaning, they were stuck in here until someone let them out. The perfect trap for catching an invader. If that door opened from the outside, everyone inside would likely be shot, no questions asked. The Shadows didn't take chances.

Fuck.

Her captor didn't respond.

"Ma'am," one of the others said, frowning. "Your palm." He nodded toward the scanlock pad beside the elevator door.

The pause only lasted a couple of seconds, but they were heavy with enough tension to make Raven cringe her shoulder up to the edge of her helmet.

By the time her captor finally reacted with a frustrated huff and a barked, "Move aside," it was already too late.

The soldiers moved, hands hovering over their sidearms. Raven caught a brief flicker of AI-blue and didn't need to read their minds to know what would happen next.

The Hawk stepped around the other prisoner, raised a hand to the pad. Fake-dark eyes found Raven again with a reckless challenge. They blew her a kiss and touched the pad.

Alarms went off overhead, flashing red lights drowned out the blue, blinding Raven, but she saw the pandemonium erupt as if in slow motion. The soldiers pulled their weapons, fumbling in the cramped space. Shots blazed out bright white, searing her retinas. She tried to pull her arm free and duck, but bodies careened into her, sandwiching her between them. They barely had room to fall. But one of them still managed to grab hold of Raven and drag her down into the pile.

Her helmet askew, she couldn't see a thing except the alarm's pulsing red lights.

Then the weight on top of her slid off, and Raven finally pulled her arm free of the restraints, yanking off her helmet. "The fuck was that!"

Ripley slumped sideways against the wall, sitting on top of one of the dead soldiers. "The plan," they grated out through teeth clenched against a lot of pain. They'd managed to take down the soldiers—or somehow make them take each other down—but not without getting caught in the crossfire. "Had to get us out of those cells."

Raven cataloged the char marks on their stolen uniform. Mostly flesh wounds and glancing burns, but they had to hurt like hell. Ripley's beautiful face was scorched across the left side, and the smell of charred flesh gagged her. She sat heavily. "Great," she said through numb lips, unable to meet Ripley's gaze. "Now we can sit here and wait for someone to come finish us off."

"Don't insult me." Ripley groaned, twisting to push up a little higher, one-handed. Raven couldn't stop a small sound of distress. Their other arm was burned off at the elbow. Noticing her gaze, Ripley attempted a sneer, but they were starting to shiver. "Now I'm only as good as you," they taunted through gritted teeth.

"Funny."

Ripley nodded toward the other prisoner sitting at the far end of the elevator with a dead soldier across their lap. They hadn't made a single sound this whole time. Remarkably calm, given the situation. Too calm. "Raven St. Clare, meet Shadow Hawk Iliana Yerrr... Yer-ranos." Shaking harder. Teeth chattering. "We bumped heads on the way here."

Without asking for permission, Ripley shoved a vision into Raven's head.

A flash of gray, and a broken hum inside their cell onboard the shuttle. Brief, disrupted impressions of life beyond the walls. Ripley sorted through them in an obsessive frenzy, their mind crawling with a need to connect but only with the right *person.*

They found Iliana Yerranos. Two levels above, halfway across the shuttle, the Hawk had a gaping hole in her memory, and her sharp mind picked at it like a scab. The Shadows might have stolen the love of her life from her mind, but she still remembered how he'd made her feel. How much she missed him. His absence was a hunger she couldn't sate.

It was perfect.

With no time to waste, Ripley quickly latched onto it and sank deep into Yerranos' psyche. They hooked into her need and stoked it so high that Yerranos couldn't focus anymore, tripping off the running track when her knees gave out.

It was a glimpse into Ripley's core ability: emotional manipulation. Love and sex. Ripley was a siren.

They found the forgotten lover's voice in the recesses of Yerranos' memory, pulled it to the surface, and used it to whisper, "Come to me…"

But the cell's Faraday shield cut them off.

Hours passed as Ripley fought to hold on to their sanity. By the time the cell glitched again, Ripley was almost on the brink. Their frantic mind raced to find Yerranos in the midst of a dream. They woke her from visions of passionate love into the empty void of reality.

As the Hawk's loneliness clawed at her, Ripley soothed it with false hope. The man of her dreams was right there on the shuttle. That's why she felt this way. She was sensing his presence. The Shadows had him in one of the holding cells—and they had no idea who he really was.

The cell's Faraday shield flickered.

Desperate not to lose the connection again, Ripley shoved so much longing down Yerranos' throat they almost choked her with it, filling her with a feverish need to act. Yerranos was a Hawk—she had full clearance on the shuttle. She could go see her man right now, walk straight past the guards in the hallway, and into his cell. No one would question her. The risk was worth it. He was worth it.

Ripley built on that conviction until the cell's Faraday shield reengaged in full and cut them off just as the Hawk pushed to her feet.

The severance was too abrupt. Ripley couldn't tell whether their siren song had taken root deep enough to hold Yerranos in the compulsion.

Waiting…

Waiting…

Then a woman in uniform opened the cell door. Physically, a perfect match. Mentally, an absolute wreck of need for her lost lover. With the cell's Faraday field disrupted, Ripley took full control. They drew Yerranos like a moth to the flame of her own desire. They siphoned her personality out of her mind, took her identity, her clothes, her entire sentience, and walked out in her place, leaving the empty Hawk sitting listlessly inside the cell.

"You stole her soul," Raven said, horrified.

"Wha's it your boyfrien' likes to say? Needed to be done." Another painful shift. A moan they tried hard to disguise. "Now listen. Don't have much time. Alarm's not just for us. Reinforce-m-m-ments have arrived—they're keeping the Shadows b-busy. One compromised elevator's n-nothing. Yerr-ranos has the highest clearance. Her hand w-w-will get you out." A deep breath. A blank mask quickly hid their twisting agony. "Use that brain of yours and *don't hesitate.*"

"What about you?"

Ripley rolled their eyes. "You wanted to make a stand? Make a difference? F-f-fight the fight? Now's your chance. Already did my part. 'f I was s'posedta make it out alive, Michael woulda t-told me. Now get the fuck out of here. I can't stand crying."

Raven dashed away her tears with a shaking hand and pushed to her feet, stumbling over a pile of tangled limbs to get to Yerranos. She didn't take off the helmet, wasn't ready to see what remained of her underneath yet. But, without a consciousness of her own, the woman was as malleable and cooperative as a zombie. With only a little nudge, Raven got her to raise her arm and shift the few inches she needed to reach the scanlock pad.

The alarms didn't shut off, but the elevator door opened.

Raven took off Yerranos' helmet, keeping her face turned away.

Ripley was breathing hard, their brow furrowed, eyes squeezed shut.

"I still hate you, you know."

Ripley scoffed weakly and flipped her off.

Taking a bracing breath, she stepped out of the elevator. "But I hate your cousin and his bullshit prophecies more. He doesn't get to martyr you for my sake." It sickened her to touch Yerranos' empty mind. Ripley had reduced it to an echo chamber of ambient noise. No thoughts, no feelings, no memories, just a cloudy awareness of the outside world. Raven grasped onto a faint remnant of will inside her and yanked it toward the surface with an order: "Get them to safety outside. Whatever it takes."

She took morbid satisfaction out of Ripley groaning, "Oh, fuck y—" before the elevator door closed, cutting them off. Yerranos had already shoved the dead soldier off her, blank eyes trained on the general vicinity of the injured telepath.

With that taken care of, Raven dropped her shields and opened herself wide, already on the move.

There were still many Shadows in the outpost who hadn't been hooked into the AI. They were trained, confident, and relentless.

But a much larger percentage of them didn't have those kinds of luxuries. The soldiers stolen out of their lives mere months ago for the AI didn't want to fight—they didn't even want to be there. But they didn't have a choice.

Raven dug into every mind she could reach. She stoked their fear, shifted their priorities, made their orders a lie, and *pushed* a new truth at them. The AI had been compromised. Green 24 was going to fall. They needed to evacuate as quickly as possible.

It worked. A good third, the ones who still had some semblance of free will, broke off from their tasks and ran. Some toward the surface and the vehicles waiting there, others down into the bowels of the facility, toward hidden shuttles and the submarine prepping to launch.

But the rest of them didn't so much as twitch. Their fear heightened, but their bodies refused to obey the urge to run. Raven couldn't break them out of the AI's hold. They panicked and burst into tears, their hearts thrashed and their limbs shook, but they never faltered from their tasks—and they were everywhere. Some already headed her way, alerted by security, and if they caught her, she'd be dead.

She needed to find Zach.

Reaching farther, Raven searched for the familiar cool metal spikes of his shields.

There! All the way at the far end of the level, in a telepathic dead spot with only one other mental signature within fifty yards.

Three soldiers approached from a side hallway near Raven. She burst into a run, grim purpose giving her speed and direction—and a target.

Gritting her teeth, she took a chance and struck out at Sandoval. He froze for a crucial instant, giving Zach the upper hand. She felt Sandoval's impact with the grated floor and stumbled to a stop, breathing through pain that wasn't hers.

Zach's furious, bloodied face hovered over Sandoval in her mind's eye. He was hurt, but the injuries had already started to heal. At the sight of him, A deep sense of hurt and betrayal flooded Sandoval.

Zach raised his fist, split knuckles healing clean before he drove it down.

Raven flinched out of Sandoval's mind, breathing hard, struggling to reorient herself in her physical space.

She never saw the Shadows coming.

A tall, powerful body rammed into her from the side, slamming her good shoulder into the wall so hard she felt something pop. She caught a brief glimpse of a shiny white helmet before a gloved hand shoved against her mouth, and a light mist sprayed up into her nose. Her head spun; her knees went weak.

The drug worked fast, melting her spine against a wall that didn't feel solid anymore. The noise in her head intensified beyond bearing. Flashes of battle assaulted her. Terror seized her by the throat and squeezed, even as fury curled around her heart, making it thrash painfully in her chest.

It wasn't hers. None of it.

The onslaught overwhelmed her, and she flailed for an anchor, her shields—anything to hold herself together.

She failed.

Two more white helmets split off from the first, and another two followed them. They danced around in her splintered vision, multi-plying and consolidating.

When they grabbed her, Raven's head dropped forward, her body as limp as a wet noodle. She had no resistance left in her.

She was shattered, each part of her churning and spinning in a different maelstrom among the hundreds of minds she'd just whipped into a heart-pounding frenzy.

65

Can't catch the ball you don't see coming. One day, there will be enough of them to put me out of business. I wish I could be there to see it. Then again, I'd rather sleep.

- The Evolutionary Gospel of Michael

Hel

They made it to the outpost with four people in Alpha, three in Bravo, and three agents of chaos, including the tattooed Yuriy. Vega refused to acknowledge his existence, but Laura was starting to appreciate the way he operated—utterly without intent. His aura was a rainbow of possibilities, all equally bright and colorful. He didn't think or make choices. He just did stuff.

Laura couldn't get a read on him, which meant no one else could, either.

Case in point: when they crashed, mowing down a bunch of AI foot soldiers, he landed his mount gracefully on top of their roof, then strolled down the cracked windshield straight at six Shadows firing at him. A plasma shield kept him safe until he got within arm's reach of one while the rest of their team shot down the others. Yuriy's target engaged with a textbook punch, his face contorted in pure horror. He had the moves, but his body, regardless of who or what controlled it, lacked the necessary muscles for a physical fight.

Yuriy ducked the swing, then casually reached out and plucked the neural node out of the man's skull. The Shadow dropped dead, and Yuriy tucked the node behind his ear like a flower. Then he came around to Laura's side, ripped open the door, and offered her his bloody hand to help her out of the transport.

Vega muttered something unflattering as she kicked her way out on the other side.

"They're pulling back," the Alpha Team leader said. Laura couldn't remember his name, but he looked like a Kenneth.

"They're reforming the line inside," Vega replied. "They'll have every advantage, and they know we're coming." She turned to Laura. "Whatever you can or can't do, I need to know now."

Yuriy bowed at the waist and motioned her ahead. But he had a plasma shield at the ready. One of his surviving men closed in on her other side with a shield of his own to cover her.

"Thank you," she told them, feeling a little safer.

While Bravo Team got the explosives in place to blast through the perimeter wall, Laura closed her eyes and concentrated.

There were still so many Shadows inside the outpost. A wall of fight-or-flight with an overwhelming level of flight. Their need to run and hide took over every muscle in her body until her knees turned weak. Her heart pounded out a wild rhythm, and tears burned behind her eyes. It was like looking into an orange supernova with long, sharp rays of blinding light. All she wanted to do was turn away and duck for cover.

A big hand closed on her upper arm. Yuriy lending her his strength to cop a covert feel. His utter lack of concern over whether or not they'd live through the next hour comforted her, in a psychotic way.

Laura grounded herself in that feeling.

The outpost's remaining Shadows weren't soldiers, no matter what had been burned into their brains. They were civilians, overwhelmed and mentally unprepared to fight, and only the AI nodes kept them in place. Laura saw them as invisible tethers leashing their true intent.

She couldn't break so many of them. But the tethers had a little give. If she pushed hard, she could bend some of them. Twitch arms a few degrees to miss their target, or delay reactions just enough to slow down responses.

"I can get us a slight advantage if we stick together. But I don't know how long I'll last, and I won't be able to split my focus if someone goes off on their own."

"Ivan," Yuriy prompted.

The man he'd called on looked like a younger, tattoo-free version of him. He ripped open the storage compartment on their crashed transport and started pulling out what looked like sidearms, but clunky, awkward, and heavy. "Impossible problem, improbable solution," Ivan said, as he handed them out.

Vega hefted the gun with a scowl. "What is this, two thousand four?"

"Good guess," Ivan said with a lopsided grin. "Two thousand ninety-eight. Shoots physical bullets straight through plasma shields. Watch the kick-back. When you run out of bullets, drop it and move on."

They must have counted on more survivors making it this far. Everyone got two guns, and there were still some left over. Laura tried to refuse, but Yuriy looped a belt around her waist anyway and stuffed a weapon into the holster on either hip. She felt like he'd just strapped weights on her to slow her down. All of her knives and sidearms combined didn't weigh as much as one of those guns.

Alpha Team retreated from the perimeter wall and took cover behind the transport. "Ready on three… Two… *One!*"

Laura turned away as the wall exploded inward, creating a hole big enough to drive a hover through.

"Go!" Vega snapped and took off, the first to breach the perimeter.

Alpha Team went in after her, and Yuriy pulled Laura in right after them.

With no time to strategize, Laura shoved her will against the AI holding their enemy hostage. Trigger fingers hesitated. Barrels shifted a few degrees up or down, sending plasma bolts overhead and into the ground at their feet. The damage was minimal, but the defensive line held, a solid wall of interlocked plasma shields shimmering in front of thirty kneeling soldiers.

Deafening shots rang out all around her as the archaic weapons went off. Soldiers dropped one after the other, creating gaps that didn't close quite all the way. The second line of defense behind the first dragged bodies out of the way, but many of them fell with ancient bullets in their skulls before they could shore up the line.

Guns dropped by the wayside, useless without bullets.

Ears ringing, Laura braced for impact as Yuriy shoved her at his partner and turned sideways to barrel into the Shadows with nothing but his shoulder.

Laura felt the wave of fear crest as the AI delivered different orders. They dropped their shields and pulled out knives and batons. Puppets on strings, shriveling beneath the kind of pain their opponents had learned to fight through without flinching.

Bravo Team managed to breach and began clearing the path into the facility, forcing Laura to shove her will farther than was safe. More soldiers filled the hallways, but they'd split up, rushing off to other parts of the facility.

Laura glared at Yuriy, who took a second out of growing his bouquet of bloody nodes to wink at her and put a finger to his grinning mouth.

There were people attacking the outpost from other sides. The second downed shuttle—they'd made it. And she'd bet her fortune that it contained more of Yuriy's reckless ilk. None of them seemed to give a shit that she couldn't do anything for them. She had her hands more than full with this group.

Laura pulled punches, encouraged fear to heights even the AI couldn't overwhelm. Three supernovas went dark when their hearts gave out. The lights around her dimmed as Yuriy hauled her over a pile of bodies and shoved her toward Vega, fighting deeper in the hallway.

"*Let's go!*" Vega barked, her fierce face covered in blood, her hair gleaming with it. She took hold of Laura's arm and pulled her into a dead run.

Hell. It was utter hell of blood, death, and dust. Sparks of light went off in Laura's vision. White hot pain seared her brain.

She was burning out.

"I can't hold on much longer," she warned, feeling something warm and wet tickle her upper lip.

Vega buried a knife in the head of a soldier twenty feet away and looked back at her, doing a double-take. She stopped their advance and grabbed Laura's chin. Tilting her face up to the lights, she declared, "You're done."

Laura shook her head. It set the world rocking around her. "Can't be. We still need to find the hub." The outpost was massive. Multiple floors above and below, where she sensed more soldiers grabbing their gear, pissing themselves on the way out the door. "You need me."

"You're done," Vega insisted. She met eyes with Yuriy, then seemed to reconsider and turned to Alpha Team bringing up the rear. It was down to two people. "Garrick, take her. I'll call in a status update and get us some backup. *Go!*"

Yuriy took Laura's hand and pressed a neatly tied bunch of bloodied nodes into her palm. "You earned these," he said, taking one of her unused guns from its hip holster.

Laura barely noticed, trying and failing not to gag. She dropped the nodes as soon as he turned to run off after Vega.

For just a second there, when he'd touched her, she'd picked up on a hint of intent from him. Vague, buried deep, but there nonetheless. Laura thought it was to cover Vega's back, but when Vega went left, Yuriy veered right.

Clearing the path. For someone else.

Panicked screams echoed in both of their wakes.

Garrick took her other gun and put a hand on the small of her back. "Come on, we need to get you somewhere safe." He was solid. All honor and duty, and grim determination. He favored his left leg and had blood seeping out of a wound on the right side of his head, but he never faltered.

"Sure, yeah," Laura agreed, leaning on him for support, still trying to figure out Yuriy's angle. "That way. There's a dead spot behind that door." It was also farther inward. Yuriy had already faded too far away to read, but that little sliver she'd stolen kept churning in her mind.

What was he after?

What did his people know that the rest of them didn't?

Garrick opened the door she'd indicated and scoped it out before he pulled her into the dark utility closet. Laura's vision still flashed orange with residual explosions of light, blinding her to the physical world. But she still had a job to do, and it wasn't to psychoanalyze a lunatic. She shook Yuriy from her mind and refocused.

Now that their forces had split, she had to concentrate on Vega, ease her way to her target. The fierce soldier's courage shone blue in a sea of sickly orange that parted before her advance.

"You let me know if you feel someone coming, yeah?"

Laura nodded without listening, pushing past the pain to reach farther. She was almost at her limit.

"Don't forget to look up and down, too," Garrick added, peeking out through the barely open door.

The reminder distracted Laura into a wider sweep.

She gasped. "Fuck."

"What?" Garrick snapped, slamming the door shut. "What do you see?"

In the heat of battle, she'd completely forgotten to watch their flank.

"Talk to me, Laura!"

She shook her head. The auric signature was fractured, unstable. She felt definite intent, but she couldn't quite read it. Almost as if its owner still hadn't made a clear decision on how to proceed. But he kept moving, slow and steady, toward a clear destination. "It's…"

"What?" Garrick knelt in front of her, his concern diluting her focus. "How many?"

"One," she said, wincing against the cool, sharp blade of something slicing through her read. He was fighting her, trying to emulate Zach's mental shield structure, but he couldn't hold it; he didn't know how. It still hurt like fucking hell to get around it.

Laura flinched.

Garrick swore and touched his com. "Come in, Shuttle Red. Come in, Shuttle Red."

Laura's eyes widened. "It's him. MacMurphy."

Garrick barked into his com, "Get Rowe down here, STAT. Laura, pull back. Shut it down."

But she couldn't.

MacMurphy was too dangerous. She needed to know what he was up to.

She grabbed hold of Garrick's arm for a physical anchor and shoved with everything she had left, slicing herself wide open.

But she got it. The target of MacMurpy's murderous solo mission.

"Laura?"

Finn?

"Laura! Answer me right now!"

He needed to know. She had to tell him.

Garrick shook her. "Hey, hey, stay with me now. Can you hear me?"

Going dark. Lights fading out, leaving her blind in the night, with too many Shadows reaching for her neck.

"He's… He's after… Griffith."

After thousands of years, you'd think people would have learned, but they keep making the same mistake over and over again, failing to grasp the most basic lesson: The weapon you forge will eventually turn against you.

- The Evolutionary Gospel of Michael

Green 24

Zach crashed into Sandoval, bowling him off his feet before the commander had a chance to brace himself. They landed hard, Sandoval already in full battle mode, swinging at Zach's face. He took the hit, felt his jaw dislocate while he relieved his CO of his sidearm, and threw it over the platform's edge. Sandoval kept his weapons biolocked to his DNA—they exploded if anyone else attempted to pull the trigger.

Another punishing blow cracked across his jaw as Sandoval reached for Zach's weapon, forcing him to break loose to realign his face. The pain faded quickly, and he spat blood as he watched Sandoval get back to his feet.

His CO didn't even glance at the weapon Zach held down to his side, confirming that he knew it was disabled. But he still went the extra mile to fuck with his head and pretend it wasn't. "You don't want to do this, soldier."

"Oh, but I really do." It was time to repay his mentor for a lifetime of ruthless instruction. With interest.

He tossed the useless weapon after the first.

Sandoval's eyes went wild as he reached for a knife.

Zach rushed him, grabbing his wrist before he'd fully pulled the blade out of its sheath, and threw his weight into an elbow strike to Sandoval's neck. Despite his age, Sandoval was in prime condition. He'd taught Zach how to fight by beating him senseless until he could hold his own. He knew every move and countermove, and he didn't hold back.

A fair fight, if ever there was such a thing, with a man like Sandoval.

They traded vicious blows, fighting over the knives still sheathed on each other's bodies. Zach twisted Sandoval's wrist to pry one loose, and got his elbow dislocated when he tried to use it. The blade clattered from his grip. Sandoval was already reaching for another, but Zach got there faster, yanking it free and burying it in Sandoval's thigh.

The CO roared, and they broke apart while Zach snapped his elbow back into alignment and wiped blood from his eyes. Sandoval pulled the knife out of his leg. Now he was armed. But unlike Zach, he was still freshly injured: cracked rib, bleeding gash over his left eye, twisted wrist that impaired his knife grip, and now the stab wound deep enough to have struck the thigh bone.

Noticing that Zach wasn't equally weakened, Sandoval released a wet chuckle. "Mindfuckers gave you more than intel, it seems."

Zach snarled at him. "Again."

Sandoval took the opening and attacked in a flurry of slashes, stabs, and jabs. Zach blocked, retreated, absorbed shallow cuts, and focused on staying on his feet. He danced them toward the ledge, then back inward, looking for an opening. His wounds healed quickly, but they still bled, making his hands slippery. Twice, he almost managed to take Sandoval's knife, only to lose his grip and end up stabbed. As long as the point missed his heart, he ignored it and fought back harder.

The knife went flying as Zach threw his CO over his hip.

"Again!" he snapped, grabbing hold of the older man's collar.

Sandoval blinked, his gaze growing unfocused, and his face slackened for an instant as if he'd had a stroke.

It didn't stop Zach from driving a fist into his face once, twice, three times. Cracked jaw, shattered nose, split lip—in that order. Sandoval's head lolled, but he roused himself from the stupor and slammed his hand into Zach's throat, sending him stumbling back.

"There's…things you don't know," Sandoval said, his focus recovered and trained on Zach. "About you…and me." He groaned as he got back to his feet and spat out a tooth. He looked unsteady, but Zach knew the mind games the man liked to play. Feign weakness and lure an opponent into a sense of complacency that he could exploit.

Zach's ribs still bore the marks of that naïve childhood complacency. He would not give Sandoval such an easy victory again.

"Never told you," Sandoval mumbled, pitching his voice low to draw Zach closer. "Bu' you deserve to know… I'm—"

"My father?" Zach cracked his knuckles, edging toward one of Sandoval's discarded knives.

Sandoval was two feet away from the other, and the only sign that Zach had surprised him was a brief hesitation on the step that brought him within reach of it.

"You really expect me to be shocked? You practically stole me straight from my mother's body—you didn't think I'd want to know why? I knew I had your DNA since I was ten. Again!"

He dived for the knife as Sandoval picked up his, and came up on one knee in time to lock blades with him. Sandoval was weakened, but he had more leverage, using his whole weight to push Zach down.

Baring his teeth, Zach ducked sideways as he released one hand, allowing Sandoval's blade to slice through the side of his neck while he delivered a vicious punch to Sandoval's side. Two distinct snaps signaled more broken ribs as they both lost balance and rolled away from each other.

Zach got up a little faster than his CO. "I have a lot of family. Dozens of brothers and sisters, brilliant cousins, even an unhinged in-law or two. One thing I don't have, and never wanted: a father."

Sandoval groaned, spitting more blood. "I made you."

"*I* made me," he growled. "*Again!*"

Sandoval threw his knife and rolled to the side. Zach caught it in his forearm. He barely felt the impact as the blade buried itself straight between his ulna and radius, nicking both, but it slowed him enough to allow Sandoval to get back to his unsteady feet. "There she is," he said, looking past Zach at the mouth of the hallway.

Not about to fall for a stupid trick like that, Zach pulled the knife free and charged him.

Searing fire burned a hole through his side, sending him to his knees.

Sandoval swayed on his feet, his gaze still locked on the hallway where the shot had come from. "You may not want me, son. But I think there's something you will want very much."

Zach turned, grateful for the burning pain of a healing plasma shot that kept him from betraying the way his heart sank. Two soldiers in white telepath-resistant helmets dragged a loopy-looking Raven between them. They brought her straight to Sandoval and forced her to her knees.

Three more came in behind them, spreading out around Zach, weapons hot and aimed at his head, white helmets strapped to their hips as if they didn't need them anymore. He didn't spare them a glance, frozen in place, every fiber of his being focused on the gloved hand clutching the back of Raven's neck, keeping her head bowed as she retched. She keened a low, broken sound that shattered through him worse than a blast of shrapnel.

His training screamed, *Fight!* It demanded that he make them pay for what they'd done to her.

Take a second and pause.

He was outnumbered and too far from Raven to protect her. Satisfying his bloodlust would get her killed.

Zach dropped the knife.

He had two more still sheathed in his boots.

He didn't touch them.

"Now," Sandoval said, sheathing his knife and straightening his jacket, covered in his own blood. "Let's try this again."

~

"Something's wrong," Deanna said, gasping as she clutched her side. Like most of the other telepaths, she wasn't used to running long distances. She had barely made it this far, but at least she'd managed to escape injury, which was more than could be said for Oliver.

Hailey bared her fangs. Blood soaked her fur, making it sticky, and there were too many more throats to rip out that she couldn't get to. She'd been made. Eight dead Shadows to her name, and the ninth one had charred a streak across the top of her spine, leaving a strip of her bare skin exposed to the cold from head to tail. The healing serum mended any wound in seconds, but it couldn't regrow hair. If it hadn't been for Captain Ahab making his grand entrance to take down the Shadow for her, Hailey might have been done for.

And that pissed her off.

They knew to watch for her now; Hailey had lost the element of surprise, and in her snow leopard skin, she was too noticeable. She should have told the others to bring her clothes with them so she could change. Opposable thumbs would be wonderfully handy things to have right about now.

"Mass," Deanna snapped to get his attention.

Captain Ahab didn't look at her. "What!" He and the other fighters were busy shooting down the foot soldiers that hurtled at them, advancing their little assault team at a steady pace of three feet per minute.

They were about two hundred yards from the outpost now. Close enough to see an awful lot of activity spilling out of its walls.

"There's too many of them," Deanna said, echoing Hailey's thoughts. "The first wave were organic, but these people are all AI puppets. We can't get through to them—can't even tell what they're planning, 'cause they aren't. They're just going through the motions."

"Lances," Ahab's buddy returned.

"Dead," Deanna growled.

That was news. They'd brought three with them, but none had been in Hailey's pod. Had they gotten shot down? She didn't exactly have a com on her, so the only updates she got were from what the others chose to say out loud, which wasn't a lot, since all of them did have coms. It was like she wasn't even—

Hailey's hackles rose as the ground beneath her paws vibrated softly. She looked around for the source of the disturbance and emitted a *ghar* sound.

Oliver noticed first, but the rest of them quickly caught on, and the shooters all paused to watch a hover rise from inside the gorge two miles away.

"Well…fuck."

"*Take cover!*" Ahab hollered.

Each of the soldiers grabbed hold of a civilian and tripped them to the ground, throwing themselves on top. Someone fell over Hailey, and her fur crackled with static as they raised a handheld plasma shield over them.

The whole world turned bright white as shots rained down on them from above in a relentless, deafening storm that melted snow and rock into puddles around them.

Her frozen heaven quickly turned into a burning, smoke-filled pit of hell.

And none of them could do a goddamn thing about it, except curl up as small as they could, and wait for their shields to give out.

67

Atonement is never easy, is it? Sometimes, no matter how much you try to make up for your mistakes, it's never enough. It never will be. It shouldn't be. Not for men like us. We wear the blood we spilled like a uniform we can never take off.

- The Evolutionary Gospel of Michael

Hel

The outpost was under attack. Strategy Specialist Matthew Gibson had been removed from his station for his safety and locked in a room filled with communications equipment and nothing else. His job was to provide intel to NARAE and keep quiet. The rest was up to the others.

It didn't feel right to be stuck in here while his brothers and sisters died out there. Yes, Gibson might be the oldest soldier on base, but he was still a soldier, dammit. He could fire a sidearm as well as the rest of them. Better, since he'd had years of actual training, unlike most of the new recruits.

Instead, he stared at the screens and watched his people die by the dozens.

Their shuttles couldn't even capitalize on a numbers advantage. Ten of them had been utterly destroyed, and the last four were disabled, their residual inertia carrying them off into space. Three were on a collision course with something bigger. They were the lucky ones.

The coms roared with hundreds of voices all reporting at the same time, as they'd been ordered. Gibson couldn't make heads or tails of the noise, but it didn't matter. NARAE had no trouble compiling all of their reports in real-time and adding them to its sensory inputs for confirmation. In return, it spat out orders to each soldier individually.

Gibson had a direct link to it. Not a node like the others, but a console he could use to speak or type his input to enhance the AI machine's directive. He was a strategy specialist, after all. You didn't get a title like that unless you could prove better insight than an AI engine with inputs from millions of troops actively engaged out in the field.

He had no idea what he was working with, but it gave him an instinctive certainty about what would happen where. He didn't hear voices, didn't see visions, he just…knew.

Like right now, he knew that outposts on Jormugandr and Fenris would fall within the next twenty minutes. Fenris would be destroyed from orbit, without a single enemy combatant setting foot onto the moon. Jormugandr already faced an onslaught of armed soldiers far better trained and far more determined. They'd leave no survivors. The weapons cache would be plundered, the vehicles seized, and all of it would be used against their forces in a future battle elsewhere.

As for Hel…

Gibson had a bad feeling about Hel. NARAE was programmed to protect itself at any cost. It had already taken most of the soldiers on base to defend itself, and so far, all they'd done was slow down the enemy's inward press. They were yards away from the primary hub chamber. Gibson had a knowing that he would somehow be instrumental in its downfall, which made absolutely no sense. Why would he want to destroy their best chance at victory?

But it was coming. He felt it like hot breath on the back of his neck. Stuck in this room, with five armed Hounds standing guard outside, all he could do was wait and turn the dilemma over and over in his head. He questioned every step he took as he paced around the room. He deliberated each input he typed to NARAE. He stared at the door for long seconds, trying to think even five minutes ahead.

Whatever this *knowing* was, it didn't work like the AI. It didn't alter its course based on new intel. He'd known this would happen the minute he'd learned that Commander Sandoval planned to retrieve his operative alive. Everything that had happened since could be traced directly back to Sandoval's failure to recognize the greatest threat to their organization and eliminate it.

Gibson had tried to alter the course. On multiple occasions, he'd given the commander several alternatives and a clear message that he was making a mistake, knowing it would do nothing to sway him. He'd entered his prediction into NARAE and let it plan for every contingency, knowing it wouldn't be enough.

What was the point of a Strategy Specialist and the most powerful AI engine ever created if the people in charge of making decisions overruled them in the end?

Another circuit around the room. More pointless questions floated through his head.

Why was he in here? Who would have known to target him if it weren't for his five-member guard squad?

What could compel him to bring down NARAE?

No matter how Gibson tried to reason it out, the outcome was always the same.

Unless…

He could kill himself. If he wasn't alive when whatever was supposed to happen happened, then he couldn't *make* it happen, could he? Unless his death was the thing that ultimately led to NARAE's demise.

In any case, Gibson wasn't keen on eating his own weapon.

The door opened.

Gibson whirled to face it, a question already on the tip of his tongue. "What are… Who are you?"

His security detail, five fully-trained Hounds were on the floor outside Gibson's hideout. A man dressed in all black crouched among them, plucking nodes from their temples. Ignoring Gibson, he nodded up to another man who stepped over the dead bodies to get inside the room.

"Who are *you*?" the new stranger returned as the door closed behind him. Something about his voice sparked a hint of recognition. He was soft with age, his hair more gray than brown and as disheveled as the rest of him. His eyes weren't just bloodshot; they were bloody. He looked like he'd been through hell, but still carried himself with authority. Dressed in a deep red uniform, he definitely wasn't one of theirs.

Telepath.

Gibson himself was armed. His primary sidearm was holstered on his left thigh, right there at his fingertips. He didn't touch it.

"Strategy Specialist Matthew Gibson." He didn't salute; it didn't feel appropriate.

The uneasy feeling in his gut intensified. He knew what was about to happen. He knew there was nothing he could do to stop it. Absolutely nothing.

But he still needed to know. "Why are you after me?"

The stranger, with his hands casually clasped at his back, took a stroll around the room to examine the equipment. He was limping. "Because you're not a strategy specialist, and your name is not Gibson."

His first instinct was to be offended by the insinuation, but something in the man's voice rang true, and suddenly, Gibson got an uncanny feeling that he didn't *know* as much as he thought he did. "Then who am I?"

The stranger faced him, his blood-clouded eyes somehow hard and sad at the same time. "Don't you remember?"

Gibson couldn't look away. That stare invaded his mind, the way he'd been warned over and over a telepath could do. He had no defense against it in here. The outpost hadn't been equipped with protective helmets. NARAE was supposed to be their answer to telepathic intrusion.

"I know who I am," he insisted. "I'm... I'm..."

A lifetime of memories flooded his brain, falling into place like long-lost puzzle pieces. Hard memories. Hard to swallow. A long career of power and influence. A bitter hatred of forces rising to take it from him. A sadistic vendetta against the man he'd once called friend.

He'd used to be somebody, once upon a time. He'd used to have complete control over so many—an entire army, including the commander he now answered to like a pet dog.

He'd used to *know* so much more.

Gibson's heart stuttered, sending arrows of lightning pain down his left arm.

"Do you remember now? Do you see what they turned you into—your own men?"

A maniacal coughing laugh tore out of his throat. "You think I didn't see this coming?" His neck went stiff, and his jaw locked. "You… You think I spent *decades* building my empire and didn't see *this*? I knew Sandoval would try to usurp me."

John MacMurphy, his one-time confidant, stepped aside as former Senator Matthew Griffith stumbled his way to the NARAE controls. The one thing he hadn't anticipated—that their collective hatred of telepaths would lead to this mechanical abomination.

"I knew he would need me too much to kill me." He watched his own hands reach for the holographic keyboard and type out a series of instructions. Nothing as overt as commanding NARAE to shut down. Only a set of predictions designed to confuse it and make the bodies under its control act erratically. A brilliant idea—one he couldn't be sure was his.

"Just like I knew you would eventually come for me yourself. Gotta tell you, John, I expected you a lot sooner." He coughed through a cardiac spasm. His heart kicked into gear for a few beats, then a few more. It was getting hard to breathe, but he still managed to face his opponent like the soldier they tried to make him into. Stubbornness fueled by wrath gave him the extra seconds he needed to speak his piece. "Then again, you were always a little too soft for your own good, weren't you? Always delaying the inevitable. Always *hoping* it wouldn't be. D'you finally find your spine, old friend?"

"I suppose I did."

"Hmph." He gritted his teeth against the pain of his lungs seizing up. Pounding himself on the chest lent him a breath. Just one. "Waited too long this time."

"I know."

But if Griffith was going down, he'd damn well take the son of a bitch with him.

His left arm was useless, but his right one still had some mobility. Knees collapsing, vision going hazy, Griffith pulled the backup sidearm strapped to his right calf and fired on his way down. His aim was true. The plasma bolt seared a hole clean through MacMurphy's chest where his heart should be.

Bastard never even moved. He…

He smiled as he collapsed.

And former senator Matthew Griffith, the original Commander in Chief of the once-fierce Shadow army, died on the infuriating thought that somehow, in some inexplicable way, MacMurphy had gotten the last laugh after all.

68

Birds of a feather flock together. There's a deadly kind of symmetry between different shades of black, don't you think? Alchemical, one might say.

- The Evolutionary Gospel of Michael

Green 24

"Oh, she is a beauty, isn't she?"

Raven heard the words echo multiple times from every direction. She tried to lift her head, but couldn't overpower the weight pressing down on the back of her neck. Her stomach heaved again, clenching in the absence of anything left to expel. She braced her hand on her knee and dug her fingers into her own flesh, groping for a rhythm, an anchor to the physical world around her.

Flashing red lights and pounding hearts. People screaming inside their heads as their bodies moved slowly and steadily through the motions of forced normalcy.

Necks wrenching, plasma weapons growing hot in the hands of soldiers whose limbs shivered out in the cold without proper clothing. Dizzy, hurting, terrified. But their aim kept finding targets to shoot down.

Raven whimpered.

Laughter echoed around her in a cackling staccato. Pain here, too, but laced with bitter satisfaction. Someone who knew he had the upper hand. Someone who took pleasure in causing pain; used it to carve a masterpiece out of inferior flesh and blood.

"Interesting, I don't recall your tastes ever being so…predictable."

Raven…

"Get up. You look pathetic."

Raven…

Everything spun and churned around her. Hundreds of realities crashed down on her. Fear and death. Fury and pain. Raven was one big exposed nerve ending, and every touch, every breath was agony.

"Look at you, so obedient all of a sudden."

A vise closed on the back of her head and yanked her upright, forcing her face into the light. Her eyes darted, tracking movement that wasn't there. Her lips formed words that weren't hers. Terror gripped her insides as she fought to blink a face into focus. Familiar features covered in blood, cold, sharp eyes staring down at her. A hard mouth twisted into an ugly sneer.

"Lovely." *Lovely little whore you found yourself. Lovely and impotent.*

—Raven!—

Her gaze snapped to the side, tracing a mental line to *him*.

Almost immediately, the maelstrom pulled her under again, away, beyond this place and this time. It wasn't just thoughts she saw anymore. Countless memories swept her into a churning vortex of lifetimes she'd never lived, people she'd never met—but they were inside her, part of her. They *were* her, and she couldn't pull herself free.

"So here's what we're going to do." *Todotodotodo…*

Heartbeats drumming a relentless rhythm. Pain and cold. Fear and fury. The feel of massive fangs tearing into her flesh; the taste of blood on her tongue.

So much death…

"I'm going to hurt her." *Tearbreakdefiledestroy…*

"Retreat!" the mind shouted, even as the body kept moving forward.

"Take cover!" the voices screamed, even as their spines refused to bend, knees locking to force a stationary target.

"And I'm going to kill her."

The snap of a neck. The squelch of a blade in the gut, ripping, tearing, spilling insides out like a nest of writhing snakes.

Cold rock meeting a broken back, stray snowflakes flurrying down onto cheeks wet with tears.

Prayers, pleas, despair, and finally, acceptance. "Mom, I love you. I'm sorry..."

"And you're going to watch."

—*Blackbird. Look at me.*— An order. A lifeline yanking her out of the churning agony back into the here and now by the music of a string instrument, dragging out its last, mournful note. Away from *them* and toward *him.*

Their eyes locked.

~

Physical sensation wasn't the key to finding Raven. Emotion was. Raw, primal terror clawed his insides to shreds as he watched her struggling on the ground, too far to do a goddamn thing. It sent Zach hurtling right into the frenzy inside her mind. There was no rhythm or order to it. Her psyche lay fully exposed, mired in the madness of countless personalities ripping her apart.

Zach threw himself into it, only half listening to Sandoval crowing somewhere nearby about how lovely his little whore was.

She was still in there. Her feather-touch swirled all around Zach, scattered to the telepathic winds, trying to latch on to something, but fading through everything.

She'd been drugged.

Raven, he called.

"Get up. You look pathetic."

Zach lost the link.

Sandoval's mouth twisted in disgust. Bleeding, unsteady on his feet, he managed to look down on Zach as if he still had the right.

Zach pushed to his feet and stood up tall, returning that stare with unbridled hatred.

"Look at you, so obedient all of a sudden." Sandoval shifted his weight to his good leg and leaned down, yanking Raven up by her hair, bending her neck back so hard she cried out.

Her eyes darted wildly. She was breathing hard, and even from so far away, Zach felt her heart racing as if it were inside him.

"Truly lovely," Sandoval said, but his words weren't praise.

Zach chased the flutter of Raven's heartbeat back into her mind, shouting her name into the chaos again and again. She heard him; he knew she did. But every time he thought he had a solid grip, the wild current of foreign thoughts wrenched her away from him again.

He forced Sandoval and his Shadows out of his mind and plunged deep into Raven's.

"So here's what we're going to do…"

Feathers brushed along his spine as she flew past him. He changed direction, through the battle and the blood, desperate prayers echoing around him as his nose filled with the smell of burning flesh and loosened bowels.

He got caught in a web of sheer helplessness, a vast network of minds that had no control over their bodies, forced to obey despite the fear tearing at their hearts. The weaker ones died in the AI's grip, their bodies betraying them and releasing them from their own personal hell permanently.

They didn't know it, but that same fear connected them all, amplifying in Raven's mind into a frequency that would shatter her.

"I'm going to hurt her."

Raven!

"And then I'm going to kill her."

Another fly-by brush of feathers, but this time he was ready for it. He snared the feeling before it slipped through his fingers and held on. —*Blackbird. Look at me.*—

"And you're going to watch."

The wild twitch of her eyes steadied, settled on him, and held.

A silent question. A hint of a request. Something he'd done before, though he couldn't quite remember how. But the blueprint was there, a mechanism his mind had constructed all on its own.

Then her gaze broke away again, and he lost her.

Sandoval stepped away, pulling a knife. "Lift her up." He leered at Raven as the helmeted Shadows hauled her up and held her between them, her toes barely touching the ground. "And hold him, I don't want him getting any fresh ideas."

Zach's guards grabbed hold of him, forcing his arms behind his back, gripping his hair to keep him from looking away. The barrel of a weapon pressed to the back of his head. "Give me a reason."

Zach watched the tip of Sandoval's knife slide down the front of Raven's shirt to where his other hand scrunched the bottom hem. He felt the prick of it against her abdomen.

She turned away, unseeing eyes desperately seeking his. Zach hurtled back into her mind. One more try. One last chance. He chased her into a vortex of final thoughts, lifetimes flashing through minds about to be snuffed out. He felt her reaching for him and threw everything he had left at the fading echo of her presence.

Contact.

Fabric began to tear, a shallow cut inching upward.

Zach clenched his teeth so hard they cracked. He didn't just grab hold. He curled himself around Raven's mind, enveloped her, pulled her into the shelter of his shields, and cut off all external stimuli.

The world shuddered, knocking him off balance.

Zach split his focus just enough to see he wasn't the only one. The Shadows holding Raven stumbled a step away from Sandoval. The ones holding Zach almost lost their grip on him.

Distracted from his purpose, Sandoval lowered his knife, turning away from Raven.

It gave them a chance.

Raven locked eyes with Zach again, this time with something that wrenched the whole of his existence off-kilter. *I'm sorry. I love you. I'm so scared… Goodbye.*

His eyes went wide, a desperate denial locked in his throat.

Too late.

She squeezed her eyes shut, took a breath, and screamed.

69

All those minds, all those pinpoints of desperate will, thrashing against the AI's control. They shimmered like a vast spiderweb of lights in her vision. There were others, though. Bright, sparkly gems of different colors dotted the darkness outside of her shining shield. Minds that had full control, unfettered by anything other than their own desires and directives.

Raven placed a hand on the smooth surface of the bubble that cocooned her safely away from them and marveled at its construct. Glassy on the inside. Spiked with merciless barbs on the outside.

So many lights out there—so many lives caught in a web that connected them all, through the unyielding force of the AI in some, but also blue veins of an artificial purpose seared into them all. The Shadow army was interconnected in ways they didn't even realize. All of them together and apart from anyone else.

And Raven never would have seen it if they hadn't stripped her mind raw.

No time to analyze how it worked—she didn't need to. That web was her target. She just had to tap into it. Back into the fray. The scorching, paralyzing torment of what the Shadows had wrought.

But Raven had an anchor now.

Better, she had a weapon.

She *was* a weapon, and her time had come.

One last look, fresh agony as she met eyes with Zach and recognized that only one of them would make it out of this alive. Sandoval would torture her for as long as he could before he snuffed her out, and he'd force Zach to watch, to make sure the lesson stuck.

He couldn't save her this time, no matter how badly he wanted to. If she tried to manipulate anyone here, the helmeted Shadows would kill her. The second Zach moved, they'd kill him and keep going with her.

There was only one solution. Not manipulation, but pain. She had to drop as many of them as she could, as quickly as she could, and hope whoever was left standing still had enough strength to finish the job—because she wouldn't.

—*I'm sorry. I love you.*— She was so scared… —*Goodbye.*—

Zach's pupils blew wide, and he strained toward her, his shields around her vibrating desperately, trying to contain her, keep her with him.

Raven closed her eyes and used the force of his fear, the power of his love, to hurl herself at the Shadow web, willing it to catch her.

Sticky electricity curved around her shields, fibers of the web tangling in the spikes. She felt the firestorm course across her nervous system, threatening to shatter her apart.

Raven screamed, spinning the bubble of Zach's shields to tangle tighter into the web until the agony stole her breath away.

I'm sorry… For waiting so long to tell him. For wasting so much time.

For robbing him of the time they might have had.

I love you… Every shadow and sharp edge. Every smile, every touch, and every second she'd had with him.

I'm so scared… She pulled it all into herself, all the moments of peace, and the harrowing pain—every morsel of her soul, as broken as it still was.

Goodbye.

Raven cut him off at the shields, tearing herself loose of the only anchor she had left…

And then she let go.

The explosion blasted her bubble apart and turned its spikes into deadly projectiles that shot out across the web, slicing through each node—*mind*—caught inside it. Bright bursts of pain lit up the darkness. Shadows screamed and clutched their heads as their brains sparked in debilitating seizures.

It wasn't enough to kill them. Not so many. But it would buy her people a few minutes to gain the upper hand. It would free Zach to finish it.

He had to finish it.

Because she was done.

~

"*Got him!*" Oliver screamed.

The onslaught of plasma suddenly stopped, and a deafening squeal rent the air above as the thumping pressure of the attacking shuttle veered sideways. Hailey pried open her eyes. Her fur was singed. The rock beneath her had grown burning hot, pools of melted stone inching closer to her vulnerable paws with every second. But she watched with unbridled glee as the shuttle tilted and dived, crashing at the edge of the gorge.

It exploded on impact, shuddering the ground beneath her. The pressure waves rolled along the shelf toward the outpost, where walls began to crack and rain dust.

But the foot soldiers shooting at them didn't stop. Taking advantage of their vulnerability, the Shadows pressed forward, those damned AI nodes keeping them on the move, walking straight through lava pools that melted their shoes. Some of them dropped, screaming in pain, but most of them kept coming.

"Return fire!" Captain Ahab shouted, raising himself up to his knees to do just that.

"Backup is five minutes out!" Deanna reported.

Great.

Only they didn't have five minutes. They were outnumbered three to one, their shields were shot, and Hailey was pretty sure their weapons were running out of charge.

Hailey needed to buy them time. She could heal; at least half of the others couldn't.

Making a reckless, split-second decision that Jer would definitely kill her for later, she dashed out sideways at full speed.

With the ground still rumbling beneath her, she raced across searing hot rock, head down, tail extended for balance, muscles burning as she pushed her body harder, faster.

Five feet away, she leaped on a soldier, bearing him down with her claws in his spine where his neck met his shoulders. Didn't waste time ensuring her kill. She launched again at the next closest one, catching her claws in his clothing and jerking sideways to throw him.

Blinding hot pain burned her left side. She'd fallen right onto a patch of melted rock. But she forced herself back up, rolling away as a plasma bolt seared the ground where she'd been seconds ago.

That bitch was her next target.

Teeth bared, she took advantage of some much-needed cover fire, distracting the soldier away from her to bowl her over. Hailey was about to bite the woman's face off when, out of nowhere, she screamed bloody murder.

Along with all the rest of them.

Thoroughly unnerved, Hailey hopped off the woman as all the Shadows clutched their heads, jerking and shaking on the ground.

In the distance, the outpost had begun to crumble, its fractured walls disintegrating beneath their own weight as the earthquake intensified. The ground itself started to crack. Massive fissures opened outward from the outpost along the edge of the gorge.

"*Retreat!*" Captain Ahab roared. "*Fall back!*"

He wasn't wrong. Looked like the whole shelf was about to collapse out from under them.

Hailey turned tail and ran, hoping to hell their people on the inside had some kind of exit strategy.

Death is one thing. Ending is something else. You can come back from death, but once it's all over... Well, let's just say I can't wait to finally get some rest.

- The Evolutionary Gospel of Michael

Hel

"Shuttle Blue on approach."

"Anyone got eyes on Laura?"

Vega swore, ducking her head behind her backup plasma shield as she and the remains of her team rushed the line of fire guarding their target. That shield was seconds from collapsing, and she didn't have a third alternate.

Pulling a couple of knives, she threw them overhand with deadly accuracy.

Too bad the AI had already learned her best moves and compensated. The blades struck arms instead of throats and, though the soldiers shouted in pain, their faces contorting with it, they kept shooting. They didn't have another choice.

The shield flickered.

Vega dived and rolled, making room for Bravo Team Leader Farasi to overtake her. His shield was still functional. Ivan's buddy Kiryl hauled her up, shoving another heavy, archaic gun against her chest. "Two bullets left," he warned, then howled like a damned animal and ran full-tilt at the soldiers, absorbing shots he couldn't possibly survive.

He cleared two feet of space and gave them three seconds to advance close enough for hand-to-hand.

"Fucking lunatics!" Loa snapped.

Vega wholeheartedly agreed.

The soldier puppets had a martial arts textbook running the show in their brains. Perfect form, perfect accuracy, shit delivery. They still gave her enough of a fight that, by the time Ivan snapped the last one's neck, Vega was bruised from head to knee, bleeding from a stab wound in her shoulder, and dragging her right leg like it belonged to someone else. There went the last five months of intensive physical therapy.

Eskel was going to kill her.

"Touchdown! We're on our way. Five minutes out."

Great timing, Rowe.

Thirty-eight bodies covered the hallway floor. Four people left to breach the hub, and ten heat signatures waiting for them inside, according to her lens. Not counting the two hundred and sixteen still alive and kicking around the facility, currently heading their way.

Vega didn't expect Rowe to make her team a priority—she wouldn't, in his place. But she also didn't have time to wait while he checked on Laura, extracted her to safety, and came back for the rest of them. If any of them were to make it out alive, they needed to disable the AI *now*. The four of them and two bullets would have to do.

Vega hoped to fuck the other assault teams out there were holding out better than this.

She motioned with Kiryl's gun. "Let's go."

Ivan placed the explosives.

Farasi pulled her a few feet farther and hunched over her, raising his riot shield to cover them both.

Loa and Ivan dropped to the floor.

The blast shook the walls and filled the hallway with noxious smoke.

The people inside opened fire immediately. Farasi's already warped riot shield wouldn't hold out for much longer. The others had no protection at all.

Except for a whole lot of dead bodies.

Ivan hauled one up before him and rushed inside. Loa, the juggernaut, grabbed two by their legs, swung, and *threw* them.

Farasi took the lead, shielding Vega as much as he could, and, miraculously, all four of them made it into the hub chamber with minimal injuries.

Vega didn't know how, and didn't particularly care as she shot two of the soldier puppets, and threw the now useless gun at a third.

The fourth barreled into her from the side before she had a chance to pull her knives, and she curled in on herself to take the impact on her back, not her head. The spinal device keeping her mobile hadn't been designed for this level of abuse. If it went, Vega would be done for.

Her opponent was built like the Hounds she was used to, but he had a node glowing bright blue at his temple, and furious eyes streaming with desperate tears. He hauled off a punch that sent his knuckles into the floor beside her head.

What the…?

Vega struck the heel of her palm against his nose, breaking it. He reared back, but not enough to free her. His legs pinned hers, and his forearm pressed against her neck. "You're killing innocent people!" He roared at her.

"So are you," she choked out. He was too heavy for her to shift, but if she could reach a knife…

Pulling back the same fist that was now bloodied and probably fractured, he punched again—at the floor beside her ear. Was he glitching? "We didn't ask for this—I have a family!"

Vega blinked, remembering what it had been like when the Shadows had first taken her. When Talon had broken her. When she'd died. "So do I," she growled. She didn't give a single fuck about these people. Willing or not, they'd killed her friends—were still killing them out there. Vega would take out every last one of them if she had to. They were nothing compared to what they were taking from her. Not even worth the memory.

Stars danced in her vision as her fingers brushed the hilt of a knife at her thigh. The last one. But it was pinned by his leg. She couldn't get to it.

Another punch, and this time, she heard his wrist break. Breathing hard, his face a mess of blood and tears, he bared his teeth at her. "Can you get it out?"

Vega looked at the node embedded in his temple, the skin around it red and swollen, and felt an unwelcome twinge of sympathy. "Not without killing you."

He ducked his head closer to hers, shifting his weight off the forearm choking her and onto his broken hand braced at her shoulder. "Issa. Ophie. Gemma. Tell them I love them."

Vega abandoned the quest for her knife. She let go of her death grip on his collar. Quick as a snap, she took hold of the node, digging her nails underneath its edge, and yanked it out.

The soldier collapsed on top of her.

Vega shoved him off, turned him over. His eyes were closed, his mouth slack. His name tag read Atwater.

She would remember him.

The hub room had gone quiet. Vega squinted through the haze of dissipating smoke to find her team still alive, surrounded by dead soldiers. Good. As long as they had a pulse, anything else was a minor inconvenience.

"She's still breathing," Garrick said in her com. *"I think she just knocked herself out."*

Fuck.

Loa offered her a hand, but his pinky and ring finger were dislocated at an awkward angle. Vega waved him away and got up on her own. It took her a few tries. Her right knee kept buckling when she put her weight on it.

"Get her out of here," Rowe ordered, and Vega heard weapons fire in the background. Her lens showed her two dozen new heat signatures spreading through the outpost—Rowe's team. But they were still massively outnumbered.

"I think this is it," Ivan said from the other side of the room, where six aisles of mechanical panels blinked with thousands of little lights beneath a tangled web of wiring.

"Are you sure?" Farasi asked.

"This looks like the primary processing unit. If we can…"

Vega tuned them out. She wasn't a tech wizard like some others she could name. She had no idea what she was looking at, but she had a strong feeling that the others were off the mark.

Something white and shiny caught her gaze in the corner of her vision. She hobbled around toward a wall of more panels like Ivan's, but this one had a small, shiny white globe embedded in it. Tiny little thing. About ten inches across, and almost completely lost in the checkered mess of that wall, but Vega couldn't look away.

The explosion they'd set off to get in here had broken shards of thick metal bars off the door's locking mechanism. Vega almost fell over picking up one that looked like a warped baton, with one end bent, twisted, and spiked.

While the others debated the best way to take down those aisles now that they'd run out of explosives, she hopped more than walked toward the far wall and the white orb. It reminded her so much of the Shadows' anti-telepath tech. White holding cells. White helmets. When Talon had them reengineered to protect his Roost on Anamtaigh, he'd mounted white orbs like that on towers inside the vault.

White for nothing. A slate wiped clean inside every Shadow—before they were painted black with all the death they reaped. All of them were puppets. Every single one. Hapless, clueless dolls controlled by forces they had no hope of escaping. Made to fight. Made to kill.

Made to destroy themselves as efficiently as everything else around them.

Vega braced her weight on her good leg and swung with everything she had left, smashing the eggshell with the force of a sledgehammer. It threw off her balance, and she stumbled into the panel, sparks flying in her face, blinding her. But she righted herself and struck again, and again, and again, smashing it all to shit until she couldn't anymore.

The bar dropped from her grip; her leg gave out from under her, and she sat down so hard she felt the impact from her hip bones to the top of her skull. She watched the lights go dark in outward ripples all over that wall. She watched the two hundred odd heat signatures coming at them halt in their tracks.

"They stopped. They're surrendering!"

"Good job, Stabby," Loa praised.

Yeah. Great fucking job.

She listened to Rowe's team discuss the takeover, their voices underscored by a lot of terrified crying in the background. Hundreds of AI-possessed civilians once again in control of their own bodies. They were free. Maybe they'd even walk out of here in one piece. More or less.

And the wave would spread. In a half-hour, the other spokes out there would go offline, and the Shadows' little experiment with mind control would be finished. Without it, what remained of the true Shadow army wouldn't stand a chance.

It was finally over.

Vega's burning rage cooled as her team joined her, slumping onto the floor around her. Nothing for them to do now, except wait for Rowe's backup to clear the outpost and turn it into a new crater.

Until then…

Vega twisted at the waist to look back at Atwater and imagined his body relaxing, finally able to let go and rest.

…they were done.

The rest is silence.

- The Evolutionary Gospel of Michael

Green 24

I'm sorry. I love you. I'm so scared.
Goodbye…
Raven screamed, and it tore a chunk of Zach's soul out of his body. It was a sound of pure agony, a final, roaring swan song.
It dropped the Shadows to the ground, screaming right along with her.
But not all of them.
The two holding her up were insulated by their helmets and when faced with an active telepath, they were trained to kill anyone and everyone affected, starting with the telepath.
An after-tremor knocked them off balance, giving Zach all of two seconds. He dropped into a crouch, spinning. The weapon that had pressed to the back of his head was right there, its owner convulsing in violent seizures. He grabbed for it without slowing, finger already on the trigger as he came back around.
One shot, one hit.

The first went through a white helmet just as its owner curled his hand around Raven's chin to snap her neck. He dropped to the ground, taking her with him.

The second went through the shoulder of his buddy, knocking his returning shot far off the mark.

Zach got up and put the seizing ones out of his misery for good measure. No loose ends. Their twitching pissed him off, anyway.

The last shot, he saved for Sandoval.

But the tremor wasn't subsiding. If anything, it built up, rattling the metal grate beneath his boots and dislodging a shower of dust and rubble off the cliff walls. Zach stumbled as one of the grate panels popped up out of the grid. Metal groaned along the edge, the massive sub shifting on its support pillars. He heard them snap just as a massive boulder broke off from the cliff, crashing through the platform behind Raven.

A blast of cool wind hit him then, scented with ice and water.

The gorge was about to flood.

The sub was already sliding unevenly downstream, ripping out the platform and crumbling more rock as it went. It destabilized the entire structure.

Zach lurched toward Raven, watching the rock above for signs of a collapse. He tripped and almost went to his knees more than once, but he kept moving. He was not about to die in this shithole, and he sure as fuck wasn't about to leave without Raven.

I'm sorry. I love you.

I'm so scared…

Another boulder dropped, blocking off the hallway exit and sending Zach's end of the grate panel up into the air. It threw him sideways, costing him time neither of them had.

And the world shook harder. Mist on the wind now. A whole lot of icy water coming in hard and fast.

Almost there.

He was reaching for her when a plasma shot burned through his shoulder. The second helmeted soldier was still alive. Zach gave him a third eyehole for his troubles.

He only took his eyes off Raven for a second.

When he turned back for her, she was gone.

Sandoval stood upright, his left eye bloody, his weight swaying unsteadily on his good leg, as he held Raven's unconscious form against his front like a living shield. "Still haven't learned your lesson, boy?" he shouted over the rumble of crumbling rock. He was two feet from the platform's edge, the metal behind him warped upward by the quake. "You get your treat when *I* say you get your treat."

Zach dropped the weapon. One shot, and Sandoval would go over, Raven with him.

The rush of water grew into a roar. Rocks the size of his head broke off from the sloped ceiling and crushed the grate platform left and right. "Look around. Your men are dead. Your factory is about to be buried. You lost. You're done."

Sandoval laughed so hard he stumbled off balance. He stepped back closer to the ledge to steady himself. "Doesn't mean you get to win."

Churning white water barreled down the gorge just beneath the platform. It kicked up sprays of white up to Sandoval's knees.

The older man grinned, a maniacal light in his eyes.

"*No!*" Zach burst into action.

Too late. Too far.

Sandoval leaned back and went over the edge, still clutching Raven.

I'm sorry. I love you.

Goodbye…

Zach's boots rattled the grate as he raced for the ledge and, with a running leap, dived after them.

He saw them hit the water. The current snatched them away in an instant, and he missed them by two feet. Freezing cold seized his lungs and every muscle in his body, but Zach forced himself to keep moving. He kicked into the direction of the current, searching for Raven in the frothing mess.

The sub barreled down the channel, slowing the water just a little, but the gorge was falling apart. Massive boulders splashed down, frothing up the surface littered with debris.

Zach caught sight of pale fabric and swam for it. He gripped onto an arm, pulled it toward him, heart in his throat.

Lab coat.

Not Raven.

He shoved the corpse away. The current was too strong already. Once the sub slipped out into the ocean, it would pick up even more. Every second that went by was a chance for Raven to drown or break against the rocks.

He struck out into the current, searching the surface, then dove below. Up and down. Lean aside to slide around an obstruction. Shove another bloody corpse out of the way.

About twenty feet ahead, something surfaced. Light and dark. Bobbing up briefly before it sank. Zach kicked furiously, racing the current.

Ten feet away. The avalanche of rock had quieted, but hadn't slowed the water in the least. A buoyant black case floated past him. It was big enough to act as a floatation device.

Zach didn't take it; he needed speed more than a buffer.

Five feet away, the pair bobbed up again. Sandoval's arms still wrapped around Raven. Blood now stained her gray prisoner's uniform. No way to tell whom it belonged to.

With one last burst of speed, Zach snared her ankle and pulled himself toward her.

Sandoval's head was busted open. Something kept him partially afloat, but it wasn't him. His eyes were closed, his cheeks puffing as he gasped desperate breaths. He'd tangled his arms into Raven's shirt to keep her with him.

Zach tore him loose, kicked him away into the path of a jagged outcropping. Sandoval's body impaled on its sharp point with a satisfying squelch moments before Zach rearranged Raven in his hold and turned to take the same, now padded impact with his back.

She was so cold. So still.

And there was no way out, except through the mouth of the river.

"I've got you."

I'm sorry...

"Just hold on a little longer."

I'm so scared...

Churning, spinning, tumbling along, Zach lost all sense of direction, other than forward. He curled around Raven, keeping her arm close to her body, her legs trapped between his, and her head stabilized against his shoulder. He could keep her away from the hardest impacts, but couldn't prevent every injury, and what little he managed cost him his control. The current batted them around in the wake of the unmanned sub without mercy. It pulled him under again and again, making him wish he'd grabbed that floating case after all.

Zach rolled onto his back, turning his feet into the current. They were approaching the outlet. The gorge didn't widen into the sea; its walls narrowed, creating more pressure that pushed the sub out like a shot.

The resulting release pulled Zach and Raven along in its wake as the sub sank beneath the waves. Zach had just enough of a heads-up to take one deep breath before the force of it yanked them down, down…

Twenty feet deep within seconds. Zach kicked out, fighting the drag that pulled him relentlessly deeper.

Raven would drown before he could get her to the surface.

Thirty feet below. He kicked harder, squeezing Raven like he could keep the water from flooding into her lungs if he just constricted them enough. Surrounded by the open sea, there was nothing in his way anymore. Eyes stinging, lungs burning, he swam as he'd never swum before, his already exhausted body struggling.

Just a little farther.

The downward pull suddenly released, and Zach propelled upward, chasing daylight. His throat worked, his lungs already desperate for air. Too long without breath. Too weak from blood loss. Jaw clenched, arms locked, he kept kicking.

One more second.

One more stroke could make all the difference.

His head broke through the surface, and he sucked in air, immediately turning Raven face-up.

She wasn't breathing.

The river had swept them a good distance out from the gorge outlet, surrounded by sheer rock on either side. No convenient beach or pier in sight, and the current was still tugging at him, dragging him farther out to sea.

Zach spotted something about fifty yards away. His vision went blurry, but that looked like a solid, flat surface carved into the cliff. He struck out for it, making sure to keep Raven's face above water. The serum was a miracle. It healed any injury, including muscle strain, but it couldn't make his body create new blood cells any faster. It couldn't clear his exhaustion or make him any less thirsty. And it sure as shit didn't counteract hypothermia.

The only thing keeping him moving anymore was Raven's weight in his arms. He couldn't feel his hands or feet. His calves locked in painful spasms, but he bore down and kept going. One more stroke. One foot closer.

It was definitely a shelf.

He timed his approach with the waves, using them to help lift Raven out of the water, then another to propel himself up onto the rocky surface beside her.

"Raven!"

Skin bloodless, lips blue. Eyes closed.

Zach put his ear to her chest. No breaths. No heartbeat. He started chest compressions, searching for any sign of an approaching shuttle. Where the fuck were they?

The last time she'd burned out, she'd been out for days, but her heart hadn't stopped.

"Come on, Blackbird, don't fly away now. We're so close."

He scanned the skies, checked her eyes, and breathed into her mouth. Still no pulse. He resumed compressions.

I love you. Goodbye…

No. No fucking way. Not happening.

"Come on!" Zach counted off the rhythm to stay consistent, fighting the darkness closing in around him. He was running out of steam.

I'm so scared…

He breathed into her mouth again, then once more.

Her body convulsed, and Zach almost passed out with relief.

He turned her sideways to expel every last drop of water in her. "There's my girl." When she was finished, Zach pulled her into his arms, sharing what little body heat he had left.

A weak pulse fluttered lazily in the side of her neck.

"There's my good girl."

She was breathing.

Still unconscious.

He didn't care.

They'd made it this far. The rest would be a piece of cake.

He felt more than saw a shuttle descend through the clouds offshore. Without his wrist unit or a com, he had no way to contact them, but there was nothing else around with four limbs and a pulse. Scanners would pick them up in no time.

There. The shuttle turned, descended lower, and a smaller pod disengaged, racing along the surface toward them. "See that? 's all good. You'll be just fine."

With Raven secure in his lap, safely away from the water. Zach leaned back against the rock, watching the pod approach.

He faded out before it reached them.

March 16, 3040 – Torrey

Silence eased Raven back to consciousness. A deep, peaceful silence, lighter than a feather, and brighter than the dawn of a new day. She listened to it for long minutes with her eyes closed, taking subtle inventory.

Her body ached from head to toe. Her mind felt thoroughly fried. There was a darkness in her memories now that burned icy hot. She turned away from it, not ready to face what it contained just yet.

"I know you're awake."

Raven pried her eyes open, shocked at how much effort it took. Then she closed them and tried again.

"You're not dreaming."

"Y' sure?" The stone walls and woven tapestries looked an awful lot like something out of Zach's imagination. Wooden rafters—check. Carved four-poster bed—check. Definitely on theme. Except maybe a little grander.

Was that a real animal pelt tossed over her fluffy white duvet?

"Yeah," Vega said dryly, "I had the same reaction the first time. Someone actually built a castle. There are a bunch of them across this region. Apparently, the locals had a pissing contest a few years back to see who could build the biggest one."

"And it's...*not* a dream."

"Want me to pinch you?"

She groaned and flipped her middle finger in the general direction of Vega's voice.

"Bottom line is, you're safe. But you are in isolation. For telepath reasons. Eskel said he doped you with something to ease you back into it when you woke up, so don't freak out if you can't read me."

Raven squinted at the window. It was too bright outside for her to make out anything other than a patch of white-blue sky.

"If it makes you feel better, you got the mountain view. Laura's stuck in the southern tower. Nothing to see out that way except a whole lot of fields."

Raven took her first good look at the other woman, and her heart sank.

"I'm fine," Vega said. She touched the armrest and maneuvered her levchair closer, turning it so she wouldn't have to twist her neck—which was in a rigid brace. "Just a precaution. Well, more like retaliation. I did some very *minor* damage to my spinal device. Eskel put me on mandatory rest until the leopard lady and her sister can figure out a fix. Spiteful asshole put me at the bottom of their list." The words, accompanied by a wave of genuine warmth, weren't nearly as harsh as she tried to make them sound.

"What happened?"

"We won," Vega said shortly. "For good this time. Or at least until some other psychopath gets high enough to start this shit all over again. Problem for another generation."

"But…what happened?"

Vega's expression hollowed a little. "What always happens in war."

That dark, burning shadow in her mind pulsed, beckoning with memories she wasn't ready to face. "Zach?"

"He's fine. Indestructible, one might say. Out on some secret mission no one knows anything about."

The dizzying relief made her glad she was still lying flat. But watching the ceiling spin and sway turned her stomach.

She pushed herself up to sit against the carved wooden headboard. "And Ripley?"

Vega shook her head. "I'm sorry. I saw their name on the casualty list. They were among the bodies recovered from the wreckage."

"No, I sent them out. With help. They should have made it."

"Might have made it out the door at some point. But the outpost collapsed shortly after your team moved on it. The entire shelf broke apart into the gorge and buried everyone within a two-mile radius. It would have been quick."

Raven swallowed hard. Fucking Michael and his fucking predictions. "How many others did we lose?"

"SU's registered civilians were all evacuated before the strike. A lot of them came here. But I think the bulk scattered throughout the Evolutionary network. As far as our fighters... We're still counting."

Raven couldn't imagine the scope. Before Green 24, the size of their combined army had been an abstract number in her mind. Something so immense that a normal person couldn't conceive of it. Now, after, she had a much clearer understanding of what even a tiny fraction of that number meant. Her bones still hummed with it. Her blood was still chilled from it.

Her mind still burned over it.

"But it's finished."

"Yes," Vega confirmed softly. "The AI is destroyed, and the intel we stole confirmed they don't have a backup. Griffith's body has been positively identified. He's dead. Looks like he took MacMurphy with him."

Raven braced herself for a punch of grief over the death of her once-beloved mentor.

It didn't come. Her mind registered the absence of him in her life the same way it did the loss of her arm. He was gone, but somehow not completely. And she found neither pain nor comfort in his loss. It simply *was*.

"Sandoval's remains washed out into the sea in a cluster of others. Beasties got to them and didn't leave much for us to recover. But we did find a partial torso that matched his DNA. He's dead, too.

"Every known Shadow outpost has been leveled. The people with nodes surrendered as soon as the AI released them. Your med team is looking into how to get those damned things out of their heads. As for the rest, Evolutionaries took a lot of prisoners for processing and rehabilitation. The SU has maybe six hundred in custody for..."

"Reprogramming," Raven offered. Those would be the people who'd joined the Shadows voluntarily because they believed in the mission and thrived on the violence. People like that couldn't be reasoned with. Their prejudices ran so deep that they defied all appeals to logic and compassion. Their defeat would only radicalize them further and make them more dangerous. Given half a chance, those would be the next generation of Griffiths and Sandovals.

Vega winced. She didn't like the word 'reprogramming' any more than Raven.

"Did they consult the rest of you?"

It would have been unconscionable not to. All of the former Shadows would view this as a potential threat to their existence. If the SU started cherry picking and deciding who couldn't be allowed to live, where would it end? What would prevent them from becoming just like the Shadows?

Vega tried to nod, winced, and straightened. "They did. We got a preview of the inside of their minds, and independent confirmation from some Evolutionary precogs—who, by the way, are the weirdest people I ever met."

Raven chuckled. She'd met a few precogs in her life, and she wholeheartedly agreed.

"Basically, the options were lifelong imprisonment under constant guard, or… You know."

Yeah. "It's kinder this way. They'll be permanently changed, but they'll live a full, happy life. With no memory of anything they'd done or been part of in the past." Beneath the duvet, Raven moved her legs restlessly. "I suppose it's not all that different from EMC, is it? But at least our way is painless and permanent."

Vega's mouth compressed into a tight line. "And if someone recognizes them? Reminds them? Or attacks them?" She tried to shake her head, but her neck brace once again stopped the motion short. The restriction seemed to claw at her worse than an actual injury, heightening her emotional unrest. "Having someone hate you so much without knowing why… A bullet to the head would be cleaner."

"They will have that choice," Raven assured her. "They always do."

And they always chose life. For all the satisfaction they derived from ending lives, murderers like that were almost uniformly terrified of losing their own.

"You know something about this."

"It's… it *was* my job."

"Did you ever hesitate?"

"Every time."

The answer seemed to satisfy Vega. "Mass told me what happened at Green 24. He said a handful of Shadows on our side got caught in your mindstorm."

Raven swallowed, holding on to her neutral mask for dear life, but she felt her face go cold and numb.

Vega noticed. "One survivor to another," she said with soft intensity, "It wasn't for nothing. Don't tie yourself into knots with 'what ifs' and 'maybes.' You did what you had to do in an already impossible situation. Not saying it won't haunt you, because it will. And the more you dwell on it, the worse it'll feel. But you did *good*. If anyone tells you otherwise, send them my way."

Raven blinked away tears. "That was a good speech."

Vega's gaze shifted beyond Raven, her ruthless expression softening. "Someone very smart taught it to me, once upon a time."

Quinn's massive stature looked downright average in the huge, ornate doorframe. He all but beamed with love and pride. "Just stopped by to check on you two," he said. "Make sure there's no plotting or scheming afoot."

"The kingdom is safe, ogre," Vega returned, sarcasm dripping from every word. "As you can see, the fair princess has awakened and requires sustenance."

Quinn grinned. "She's not the only one. Lunch on the terrace?"

Vega gave him a nonchalant shrug. "I could eat."

"Raven, it's good to see you doing better."

"Likewise," she said.

"I'll track down Eskel and send him up here with some food. Now you'll have to excuse me." He turned sideways in the doorframe, extending a hand. "I have a very important date with my wife to get to."

Vega rolled her eyes. "You are such a mother hen."

"You're welcome."

~

Eskel came and went, leaving behind a tray of delicious food, a full bill of health, and a detailed therapy program for her body and mind.

He deemed her not quite ready to jump "full brain ahead," as he said. Probably because she kept asking him not to think so loudly. He gave her a small injection to re-up her neural blockers, and off he went again, back to saving lives and limbs in the *castle* infirmary.

That bit still didn't quite compute. Raven was in a castle. A real, sprawling castle with so many rooms, her little tower sanctuary was basically an afterthought. It made her wonder about the kind of people who inhabited Torrey, that they would build castles instead of high-rises, and grow their own crops instead of manufacturing them.

She ate her lunch slowly, working her limbs a little between each bite. When she finished, Raven took a bracing breath and slipped out of bed.

Her knees held somewhat steady all the way to the window—excellent progress.

Wow, Vega hadn't lied about the view.

The castle was built at the edge of a body of water so vast that she couldn't tell if it was a lake or a sea. Boats docked at a wide pier lined with wooden pillars. Some were hung with colorful banners, others streamed with bright ribbons that billowed out on the breeze.

She saw green everywhere, riotous and colorful in the most natural way. A few miles to the north, the mountains rose into the sky in stark contrast, their dark peaks dusted with bright white snow.

If the sanctuary of Zach's mind was the darkness of a winter's night, this was what it looked like when the sun finally rose on a spring thaw. And it took her breath away.

Raven found the washroom attached to the suite and made use of every old-world luxury, starting with a hot bath. Someone had also provided clothes. She selected a long skirt that turned out to be cleverly designed pants, and a soft, long-sleeved tunic.

Her energy depleted on the way back out, forcing her to sit in the cushioned chair someone had helpfully positioned right beside the washroom door.

Raven was an absolute mess. Weak as a kitten, telepathically compromised, her entire being depleted after the last month. She ought to be in bed, resting.

But it was too quiet inside her head, and her skin was starting to crawl. With the neural blockers, she should be safe to venture out among people for a little while. Vega would have told her if anyone else she knew had fallen—she had too much integrity to keep something like that from her. But Raven still needed to see for herself.

She needed to see Zach.

It belatedly occurred to her that Zach had been on his own for most of his life. He'd chafed badly in the crowded community of Lavari Dolmi, especially with Quinn and Vega constantly teasing him about being family. It would be so much worse here, with ten times that many people under one roof, even if it was inside a castle. Even from two stories above the nearest inhabitants, Raven heard them all down there, talking, laughing, shouting—*living*.

What if it was too much? What if he'd left? Not on any mission, but just…left?

The thought got Raven up and moving again. She held on to the wooden railing for dear life, her legs quivering with each careful step downward. It took her ages to get down one landing, where the narrow window looked out over the lake.

Her head swam. Things went blurry here and there, but she definitely saw people down there on the pier. A welcome party of some kind, and travelers disembarking from the ship. They had giant levpads to transfer massive crates from the ship to the pier, and a team of workers maneuvering them around the small gathering.

Raven waited there until her legs felt a little steadier, and then she kept going.

On the topmost floor, a deep red carpet ran the length of the hallway, and windows lined one side while tapestries covered the other. A couple of kids raced from one end to the other, squealing with laughter.

Raven couldn't help smiling.

Until a giant black panther jumped out from an open doorway into their path and roared.

The kids screamed, skidding to a halt. One of them managed to pivot and make a run for it, but the smaller boy barreled straight into the panther. With a massive paw that covered half of the child's back, the panther righted the boy and nosed him around to go after his friend.

Raven stared, frozen to the spot.

The panther's tail stopped swishing, and it turned to spear her with a piercing golden gaze. She could have sworn it huffed a grunt and nodded at her before slinking back where it had come from.

Not a dream, Vega had said.

She knew that.

Of course.

She knew that Dr. Chase-Calen was a mutant hybrid who turned into a feral snow leopard. She knew that there were others like her. Not many, but they did exist. She'd understood that and made peace with it back in Lavari Dolmi.

But *knowing* and *seeing* were two very different things.

Raven closed her gaping mouth and decided it would be best not to linger. Just because the panther had been friendly to kids didn't mean she rated the same consideration.

The staircases between levels didn't curve anymore—a small blessing. It still took her a while to reach the next floor down. This one had a distinct scent. Disinfectant. No red carpets here, just polished wooden floors for easier cleanup. No tapestries, either. Instead, next to each doorway, a holographic screen flickered with medical information.

This would be the infirmary.

Not wanting to get in the way, Raven went another floor lower.

Voices became louder and multiplied. Several groups of people conversing simultaneously. She recognized a familiar laugh briefly rising above the rest, and her heart gave an extra thump.

That last step almost sent her to her knees, but she clutched the railing and kept herself upright.

There he was, the Hawk who'd turned the tide of war. Dressed in crumpled slacks and a white shirt opened at the collar, the sleeves rolled up to his elbows, Zach stood in a pool of golden sunlight, talking to a beautiful young woman with long gray hair and rich brown skin. Beaming at her. And she smiled right back at him.

Raven pressed her back against the wall and locked her knees to stay upright.

She could do this. She'd just gone through several circles of hell, and none of them had bested her. Whatever this was, she'd handle it like she'd handled everything else: have a breakdown, self-isolate for a few weeks, then drag herself back out into the world and keep going.

No big deal.

Zach was touching her! He had his hand on the woman's elbow, steering her—

Shit!

—in Raven's direction.

Shit, shit, shit! She couldn't do this. She had to get back to her room—*crawl* up there if necessary.

But then he looked up, and everything stopped. He dragged a step, his words pausing mid-syllable as their eyes met.

And Raven couldn't move.

She saw him again as she had the first time they'd met face to face, in a sterile holding cell deep underground, cocky, flirtatious, and deadly. She remembered him floating in the detox tank. Standing out on that frozen balcony back in Petrus. Snaring her with the relentless intensity of his gaze on the rooftop in Lavari Dolmi. He'd looked at her then as if nothing else existed; watched her as if to make sure she didn't stumble, ready to step in and catch her if she did.

He was looking at her that same way now as he let go of his companion and kicked time into forward motion again, crossing the distance between them.

Raven pushed away from the wall, determined to stand on her own for whatever came next. "Hi—*oof!*"

Zach snatched her up off her feet before she could properly finish the one-syllable word. With his face buried in the crook of her shoulder, she didn't quite catch what he said, but she got the gist of it.

"Yep, awake and in full possession of most of my senses."

His companion joined them, grinning. "You must be Raven." Even her voice was beautiful. Low and husky, with a light, lilting accent like a soft lullaby.

"Yeah," she said, "that would be me. I'd shake your hand but—can you put me down please?"

That response she understood loud and clear.

Zach came up for air, turning sideways the wrong way, pulling Raven's extended hand away from where the other woman had reached up to shake it so it would curl around his neck instead. "Zia, this is my wife, Raven VanWarren. Raven, meet my very good friend, Dr. Zia Goabi, Chief of Medicine at the Jericho Institute for Occupational Bionics. Zia and her team set the standard of care for bionic limb grafting."

"Our success rate for achieving full neural integration is ninety-nine-point-nine-nine-seven percent," the woman said, and somehow made it sound genuinely humble.

Raven's jaw went slack, and she was suddenly grateful for Zach still holding her up.

"When I told Zia what we had going on here with the Chase sisters and Eskel and all the wounded, she couldn't wait to get in on it. She brought her entire lab and all her assistants with her, too. And *you* are the very first one at the tipity-top of her patient list."

She was staring. She felt like she was staring. And possibly drooling. But Raven couldn't muster enough brain power to manage a single word.

"It's a pleasure to meet you," Dr. Goabi said, filling the awkward silence. "Ian… I'm sorry, *Zach* now, gave me access to your medical file and made it very clear that you were to receive the highest level of care. From what I've read, you've been stalled for treatment for a very long time."

"I—uh… Well—"

"I can translate," Zach offered. "She says it's nice to meet you, too, and she looks forward to talking more in-depth once you're all settled in. But she needs a few more days to recover from her latest ordeal first."

"I understand completely," Dr. Goabi said, her pretty eyes dancing. "I'm told that accommodations have been arranged for me and my team in town, but the lab will be set up in the castle, so I'll be here whenever you're ready. You are in very good hands, Raven. And I'm not just talking about mine."

"Thanks, Doc." Zach had already turned away, Raven's feet still dangling several inches off the floor.

Dr. Goabi watched them leave with a wry smile and a shake of her head.

"T-that was the secret mission you were on?"

Already on the infirmary floor, Zach waved to Eskel, who didn't even raise an eyebrow to see him literally carrying Raven up the stairs. Although she did pick up on a hint of, *How did she get down there?* The neural blockers were starting to wear off again.

One more floor up, Zach swerved around the black panther heading down. He didn't miss a beat, greeting it with a nonchalant, "Cat."

Said cat huffed with equal disinterest as it slinked downstairs.

In three minutes flat, they were back in the tower room, and Raven almost hated him a little for not even being out of breath. He kicked the door shut behind him and sat her on the bed, hands braced on either side of her hips as he glared into her face from three inches away. "You were out for the whole four days it took to get here. Then they put you in the detox tank for another week."

Raven winced. No wonder she felt all wonky.

"I leave for two days, and you wake up without me. Unacceptable."

"What?"

"How's your head?"

"Uh, a bit achey but not too b—"

"Do you remember your name?"

"I thought I did." Until he'd just introduced her by a different one. As his *wife*.

"Do you know where you are?"

"Torrey." The rapid-fire questions gave her mental whiplash.

"Do you remember what happened?" Softer this time, more cautious, that steady gaze searching hers.

"Some of it. Up to a certain point, it even makes sense."

He dropped forward on an exhale, thumping his forehead against hers. "You scared the shit out of me."

"Scared myself a bit, too," she confessed.

Zach made a rough sound, got into bed with her, and pulled her back into his arms. And legs. He just wrapped himself around her and put his nose to the crook of her neck again. "For future reference, 'goodbye' is no longer part of your vocabulary. I can handle, 'I'm scared.' I'll be demanding 'I love you.' But try to tell me 'goodbye' one more time, and I guarantee you will not be going *anywhere*."

Raven melted. All the fear of the last few years, all the pain, grief, and sorrow faded far into the background, leaving her completely drained. But she wasn't empty. Warmth now filled the parts of her that had gone cold, and safety replaced the loneliness she'd felt for so long. She curled her fingers into the back of Zach's shirt and held on as tight as she could.

"The war's over," she said. "What do we do now?"

"I, for one, don't plan to move from this bed for at least the next eleven days."

The sheer petulance in his voice made laughter sparkle in her chest like champagne bubbles.

"After that, my dear, we are VanWarrens, with more money than a small country could spend in a hundred years. We can do whatever we want, and then some."

Raven pulled back to look at him, ignoring his disgruntled growl. "The Shadow accounts. You never handed them over, did you?"

He put forth a valiant effort to keep a straight face, but his sinful dark eyes sparkled with pure mischief. "I don't know what you're talking about. I'm just a very distant relation of a very wealthy clan. Ask my cousin—he'll tell you."

Raven laughed. "Raven VanWarren. Sounds important."

"Vital," he said. "The kind of name a normal guy can't live without. Wanna keep it?"

"For now," she decided. "But I refuse to make any final decisions until I see the Christmas tree."

And she could tell by the quicksilver glint in his eyes that he would spend the rest of the year planning the Christmas to end all Christmases.

She couldn't wait.

EPILOGUE

December 25, 3040 – Torrey

Zachary VanWarren was no longer a normal guy. As soon as his name popped up in the public's awareness, he and the rest of the VanWarren clan once again became front-page news. Except this time, no one cared about the disgraced entertainers still shrieking for their lost fortune. They wanted to know about the heirs leading war recovery efforts on multiple worlds.

Quinn and Vega took it upon themselves to coordinate the rebuild of vital communication relays that had been damaged or destroyed during the last four years. The massive project was part of a larger goal. While the SU's medical experts studied the AI nodes in hopes of eventually removing them from the implanted survivors, no one had time to consider those who'd died.

Vega had become a bit obsessed with tracking down their surviving relatives to give them closure and offer financial assistance. It turned out, the thousands they'd identified via rosters pulled from the Shadow databases were only the tip of the iceberg—the ones who'd lasted long enough to warrant having their names on record. Vega had found Shadow processing centers on multiple worlds with crude counts of so many more who hadn't survived the initial implantation procedure. Their bodies had been incinerated on the spot, effectively erasing them from existence.

The cruelty of it only seemed to fuel her more. Her self-appointed quest kept Vega and Quinn on the move, rarely staying in one place for longer than a couple of months, but they kept in touch and sent little presents whenever they could.

Meanwhile, Raven and Zach had established the Tessa Sinclair Medical Fund to support research into chem-resistance and the debilitating defects and conditions associated with it. They held fundraisers among the wealthiest echelons of society and matched all donations credit for credit.

Not only had they managed to cast a glaring spotlight on the loopholes and cracks within the healthcare system that often left chem-resistants without necessary treatment, they'd also made the general public care enough to get involved within their local communities. Thousands of people sent messages every day, sharing stories of their struggles and successes, seeking advice on organizing their own drives and finding medical assistance for rare cases. Several leading scientists in the medical field had also joined the cause, working closely with the SU heads of medicine and openly sharing their breakthroughs with treatment centers worldwide.

But today was not about work.

Today, Zach walked into the great hall dressed in his finest black suit with his stunning wife on his arm. In honor of the occasion, Raven wore a sleek, strapless red gown with white rhinestones at the top of her bodice, mimicking snow falling from the sky. The scars from her surgery had already faded, and her bionic arm was as dexterous and sensitive as if it were her own flesh.

"Would you look at that tree?" she said, staring wide-eyed at the twelve-foot monstrosity taking up one corner of the great hall.

He shrugged. "I guess it's fine." The one he'd brought home for her was so much nicer.

To prove his point, he sank into his mind and let his heart lead him to Raven's. Ever since Green 24, she'd kept the door open for him and encouraged him to practice walking through it. He'd explored the maze of her memories a hundred times now and knew exactly where to find her by the trail of feathers she always left for him.

Zach matched his vision to her view of the glittering star on top of the giant Christmas tree in the great hall and turned them both away from it, leading Raven to the memory of seeing their new home for the first time.

In a luscious valley beneath the jagged peaks of Monte Erebus on

Mai, their little cottage crouched at the northern edge of the pictur-esque Kamik Village. Tall pine trees stood sentinel on either side, decorated with warm lights that shone clean through the snow on their branches. A small stream meandered around the front, turning a decorative wooden water wheel that creaked and groaned into the soft silence. Hoofprints dotted the snow where local animals had wan-dered through the yard to the covered wooden troughs filled with hay.

From the outside, the cottage looked quaint and simple, with its whitewashed walls and painted window frames.

Inside, the floors were layered with woven rugs. Cut and polished tree trunks shot up in place of pillars, with thick branches forming beams across the living space. They supported a pitched roof made of heated observation glass that melted the falling snow and never fogged over. The couch seated ten, and the fireplace could spit-roast an entire pig.

And by the window that overlooked Monte Erebus, their first Christmas tree twinkled in all its old-age glory. He'd commissioned two dozen artisans to handcraft the ornaments. The topper was a twenty-sixth-century ceramic star, hand-painted on Earth.

Raven sighed, leaning into him, a puzzle piece settling into place.

This was it. Their prize at the end of the long, dark tunnel. Home. Safety. Love.

Point made, Zach returned to himself and crowed, "See? My tree is way better."

Raven jabbed her elbow into his side. "It's not a contest."

Like hell it wasn't. "Theirs doesn't even have furs underneath it. Remember how much you liked the furs?"

Raven narrowed her eyes at him. "Not as much as you," she said and then took over his mind, shoving him back into the memory. Only this time, he was lying on said furs beneath the tree, watching the lights play across Raven's flushed skin as she rode his cock.

Zach cleared his throat. "Touché." Now he was sweating, and they hadn't even made it ten feet past the door. He loved it when she played like that. It made board meetings and funding negotiations so much more entertaining.

The long tables were spaced out to accommodate over three dozen guests, and each place setting had a little wrapped gift sitting on top. Everyone here knew each other. Most of them, Zach considered family. Whether they knew it or not.

This was the first annual Christmas reunion gala, and the first event of its kind hosted by the no longer "Acting" SU Director Emma Wayland. She'd planned a whole month of convention-type activities for all of the combined SU-Evolutionary-ex-Shadow survivors. But tonight was only for the coalition's beating heart.

Zach led Raven over to Quinn and Vega, tearing them away from a conversation with their Anamtaigh crowd to exchange hugs and brief stories. Laura and Finn were nearby, so, naturally, they came next, followed closely by John and Emma herself.

They must have been among the last to arrive, because Emma led them to their seats at her table, with Hailey and her handsome husband across, and her sister Amelia with her husband Gabriel right next to them. Zach gave the panther shifter a wordless nod, which the man returned in a way that could only be described as sarcastic before he rolled his eyes and shook his head.

They were well on their way to becoming the best of friends.

As they sat, the rest of the gathering took their cue and drifted to their own tables. For the next two hours, they took part in lively conversations and enjoyed some truly excellent food with soft music providing a mellow backdrop.

"I could get used to this," Raven said in his ear.

"Six-course meals with three dozen people, and a gaggle of scream-ing kids?"

She shrugged. "Families are loud. But it's a good kind of noise."

Zach looked around and saw exactly what she did. Joy. Color. The chorus of familial love. There were no drab gray walls here; no dark, echoing rooms. Every corner was filled to the brim with a kind of magic that didn't sparkle on the outside, but made you flutter on the inside.

Three dozen people and a gaggle of screaming kids, and not one of them a stranger. Everyone belonged here, including him.

"Yeah," he decided, "I can see the appeal." He turned to Raven to find her watching him with a small smile playing on her lips. Her feather-touch sank into his mind, and for just a few minutes, even surrounded by loud, boisterous people, they were all alone, curled up on a cushy couch in front of the blazing fireplace.

A chair scraped over the floor, jarring Zach out of the vision. Emma had stood up to stare wide-eyed down the table at the grand entry, where an unfamiliar group had just walked in. The man was built like a Shadow, his dark hair streaked with white and a muted orange. Interesting choice, but Zach wasn't one to judge. The smaller, kind-faced woman beside him looked shy, as if she wasn't sure of their welcome. They each held a child by the hand; the boy hid behind his mother, while the girl stared down Zach with enough spunk to raise an eyebrow.

Zach had never seen them before in his life. But even without the people closest to him whispering the names Tristan and Dara, he would have known exactly who they were.

"The fluffy one has come home," Emma said into the shocked silence, smiling with equal measures of joy and relief. "Everything will be all right now."

THE END

ALIANNE DONNELLY is an avid lover of stories of all kinds. Raised on a healthy diet of fairy tales in a place where they almost seemed real, she grew into a writer who seeks magic in the modern age and enjoys sharing a little bit of it with the world through every story she writes. Her books span the spectrum from fantasy to science fiction with varying degrees of romance sprinkled throughout. Alianne now lives in California, where she spends her free time reading, writing, and daydreaming.

Keep turning the page for
an excerpt from Wolfen!

Man's quest for genetic perfection has led to the creation of new subspecies. Wolfen were the pinnacle of scientific achievement, redefining the limits of what it means to be human. Their counterparts, in turn, grew into the ultimate predators. Incapable of higher thought, converts were unstoppable in their need to breed and devour, and when they escaped, they brought the world to its knees.

Almost two decades later, humanity is on the brink of extinction and only the heartless survive. Rescued by two Wolfen brothers, Sinna must now brave the treacherous wastelands of North America in order to reach safety and the promise of a better life. But when an unexpected gambit forces them to separate, a genetic advantage becomes a liability, and the worst monsters turn out to be the ones who don't have claws.

In the game of survival, Wolfen were created to be champions. No longer. The enemy keeps evolving, rendering old tactics ineffective, and the only rule left is to endure at any cost.

THE END

"You can always tell the Wolfen children from the inerts. Although the term is misleading, given the broad spectrum of animal traits mixed in vitro, they truly do behave like a pack. The two oldest of this batch, Alpha Seven and Beta Twelve, are growing like weeds, and their intelligence quotients are off the charts."

Dr. Leslie Gerome watched the two boys on screen, playing quietly in one corner of the playroom, while the rest of the children chased each other and fought for toys. Her smile ebbed. "It worries me sometimes. I can see it in their eyes, they just…know."

She set her voice recorder down, popped a piece of gum into her mouth, then tossed the wrapper in the general direction of the trash bin. Orderlies normally kept the lights on in the room, but Leslie preferred the dark. It was more intimate, and it forced her to pay attention to the monitors and nothing else. "Dr. Hallemann's file said that during the last round of tests, Alpha Seven noted a mistake in his serum formula. He'd pointed out that, at those levels, the acid content would burn a hole in his arm when injected." Leslie chuckled to herself. "Hallemann's recordings show him arguing proper test administration techniques with a ten-year-old. The child turned out to be correct."

Alpha Seven and Beta Twelve were brothers—the genetic equivalent of fraternal twins, born three years apart, and the only instance in which a particular cocktail of DNA fragments resulted in more than one viable embryo. Now, they were Chernobyl den's pride and joy, playing with construction puzzles, building intricate towers and castles. Every so often, one of them looked up to survey the playroom, his eyes catching the light like an animal's.

Such serious children they were. They never smiled anymore, not since the regeneration experiments had begun. And although Leslie knew them to have vast vocabularies on par with college students, the brothers never spoke, unless absolutely necessary, as in the case of the mistaken formula.

"The psych team has declared them at risk of being compromised, but fit to continue being tested—with caution. They're to be monitored closely during interactions with other children, but they rarely play with anyone else."

Sometimes a younger child would approach them for help with a puzzle, and they would help. But once the puzzle was solved, they'd turn their backs and let the child wander away. "They're deliberately setting themselves apart," Leslie said. "I'm sure they have a reason for it, but I can't for the life of me figure out what it is. It goes against their social nature, and has to be hard on them…"

She trailed off when one of the inert boys pushed a Wolfen girl, making her lose her balance and fall over a pile of hard wooden blocks. When the girl broke into tears, the brothers paused and looked up at the same time. The culprit faced them immediately, and as the brothers stared at him, he stared right back.

None of the other children noticed the three holding preternaturally still, but Leslie gaped, held her breath, and waited.

After a full sixty-seven seconds, the brothers exchanged a speaking look, then ducked their heads back to their own game. Too easy. This was in no way over.

Leslie frowned. "Their protector instinct is strong. They do not tolerate dissent within the group, but pick their battles and only engage when they can get away with it. Technical note: Move cameras in the play den. They've found them again."

The lights flicked on, blinding her for a moment. Leslie rubbed her eyes and swiveled away from the monitors to give the intruder a piece of her mind, but stopped short when she saw her colleague darkening the doorway.

Dr. Sallinger was a distinguished intellectual with a pair of glasses on his nose and another on top of his head, overdressed in a starched white lab coat. His real name was Dimitri Andreyevich Roskoff, but he liked to pretend he was a man apart. Tablet in hand, he barely looked up when he announced, "Sigma Nine is to start testing today. Have her prepped and ready in an hour."

It took Leslie's mind a moment to redirect and catch up. "So soon?" she asked. "She's only just transitioning."

There were certain biological thresholds which marked the end of childhood in all things. In humans, it was puberty. In these children, it was a little more complicated. Generally speaking, a conversion could be considered a threshold to failure. Children who converted were the result of a destructive combination of DNA flaws; they became more animal than human, incapable of higher thought function. They were incredibly fast when they wanted to be, yet had a lumbering gait that bespoke of an inner ear defect, which also accounted for their poor hearing. Having observed several of these for a number of years, Leslie recognized them for what they were. Monsters.

Another threshold distinguished Wolfen from inerts, and it was determined by a measure of pheromones. A higher level in one or the other usually predicted which way a child would develop.

Sigma Nine had only shown an imbalance of pheromones last week. It was tentative at best, so they'd been holding off further testing until she'd matured a little more.

"Apparently there's some confusion in her blood tests," Sallinger said. "We need to know where she falls."

"Why?" she demanded, mentally preparing for an argument. She couldn't help it. Sigma Nine was only four years old.

"Don't know, don't care." Sallinger lowered the tablet with a put-upon sigh, and deigned to look at her. "Will you do it, or shall I call in Michito?"

Leslie frowned. "Michito is here?"

"Tick tock, comrade." Sallinger made a face and tapped his wrist. He didn't close the door behind him when he left, a signature Roskoff passive-aggressive jibe to get her moving.

The voice recorder was still on. With a sigh, Leslie spoke into the mic. "I've just been informed that Sigma Nine's timeline has been expedited, so... I guess I better get going." She was reaching for the stop button, when the Wolfen brothers caught her eye. Jonah had stepped out on break, and the brothers were putting their puzzles aside, watching the inert boy who'd hurt the Wolfen girl.

An odd thought occurred to Leslie. "Observer commentary: A few months back, we received a message that the Fukushima den was having issues. I know the protocol is to limit contact, but we haven't had any updates or progress reports since then. Now one of the Japanese team leaders is here, and this thing with Sigma Nine…" She rubbed her brow. "I don't know, maybe I'm being paranoid, but something just doesn't feel right. My gut tells me Michito wouldn't be here unless something was wrong." She chuckled at herself. "Listen to me. A seasoned geneticist having *feelings*. Ignore that last remark. It's apparently been a longer day than I realized."

Leslie turned off the voice recorder as Alpha Seven and Beta Twelve closed in on the inert boy. The others instinctively moved out of the danger zone. Fights like this occurred regularly among the subjects, and they were allowed, considered as an integral part of development. Unless blood flowed, the orderlies did not interfere.

But this was different. When the first blow came, it wasn't the childish slap Leslie would have expected. Alpha Seven drew back a fist, fingers tucked in like a champion boxer, and drove it into the boy's midsection. The inert boy went down, curling in on himself, and already the brothers were easing away.

It should have ended there. But instead of staying down and accepting defeat, the inert boy pulled himself up and faced off with Alpha Seven, a mean gleam to his eye.

Beta Twelve cocked his head and leaned in to sniff the inert boy. He met eyes with his brother and both nodded.

Leslie frowned. Had she missed something?

She was about to page Jonah to get back into the playroom, when Beta Twelve curled his fingers into claws and slashed them across the inert boy's neck. Quick as a snap; one swipe, and blood sprayed, sending the other children into a screaming panic. Leslie gaped. She couldn't have just witnessed a seven-year-old commit cold, calculated murder against another.

She zoomed in on the inert boy gurgling blood on the floor. The pool spreading around him was too bright to be healthy. Pressing a shaky hand to her mouth, Leslie sat back. He'd converted. And the Wolfen boys had smelled it on him.

But he'd tested safe!

Children weren't allowed into social units until doctors determined them either safely inert or Wolfen. How could he have converted so late?

By the time Jonah came back, the brothers had wiped off the convert's blood and returned to their game. Though still visibly shaken, the other children seemed to sense the threat had been eliminated, and following the brothers' example, quieted as well. They went back to their smaller groups, giving the now-dead boy a wide berth. Inert or Wolfen, they all trusted the apparent alphas of the pack, instinctively adhering to the subconscious social structure. Amazing.

Jonah herded the children out of the room and away from the corpse. He looked uneasy, as well he should. None of the children moved until the brothers did, recognizing their authority over them as greater than Jonah's.

Leslie was still pondering this as she walked down the Green corridor to the nursery. The hallway was quiet. This level didn't usually see much activity, what with nothing here but the guts of the facility—control rooms, nurseries, and incubation chambers. A horizontal green line ran its length as a directional. At the next intersection, a red line ran down another hallway that led to the convert testing rooms and loading/unloading docks.

Leslie glanced sideways at it as she passed, and waved to an orderly jogging to get somewhere. He didn't see her. She shrugged, and kept going to the nursery. This chamber was separated into halves, with the far side walled off for newborns and an antechamber that served as the sleeping quarters and playroom for the one- to five-year-olds. It had gray walls and black floors; a deliberately bland environment to encourage imagination and mental development, while curbing overt excitement.

Sigma Nine sat at one of the plastic tables, coloring with crayons. Her brown curls fell over her forehead and she kept blowing them back with frustrated huffs. The cutest little angel. She still had her chubby cheeks, but Leslie could tell it wouldn't be long before Sigma Nine hit her growth spurt, and when she did, the girl would be a show stopper.

"Hey, Sinna," she said.

Sigma Nine looked up and gave her a ten million megawatt smile. "Hi, Gerry! Are you here to play with me?"

Oh honey, how I wish I could. Leslie struggled to maintain her own smile. "Not today, sweetie. I need to take you to do some tests. Is that okay?"

Sigma Nine pouted. "Will it hurt?"

"Maybe a little."

"Do I have to?"

Leslie nodded.

Sigma Nine bowed her head, put down the crayon, and came forward, holding out her hand for Leslie to take. She kept her gaze on the floor, but didn't drag her feet, as docile as a trusting little lamb despite her apprehension, and it broke Leslie's heart.

When they reached the lab, Leslie lifted Sigma Nine onto the exam table and performed a quick routine physical, noting the results on her chart.

She was just finishing up with the initials when Dr. Sallinger arrived. He checked the chart, scrubbed up, and held his hands out for gloves. His face mask, as always, hung around his neck, ready to be donned in a hurry. He pulled it up, saying, "You may begin, Dr. Gerome."

Leslie stared at him. "Me?"

"Did I not make myself clear?"

Leslie swallowed hard. Sigma Nine was watching her with an eerie calm. She couldn't make herself move.

"Are you unfamiliar with the procedure?"

Leslie shook herself. "No. I mean, I know what to do."

"Then what are you waiting for?"

She stepped up to the table and pulled the instrument tray closer.

"Secure the arm," Sallinger instructed, and she did, hating that he felt the need to talk her through this. "Now, disinfect the area. That's right. You'll want a number eighteen scalpel. Make a six-centimeter incision parallel to the ulna, beginning one centimeter from the styloid process."

Leslie's head snapped up. "Six centimeters?"

"Need I remind you we have two hundred and forty-seven other children to see to? I do not have time for this. Now, make the incision. Six centimeters parallel to the ulna, beginning one centimeter from the styloid process."

Again, Leslie swallowed hard, and tried not to look at Sigma Nine's face when she pressed the blade tip to the inside of the girl's arm. She made the cut smooth, but not fast enough to spare the girl pain, and Sigma Nine gasped and moaned. She started crying, but like all of the children, she was trained not to move during testing. With a scalpel so close to her delicate skin, a sudden twitch could kill her.

"Starting timer," Sallinger said, as blood began to flow. "Five seconds… Ten seconds…"

Leslie frowned. "She's not healing."

"Give her time. Fifteen seconds…"

Sigma Nine sobbed, her heart rate rising with her distress. And she kept on bleeding.

"Twenty seconds…"

Leslie shook her head. "Enough of this." She grabbed a bunch of gauze and pressed it to the wound.

"What are you doing? I did not tell you to arrest the—"

"She's not healing! I am not letting her bleed out on the table."

Sallinger tore off his mask and gloves. "You have just contaminated the test and wasted my time, and you have achieved nothing except to ensure the test will need to be repeated."

"Get out," Leslie snapped. She'd been careful to make the cut shallow, but Sigma Nine was still losing too much blood. Pinching the girl's skin together, she applied a clear solution to glue the edges closed. It wasn't normally used for lacerations this long, but Leslie didn't want to mar the poor girl with rough stitches and an ugly scar. It would have to be enough.

"I will see you fired for this—"

The lights went out with the disconcerting sound of a power-down as the entire facility sighed into darkness. Five seconds later, emergency generators kicked in and red bulbs flared, illuminating the room and the corridors outside.

"What's going on?" Leslie demanded, winding a sterile bandage around Sigma Nine's arm.

Sallinger cast her a dirty look. "Probably just a power outage. Stay here."

"Gerry?"

"It's okay, Sinna. Just hang tight for me, all right? I'm so sorry I hurt you. I promise it'll never happen again." There was no reason; her lack of regenerative abilities confirmed her status as inert.

That's what you thought about the dead boy, too.

She pushed the thought aside. If she studied the boy's behavioral history, she'd probably find clues about his convert tendencies beginning from an early age. Sigma Nine was too gentle, too sweet. No, she was inert—for all intents and purposes, human.

When she finished with the girl's bandages, Leslie freed her arm and sat her up, pushing her curls away from her face. "How are you doing, sweetheart?"

Sigma Nine's chin wobbled, and more tears spilled.

Leslie hugged her tight, rubbing her back for comfort.

That was how Sallinger found them when he came back. His hair was disheveled and he was missing one pair of glasses. Gasping for air, he slammed the door shut and locked it. "They breeched the holding pens," he said, heading for the security console.

"What?"

It took him three tries to enter his code, then the screen split into nine, showing security feeds from their wing. "I knew I shouldn't have signed off on the transfer," Sallinger rambled. "My God, they'll kill us all!"

The break in his voice sent a chill down Leslie's spine. "W-what are you talking about?"

Sallinger rubbed his sweaty face, shaking as he watched the screen. Two of the nine feeds showed groups of scientists herding several children in one direction. Two more showed the convert holding pens—empty. "The crazy Japs! Michito didn't come alone. Fukushima den was compromised. They were storing too many fully grown converts, and they broke free. Michito didn't want to lose twenty years of research, so he captured several of them and brought them here."

"Is he insane?"

Sallinger trembled so hard, he knocked his glasses off his nose trying to adjust them. He wheezed, on the verge of tears, and his distress sent Sigma Nine into wailing fits. Sallinger froze, staring at the child. "She knows," he said. "She can sense them. We can use her to get out."

"Don't you dare!" Leslie twisted to keep Sigma Nine away from him, but her gaze was fixed on the screen and all of those people nervously looking over their shoulders.

"Didn't you hear what I said? We're going to *die* if we don't get out."

Leslie circled around Sallinger to get to the screen. Her thumbprint would be enough to signal distress in the lab. "You're panicking over nothing. The guards will take care of this." They were highly trained mercenaries, paid well for their service, and their response time was usually less than seventy seconds. Of course they could handle this. She was certain of it. They'd come and escort the three of them to safety.

But Sallinger shook his head. "They're all dead! Fully grown converts are not like the children, Gerome. They feed and they breed, and they're unstoppable when the urge hits them. It's like a hive mind effect. The Fukushima ones were starved, and their frenzy riled up the converts here. The den is overrun!"

No. That couldn't be. He was in hysterics. When he calmed down, he'd realize how crazy that sounded. A small army of guards, dead? No way. She'd show him.

Adjusting Sigma Nine in her hold, Leslie typed one-handed, looking for a duty roster. Everyone on active shift could be reached directly in an emergency through a tracker in their radio unit. She called them with her digital page, one after the other, but no one answered. Throat suddenly dry, Leslie shook her head and tried again. One by one, the signals disappeared as if deactivated. Either every one of those radios had gotten smashed, or someone—some*thing*—had damaged the main controls in the lower level server hive. She couldn't call out. No one was coming. They were on their own.

Apprehensive and irritated by the red lighting, Leslie backed away from the screen. "What about the others?"

Sallinger hesitated.

"*What!*"

He jerked his chin toward the screen just as the last group disappeared from the shots. "They're already evacuating. The researchers and orderlies are gone, along with whatever children they had with them at the time. The rest they left for dead."

Leslie's knees buckled and hit the floor so hard, the impact jolted through to the top of her head. Sigma Nine clutched her, whole body shaking with sobs.

"Listen to me," Sallinger said. "There's an escape hatch at the end of the corridor. We can make it. If we can get to the surface before they detonate the charges, we'll be fine. We just have to get there. Give me the child."

None of his words had penetrated Leslie's haze of fear, but when he reached for Sigma Nine, something snapped. Why did he want her so badly? "No." She moved out of the way. "I'll take her."

Though he looked ready to throttle her, he somehow pulled himself together and nodded. "Very well. But you must calm her down. They will hear us."

A flicker of movement on the screen caught her eye, but she refused to look. "Give me a minute."

Removing herself to one corner, Leslie rocked Sigma Nine, crooned to her. "Easy, sweetheart. Breathe. You're okay. You're going to be just fine. I won't let anyone hurt you."

"Hurry up," Sallinger hissed, nervously watching out the window.

Leslie hummed and rubbed the girl's back until her sobs eased. "That's my girl. That's my brave girl. Now, we're going to play a game, okay? I want you to close your eyes, and stay as quiet as you can. We're going to pretend we're hiding from monsters."

"Will they hurt me?"

Sallinger gasped. "Move it!"

Leslie glared at him. "No, baby. No one's going to hurt you again, I promise. Are you ready?"

Sigma Nine sniffled and nodded against her shoulder.

"Good girl. On three, okay? One…"

She signaled for Sallinger to open the door. He did it slowly, peeking out to make sure the path was clear.

"Two…"

Silence out in the hall—no hum of artificial lights, no pitter-patter of rushing feet, not even alarm sirens. Just total, dead silence. And that terrified her. They were truly all on their own. Gritting her teeth, Leslie walked when Sallinger beckoned, and stepped out of the room.

"Three," she whispered.

The race was on. Leslie focused on the ceiling hatch some thirty yards away. She headed straight for a wall ladder leading up to it, heart pounding, and Sigma Nine sitting heavy in her arms.

Of course, Sallinger noticed her readjust her hold. "Let me take her," he offered. "I can carry her more easily."

Leslie shook her head and quickened her step. Almost at the ladder. Shuffling noises from the other end of the corridor made her look back. "Oh, no…"

Two converts, an adult and a child, lumbered toward them. They looked marginally human, with patchy hair and thin bodies corded with lean muscle. But their long limbs ended in clawed fingers, and they had fangs instead of teeth. Because of their cold-blooded nature, their skin held a grayish tinge, but this condition didn't seem to affect their metabolisms in any significant way, acting as a cloaking mechanism only. Matching body temperature to their surroundings made them invisible to heat sensors and infrared cameras.

Monsters. Boogeymen out of nightmares. Mindless, ravening beasts.

And they were coming closer.

"Climb!" Sallinger shouted.

"Hold on to me," Leslie told Sigma Nine, and then she climbed.

The converts stopped and sniffed the air. Although their hearing was impaired and their eyesight compromised by the flashing emergency lights, their sense of smell remained unequaled. The moment it scented prey, the adult convert tossed its head back and screeched.

Several others answered from a distance.

Then it ran forward.

"Climb! *Climb!*" Sallinger shrieked.

Leslie climbed as fast as she could, arms burning with strain, Sallinger right on her heels. But they could only go so far before Leslie had to stop to open the latch. Sallinger clambered on top of her as high up as he could manage.

It wasn't far enough. He screamed as the adult convert sank its claws into his leg and dragged him down to the floor.

"Keep your eyes closed, Sinna." Leslie trembled, vision blurry with tears, but she didn't dare take her eyes off her target as she touched the thumbprint pad to activate the latch mechanism. *Don't look down. Don't look down!* "Just hold on, baby girl," she whispered as monsters tore into Sallinger below. The sounds he made…

Please, God, get me out of here.

The heavy escape hatch slid open, and she moved, climbing higher to reach the pad on the other side. *Don't look down.* Just a few more rungs. Almost there. *Don't look down…*

Got it!

The three-inch metal hatch slid closed, sealing off all sight and sound. Leslie pressed her forehead against the ladder, too shaken to keep going. They were still thirteen stories below the Chernobyl disaster site. To this day, few came to these parts for fear of radiation poisoning. Just as with Fukushima, it had been the perfect hiding place, with all contingencies accounted for.

Except for the crazy Japanese.

If Sallinger had been right, then somewhere on the surface, a researcher had his twitchy finger on a detonator that would entomb this place forever. Leslie had to get moving or she and Sigma Nine would be buried right along with it.

"Gerry?"

"It's okay, Sinna, we're safe. You can open your eyes now."

"I can't see anything."

"That's because it's dark." Leslie looked up. Twelve stories above, a small green light marked the exit—her north star. "I'm going to get us out of here," she swore. "We'll get out, and catch a plane to San Francisco. We can go check out the sea lions at Pier 39, would you like that?"

Sinna nodded.

"Good. Now just hold on."

Keeping her eyes on that little green light, Leslie reached up for the next rung.

Look for Wolfen at your
favorite online bookstore!

www.ingramcontent.com/pod-product-compliance
Lightning Source LLC
Chambersburg PA
CBHW031434200726

48289CB00001BA/48